CAMELOT'S SHADOW

Sarah Zettel was born in California in 1966. She is the author of the acclaimed *Isavalta Trilogy* (*A Sorcerer's Treason*, *The Usurper's Crown* and *The Firebird's Revenge*), a romantic fantasy based on the folklores of Russia, China and India, and has also written four science fiction novels and many short stories in various genres. She currently lives in Michigan with her husband and their son.

By Sarah Zettel

SARAH ZETTEL

Camelot's Shadow

HarperCollins*Publishers*

This novel is entirely a work of fiction.
The names, characters and incidents portrayed in it are
the work of the author's imagination. Any resemblance to
actual persons, living or dead, events or localities is
entirely coincidental.

HarperCollins*Publishers*
77–85 Fulham Palace Road,
Hammersmith, London W6 8JB

www.harpercollins.co.uk

Published by HarperCollins*Publishers* 2004
1 3 5 7 9 8 6 4 2

A catalogue record for this book
is available from the British Library

ISBN 0 00 717108 0

Typeset in Meridien by Palimpsest Book Production,
Polmont, Stirlingshire

Printed and bound in Great Britain by
Clays Limited, St Ives plc

To all those down the years who have told the tale.

ACKNOWLEDGEMENTS

The Author would like to thank all the members of the Untitled Writers Group, and most especially Karen Everson and Jonathan Jarrard, who took it upon themselves to read the whole book. She'd also like to thank Susan Shwartz and Jane Yolen and all the women of the SFF-WFS list who answered her numerous questions. And finally, Matrice, Shawna, Sarah and Danny, without whom this book would not have happened.

PROLOGUE

The rain pelted down through the trees as if to make a second Flood. Its noise muffled Jocosa's moans. The oaks had provided some shelter when the rain fell softly, but now they were as useful for stopping the water as a sieve.

Lord Rygehil eased his horse backward a few steps and lifted back the curtain of Jocosa's litter. Rain ran in rivulets down onto the cushions and their occupants. Jocosa tossed restlessly beneath her woollen cloak, lost in her own tortured imaginings. The two maids who flanked their fever-racked mistress looked up at him in mute distress.

Rygehil's throat closed on his breath. He let the curtain fall.

Curse this rain. He pounded his fist against his thigh and glared at the darkening sky from under the hood of his cloak. *Curse King Arthur and his coronation, curse his useless physics and curse me, curse me for taking Jocosa so far from help!*

The rain fell implacably on his head and shoulders. His horse stirred restlessly under him, shaking its mane and stamping its hooves. The animal was soaking wet, and no doubt cold. He could smell, rather than see, the steam rising from its back. The men-at-arms around him were at least as badly off, if not worse.

Forgive me, God. Forgive me. Rygehil bowed his head low over his horse's neck. *Mother Mary deliver my wife. I love her, I love her. Take me. I'll go gladly to the grave, but spare my Jocosa, the radiant, the incomparable. I beg of you!*

'Hoofbeats, lord,' said Whitcomb. Rygehil jerked his head up. 'Liath is back with us at last.'

Without waiting for an order, Whitcomb urged his horse out onto the road. *Sea of mud, more like,* he thought ruefully as his horse sank up to its fetlocks in the mire.

Even though the clouds had brought night down far too early, Rygehil could make out young Liath, urging on his dun pony for all the poor beast was worth.

'A fortress, my lord!' Liath cried as he drew close. He brushed at his hood and sent an additional gout of water down his own shoulders. 'An old Roman garrison. The roof is still good in spots. We shall have some shelter at least, and a place a fire can be made.'

Hope sparked in Rygehil's heart. A fire, a dry place to rest, it could make all the difference to Jocosa.

'Lead on, then, boy.' Whitcomb's voice called before Rygehil could get the words out. Rygehil glanced behind to see Whitcomb checking the thongs that held the litter to the mules' backs.

'On the road, then,' Whitcomb cried, with one eye on the litter and the men and one on his lord. 'Be quick, and careful with my lady!'

Rygehil let his men-at-arms pass him by. They were so soaked that even their mail no longer jingled. He took his place beside Jocosa's litter and rode at the very edge of the road. The thrashing of rain, the squelch of hooves in mud and the hundred small thumps, rustles and mutterings that filled the night kept him from hearing whether she still moaned or not.

Surely, she has not fallen silent yet, not within moments of shelter and warmth. No. She is not that weak yet. Not yet.

His mind filled with a thousand memories: of how the sight of her beauty struck him a blow when he first saw her; of how his heart soared when he first kissed her lips; of how she moved about his hall with such grace and confidence, ordering everything to the very best advantage; of waking from a long, slow fever to the sight of her brown eyes gazing down at him.

Rygehil's heart squeezed tight inside his chest. He had been chided many times by his father and brothers for laying so much store by one woman. He had never even wanted to listen to their words.

Rygehil forced himself to look away from the litter and its limp curtains. He pointed his attention down the mired road, hoping to catch some glimpse of Liath's fortress.

The road took a turn and dipped down a small hill. The men cursed as they tried to negotiate their horses' way down the mud-swamped slope.

'Just here, my lord!' Liath hastened his pony on, although the creature started to balk under him. At last the beast gave up resisting, tucked its hind legs under its tail and slid straight down the hill. Liath gaped like a fish but kept his seat, even when the pony hopped back onto all fours at the slope's bottom. Rygehil took a moment to wonder if the boy was an extraordinary horseman or a very stupid one. As frantic as he was for Jocosa, he let his mount find its own way down. He could feel its muscles bunching and rolling as it struggled to stay upright. Rygehil tried to tear his attention away from the litter long enough to work on keeping himself in the saddle.

The trees parted at the bottom of the hill, opening on a meadow that sloped gently away from the road. At the top of the rise, Rygehil saw Liath's shelter. His first thought was that it was far too small to be a fortress or garrison, but the shadows seemed to thicken as he stared at it and he grew uncertain as to which part was wall and which was twilight. But still, he could see the gate right enough. The building looked to be two storeys tall with a peaked roof that in the day's last light appeared sound. A villa maybe, or an old temple that someone had turned into an outpost or hideaway before Arthur had spread his peace across the isle.

As the horses laboured up the muddy slope, the rain redoubled. Rygehil could see no more than a hand's span in front of him. Behind him, Whitcomb was trying to direct the men minding the litter. He had to shout to be heard above the torrent. Rygehil dismounted his horse and handed the reins to Liath. Shouldering away the clod who was attempting to handle the balky litter-mule, he caught up the beast's halter. With a firm hand and soothing words, he led the mule forward. Whitcomb took charge of the other and together they slogged towards the shelter.

After what seemed a thousand years of drowning rain and fading light, Rygehil heard cobblestones clatter under hooves. He lifted the edge of his hood and saw their chosen shelter looming against the dark sky, a black shadow against the thick grey. He could just make out the covered porch and, to his surprise, the open door.

'Unfasten my lady's litter,' ordered Rygehil. 'Liath, see if you can find some stabling for the animals. You and you,' he pointed at two indistinct figures. 'Help with the horses. If nothing else can be done for them, bring them onto the porch.'

The men undid the litter's fastenings with fingers clumsy with cold. Una, Jocosa's maid and dearest friend, peeked out from behind the litter's curtain, taking in the situation with a shrewd eye. She jumped down at once in a cloud of skirts and veils. She was drenched in a second, but if her scolding was any sign, she cared nothing for it.

'My lady must not be jostled, be careful you oaf, my lord, my lord, you must have greater care how you heave my lady about . . .'

With her fussing about them like a flustered hen, they gained the porch. Stepping under its roof was like emerging from the ocean. Rygehil shook his hood back, and felt a stream of extra water pour down his back.

They manhandled the litter through the black and open doorway. Rygehil smelled mould and dirt and confinement. His boots thudded on a dirt floor. His eyes all but burst from their sockets in an effort to see through the gloom.

'Here seems clear enough, my lord.' Whitcomb's voice sounded strangely harsh in the darkness.

'Yes, yes, put my poor mistress down.' Rygehil heard a flopping noise and imagined Una wringing her skirts out. 'Oh, not there, for shame, 'tis right in the draught. Here, here.' Rygehil made out her shadow and guided the litter towards it. She was right. Jocosa would be better in a corner out of the doorway's draught until they could get some sort of fire alight.

He and Whitcomb set the litter down as gently as they could. He heard the curtains rustle damply. A form scrambled out. Maia, who was but lately entered into Jocosa's service, young and plump and gasping from her efforts.

Rygehil took a deep breath. 'How does your mistress?'

'I . . . oh, my lord . . .'

Rygehil dropped to his knees beside the litter. He tossed his gloves aside and lifted up the sodden curtain with a trembling hand. He could not see anything. He reached out blindly and his fingertips brushed skin as cold as marble.

'No,' he whispered. Jocosa's arm lay under his palm, icy cold. He felt his way along its length to her shoulder. She was so thin, so drawn. He could feel the bones right under the skin. He reached across to her breasts, her beautiful, pale flesh that he had kissed and stroked so many times. Now he lay his hand flat and heavy against them to find her precious breath. But her bosom lay still and fear strangled his heart and brain.

Then, her chest heaved once under his hand, and again, and yet again.

'She lives,' he blurted out. 'She lives still.'

'Praise be to God!' cried Una. 'Haste, now, haste, you men and see what fire we can make. There must be something to be found that can burn. Maia, hold up your cloak, girl, and shelter me from the sight of these ruffians. My shift is yet dry. We can strip off my lady's wet garments and wrap her in that.'

'My lord?' Whitcomb touched Rygehil's shoulder.

Rygehil lifted his head. Some twenty paces away, towards what Rygehil had assumed to be the back of their shelter, stood an arched doorway. Through it, golden firelight flickered against stone walls and showed a staircase leading down.

Rygehil got slowly to his feet. 'It seems we are not the first to take shelter here.'

'Hallo!' called Whitcomb. 'Hail fellow traveller!'

They waited for the echo of his voice to fade. In the silence, Rygehil noted how little the new light revealed. He could see the doorway, he could see the first few stairs, but nothing else. He could not see the walls of the room he stood in, nor the doorway behind him. He could not even, he noticed with a start, hear the rain outside anymore.

What is this? He restrained the urge to cross himself. This was a place with a fire for Jocosa. A fire she must have to stay alive.

'Una, Maia, look well to my lady.' Rygehil laid a gentle hand on the litter curtain. 'Whitcomb, you and I will go speak with the maker of that light. The rest of you, stand

ready.' He touched the hilt of his sword as if it were a piece
of the True Cross and started forward.

'My lord . . .' Rygehil turned to look at Whitcomb.
Whatever he meant to say, he evidently thought the better
of it, as he closed his mouth and followed silently after his
master.

The light dazzled his eyes that had been too long in darkness. Rygehil had to touch the wall to be sure of his way.
The stone was smooth and cool under his hand, and solid
under his boots. When his sight cleared, he saw the hollows
worn in the centres of the steps from years of feet passing
this way. This place was old, whatever it was.

Rygehil counted fifteen steps before his boots found dirt
again. They stood in a short corridor of stone that opened
up ahead and to the left. Strangely, this cellar smelled cleaner
than the room upstairs. It felt dry, and was wholesome with
the sharp scent of wood smoke. The flickering light of flames
turned the stone walls orange and red and gold.

'Who is there?' called Rygehil as he moved forward. Again,
silence answered him.

He reached the opening in the wall and peered into the
chamber beyond.

First, he saw the fire blazing in its central pit. Its heat
wafted over him like a welcome dream. Black against the
golden fire stood the silhouette of a tall man. His robes hung
in heavy folds all the way to the floor. Rygehil could make
out the profile of a craggy face and deep-set eyes, but little
else. The man stood completely still and gazed into the fire
as if it held the secrets of Heaven.

Gradually, as his eyes grew accustomed to the play of light
and shadow, Rygehil began to make out other details of the
chamber. Along with the strange, rapt man and his blazing
fire, it held a large number of trestle tables. These were
crammed with braziers, alembics, retorts, various squat

beakers of clay. Among them were vessels made of clear
blown glass, more than Rygehil had ever seen in his life.
They also held lumps of raw minerals, twisted pieces of metal
and other forms he could only guess at, but a raw, animal
stench reached him over the clean smell of wood smoke and
he decided he would be glad not to draw closer. More beakers
hung from the cellar's wooden roof beams, along with
bunches of dried herbs and here and there a dead bird or
hare.

All at once, the man turned and fixed Rygehil with a
piercing stare. To his shame, Rygehil took a step back and
laid his hand upon his sword hilt.

'Your woman is very ill.' The stranger's voice was soft and
dry, but its tone was almost musical.

Rygehil swallowed hard. 'Who are you, Sir, that you know
of her trouble?'

The stranger smiled thinly. 'I am called Euberacon Magus,
and, as you see, I am master of this place.' He waved one
long hand to indicate the room about him. 'I know all that
occurs within its confines. Thus, I know that your woman,
your lady wife, I believe you term her, is in danger for her
life.'

Rygehil realized his hand was still on his sword hilt. He
left it where it was. 'She needs shelter, and a fire. Sir, since
you are provided of both, I beseech you to allow us to tres-
pass upon your hospitality . . .'

'She needs more than that.' Euberacon turned his gaze
back towards the fire. 'Death on his pale horse seeks her in
the storm outside. He may yet find his way here, if nothing
is done to prevent him.'

Rygehil's stomach knotted painfully at these words. At the
same moment, Whitcomb touched his shoulder. 'My lord, I
do not like this. I do not like this man and his guesses and
secrets. There is something unclean about this place.'

'Your man is right to urge you to caution.' Euberacon turned to them again, with his thin smile showing on his long, lined face. 'All art, all science and all practitioners thereof should indeed be approached with caution.'

Rygehil waved Whitcomb to silence. 'Are you a philosopher, Sir? Have you some skill as a physician?'

Euberacon inclined his head modestly. 'I have, Sir. Bring the woman to me. I will see what may be done.'

'My lord,' breathed Whitcomb again. Rygehil ignored him.

'I thank you, Sir. We will bear her here directly.'

He started up the stairway again. He felt Whitcomb at his back, bursting to say something more.

'Here is hope for Jocosa, Whitcomb,' he said softly. 'What more am I to care for?'

'I fear here may be more peril than hope,' muttered Whitcomb. 'If she dies now, at least her soul and yours are safe.'

Despite the close quarters, Rygehil whirled around. 'Speak so again, Cein Whitcomb and I will have your heart out of your body. Jocosa will not die. She *will not* die.'

He hurried up the remaining stairs to the darkness of the upper chamber. His company received him without a word. They had doubtlessly heard his outburst, but he did not care.

'We have met the master of this house. He is a philosopher and may be able to aid my lady. We shall take her to his chamber.'

It was impossible to fit the litter down the narrow stairway, so Rygehil scooped Jocosa tenderly into his arms. Her maids had wrapped her in Una's dry shift and found a cloak that was still dry inside. Despite this, her skin was damp from her own perspiration and she lay far too still for a living being. She made no sound as he lifted her. Her head fell back against his chest. He bent to press his lips to her brow and felt the heat of the fever like a fire there. The only sign of life inside her was the all too infrequent rise and fall of her breast.

He carried her down the stairs with Whitcomb and Una at his heels.

Euberacon had moved from his place at the fire. Now he stood beside one of the trestle tables that had been cleared of its instruments and flotsam and covered with a clean, bleached cloth. Rygehil laid Jocosa down and stepped back.

Euberacon looked first at him, then at Whitcomb, then at Una.

'Send the dross away.'

Rygehil faced them. 'Return to the upper chamber. I will send for you if there is need.'

'My lord . . .'

'But my lord . . .'

'Go!' Rygehil ordered sharply. 'All will be well. I will attend to all that is needful.'

They did not protest anymore, but Rygehil could tell they wanted to. When the sound of their footsteps had vanished, Euberacon looked down at Jocosa once more.

For a time he examined her closely. He bent his ear to her mouth and listened to her shallow, sparse breaths. He laid a hand on her brow and measured her fever. He touched her hands and feet and felt the coldness of them. He lifted first one lid and then the other and peered into her blind and staring eyes. He laid a hand on her belly and stood as if listening to some faraway voice.

At last, Euberacon straightened up. 'Death has almost found her. There is none of man's physic that will save her from him.'

It seemed to Rygehil that the world split in two. 'There is nothing you can do?' he heard himself ask.

'I did not say so. There are things that may be done, but for them, I will demand a price.'

Whitcomb's remark about souls came echoing back to Rygehil. 'What price?'

Euberacon smiled his thin smile. 'Compose yourself. I am not the Devil. I have no interest in souls in that way.' Rygehil wanted to bridle at that, but he looked again at Jocosa, pale and still in the firelight, and did not dare.

'Your wife carries a daughter in her womb. I claim the life of the child in return for the life of the woman.'

Rygehil opened his mouth to say 'How do you know? How dare you? What manner of man are you?' But he looked again at the room with its jars and mortars and nameless shadows. This stranger who asked for the life of his child. His child who waited within his wife . . .

His wife who would die, and presently. He felt it as he felt the blood and fear roaring through his veins. What was one child? They would have a dozen. It was nothing, such a bargain. There were many solutions that could be found before then. This man, this sorcerer, might be satisfied with gold or land or some servant woman. It was nothing, this promise now. It was everything. It was Jocosa's life.

'If that is the price, I will pay.'

Euberacon's dark eyes glittered. 'Very well then.'

The sorcerer melted into the shadows and returned with a piece of parchment. He spread it out on one of the work tables. From overhead, he selected a gourd and untied the thong that held it to the roofbeam. He unstoppered the gourd and instantly the room filled with the scents of myrrh and rich resins. He poured some of the powder out into a shallow dish.

Euberacon picked up a small knife from the table. With one sharp stroke, he scored his own palm. Rygehil gasped. The other man gave him a look bordering on contempt and held his wound over the dish. Bright blood dripped into the powder. From a bundle of plumes on the table, Euberacon plucked up a crow's ebony feather. With delicate strokes, he mixed the blood and powder into a dark ink. He laid by the crow's feather and selected the feather of a white swan. With the same knife that had cut his hand, he trimmed the quill into a point. He dipped the pen into the ink. Despite the blood, its point came out blacker than Euberacon's rich robe. The sorcerer bent over the parchment and began to write.

Rygehil tried to see what words Euberacon laid down, but he could make no sense of the waving lines and dots. He had seen some Hebrew written once and thought it might be that, but it did not look quite right.

Whatever he wrote, Euberacon was soon finished. He sprinkled sand over his work and brushed it away. Then, he blew gently across it. Apparently satisfied, he reached for a glass beaker that seemed to contain nothing but the purest water. As he stretched out his hand, Rygehil saw his palm. The wound was completely gone.

Rygehil resisted the urge to cross himself. *It is for Jocosa's life. Her life.*

Slowly, carefully, Euberacon poured the water from the glass across the words he had written. He tilted the parchment so the liquid flowed down into a brass bowl. When all the water had crossed all the words, he set beaker and parchment down and picked up the bowl.

'Hold her head,' he instructed Rygehil. 'Open her mouth.'

Rygehil cradled Jocosa's head in the crook of his arm, and as gently as he could, prised open her mouth with two fingers. Euberacon set the bowl to her lips and tipped it forward. The liquid ran into her mouth. Euberacon stroked her throat.

Jocosa coughed, once, and then again. Her eyelids flew open. Euberacon clamped her mouth closed. She stared wildly up at Rygehil for a moment and then he saw her throat move as she swallowed. Almost at once the fear left her as she looked at him, and recognized what she saw.

Euberacon withdrew his hand.

'My lord?' whispered Jocosa. 'What day is this? How long have I lain asleep?'

'Lady!' Rygehil fell to his knees. His hand trembled as he touched her brow. The fever had departed and her skin was once again warm and dry. 'Oh, my love.' He bowed his head to her hand and could not speak another word.

Above him, Euberacon's voice spoke.

'You and your people may rest the night here. Be on your way in the morning. And do not forget your promise. When the child is of age, I will come for her.'

'I . . .' Rygehil looked up.

Euberacon was nowhere to be seen.

Rygehil swallowed hard. Jocosa touched his hand. 'What was that?'

'Nothing,' Rygehil embraced her. 'Nothing at all, my love.'

ONE

Rhian of the Morelands was in the yard when her father told Vernus to remove himself from the hall. Normally, she would have been lurking around a corner or in the shadows of the gallery, but this time she found she could not bear to hear the pre-ordained reply.

So, she stood in the grassy yard with the fresh spring sun warm on her skin. Around her, vassals drove geese and goats to pasture and pigs to root in the forests. Servants toted bales and baskets into the hall and the outbuildings. In the distance she could hear old Whitcomb berating one of the new squires for being slow, or slovenly, or both. All was busy life and full activity.

Except me. She twisted her fingers together. Her handmaid, Aeldra, stood a respectful distance behind her, but she could feel the woman's quiet disapproval. She should be at loom or spindle. She should be down in the cellar helping with the brewing, or seeing how Gwyneth and her new baby were getting on. She should be doing any of a thousand things.

It is like a verse from a country ballad.

'And the maid went to her father,

And her knees she bent.
Begging, "Father, dearest father,
will you please relent?"'

She stared at the cloudless sky. *Mother Mary, I beg you. Soften his heart.*

'Lady Rhian.'

The sound of Vernus's voice turned Rhian around. He emerged from the doorway and crossed the yard to her, side-stepping a cluster of squawking chickens. When Rhian saw his shoulders set square and level, she felt her heart rise, but in another moment he was close enough for her to see his face. The lines of bitterness on his brow and around his broad mouth showed clearly.

'It would seem I have failed in my suit to your father.' He squeezed his riding gloves in his hands and spoke to the tips of his boots. 'I am to take myself away and not return.' He looked up at her. 'Especially not with an offer of marriage.'

Rhian felt tears sting her eyes even as anger drove the blood to her cheeks. Cruelty. Sheer miserable cruelty. All the worse this time because Vernus was not just some faceless stranger who had sent a letter and gifts. He was a friend from her childhood, who had grown into a tall and handsome young man, well worth the position he would hold in the world. He had even been to Camelot and been presented to the king.

But no. She was not to have him.

'My father seems determined I should die unmarried and go to run with the apes in Hell,' she sighed. 'Vernus, I'm truly sorry.' *And sick and sad and burning with fury. Perhaps I shall burst my heart with grieving and that will be an end to it.*

'Could you speak to your mother? Your father sets much by her counsel, perhaps she could persuade . . .' his words trailed away as Rhian shook her head.

'Not in this, she cannot.' Tears threatened again. Rhian dropped her gaze to the ground and blinked hard. 'My father has been turning away my suitors for five years now, and for five years my mother has tried to persuade him of the worth of each of them. But he will not hear of it.' The heat of her anger dried up her tears. She stared hard at the window of the hall. 'He will not hear anything from any of us.'

'I will speak to my father. Perhaps he can persuade Lord Rygehil to part with you.'

Rhian felt a weak smile form. She wanted to touch his hand but decided she had better not. 'Thank you, Vernus. Perhaps he can.'

Your father will marry you to Melina of White Hill whose father is not insane, and we both know this. Please go away, Vernus. I cannot stand here trading empty words anymore.

'I must go, Rhian.' He bowed to her. 'But I have not abandoned you.'

'Thank you, Vernus.' She dropped a curtsey. 'God be with you.'

'And with you.'

His cloak swirled as he turned away and marched towards the stables, cutting a straight line through the myriad activities of the yard.

Rhian watched his back for as long as she could stand it. She dropped her gaze and caught sight of her reflection in the horse trough. Her eyes were a pleasant blue and since the age of fifteen, her figure had been rounded and full. She had seen the stablehands and foster boys casting glances at her so she knew she was not uncomely. Her hair was her crowning glory. It was red-gold in colour and even tightly braided as it was, it fell to the backs of her knees.

But it seemed she would have no use for what beauty she might have if her father continued to have his way.

'Aeldra,' she said to her maid. 'Fetch my bow and arrows,

and send a boy for my hounds. Meet me at the gate. I expect I shall soon want to be elsewhere.'

She lifted the hem of her skirt and strode into the hall.

It took her eyes a moment to adjust to the dim interior after the bright daylight, but her ears immediately caught the sound of preparations for the midday meal.

He did not even let Vernus stay to eat. Rhian's teeth clenched together. She stood aside for the servants setting up the trestle tables and bringing the benches away from the walls. Kettles of fragrant stew hung over the fire pits and a sheep's carcass turned on a spit tended by ancient Cleve.

Her father, Lord Rygehil of the Morelands, sat slumped in his carved chair at the end of the hall. A wooden goblet dangled from one hand. He looked up when she came to stand before him and dropped the curtsey that respect demanded.

'Yes, Rhian?' he said in a tired voice.

> *'And the maid went to her father,*
> *And her knees she bent.*
> *Begging, "Father, dearest father,*
> *will you please relent?"'*

But she would not beg. Not this day.

'Why?' she asked instead.

He sighed and straightened his back a little. His features fell into the hard lines she had come to know so well. 'Because I did not choose to give you to him.'

As if that were not evident. 'Lord Father, may I know the reason?'

He looked into the depths of his cup. 'More ale!' he called out and one of the servants hastened forward with a pitcher. Rhian wondered how much of that pitcher he had already drained.

'Lord Father . . .' she began again.

He pointed to her with his free hand. 'Your place is not to question me, Rhian, it is to be silent and obey.'

He downed a prodigious portion of his drink, and when he lowered his cup, Rhian saw something unexpected in his face. Regret, as plain and full as the resentment had been earlier.

She opened her mouth, but all her earlier thoughts had fled her. 'If you would just tell me what I have done, Lord Father, to merit this treatment.'

He shook his head heavily. 'Nothing, Rhian. You have done nothing.'

He turned his attention back to his cup.

I have lost. I am lost. Rhian curtsied reflexively. When she lifted her eyes, she saw her mother, Jocosa, standing in the threshold between the great hall and the living rooms. Jocosa gestured to her. Rhian set her jaw again and followed her mother as she walked up the stairs of the stone tower and into the sun room.

'Now then,' said her mother, sitting herself down on a cushioned chair. 'I suppose you will run away and shoot at birds and hares until dark to ease your disappointment.'

Rhian felt her cheeks heat up. 'That was my intention. What else should I do?' She threw open her hands. 'My father consistently denies me other employment for myself.'

'I know.' Jocosa took her daughter's hand. 'You will forgive your foolish mother. I fear one day you will run off and not come back to us.'

Rhian squeezed her mother's hand. It felt as worn by years as her face appeared worn by care. In a chest in the treasury Rhian had once seen a miniature of her mother as a young woman. She had been lovely. As a girl, Rhian had wondered where all that beauty had flown. Now, she thought she knew.

'On my soul, I would never leave without telling you, Lady Mother.' Rhian let herself smile. 'Where would I go, in any case? What neighbour would take me in knowing my father?'

Her mother pulled her gently down until Rhian sat upon a footstool. 'I know, I know, my dear. Perhaps if one of your brothers or sisters had lived, he would not guard you so jealously. Perhaps . . .' she stopped herself. 'Go off to your woods. Shoot what you may. Come back before dark. Then you can amuse yourself with your other skill. Lurking in doorways.' Rhian opened her mouth to protest, but her mother patted her hand. 'Do not attempt to beguile me, my lamb. I know in Aeldra you have had an excellent tutor in such matters.'

As hard as she tried not to, Rhian fidgeted. 'And why, Lady Mother, should I give way to that practice this evening?'

For a moment, her mother's gaze drifted over Rhian's shoulder and she seemed to be studying the grey stones of the wall. 'Because tonight, I mean to have your father announce to you he has reconsidered the suit of Vernus of White Hill.'

Rhian's heart leapt into her throat. 'Mother, how?'

Jocosa's shoulders slumped. 'Tears, extortion, hysterical fits, threats to bar him from my bed if necessary.' Her voice sounded drained and dull. 'I have never, never had to work upon him thus before. Such gross artifice is to be despised. But in this matter, I am afraid your father's reason has failed him.' Her gaze came back to Rhian's face. 'So now, mine must fail me.'

Rhian said nothing for a moment, she just squeezed her mother's hand. 'But,' she licked her lips. Her mouth had gone unaccountably dry. 'Forgive me, but why would you want me to witness this . . . conversation?'

Her mother smiled and some life returned to her voice. 'Firstly, so you do not hear about it through the general gossip. Secondly, because if nothing else, I am going to force my lord to give his reasons for forbidding you to marry. I want you to hear them from him, whether he knows he is giving them to you or not.'

Rhian let go of Jocosa's hand and walked across to the window. She stared out across the yard with its people and animals strolling to and fro.

'I do not like this, Lady Mother.'

'No more do I,' said Jocosa. 'And if you can tell me what else can be done, I am willing to hear you and act.'

Rhian had no answer for her. 'I will be back before dark.' She gathered up her skirt and left.

The whirling in her mind did not clear even when she reached the gate in the wooden wall that surrounded the hall and its yards and buildings. Her three long-legged grey-haired hounds leapt to their feet, wagging their tails and baying and straining at their leashes. The boy, Innis, struggled to hold them in check. As she approached, they thrust their noses into her skirt and against her hands. She patted them absently. Aeldra frowned at her, but Rhian did not say anything. She just took her bow and quiver from her maid's hands and slung them over her shoulder. Innis bowed until his scraggly forelock almost touched the ground.

'Let us go then. I would see if there are any partridge we can catch unawares today.' Rhian nodded to Innis and again to the guards who saluted her from either side of the gate. She tucked her skirt into her belt, set her gaze on the meadow past the earthen outer wall and followed the boy through it.

The dogs loped happily forward through the knee-high grasses towing Innis behind them.

'Let them loose, Innis.' Rhian unslung her bow and tested the string. 'Let us see what they find.'

'Yes, my lady.' With some difficulty, Innis hauled the dogs

to him so he could unfasten their leashes from their collars. With yelps of pure joy, all three sprang into the grass, free to run where they pleased. As she nocked an arrow into the string, Rhian found it in her heart to envy them.

In the next heartbeat, a great flurry of wings sounded from the burgeoning grass. Three brown partridge shot up towards the sky. Rhian drew her string back to her nose and sighted along the arrow's shaft. She loosed and was rewarded by the sight of one of the birds plummeting back to earth and landing with a loud thud.

'That one is for Vernus,' she whispered. 'And the next is for Aelfric, and the next for Daffydd, and the next for Shanus, and the one after that is for me.'

'If my lady is thinking of counting her disappointments with arrows, we will be out here all the rest of the year,' said Aeldra, puffing up behind her.

'What would you have me do then?' Rhian watched Innis crouch over the bird and pull out the arrow.

'It is not for me to say, of course, my lady,' said Aeldra with the false modesty that irritated Rhian so easily. 'But there are ways to ensure your father must say yes to your suitor.'

Rhian rolled her eyes and sighed. 'And don't think I haven't considered them Aeldra. But I would have to face my mother also and I'm not yet certain I could.'

All at once, one of the hounds bayed at the edge of the woods. Something flashed white and immediately there was a great crashing of underbrush and bracken as the creature, whatever it had been, fled into the forest. All three hounds barked and howled. They dived forward into the trees. Rhian ran after them.

What is it? A deer? No, it is too white for that . . .

She broke the treeline and was engulfed in the sun-dappled twilight of the forest. She saw the dogs' grey backs plunging on ahead of her and again glimpsed the fleeting white form.

The dogs ran into a thicket of fern fiddleheads and Rhian lost sight of them. The wind blew through the forest, rustling the greening underbrush and confusing her further.

'Orestes! Orion! Orpheus! Here, boys!' she called, dashing forward. Somewhere behind her she heard Aeldra calling her name. Rhian ignored her. She wanted to find her dogs. She wanted to see that mysterious white quarry they had flushed.

All at once, she broke into a sun-soaked meadow. The sudden light dazzled her and Rhian stumbled to a halt, blinking hard.

When her gaze cleared, she looked around to take her bearings, but then found herself gawping in surprise.

In the centre of the clearing stood a broad, gnarled stump. On it lay a flat board covered with red and white figurines of extraordinary delicacy. Not one of them was taller than Rhian's hand was long.

To one side, on a fallen tree, sat a gigantic man all of a sparkling green colour, as if he'd been fashioned out of a monstrous emerald. One of his hands could have engulfed Rhian's waist. The crown of his head brushed the leaves of the oak tree he sat under. Skin, hair, eyes, all shone greener than the sea. His plaited beard might have been grown from dewy meadow grass. His jerkin, mail and hose were so green the fresh leaves paled next to them. Beside him on the ground lay a battle-axe of the same brilliant colour.

Rhian was rooted to the spot, unable to move or think. The great, green giant smiled so broadly she could see that his teeth were indeed emeralds that flashed in the sun.

'It's called chess,' the giant's voice boomed all around Rhian's head. 'And a merry game it is too.' His eyes glittered as if he had caught two stars in them. 'Would you learn this game of nations and of power, pretty maiden? Step forward, then.'

Rhian found her feet moving. Without any thought or help from her, they carried her body into the sunlit meadow until she stood over the board. Now she saw the figurines were people, men and women all standing on a board inlaid with neat squares of ebony and ivory.

'Now, then.' The giant winked at her. 'Which side for you, pretty one? The red?' He pursed his lips and wrinkled his brow. 'I think not, though the red king knows you passing well.' He plucked a scarlet figurine from its place and Rhian saw a man with a lean, lined face and hooded eyes who wore long robes like a nobleman, or a monk.

'The white is your side, and the white queen is your protector, I think.' Another figurine lay nestled in the hollow of his enormous palm, although Rhian didn't see him put down the first. This one was a woman, perfectly formed, with a circlet on her long hair. Her eyes were wide and her face was wise, somehow. 'And with her, the white king, but not before the white knight.' Another figurine appeared in his palm. This was a man on a horse, holding his spear aloft and his shield before him. Rhian could not see his face, but she clearly saw the five-pointed star carved on the shield.

'Will these three keep you from the red king and the red castle?' The giant shook his head gravely. His palm was empty.

'You do not speak, pretty one. Perhaps chess is not the game for you?' The sparkling green smile grew fierce. Rhian felt her heart fluttering against her ribcage, but still she could not move. 'Perhaps you prefer riddles? Excellent!' The giant slapped the stump and all the figurines rattled on their board. 'Now, answer me this and be quick, pretty one,' he leaned over her, blocking the sun with his great, green head. 'What is it every woman wants?'

The scene in front of her began to fade and blur, as if her eyes had filled with tears. The giant laughed again 'Answer!

Answer!' he ordered. 'Answer, my pretty one!'

A noise. From the forest. A sharp, high barking. Drawing closer. The dogs. The dogs had found her.

Rhian found her tongue could move.

'Sweet Mother Mary, save me!' she screamed.

And she was alone.

All the strength fled from Rhian's body and she fell backward onto the forest floor.

For a long moment, she lay there blinking stupidly at the leaves above her. She heard the barking coming closer. All at once her hounds swarmed over her, whining, nosing and licking. They put their heavy feet on her stomach, squeezing out what little breath she had.

'Off, off,' she grunted. She managed to heave herself upright.

'Lady Rhian!' Aeldra's voice drifted through the trees. 'My lady, where are you?'

Rhian got to her feet. Her gaze swam, but steadied. The clearing was empty save for herself and the nosing, wagging dogs.

It was nothing. A dream. I have been too long out in the sun. I fainted, perhaps, or sat down to rest and dreamed.

But then her gaze drifted across to the rotting tree stump and she saw on it two figurines, one red, one white. Her heart in her mouth, she crossed to look at them. The red one was a tall woman, the very essence of beauty and perfection. She wore chains around her neck and bracelets on her arms. Her robes fell in heavy folds over her feet.

The white figure was a hag. It stooped to half the red lady's height. It was a grizzled, toothy horror gaping up at Rhian with a pig's glaring eyes.

'My lady!' A crashing and thrashing sounded through the brush behind her. Heavy-footed and out of breath, Aeldra waded through the grass. 'Where have you been? I . . .' she stepped up beside Rhian and saw the figurines.

'What are these?' Aeldra reached out one hand towards the red lady.

'No!' Rhian smacked her hand away. 'Leave them. They are cursed. I'm sure of it.' She took Aeldra's arm with one hand and the hem of her skirt with the other. 'Let us leave here, Aeldra, and find Innis. I would be back at home.'

Rhian set off between the trees. She very carefully did not look back.

Harrik, Hullward's son stepped into the council tent. As his eyes adjusted to the gloom, he surveyed the gathering. There were a dozen men, all Saxons, like himself, most battle scarred, also like himself. They squatted or lounged on piles of furs around the smoking central fire.

Dogs, Harrik thought. *Dogs at the feet of their master*. He lifted his gaze.

Wulfweard, called Wolfget by those who knew his vicious nature, sat in a slatted chair. He alone of the gathering was armed. A naked sword lay across his thighs. The symbol was hardly needed. The menace in Wolfget's hooded blue eyes shone plain enough.

'Be welcome to this assembly, my Lord Harrik,' said a musical voice.

Harrik started. A woman, clothed in a gown of smoky red circled the fire towards him. 'Let me offer you the guest cup and bid you know my Lord Wulfweard wishes you to sit at his right hand.'

Harrik struggled to keep himself from gawking like a boy. Wolfget had never before taken a wife, let alone one so blindingly lovely. Her golden hair hung to her waist and was plaited with a thread of silver. Her face was smooth and round with blue eyes set wide above a slim, straight nose. Her breasts and hips swelled amply beneath the dark red of

the gown which hung from her shoulders as if to call
attention to their perfect roundness.

Harrik mastered himself and took the wooden cup from
her soft, clean hand.

'My thanks.' He took a swallow of the mead.

Wolfget was flanked by two empty chairs. Harrik took his
place in the right-hand seat as invited. The woman took the
left.

Wolfget swept his cold gaze across the assembly.

'Brothers.' His voice was hard. 'It is ten years since the
defeat at Mount Badon scattered our strength. Since then,
Uther's upstart bastard has held us as his vassals, claiming
our lands, our sons, our very bodies as his own. We have
submitted in silence, knowing ourselves to be weak and
divided.' He laid a thick hand on the sword's hilt.

'Wounded to the death as we were, we were wise to do
so. But now, our wounds are closed. Our sons grow tall and
strong. Our brothers eye the rusted swords and axes hanging on our walls with restless anticipation. Now is the time
to force Arthur the Bastard to pay for what he has stolen.'

An angry rumble of assent rose from the assembly. Wolfget
smiled and Harrik felt a chill cross his skin. He cast a glance
towards the woman. All her attention was fixed on Wolfget
in an attitude of rapt adoration. Harrik's chill deepened. In
the flickering firelight he could see the stump of the ear
Wolfget had lost at Badon. Harrik himself was missing two
fingers from the same battle. The ghosts of them twitched
in memory of the blow.

Kolbyr, who'd seen both his brothers ridden down by
Arthur's captains, got heavily to his feet. 'My heart is with
you, my Lord Wulfweard, and I would sooner die in battlefield mud than a vassal's bed, but how can we wage such a
war? The Bastard sits secure in Camelot with a hundred
captains who will leap into action at the flick of his little finger.'

'Truth, truth,' said Ehrin, whose jaw had been so broken his words slurred in his mouth. 'Strong of purpose we may be, but we are not so strong of arms and warriors.'

'Our course is simple,' said Wolfget. 'Does the Bastard think us divided? Divided we will appear. In our separate lands we will strike here, there, take this town and that. He will respond with men and arms, as he must to preserve the peace that so boldly bears his name. We will harry those men, wear them down, kill all we can and withdraw. Soon, the Bastard's forces will be weakened by so many small cuts, they will not be able to defend themselves when we are ready to give the death blow.'

Harrik frowned. This was not the brash, heated Wolfget he knew from the wars. This stranger was a calm-hearted strategist. With a beautiful woman at his shoulder. Harrik glanced at her again. Had he been a young man, he would have stood up and made some fearless speech about rushing into battle, not for Wolfget's sake, but for hers.

Which was a point to be considered closely.

'Harrik you sit as silent as stone.' Wolfget's soft voice broke Harrik's reverie. 'What are your deep thoughts?'

'My thoughts are of Badon,' he said, looking into the depths of the guest cup. 'My thoughts are of lands, and of my son, hostage in Camelot to my word. And he is not alone there.' *Let me see your eyes, 'brothers', how many of your sons does Arthur hold?* 'I am thinking of the thousand thousand ways Arthur is entrenched on this island. I am thinking of the kings who are his neighbours and who pay him tribute.' He gave them all a grim smile. 'I am thinking we could have more easily bested all the Roman legions than this king.'

To Harrik's surprise, Wolfget nodded. 'Your words are sound, Harrik, and they should be weighed carefully. But think of this. Does the Bastard have neighbours and friends? Yes. But so do we. The terms of Arthur's peace have been hard on many, and many would be glad to see it broken. We have our secret friends in every town and fortress. Do arms and men flow from Arthur? They will flow into our hands.'

Harrik looked around and saw how the eyes of the men on the floor shone with eagerness. He knew then how it would be. There would be hours of talk, some close questioning of Wolfget, perhaps even a few words of wisdom spoken. But in the end, they would all pledge their lives on Wolfget's naked sword.

Feeling like an old man, Harrik got stiffly to his feet. It would be better if he stayed, of course, if he lied and flattered and foreswore himself. But he could not. He would not.

'What ails you, my Lord Harrik?' asked the woman softly.

'Old wounds, my lady.' Harrik bowed to her. 'This assembly will do as it will. We have been brothers in arms before this. I have been proud to say so. But I myself must consider carefully whether the peace that came when we laid down those arms has not benefited our people as it has the Britons.'

He left the tent amid a stony silence. Out in the open air he called for his horse and his sword. The animal was brought to him by a sour-faced man with Wolfget's blazon on his tunic. Harrik mounted and urged the horse into an easy canter until he was well out of earshot of the assembly encampment.

When he judged he had gone far enough, he pulled up on the reins. The horse halted and Harrik climbed down. Looking sharply about him, he led the animal into the thick of the forest. There, he tethered the horse loosely to an elm tree. He did not want the animal trapped if he did not come back. He tightened the laces on his scabbard so his sword would not jingle. Then, one careful step at a time, he made his way through bracken and fern back to the camp.

He had been uneasy when Wolfget sent his messenger with the invitation to this secret council. He had grown more uneasy each time he contemplated it. It was folly, this idea that the handful of Saxons who remained on the Isle of Britain could defeat Arthur. Worse, it was suicide.

But is it enough for what I do now? Harrik glimpsed the fabric of the tents and the sparkle of studded leather through the trees. Slowly, he lowered himself to the ground. Trying not to rustle the carpet of leaves beneath him, he crawled forward on his hands and knees. *Is it truly enough to turn spy on your own people?*

Apparently, it was, because he lay prostrate on the ground with fern leaves tickling his brow and nose, watching the camp carefully.

And we'll see who stays and goes, and when and how. If I am wrong about how it will go, so much the better. But if I am right . . .

He composed himself to patience. To keep his mind from the incessant itch of the ferns, he set about studying the sentries, thinking how he would have posted and armed them in Wolfget's place.

Men came and went. Servants brought wine and meat into the tent. The guests came out to relieve themselves or check on their horses. The sentries paced, or lounged about. The lounging became more frequent as the time wore on. Harrik shook his head minutely. Wolfget was not well served.

The tent's flap lifted again. This time, it was the woman who came out. In the full daylight she was even more shatteringly lovely than he had thought. His heart and loins both began to ache with an urgency he had thought himself past.

The woman looked about her. Evidently, she saw nothing that displeased her. She raised one hand and spoke a word Harrik could not understand. In the next breath, he heard the flapping of heavy wings. A raven glided down from the trees and came to rest on the woman's waiting wrist.

She brought her wrist down until the bird's eyes were level with her own. She contemplated the raven for a long time, and it stared back unwinking, which a beast should not have been able to do. At last, the woman opened her mouth.

The raven thrust beak, head, and neck well down her throat.

Harrik jerked backward, forgetting the need for silence. The woman and the bird stood still, its head in her mouth, like some foul statuary. He realized the muscles of her throat swelled and contracted. Not swallowing, but pushing something out.

Harrik's own throat clamped down around his breath.

The raven pulled its head free of the beauty's mouth. She smiled broadly and lifted her wrist again. The bird spread its shining wings and flew away.

She watched her pet vanish into the sky, turned, and went back inside the tent.

Harrik, struggling to keep his breathing under control, crawled back into the woods on his hands and knees. He moved as far and as fast as he could, but finally, he had to stop and vomit at the roots of a birch tree.

What manner of secret friends have you, Wolfget? He raised his head and wiped a shaking hand across his mouth. *What alliances have you made for us?*

He sat and listened for a moment. No sound of pursuit cut through the small rustles of wind and the forest life. Harrik forced himself to get to his feet and take his bearings. As soon as his knees had stopped shaking enough that he could be sure of his footing, he made his way back to his horse.

The animal was still there, chewing thoughtfully at the undergrowth. Harrik led it back to the road and slung himself into the saddle. To his shame, he found he had to work to keep himself from taking the horse to a gallop to escape as quickly as possible from what he had seen.

You are a fool. A fool! He admonished himself. *You have seen far worse things in battle.*

But the truth was, he had not. He had heard stories of such horrors, of course, and told a few himself, with great relish. Witches and wizards had their ways and everyone knew it. Did not Arthur have Merlin to advise him and keep watch over his captains and capital? But to see so unnatural a thing . . .

I grow old. I grow dull. Perhaps this role of spy and traitor is all I am fit for anymore.

The forest thickened around him. The sound of his horse's hooves became muffled by the unbroken carpet of leaves. The wind freshened and Harrik tried to catch a glimpse of sky between the leafy branches overhead. There might be rain before long, but without a clear view of sky there was no telling. The prospect of concluding his business in a downpour, further darkened his mood, but he rode on.

Up ahead, the road forked, one branch bearing west, the other continuing north. At their crux, a man tended a small fire. A great, pale horse was tethered nearby. Green trappings hung from its reins. A bay palfrey stood beside it, nuzzling a patch of fern. Its reins were also hung with green. The studded shield propped against a tree was covered in green as well.

The man himself was no longer a youth, but neither was he old. He was dark in hair and eye. His beard had been shaved clean off. His shoulders and arms were powerful. Here was a man who had not led an idle life. He could not be taken for anything but a Briton lord. He looked up at Harrik's approach and raised a friendly hand.

'God be with you this day, good sir.'

'God be with you,' Harrik answered. 'I'd be glad of a rest. May I share your fire?'

'You may,' said the man. 'If you can tell me my name.'

Harrik gave a show of consideration. 'I think you are my Lord Gawain, captain of the Round Table and nephew to Arthur, the High King.'

Gawain smiled and got to his feet. 'My Lord Harrik,' he bowed deeply. 'You are most welcome.'

'And I am most honoured.' Harrik dismounted and tethered his small hairy horse next to Gawain's animals. 'I was stunned to receive word Arthur would send his nephew to me.'

'He means it as a token of his good will.' Gawain opened one of his saddlebags which lay on the ground beside his shield. He pulled out a folded sheet of parchment. 'As you will find written here.' The document was sealed in red wax impressed with the dragon rampant that was Arthur's sign.

'You may assure His Majesty that I will read this with great attention.' He tucked the document into his shirt.

'But now you have other news for me?' Gawain folded his legs and settled by the fire again.

'I do.' Harrik sat beside him. He watched the fire for a moment, gathering his thoughts. He opened his mouth to speak, but the words he wanted would not come.

'I have a son at Camelot,' he said awkwardly. 'My only boy. They have taken him well in hand there. I visited him not three months ago. He has been taught to read and write Latin. He can use a sword and ride better than I could at his age. He grows into a strong and reasoned man.' He paused. A stick in the fire snapped in two. 'Not a brute. Not a barbarian. Not like the men I knew when I was a boy, a world away from here.'

Gawain nodded. 'I think you will find word of your boy in His Majesty's letter. I believe my brother Geraint intends to take him as squire.'

Harrik touched his shirt. 'I like this peace of Arthur's. I

like this land. I do not . . .' He clenched his fist. 'I will not see it die to feed Wolfget's blood-lust.'

'You too are a strong and reasoned man,' said Gawain softly. 'I ask you, of your courtesy, tell me what you have seen.'

Harrik spoke slowly, sketching the events of the council. Gawain listened attentively. When Harrik named each of the men he saw there, Gawain asked pointed questions about where their lands were, how many men they commanded, and who their allies were. Harrik could see the knight sketching a map of the treachery in his mind.

Then, Harrik told him of the woman and the raven.

Gawain's eyebrows lifted. 'That, friend, is an unwholesome thing.'

Harrik gave one short bark of a laugh. 'Those are milder words than I would use, my lord.'

Gawain smiled. 'You have not seen the inside of Merlin's workroom. No,' he held up his hand. 'Pray do not ask me. I was a youth when I had my glimpse, and more of a fool than I knew.'

Harrik dismissed the suggestion with a wave. 'I have no intention of questioning you. As it is, I know more of magic than I care to.'

'That shows your wisdom as clearly as anything you have yet done,' said Gawain soberly. 'My Lord Harrik, it was my intention to linger in this land for a day or two to see what else I could learn, but what you have told me, both about Wulfweard and his nameless lady, shows me I must return to the High King without delay.'

Harrik stood. 'Let me take my leave of you then.'

They clasped hands and each commended the other to God. Harrik rode away feeling moderately better. The High King's letter crackled in his bosom. His old loyalties sold for new safety and peace, and his son's life.

All at once, his horse stumbled. A curse slipped out of

Harrik's mouth. The animal recovered its gait, but not completely. It limped now, favouring its left foreleg.

'God's legs,' muttered Harrik, as he halted the beast and climbed to the ground. He bent down and with a practised hand, coaxed the horse to lift its hoof and show him the bottom.

There, a round stone shoved deep into the soft frog of the hoof. Harrik retrieved the hoof pick from his pack and swearing in each of the three languages he knew, finally managed to pry it loose. There was no question of being able to ride any further, though. The animal was lamed. He would have to walk the rest of the way.

He let the horse drop its hoof and looked at the stone. It was a round-bottomed, sharp-edged chunk of flint that had done the damage.

How does such a thing come to be in a forest? This belongs on some low riverbank.

He drew his arm back to hurl the thing into the bushes.

But as he looked where he aimed, he saw a huge black raven sitting on the branch of a maple tree. The bird gave a rough, mocking croak and flew into the air.

Harrik's fist closed around the stone. His heart grew chill and inside him a small quiet voice told him the horse's lameness did not matter now. Harrik, Hullward's son, would not reach home after all.

TWO

The evening meal was a mostly silent affair. Rhian, still disturbed by the events of the day, had no appetite. She could only force down a piece of bread sopped in gravy from the mutton, and for once her mother did not chide her for it. Father attended to his drinking and little else. At last, Rhian excused herself and fled the hall. Aeldra rose primly to follow her, but Rhian waved her maid back to her seat. She did not want that nosing, talkative presence now. She wanted to return to her chamber, to sit alone and try to regain some composure. But as she mounted the narrow, spiralling stairs she paused, one hand resting on the cool stone of the wall, and she remembered what her mother had told her.

She did not want to spy on her parents to find out what it should have been her right to know. But mother had spoken truthfully. If, after turning down five separate suitors, father had not told her what his reasoning was, he had left her with no choice but to gain that understanding by artifice.

At the top of the stairs, Rhian turned right instead of left and entered her mother's sitting room.

The room was empty. All were still at board. The great

embroidery frame with its partly completed scene of a lion and a unicorn kneeling before the Virgin waited for its mistress's touch. Other tapestries, some completed by her mother's hand, some by ladies gone before, hung about the room. Scenes of hunts, pastoral weddings and orchards blocked out the worst of the draughts and dressed the bare stone with summer colours. After a heartbeat's indecision, Rhian lifted the corner of the orchard tapestry and ducked behind it, drawing her hems in close to her body so they would not peep out and give her away.

She felt completely ridiculous; a naughty child at some mischievous game.

Think of Vernus, she counselled herself as she attempted to find the patience to wait. The tapestry smelled of old dust, and the crowning of this whole nonsensical affair would surely be if she gave herself away with a sneeze.

Think of finally knowing why you are being forbidden to marry. Think of becoming mistress in your own house. Vernus was kind, and had beautiful eyes. He would be good to her, as mother swore father had once been. But Vernus would not change as father had. Surely he would not.

Rhian bit her lip and tried to compose her agitated spirits.

Fortunately, she did not have long to wait. Light footsteps soon sounded against the floor, signalling the arrival of Jocosa with her faithful maid, Una.

'Una, please ask his lordship if he will attend me here. Then you may retire.'

Cloth rustled, indicating, Rhian was certain, Una's small curtsey. 'Yes, my lady. Are you sure though . . .?'

'I will send for you if I have need.' Jocosa's voice was tired.

'As you wish, my lady.' Rhian thought Una sounded a little hurt. It was a day for bruised feelings.

Rhian did not directly hear Una's departure. She inferred

it from the sound of her mother's sigh, from the brush of cloth as she crossed the chamber, the gentle scrape of her fingers against the uncompleted tapestry, the soft pop of a needle through cloth and the drag of thread behind it as she completed a single stitch. Rhian wondered if she should reveal herself, but decided against it. There was no telling when father would walk in, and should the unthinkable happen and the scene turn truly ugly, she wanted to be able to say mother had no idea she had concealed herself in the room. That much, at least, would be true.

Boots slapped against stone. Hinges creaked. Rhian held her breath.

'You sent for me, Jocosa?' Father's voice was heavy with more than just an overindulgence of ale.

'I did, my husband.' Mother's voice was crisp, efficient, as when she was giving orders to the servants. 'I am told that young Vernus was sent away with his hat in his hands.'

Wood creaked sharply as father dropped himself into a chair. 'It is not time for our Rhian to marry.'

'Tell me, pray, when will it be time?' Each of mother's words took on a sharp edge. 'She is fully nineteen and a grown woman. She is ready to be mistress of her own house and mother of her own children.'

'Vernus is not for her.' His reply was dull. Rhian wondered if he even looked at mother.

'Why not?' Rhian imagined mother throwing up her hands in wonderment. 'His rank and heritage are good, his father's standing with the High King . . .'

'I say Vernus is not for her! Be content!' roared father, his fist thumping hard against the chair's arm.

'How am I to be content?' demanded mother. 'When I watch my daughter sink into melancholy and my husband sink into a pitcher of ale?' Cloth rustled and Rhian knew mother strode across the room. 'What has happened to you,

Rygehil? Where is the man I loved more than life itself?'

Silence stretched out, long and heavy before her father spoke again in his thick voice. 'I did not think it would be thus. I thought there would be other children.'

'God has left us Rhian,' said mother, puzzled.

'No.' To her shock, Rhian heard tears in her father's voice. 'He has not left her to us.'

Again, a rustle of cloth. Did her mother kneel? Retreat? Rhian longed to see, but forced herself to hold still.

'I do not understand,' said mother.

'I . . . she . . . oh, Jocosa . . .' emotion made father's voice tremble. 'I made a promise, Jocosa. I did it for you, I swear, I thought there would be other children. I did not know. I would undo it if I could, I swear. I have tried . . .'

'Husband.' Mother spoke the word firmly, but Rhian heard the fear in her voice. It echoed the fear causing Rhian's breath to flutter in her throat. 'Contain yourself.'

Father, what have you done?

Neither drink nor grief permitted father to gain coherence. 'We were returning from Arthur's coronation. I didn't know you were with child or I never would have taken you on the road. You were sick to death, Jocosa. I was so afraid I would lose you. You were everything to me. I was weak, and afraid. I . . .'

'Rygehil, what are you saying?' Rhian thought mother must have shaken him then. 'I cannot understand you.'

Rhian listened, her heart growing cold and tight with fear, as her father told of taking shelter in the old Roman garrison, of finding the sorcerer there, and of making his bargain. Rhian's life in exchange for Jocosa's.

'No,' whispered mother, her voice trembling as badly as Rhian's hands at these impossible, terrible words. 'Say this is not true. Say it is the drink, some madness. Anything but that you sold our daughter away to a black sorcerer.'

'I did it for you, Jocosa. You were going to die!'

'Better I had died!' shouted mother in return. 'Better Rhian had never been born than you should do so impious a deed!'

'You will not so speak to me!' bellowed father. 'Ungrateful woman!'

'No!' screamed Rhian, unable to contain herself a moment longer. She shoved the tapestry aside to see what she had suddenly feared; father towering over mother, his strong hand raised to strike her pale face.

'Rhian,' he breathed. He truly was very drunk, the effects of the ale causing his emotions to ebb and flow without warning. In a heartbeat, he had gone from rage to guilty pleading. 'Daughter, you should not be here. This is not for your ears.'

'Then for whose is it?' Rhian was too afraid, too infuriated to be placated. She interposed herself between her parents and squarely faced her father, turning her face up so he could strike it if he so chose. 'Can you at least tell me what I have done that I should be sold off in this manner? Have I ever been unfilial or impious? What crime could I have possibly committed that you would thus condemn me out of hand?'

'This is no fault of yours, Rhian.' His breath smelled of the excess of ale he had drunk but he was struggling to rise above it. It was a terrible sight, as if she were watching him drown. 'I acted as I thought best. Look at your mother. It was her life I sought to save.'

Rhian did look at her mother, the gaunt, lined woman who had spent years trying to understand why her husband held himself at such a distance from her. Now she had her answer, and her gentle brown eyes were full of the horror of it.

'We must seek this man out,' said mother, twisting her hands together as if attempting to rip a solution out of thin air. 'We must offer him some other bargain. Any other . . .'

Father shook his head. 'I cannot find him. I have searched the countryside for him, thinking to trade my life to break the bargain.'

'Then go to the High King,' urged Rhian. 'Tell him what has happened. Surely, he will not hold you to so evil a contract.'

But father just turned away. 'This is not a matter for the laws of men, not even for kings. The sorceries here are too deep for that.'

Rhian thought of her vision in the forest and shuddered.

'Return to your room, daughter,' said father without looking at her. 'The bargain is made and may not be undone. Ask no more after marriage and commend yourself to God. Only He can help you now.'

Stunned and sickened to her core, Rhian found words died in her throat. She looked helplessly to her mother.

'We cannot leave it at this,' mother said.

'We will, because we must.' With those words father departed from the room, the tread of his boots echoing off the stone walls.

'No!' cried mother. 'No, husband . . .' Gathering her skirts, Jocosa ran from the room, following her husband, to cry, plead or threaten.

For a long moment, Rhian found herself unable to move, and when she did, it was as if her body had undertaken the decision of its own accord. She walked down the cold, stone hall, past the stairs and into her own chamber. There, Aeldra stood among so many familiar things; her spindles and threads, her sewing and embroidery, her paints, the small inlaid table that held her jewellery box, the carved bed she had slept in since she was a child. It all seemed hollow, drained of substance, as her life had suddenly become.

'Mistress?' said Aeldra, tentatively. 'Are you well? Shall

I fetch you wine? Or a cloth for your head?'

'No,' Rhian managed to say. 'I want nothing.'

'At least sit then.' She felt Aeldra tugging at her arm and permitted herself to be guided to a chair and made to sit.

Her mind was too full to perform these simple actions without assistance. The same thoughts rang over and over, like church bells on the Sabbath. She was promised, to a sorcerer, who had asked for her before she had even been born, and her father, her father whom she had loved and trusted all her life, even when she did not understand him, had given her over, and had done it for love.

She tried to understand a love that would make such a bargain, that would demand so much. It was passion such as the bards sang of. It knew no limits. It would sacrifice all for the beloved.

And in the ballads, it sounded very fine and noble, but what of the one who must be the sacrifice? What of the child she had been and the maiden she was now? Was it her duty to go meekly with this stranger who had demanded so evil a price from a desperate man and a dying woman?

That thought broke the paralysis that held her.

'No,' she said, looking up at Aeldra. 'It is wrong and it is wicked.'

'What do you mean, my lady?' asked Aeldra, confused.

Rhian's mind felt as clear as it had been cloudy before. She would not be handed over like a bribe to a corrupt seneschal. She would not stay and watch her father do this, nor would she watch her mother break her heart over what her husband had done.

'Aeldra.' Rhian gripped her maid's hand. 'Aeldra, are you my friend?'

Aeldra stiffened, shocked at such a question. As she looked into Rhian's eyes, however, a measure of understanding came to her. 'I hope my lady knows how well I regard her.'

'Then as a friend, much more than as my maid, I am asking for your help. You must bring old Whitcomb here to my room. Neither of you must be seen, by anyone, but most of all not by my father, do you understand?'

She did not. The expression on her lean face said that plainly enough. She folded her hands primly before her. 'I am sure my lady knows what is best . . .'

'No, she doesn't.' Rhian shook her head. 'Your lady is terrified, for her life and her soul, and she is trying to save both. Will you help her?'

Again Aeldra searched Rhian's eyes, looking deeply. 'Very good, my lady.' She curtsied. 'I'll see to the matter.'

Aeldra shut the door behind her. In the silence left in her wake, Rhian fancied she could hear her own heart beating like the hooves of a galloping horse, spurred on by the temerity of what she meant to do.

Whitcomb was her dearest friend among her father's servitors. Where her father would not, or could not, love her, Whitcomb had. He was the one who had taught her to shoot and to ride. He had helped her train her hounds and taught her to hunt. He told her all manner of stories he'd learned from the freemen and serfs, most of which Rhian was quite certain her mother would have been appalled that she knew. But despite years of such daring secrets, Whitcomb was always the first to insist she learn to be a proper, God-fearing lady and be a source of pride to her parents.

But at the same time he was staunchly loyal to his lord. Rhian bit her lip. There lay the danger, but she needed him. He could go without question where she could not, no matter how dark the night or how thoroughly she disguised herself.

Rather than simply pace about, Rhian sought action. She pulled a square of fine linen out of her sewing basket. She had meant to broider it into a veil. Now she upended her jewellery box into it. She did not have much, but she had some gold, a string of amber beads, a brooch of pearl and rubies, and several rings, one set with a square emerald the size of her thumbnail her mother said had come all the way from Rome. The whole of her wealth. She tied the cloth tightly and stowed it in the leather satchel she took with her when she went out shooting.

She'd have to leave her hounds behind. Rhian's heart twinged at the thought. Odd – it was a small thing compared to leaving her parents. She rubbed her forehead. She must not distract herself with such thoughts. She must keep her wits about her, or she was lost.

A soft knock sounded on the door.

'Come,' she called.

The door opened. In the threshold stood old Whitcomb. He had been her father's right hand for longer than Rhian had been alive. His hair and long beard were iron grey turning to white, but he was still a bluff man with hard hands and eyes that could see a lazing stablehand through a stone fence.

Those eyes took in the bulging leather satchel as she beckoned him inside, and they surely saw how white her face had gone.

'So,' he said with a sigh as he closed the door. 'It's come home at last, has it?'

Rhian started. 'What do you know of this?'

The lines on Whitcomb's kind face deepened until he looked as old as Methuselah. 'I was there, my lady. I heard your father speak his bargain with that black sorcerer. I knew one day there would be a reckoning.' His gaze hardened. 'I have searched the land whenever I had leave, hoping I might find him and put an end to this thing one way or another before . . .' It seemed he could not make himself finish.

Rhian felt her hands begin to shake once more. 'I thank you for all you have done for me, though I knew of none of it. Now I must ask for your help again.' She took a deep breath. 'I mean to leave tonight to seek sanctuary with the holy sisters at the monastery of St Anne. I will take holy orders if I must.' She laid her satchel down beside the empty jewellery box. Surely there was enough inside to dower herself to Christ, if that was the only way the Mother Superior would shelter her. 'I need you to go down and saddle a horse for me. Not Agamemnon,' she said, with another pang of regret at leaving behind her favourite steed. 'That would cause too many questions.' Whitcomb could make a hundred excuses to ride out at any hour. She could not. It would be hard enough for her to sneak out into the yard without being seen. To ready a horse in the stables with the hands sleeping in the loft, or playing bones in the stalls would be impossible.

If she was seen, she would be stopped, she was certain of that. Whitcomb was her one chance.

'I will see to it, my lady,' said Whitcomb gravely.

'Thank you.' She grasped both his hands and kissed him swiftly on his rough cheek. 'I will be behind the brewing shed as soon as I may after the household goes to sleep.'

'I will not fail,' he said, squeezing her hands.

With that, he turned and opened the door. He looked sharply left, then right before he stepped into the corridor, leaving Rhian alone once more.

Rhian swallowed. All her limbs felt suddenly heavy as lead. *Are these my choices? To be taken away by a black sorcerer to live or die at his whim, and who knows which would be worse? Or to live in silence behind stone walls swaddled in black and grey and to know only work and prayer?*

She squeezed her eyes shut, to stop the tears that threatened to flow freely. *Mother Mary, there must be another way. I beg you, send me a sign, some messenger that I may know what to do.*

But if the Holy Virgin had an answer for her, Rhian could not hear it.

*   *   *

Harrik opened his eyes. Light flickered against pale canvas. Outside the wind whistled through the branches of the trees, rustling their new leaves. He lay on a bed of furs. A good fire burned in the centre of the pavilion, scenting the enclosure with smoke . . . and something else. Something rare and unfamiliar that at once disturbed his mind and made him feel profoundly awake.

Harrik sat up. His hands were not bound, which he would have expected, for surely he was a prisoner. He had no memory of how he had got here. He remembered finding the stone, and seeing the raven, but then all was darkness.

The unfamiliar scent reached him again and he breathed it in. It was like cloves, and like amber, but neither of these. It appealed, like the scent of a good meal just cooked, or, even more, the scent of a woman close by.

Harrik shook his head. It was distracting. If they had left him his hands, whoever brought him here, they would learn they should not, even though they had thought so far as to deny him his sword.

He got himself to his feet, but before he could take a step, the pavilion opened to reveal a woman. The rich scent grew suddenly sharper, as if she carried it with her, and for a moment Harrik felt dizzy. Then he recognized the slim form and the golden hair. This was Wulfget's woman. What was her name? Had he even heard it?

But it meant that Wolfget held him, and it meant he must be careful still what he said.

The woman, however, spoke first. 'Welcome Harrik, Hullward's son,' she said and her voice was low and clear, and truly did seem full of welcome. Her eyes that reflected the firelight also seemed to hold welcome, but of a very different sort.

Harrik reminded himself again that he was not a boy nor a fool and pushed himself to his feet. He towered over her.

She had not seemed so small nor so delicate when he had
seen her before as she did now, moving to a table where
cups waited with a skin of wine. Harrik stared, fascinated.
He had not remembered her skin being so fair either, nor
her hands so supple as they lifted the skin and deftly poured
the wine, red as blood, red as her gentle mouth, into the
cups for them to share.

'Why have I been brought here?' he remembered to ask.
'Where is Wulfweard?'

'My husband will be along presently.' She lifted a cup in
her pale hand and held it out to him. She seemed lumines-
cent, absorbing the firelight and returning it softened and a
more pure white than it had been. Her mouth was so red
. . . had she already drunk some wine? Was that what stained
her lips and turned them so inviting a shade?

She saw where his gaze lingered. How could she not?
Harrik cursed himself and tried to look away, but she moved
towards him with the grace of a doe. Her dress was simple,
a plain fawn wool. It outlined her round breasts and a flat
belly that had never yet known children. The braided belt
served only to draw the skirt more tightly over her full,
smooth hips that swayed ever so slightly as she approached,
bringing all the scents of wine and spices, smoke and amber
with her.

'Will you drink with me, Hullward's son?' she asked softly,
her eyes dipped, almost shy as she held out the cup. He
should not take it. He must not. There was something wrong
here, in the air, in his blood, in this woman's presence. He
tightened his hands into fists. If only he could think what it
must be. If only her perfume were less strong, if only she
herself were less lovely.

'Surely there is no harm in sharing what is offered?' she
said with a small smile. 'I shall drink myself and you will
see.' She lifted the cup to her full and smiling mouth. Harrik

could not help but watch the way her tongue parted her red, red lips just a little in anticipation of the wine's touch. She sipped delicately but long. He watched the way light and shadow played across her throat as she swallowed and his clenched hands ached to trace the wine's path down between her breasts to her belly and lower yet, to know what she kept between her round thighs, to hear what she said in love . . .

'Now, you drink for me, Harrik.' She held out the cup and looked boldly into his eyes, her mouth still parted just a little so he could see her white teeth. A drop of wine clung to the corner of her mouth. It shimmered there like a ruby and he stared at it, mesmerized.

The woman noted that his gaze lingered there on her mouth, and her eyes widened, playfully, knowingly. With her free hand, she reached up and wiped the drop away, then held up the tip of her wine-stained finger before him.

'Drink, Harrik,' she murmured, her voice rich with promise. 'Let me know what manner of man you are.'

Slowly, as in a dream, Harrik touched his lips to the tip of her finger. The wine tasted sweet, like honey, and her skin beneath was soft and warm. She sighed at his kiss, her eyes closing in pleasure. He took her hand between his own. It was light as the petal of a white rose and smooth as silk. Like silk, it was sensuous to the touch, inviting the hands to caress it, to press it, to wrap one's whole self in its luxury.

She opened her eyes and all her pleasure of him seemed to shine in the sparks lit by the fire.

'Take what you want,' she whispered to him. 'It is all before you, and then I will be yours and you will be mine. Come, Harrik my love. Hold nothing back.'

Her words undid him. Harrik laced his fingers in her golden hair and pulled her to him, kissing her hard. Her mouth opened eagerly to his, her tongue touching lips and teeth even as she made a sound like a laugh and threw her arms around him. She tasted of wine, salt and myrrh. Harrik felt himself rise and harden and his blood sang as the whole of her body pressed against him, rubbing, teasing, promising, ready. He could think of nothing else, desired nothing else but the silken warmth of her skin, the salt and sweet of her body. The thought of her surrounding him aroused him as if he were a youth again, and as she laid herself down onto the furs, he knelt as if in fealty and followed willingly where she led.

Daylight faded from the world with painful slowness. Rhian lingered over her sewing while the rush lights and the hour candle burned low around her. She sent Aeldra running for wine, for a posset, for a lavender-rinsed cloth for her brow, pretending that a headache kept her from seeking sleep.

At last, because she could think of nothing else, she sent Aeldra for a bed warmer. Alone, she tried to think. Rhian did not want to tell Aeldra any more than she already knew. When the household discovered Rhian gone, Aeldra would be the first one questioned, and Aeldra would not lie to her lord and lady. To do so was to risk being turned out of the hall to fend for herself in the hedgerows. Which left the question of how Rhian could send the maid away long enough to make her escape. She could not even allow herself be put to bed in her nightclothes, because she would have to dress alone and in the dark afterwards. It would take an age when every second would be precious.

Aeldra, however, solved her dilemma for her. She returned, not with the bed warmer, but with a brown cloak draped over her arms.

'If my lady were to choose to wear this,' Aeldra said quietly. 'Anyone who saw her might think they were seeing one of the serving women instead.'

Stunned, Rhian accepted the cloak, a lump rising in her throat. 'They will question you.'

Aeldra folded her hands in her familiar way. 'And I will say my mistress said she went to meet young my Lord Vernus in the charcoal burner's shed by the well of St Ethelrede.'

'It will be a lie,' Rhian whispered.

'Not if you say it now.'

Slowly, Rhian repeated her maid's words. 'I'm sorry, Aeldra,' she said, laying the brown cloak in her lap. 'I knew you were my friend, but did not realize how true a friend.'

The maid's smile was kind. 'Young women seldom understand such things. Especially when the friend is apt to be exacting and sharp of tongue.'

Rhian glanced at the slash-marked candle beside her bed. It had been burning for three hours, and had been lit at twilight. 'Is it safe now, think you?'

Aeldra leaned towards the door and put her hand to her ear in a practised gesture. 'I hear no one.'

Rhian drew the cloak about her shoulders. A full handspan of her dress showed out underneath it, as she was some inches taller than Aeldra, but hopefully no one would be able to discern the colour or quality of the exposed fabric from one swift glance in the dark.

Aeldra fussed with the carved bone clasp and then, unexpectedly, kissed Rhian on the cheek. 'God be with you, my lady.'

'And with you, Aeldra.'

There was no time to linger. Rhian squeezed Aeldra's hand, claimed her satchel, and opened her chamber door. The corridor outside was still and dark. She could not risk a light. She laid her hand on the cool stones of the left-hand wall and hurried ahead, trying to step only lightly on the rushes underfoot.

Behind her, Aeldra closed her door, cutting the golden

candlelight off sharply, and leaving Rhian alone in the dark.

Rhian faltered only briefly. She called to mind what awaited her if she were caught, and that thought lent her speed. Her fingertips found the threshold leading to the staircase and her foot found the first stair. Feeling her way carefully, she began her descent.

Light flooded the world suddenly, making Rhian blink and miss her step. She stumbled, and looked back before she could stop herself, and found she looked up into her mother's face.

Mother stood at the top of the stairs, frozen in the flickering light of a tallow candle. Only her eyes moved, as she took in the maid's brown cloak, the satchel, and Rhian's face peering out of the shallow hood. Rhian lifted her chin.

A single tear glistened on Jocosa's cheek. Her mouth shaped words. Rhian thought she said, 'God be with you.' Then, her mother turned back the way she had come. Within two heartbeats, she vanished into the corridor's shadows.

Rhian drew the hood down further over her face, more to hide her tears than her visage, and hurried out into the cool spring night.

Whitcomb had indeed not failed her. Rhian rounded the corner of the brewer's shed to see him standing in its shelter, well out of the silver-grey light the curved quarter-moon sent forth. His gloved hand, however, held the reins for not one horse, but two. The first was Thetis, a grey mare, the horse Rhian had learned to ride on. She was no longer so fast or so spirited, but she was still strong and steady, and she knew Rhian well. The other was Blaze, a chestnut gelding with a white forehead and fetlocks that Whitcomb often rode as he surveyed the lands for her father.

Rhian stared accusingly at Whitcomb, now seeing that he wore his old leather hauberk and hood, and that he had his long knife at his waist and his bow and quiver of arrows slung over his shoulder. He said nothing, but even in the darkness she could read his face plainly enough.

I am coming. I will not let you do this alone. If you order me back, I will follow you.

'Father will be angry with you when he finds out,' she murmured.

'I have braved my lord's anger before,' replied Whitcomb with a grim smile. 'And never with greater cause.'

There was no time for argument. The moon was already well up, and if mother had been stirring, others might be about. In truth, Rhian had no heart to try to order him away. His solid presence would make what she must do less lonely.

Whitcomb held Thetis's head while Rhian stowed her satchel in the saddlebag. Inside she found a number of small but useful items Whitcomb had thought to add – a hunting knife, a spare bowstring, a pair of riding gloves. She mounted the horse and Whitcomb passed up her bow and quiver and handed her the reins. Then, expertly, if a little stiffly, he swung himself up onto Blaze's back. The horses were long-time stable mates and old friends with their riders, so they stepped up quickly in answer to the lightest of urgings. Despite this, their hoofbeats on the packed earth of the yard sounded to Rhian like thunder. She could not help but glance back towards the hall that had been her only home. No light shone in any of the windows, not even her mother's.

Tears threatened again, and Rhian turned her face quickly towards the night beyond the yard.

They rode across the cleared fields where the damp air was heavy with the scent of freshly ploughed earth. They crossed the chattering beck, its clear water flowing like liquid moonlight over round stones. Both deeply familiar with the countryside, they had no difficulty in finding the track through the forest that would lead them down to the broad Roman road. The rustles of the night-waking animals accompanied them. An owl hooted once overhead. The stars in all their millions filled the sky with glory and the wind blew chill, but soft, across Rhian's skin. Slowly, she felt the ache in her throat begin to ease.

Perhaps it would not be so bad. Perhaps the Mother Superior of St Anne's would shelter her without requiring that she take vows. The emerald ring and the rest would, after all, buy a small convent much that it needed. Perhaps Whitcomb could find some excuse to travel alone again and visit her there, bringing Vernus with him. Perhaps a small deception could be given out that would ensure the priest who came to hear the sisters' confessions would agree to marry Rhian to Vernus on the spot . . . then they could have their wedding night, and make sure the deception became the truth. Then no one would have to know what father had done, and she would not have to be the cause of his dishonour. For despite all, she found she still had love in her heart for him.

Perhaps mother could make father see reason after all, and Rhian would be able to go home and live in peace again without resorting to such elaborate games to keep her freedom.

Games. Played on a board of ivory and ebony. What is it every woman wants?

Rhian closed her mind tightly against these thoughts. It had been a dream, after all. A dream. She could not let it distract her now.

Ahead, the black trunks of the trees parted just enough to show the stretch of road the Romans had laid, still straight and flat even after all these years. But Rhian's eyes, which had become well-accustomed to the dark, picked out something standing just at the point where the track met the road. It was not a tree, nor yet a road marker. It might have been a standing stone, but there had never been any such in this place.

Whitcomb urged Blaze into the lead. Past him, she saw
the wind catch hold of cloth, and realized that what she
saw was a tall man wrapped in a dark robe.

'Who is that?' Whitcomb demanded.

The figure spoke, and its voice was low and cold. 'I am
Euberacon Magus, and you, old man, have what is rightfully
mine.' Euberacon turned towards her and in the light of the
waxing moon she saw his hooded eyes glinting like a serpent's
– cold, inhuman, and filled with the knowledge of death.

Rhian's mouth went instantly dry. She pulled Thetis to a
halt. She did not ask how this could be, she did not have
thought enough in her head for that. She only knew deep
and sudden fear at the sound of that voice and the dark
sheen of those hooded eyes. This was the one to whom her
father had promised her life, and he had come to collect.

Thetis whickered and stamped. Rhian pressed her knees
into the grey mare's ribs. Thetis balked, but began slowly to
back. The track was narrow here, and there wasn't enough
room to turn her easily.

'Stand aside for my lady,' Whitcomb commanded. 'Or do
you relish the thought of being run down by a pair of
horses?'

Now she could see that the dark-robed man had thin lips
and that they twitched into a smile. Whitcomb dug his heels
into Blaze's sides and the horse started forward.

No! she tried to shout, but no sound came.

Euberacon raised his hand, and Blaze reared up high,
screaming in sudden, unbearable terror. Utterly unprepared,
Whitcomb crashed to the ground. Blaze fled into the darkness, running in blind panic past the sorcerer who stood still
as a stone, caring not a bit as his robes rippled in the wind
of the terrified animal's passing.

'I can make that creature run itself to death,' said
Euberacon calmly, as if remarking on the weather. 'I can do

the same to a man. Shall I prove these things to you, so you will see I may not be brooked or gainsaid?'

Whitcomb groaned and tried to rise. The sorcerer glanced down at him, distantly, as if the fallen man were no more than a stick of wood.

Anger overrode the fear that filled Rhian. 'Leave him be!' She flung herself from Thetis's back. The sorcerer did not seem concerned for her shout or her sudden movement. Steel glinted in the moonlight as he drew a wickedly curved knife from his belt. The sight of it stopped Rhian's heart. Whitcomb rolled, trying to get away, trying to rise, but although he pushed himself up on his arms, it was only to fall again. Rhian pulled her bow off her shoulders and an arrow from her quiver.

'Do not touch him!' she cried as she nocked the arrow in the string. 'Can you make a beast run itself to death? I can hit a mark at fifty yards.' She drew the string back next to her ear, sighting along the shaft. Even in the dark Euberacon Magnus would be an easy target.

'Run,' croaked Whitcomb, rolling to his side again, struggling still to rise. 'Run!'

She did not heed him. She would not abandon Whitcomb to this devil. 'Leave us, sorcerer. I belong to none such as you!'

Euberacon turned his inhuman eyes towards her. They glinted like the steel of his knife. Rhian braced herself to let the arrow fly.

The bowstring snapped in two.

The arrow fell soundlessly to the ground. Rhian stared dumbfounded, unable to understand what had happened. Euberacon bent over Whitcomb, who swung out feebly. The sorcerer avoided the blow with ease. Rhian rushed forward, but it was too late. The sorcerer lifted his dagger and plunged it straight down into Whitcomb's heart.

Rhian screamed. Whitcomb cried out, a long wail of terror and pain, as his blood poured out onto the ground. Rhian threw herself at the sorcerer, grappling with him, but he tossed her back easily. She scrambled backward, groping for a branch, a stone, anything she might use for a weapon.

Whitcomb's cry fell silent, and all his struggles ceased.

'No!' wailed Rhian, pushing herself to her feet. She could not see Thetis. She could not see the road. She could not see anything but Whitcomb dead on the cold ground, and the sorcerer bending over him as if to examine his work for flaws.

'Demon!' She still had no weapon, but in that moment she could have torn him apart with her bare hands.

'Cease this nonsense.' Euberacon straightened up. His robes were so black that she could not even tell if he had any blood on them. 'Come to your master.'

Rhian's breath froze in her lungs. Unseen hands seemed to catch up her limbs, compelling her forward even as a fog descended over her mind, disordering her thoughts and confusing her senses.

'No!' she screamed, straining to hold herself still. 'Mother Mary save me!'

Euberacon laughed, and the sound filled her like winter's ice. 'No mystic virgin can hear you now, little girl. All ears, all eyes here are mine.' He was close enough that she could feel his breath on her skin. How had she moved so far? Her hands and arms had gone numb. 'For you now there is no God, no saviour, no father, no mother, no protector save for me.'

'You lie, villain!'

Hoofbeats shattered the stillness. Sensation returned in a rush and Rhian jerked her head up to see a figure on a grey horse thundering towards them, a flashing spear raised high. Euberacon yanked Rhian sideways, but she twisted in his grip, grabbing at his little finger and forcing it back. He cried in pain and his hold broke. Rhian dived forward just as the mounted figure cut the night between them. She rolled, getting tangled in her own skirts, but somehow managing to get her legs free to stagger to her feet.

The horseman wheeled his mount in a tight and expert turn. Moonlight sparkled on mail, on harness, on spear's tip and on shining dark hair. Euberacon's face had broken into a snarl, and he raised clawed and empty hands. The horseman wasted no time digging in his heels and charging the sorcerer again. At first she thought the spear must have caught him square in the chest, but he only spun back, and did not fall.

Rhian did not stand and stare, for the moonlight also showed her where the sorcerer's knife had landed. She snatched it up and held it out low by her waist as she had seen Whitcomb do while helping train young men who came to her father for fostering. Her flesh seemed to recoil at the touch of its smooth, warm hilt but she clutched it tightly nonetheless.

Again, the horseman wheeled. This time, the blow struck Euberacon flat on the ground. Now it was his turn to struggle to rise. Blood stained his temple black and he clawed at something under his robes. The horseman pulled his mount to a halt and leapt from its back, sword in his hand. Euberacon looked directly at Rhian with his snake's eyes and she raised his knife defiantly.

'Do you yield?' demanded the horseman as he put himself between Rhian and Euberacon.

In answer, Euberacon's mouth curled into a smile, and he made a gesture as if to throw something at them both. Suddenly, there was a roaring wind and a foul cloud of smoke. The gale knocked Rhian off her feet and she lay coughing in the damp grass, unable to do anything for a long moment but squeeze her eyes shut and clutch at her mouth and try not to breathe.

At last, there came silence and stillness.

Rhian opened her eyes and scrambled to her feet. A thick lock of hair had come loose and tumbled in front of her eyes. She pushed it aside and for a moment saw only a man's broad back, corsletted in a leather coat with bright mail rings over it. He was breathing hard, and staring at the place where Euberacon had been. Soft sounds she suspected were oaths came from him.

Of the sorcerer, there was no sign.

The horseman turned towards her and for the first time, Rhian could see the whole of her rescuer. Broad and strong, he stood against the night. Behind him, to one side, her bewildered eyes saw his white horse and his shield that hung from the saddle. Its device shone clearly; a five pointed star of green on a silver field, the symbol of the Virgin Mother.

It seemed that her prayer had been heard after all.

To the other side of him lay Whitcomb, her dear friend and protector, still as stone, his eyes open and staring at the stars, but seeing Heaven.

It was too much. Relief, wonder and sorrow poured over her and Rhian began to cry. Not quietly with a maiden's gentle grief, but in great, inconsolable sobs that shuddered through her frame. The strength in her legs gave way, and, still sobbing, she fell to her knees on the cold and sodden ground.

THREE

The violence of the maiden's weeping shook the whole of her body. Gawain tightened his arm around her shoulders to keep her from throwing the whole of herself into the mud. Sudden violence, fear and loss had clearly robbed her of all composure.

'My lady, do not grieve so,' he murmured, not knowing if she could understand him in her state, but hoping the sound of his voice would bring her comfort. 'You are safe now, I swear it. On my life, I swear it.'

Even as he spoke those words, his eyes searched the shadows of trees and bracken that crowded this disused length of road. There were too many places to hide here, too many ways to watch unseen. Sorcerers were full of more tricks than man could number, and there was no knowing if her attacker had taken himself miles away, or simply vanished into the trees behind the cover of his smoke.

He had to get her safe away from here.

But having begun to weep so hard, she did not seem to be able to stop herself. Her tears ran down in rivers and her sobs clogged a throat that seemed too tight to release them all.

'Come away, lady. Come with me.'

She lifted her head, her tears coating her cheeks like a layer of ice. She looked not at him, but at the dead man stretched out before them. 'I cannot leave him like this.'

Cursing hard necessity, Gawain took her hands in far too familiar a fashion so that she looked from the corpse to him. 'Lady, there is nothing more that can be done for him, and we do not know where your assailant has gone. He may be nearby and waiting.'

That broke through her grief and she looked up at him with stark terror in her eyes. Gawain berated himself inwardly for frightening her further, but she did not protest as he raised her to her feet and led her to her mount. The lady's horse, fortunately, had not bolted, evidently deeming it a safer thing to stay with her mistress, rather than brave the dark forest.

The lady suffered him to help her onto the horse's back. She huddled in the saddle. The moonlight showed him fair skin and regular features, and a lock of waving hair that had come free from a braid that was as thick as a man's wrist, but it also showed him a face gone far too pale.

And if you stay here staring, Gawain, she will succumb to the cold as well as her shock. The early spring night was almost as chill as a winter's day. Trusting the mare to hold steady under her mistress, Gawain went back and retrieved the bow from where it had fallen. He gave it into her hands, and she clutched it like a talisman, which was what he had hoped, because it would keep her from trying the reins. No doubt she could ride well enough, but her eyes had turned glassy and staring. There was no telling if she could guide the animal in the state she was now, nor where she might attempt to lead it. He also retrieved the vanished sorcerer's knife. There was no point in leaving a weapon lying where it might be taken and used by any who passed.

'Now, Mistress Horse.' Gawain took hold of the mare's bridle and stroked her neck. 'Shall we be friends you and I? Your good lady is in need of aid from us both.'

The horse seemed to find this a reasonable request under the circumstances and remained quiet. Gawain looked again to the dead man on the ground. It was unseemly to leave him this way, but he must help the living.

What story is this? he wondered as he caught up the reins of his stallion, Gringolet. He had no answers, nor would he until the maiden had more fully recovered herself. It stank of magic, all of it. He'd set the sorcerer's head on a platter, if he got his way, and that of Harrik's witch beside it. The thought of Harrik reminded him afresh of the urgency of his errand though, and Gawain gritted his teeth.

God grant we find your friends soon, my lady. Gawain glanced at the sky where the stars shone down clear and brittle. The moon had almost set. *For I must be gone come the day, but I would not leave you alone.*

Gawain led the horses down the high road, the half-frozen mud muffling their hoofbeats and their breath making silver clouds in the deepening dark.

Euberacon, shrouded by night and magic, watched the rider hoist the weeping woman onto the horse and lead her away. The glittering light of moon and stars gave him a clear view of the device decorating the shield hanging from his horse's saddlebow.

Well, my Lord Gawain, what do you think of the prize that has fallen into your purse? Is it not lovely and rare? Does it not fill your heart with tender and possessive thoughts?

Under Euberacon's watchful eye, Arthur's captain turned down the forest road, leaving behind dark trails of prints. Euberacon smiled briefly, and then turned back to the dead man. There was profit yet to be taken from this night's work.

The deep gouge in Euberacon's chest where the knight's spear had stabbed him was painful and the exposure of his ribs made him feel a little dizzy and weak, but it would close soon enough. The source of Euberacon's life was no longer in his heart, and those who sought it there were bound to be sore disappointed. There was no reason to hurry home. The heart and eyes, the tongue and left hand, these were things not to be wasted. Euberacon drew his second, sharper knife and bent to work.

In the light of the setting moon, Gawain could barely make out the tiny roadside chapel where he had taken shelter for the night. It was a rude and neglected place. Piles of twigs and leaves in the corners and the char on the uneven flagstones told him it had lately been more a house of travellers and wild creatures than of God. But the thatched roof and stone walls were still whole and while the presence of another horse and another human would make for a cramped and slightly comical congregation, they would also add greatly to the warmth, and warmth would only aid the lady in her recovery.

'Come my lady.' Gawain held out a hand. Her hand was ice cold in his and he had to grip it hard to help her down because she had no strength to hold onto him. Trusting that her horse would not stray far, he led the lady through the low, narrow door. Inside, the dying coals of his little fire provided just enough illumination to show the dusty altar and chipped cross. The whole place smelled heavily of horse, and his palfrey whickered and stamped as he entered.

'Rest you awhile, lady. I will see to the horses.' Keeping hold of her hand, Gawain lowered himself onto one knee so the maiden would be able to steady herself as she sat by the fire. He felt her tremble as she did, her free hand automatically tucking her cloak and skirt under her to guard her from the cold of the cracked flags. He took that as a good sign. He had seen men after battle become like this, too stunned by what they had been through to see the world in front of them any longer. Fire, drink and a time of quiet rallied most of them. He prayed it would be so with her.

Outside, Gringolet stood alone, nibbling at the bracken. Gawain cursed under his breath and circled the chapel, to find that the mare had sniffed out a springlet and decided to help herself to a drink. He waited somewhat impatiently until she raised her dripping head and allowed him to lead her into the chapel, balking only slightly at the narrow doorway.

Inside, the lady had fallen, stretching out to her full length on the flags. Gawain dropped the mare's reins and ran to her side, turned her, thrusting a hand under her cloak and leaning close, to search for breath and heartbeat.

To his immense relief, her heart beat steadily under her cloak and her warm breath brushed his cheek and mouth. For a moment, he inhaled a scent like summer itself. This close, he could see the colour was beginning to return to her white cheeks. Simple sleep then, was what had claimed her, and Gawain thanked God and the Virgin for it. That would heal her more than any clumsy words he could offer.

As gently as he could manage, he laid her back down and stood, running his hand through his hair and looking at the face the firelight revealed to him. Her cheeks were round and full, her features regular and delicate. Her hair underneath her veil was the colour of the flame, a reddened gold that shone like the setting sun. The few tresses that had come free of the braid trailed almost to her ankles. Her eyes were set wide beneath her clear, white brow, and he wondered what colour they would be when they opened.

He also noted that she was full and fairly grown. No wan

and wilting flower she. Then he realized that he was staring, and he turned quickly away.

The horses were in urgent need of attention. Gringolet
had not been unharnessed the whole hard day. The lady's
mare seemed to be fairly fresh, so wherever they had come
from, it was not far. He thought again on the dead man left
in the wood. Perhaps he could take word to the king of whatever injustice had come to pass here.

Unsaddling and unharnessing the horses and wiping them
down took some time. The lady did not have much gear with
her. A quiver of arrows, and the bow with the broken string,
and a single saddlebag. Had she been hunting and become
lost or distracted? The bag was heavy, but a cursory investigation of it showed she had not brought provisions, not as
much as a skin of water or wine, which only deepened the
mystery about her.

Gawain glanced back at her. Instinct had caused her to
curl closer to the fire's warmth. His exercise had kept him
from feeling the deepening cold, so Gawain unclasped his
cloak and laid it over her like a blanket. He leaned close to
see if any token of fever clouded her clear brow. But there
was only the summer scent of her, and the deep, regular
breathing of a peaceful sleeper.

Against his will, Gawain remembered Pacis. Her skin had
been white like this, her cheeks and shoulders this round as
she lay sleeping beside him, before she had woken and kissed
him lightly and bid him begone before her husband returned.

Before she had laughed when he had begged her to come
with him.

Gawain busied himself with the fire to distract himself
from those deeply unwanted thoughts. Before he had to look
any longer at this beauty who reminded him so sharply of
that other.

Agravain would have a whole sermon to preach if he could but see you now, he thought ruefully. Of his three brothers, Agravain was closest to him in age, and his harshest critic. Gawain had once heard that when the ancient emperors of Rome rode through the streets to display their spoils of battle, a man rode beside them whose job was to whisper in the conqueror's ear 'remember thou art mortal'. Agravain seemed to have taken that role on himself with respect to Gawain.

What will you do when one of your dalliances forgets her undying love for you and shows up at court in tears with a big belly and a witness to your pretty words? Agravain would say, and had said, more than once, his sharp face creased with anger. *How much will our uncle have to settle on that cuckolded husband, or petty chieftain's daughter? You could always refuse to acknowledge the truth of their claim, I suppose, but that would stain some of that virtue you polish up like your arms before you go into battle . . .*

The situation was only made worse by the fact that Agravain's scoldings were not without merit. Gawain poked at the fire with one of the damp sticks he had gathered and frowned. It wasn't that he was unmindful of his responsibilities. He took them most seriously. Arthur was a great king and a great man. Living up to his example was a life's work which Gawain set himself to with a good will. If it was love that led him astray, surely there were others who had done far worse?

Gawain grimaced as he thought of the colours Agravain's face would turn if he spoke that light verse. And there were others who would not approve. He winced and glanced up at the cross above the altar.

Penitent, Gawain knelt in prayer, hands clasped before him. He carefully recited his pater noster and added, *Father, forgive my sins and help me strive to be more worthy of the grace You showed through your Son, Jesus Christ. Mother Mary, guide this foolish sinner and show him how he may amend his faults. Amen, amen, amen.*

Gawain crossed himself. Resolutely, he sat down facing the door with the fire and the lady at his back and his sword naked on his lap, in case the villain who pursued this maiden and killed her protector should attempt to return, and so that he would not have to watch her sleeping there and think again of Pacis.

Rhian woke slowly and reluctantly. The first thing she saw was a low fire smouldering on a floor of rough flagstones. The smell of horse hung in the air, overwhelming the smell of smoke.

Memory rolled over her like thunderclouds across a summer sky. She pushed herself instantly upright and became aware of a stiff neck and a sore back. A cloak slithered off her shoulders, but she paid it no mind. Across the fire she made out Thetis standing beside a great white charger and a small bay palfrey. The saddles and tidy piles of harness waited beside the splintered wooden door.

'God be with you this morning, my lady,' said a man's voice, pleasantly, as if she had just walked into the great hall to break her fast. Rhian nearly jumped out of her skin, and she stared. Beside her sat the rider who had come to her aid. He regarded her with patient courtesy, and in the firelight Rhian could see that his eyes were the colour of dark amber, warm and deep. His grecian nose was somewhat crooked, having been broken at least once. His chin was clean-shaven in the old Roman style but it had clearly been several days since he had seen a barber. His mouth was wide and his black locks brushed the shoulders of a plain brown tunic trimmed with simple blue embroidery.

Rhian realized that her own cloak lay beneath her, protecting her from the cold stones of the floor. It was this man's mantle that had fallen from her shoulders.

She tried to bring some order to her thoughts, but her

mind did not seem fully hers to command yet. She swallowed to clear some of the sand that seemed to clog her throat. 'God be with you, Sir.'

She meant to add, 'where am I?' but the sight of a cross over an ancient and dusty altar answered her question, at least in part. Before she could stop herself, she thought to tell her father this place was in need of repair so he could send Whitcomb to see what could be done.

Whitcomb, helpless on the ground, the flash of a knife in the moonlight . . .

For you now there is no God, no saviour, no father, no mother, no protector save for me.

A man on a tall horse, his spear held high . . .

Whitcomb still and dead, his blood staining the ground black.

That evil memory robbed Rhian of any polite words. As if discomfited by the silence, the white warhorse stamped once. The knight got to his feet and went to the charger, patting its sides.

'Gringolet reminds me he has not yet broken his fast,' he said in that same pleasant, comfortable way. 'With my lady's permission, I will take the horses outside to see what they can make of the foraging nearby.'

Rhian nodded dumbly. The man pulled a light halter from the pile of gear. He looped it over Gringolet's head and led the animal out into the crisp, grey morning. Thetis and the palfrey both followed, docile and comfortable, leaving the room more airy, but also much colder. Rhian wrapped her own cloak more tightly around her shoulders.

What have I done? Oh, Whitcomb, my friend. I have been the death of you.

Peace, she counselled herself. *The fault was none of yours.*
Was it not?
No, she told herself firmly. *It was the sorcerer who held the*

knife. It was he who corrupted your father and broke your mother before you were even born.

The chapel door opened again and Rhian's head jerked up, startled. The man paused in the doorway.

'My lady.' He bowed. 'Your humble servant can only hope it was not he whom you were thinking of with such fury.'

Rhian blinked and tried to smooth her features. He was tall, this man. He'd had to stoop to enter the chapel and his shoulders almost filled the doorway. His mail shirt and other arms lay beside the horses' harness, but he still wore his sword at his narrow waist.

And she had slept the night away beneath his cloak.

Rhian almost wanted to laugh, but she knew if she began, not only would it be hopelessly rude, but it might swiftly turn to tears. She cleared her throat, and tried to remember her manners. First of all, she stood, and picked up the cloak he had graciously loaned her. It was a rough wool, but well dyed a deep green and lined entirely with fur. Not at all the garment of a poor man. 'I would know, Sir, to whom it is I owe such thanks. You surely saved my life this night.'

The knight bowed, a smooth and studied gesture. 'I am Gawain, son of Lot Luwddoc of Goddodin, and companion to Arthur the King at the Round Table.'

Surprise tightened Rhian's fingers around the cloak. This was Gawain? Nephew and heir to the High King? The acknowledged champion of all the High King's chosen and the one who sat at his right hand when the cadre of the Round Table met together?

'Have I said something to give offence to my lady?' inquired Gawain, as he straightened up.

'No . . . no . . . I . . . forgive me.' Rhian cursed herself for her stammering, and for her inability to stop staring. 'It's just . . . I had not heard word of your being in this country,' she finished. Feeling the fool, she held the cloak out to him. She could think of nothing else to do.

Gawain's smile was small, and the arch of his brows said he knew this was not what she had first thought to say, but he was too polite to remark on it. 'I am glad to hear that. I am meant to be travelling in secret.' He smoothly accepted the cloak and slung it around his shoulders. He must have been freezing without it all night, despite the warmth the horses provided. Rhian felt her hands would go numb any moment. 'As there are none here to introduce us properly, lady, may I be so bold as to ask the favour of your name?'

Manners, forgotten again. 'I cry you mercy, Sir, for my country ways,' she said, dropping her gaze and reminding herself sternly that she did in fact know how to comport herself before visitors of rank. 'I am Rhian, daughter of Rygehil of the Morelands who is the barown of this land. My lord, I render you humble thanks for all you have done.' She spread her skirts and curtsied deeply.

Gawain acknowledged the gesture with another stately bow. 'I have heard Rygehil of the Morelands spoken of most fairly.' He crouched down before the fire, poking renewed life into the modest blaze with a charred stick. 'If my lady would care to refresh herself . . .' he handed her a wineskin that had been warming by the coals.

Rhian took it with thanks and drank the sweet, watered wine gratefully. It coursed through her, strengthening her blood and clearing her mind. She lowered the skin to find Gawain watching her thoughtfully. In the daylight streaming through the open chapel door, she could see his eyes were lit from within by sparks of wit, and, for all his courtly words, a bit of wariness.

'Was it your father you rode with last night?' he asked.

Rhian set the skin down. 'No.'

'Your husband then?' The wariness in him became ever-so-slightly more marked.

Rhian wondered briefly if she should lie, but found she did not have the heart for it. 'No. My father's steward.' *Whitcomb*. Fresh sorrow filled her heart.

Her answer caused Sir Gawain's brows to arch sharply, and Rhian dropped her gaze again.

'Would my lady consent to share her tale with her humble servant?'

Rhian bit her lip. The tears which had watered the ground beside Whitcomb's corpse had made her rage against her father fresh and green. Still, it was hard for her to think of speaking openly to a representative of the High King. To tell this story would bring shame not only upon father, but also upon mother. But, it was not only that. To her surprise, a part of her still longed to hear her father's horse outside, to have him come to tell her it was a mistake, that all was forgiven, that she could come home now and she would be safe, and all would be well and right. That part still knew the love between father and daughter, and could only weep.

Seeing her hesitate, Gawain said delicately, 'If my lady prefers, I could simply escort her back to her father's hall. . .'

'No!' The word was out before Rhian could stop her tongue.

Gawain bowed his head in acquiescence. 'Then, my lady, you must tell me how I may best be of assistance.'

Rhian looked at him again. This was a man of whom songs were made. No doubt they exaggerated freely, but still, if he was even half as noble as the tales claimed, he would take serious note of her distress, and there were advantages to him being the king's man. He could order the convent to take her, where they might not take a woman alone . . .

He could help make sure Whitcomb got a Christian burial.

And if he did decide to take her back to father after all?

The thought stiffened Rhian's spine even as it brought on a fresh wave of fear. Well, these were woods she had known since she was a girl, and Gawain was on some important errand. He would surely tire soon of trying to chase her through them on horseback.

'My lady,' said Gawain once again, this time with a trace of exasperation in his voice. Impatience seemed to bring out the extremes of formality in him. 'Forgive your servant, but, his errand is urgent, and he fears if he must endure the steel of your gaze any longer he will be wounded so gravely that he will be unable to complete his appointed task. I ask you again, for the sake of that God we both love, how can I be of service to you?'

Rhian drew the shreds of her composure together. She had to answer him.

It was pride and nothing else that also made her choose to match his formality of speech. 'Again I cry you mercy, noble sir. I would have answered you before, but I must speak of dark and shameful matters, and I hesitate to bring dishonour upon one whom the Lord commands I should honour above all save Christ.'

His expression flickered, and Rhian thought for a bare instant he looked impressed. 'Speak freely, my lady,' he told her. 'Be assured your servant will listen discreetly and advise you as best he may.'

So Rhian squared herself against the tumult within her, and told Lord Gawain all that had happened to her the day before – how her father had refused her best and final suitor, how her mother had arranged matters so that they came to know the strange and dreadful promise her father had made, and how Whitcomb had agreed to help her in her flight.

As she spoke of how the sorcerer Euberacon had waylaid them on the road, the memory of his hooded eyes, and how he seemed able to take command of her, sent a deep chill through her, but she still forced herself to speak calmly. She felt glad that Sir Gawain had seen the sorcerer vanish as he had. Otherwise he might think her a mad woman, or worse, a witch.

As he promised, the knight listened discreetly. In fact, he scarce moved a muscle for the length of her tale. Only his eyes narrowed. Did he accuse Rhian of having steel in her gaze? His own was nothing less than cold iron.

At last, there was nothing more to tell. Gawain turned his eyes away and stared a long while out of the chapel door.

When he finally spoke, he said, 'Lady, these things you tell me of are most strange and of grave import. I am not sorry I came to your aid.'

Despite the return of her fears, Rhian felt her mouth quirk up. 'And I am right glad to hear it.'

Her tart remark startled Gawain. For an instant he looked annoyed, caught out, but then a smile spread across his face. Rhian felt her throat tighten. She had thought him fair before, but that smile of his brightened the very air around him.

'Now it is I who must cry you mercy, my lady.' Still smiling, he gave a small bow where he sat. His wry humour, though, quickly faded. 'But you give me tidings that match with those I already carry to the High King. I have just heard tell of a witch from a man I trust, now you speak to me of a sorcerer. I must make haste back to Camelot. There are darker councils abroad in this land than Arthur suspects.' These last words he spoke more to himself than to her.

'Then, Sir, we must not linger here. If you can delay your errand long enough to see me to the sisters . . .' Rhian tried to keep the plea from her voice.

'I fear I can do no such thing, my lady.' Rhian's heart plummetted. 'I must be importunate and instead ask you to ride with me to Camelot and give witness of these matters to the High King.'

And what would King Arthur do after that, but send her back to her father? Panic squeezed Rhian's heart.

Her thoughts must have showed plainly on her face, for Gawain said, 'At court you may plead your case to Queen Guinevere. Her Majesty is of a generous and discerning heart. I promise, she will not fail to hear you.'

The queen will hear, and the king will hear, and all the world will know what father has done. God and Mary why do I care? Let him reap the shame he has sown, and let us be gone, because it is morning. He will be searching for me by now, if he cares even that much.

She wanted to be able to hate. She wanted there to be nothing in her but anger, but other feelings twisted inside her, bringing with them nothing but pain.

Beyond this, there were other matters of cold law that might remove from her hands what little hope she still clutched. 'And if it is judged that I am my father's and his to do with as he pleases? What then?'

For a moment, bare anger showed in Gawain's eyes, as if she had spoken insult. 'You do not know Her Majesty, or you would not speak so,' he said, and his words had an edge to them. Belatedly, he seemed to notice this, and his voice grew gentle again. 'She has never turned away any who ask for her protection.'

Rhian swallowed. There was no time to argue. The sky outside was brightening. She could see it through the cracks in the chapel's roof. Whitcomb would already be missed. A search would be sent out soon, and there would be fresh tracks on the muddy road for them to follow.

'I will go with you, then, Sir,' she said, glancing at the chapel door as if she thought the sorcerer's shadow would cross the threshold at any moment.

Gawain did not miss the gesture. 'If my lady will permit, I would say we ride on to the town of Pen Marhas. The master there is Arthur's man and will give our horses and ourselves good rest before we reach the final road to Camelot.'

'With a good will, Sir,' said Rhian, although she felt none. She did not want this. She only wanted the impossible – for all of this not to be. She wanted to be home in her bed and waking up to find that father had consented to let her marry Vernus after all, and for mother to be planning the betrothal feast.

Furtively, she looked at the neglected cross. 'May I pray a moment?'

'Of course, my lady,' said Gawain. 'I will see to the horses.'

Rhian knelt on the stones, clasped her hands together tightly, bowing her head and squeezing her eyes tightly shut. She heard Gawain's footsteps as he came and went, heard the gentle ring of harnesses lifted, settled and tightened over the stamping and mild protest of the horses.

She meant to pray. She tried. She wanted to call up images of the Virgin's serene face, of Christ's noble suffering, but all she could see were the eyes of the sorcerer, and how he called and compelled.

Was it he who sent the vision of the Green Man to frighten her into a faint? Had he already begun his possession of her then, and his laying his claim on her at the crossroads was the end of it, rather than the beginning?

Fear wrung a single tear from Rhian's eye, and it trickled down her cheek.

Was there any man, king or companion who could keep her safe?

And yet, she had prayed before in the darkness, and there had come Gawain, who had caused the sorcerer to flee before him and brought her back to herself.

With that thought, the fear eased, and Rhian found her fingers loosening a little from each other.

Mother Mary, if this man truly is your servant, I beg you watch over us. Help me to know that I am doing the right thing. And watch over Whitcomb until he may rise again at the Day of Judgement. Amen.

A little peace came to her then, and hope grew a little stronger. She was able to rise and walk outside without flinching. Dawn shone through the trees, doing little yet to dispel the night's cold, but at least there was light. Gawain was working among the three horses. The glance he gave her was only mildly inquiring, leaving her the privacy of her thoughts.

Thetis was already saddled. Rhian's bow with its broken string protruded from the quiver hanging from the saddle. Rhian tried not to look at it. She tried to hang on to the peace of prayer as she mounted Thetis. She would not be abandoned now. Surely not now.

Gawain mounted his palfrey. The warhorse's reins had been tied to the smaller horse's harness. It was obviously used to this arrangement for it started forward peaceably enough when Gawain nudged the palfrey into a walk and then into a trot.

There should have been a squire, Rhian realized, shocked that she had not noticed before. He had said his errand was urgent, but what was so urgent that the High King's nephew would travel without even one servant or companion?

The unwelcome sensation of being watched stole over her. Rhian shivered and knotted her fingers into the reins as she urged Thetis forward to follow Gawain onto the highway.

Neither of the travellers looked back to note the pair of ebony ravens perched in the bare oak tree. Nor did they see that while one flew off to the east, the other flew to the west, as if to join their party and travel alongside them.

*   *   *

'There, Sir!' The boy running ahead of the mounted men pointed as he cried out.

Rygehil squinted. The dawn had not completely penetrated the thick trees yet and they rode through twilight. The shape that the boy pointed out was little more than a mound of darkness on the bed of last year's fallen leaves. But for the crows, it might have been a log or a faggot dropped by some peasant out cutting fuel. The ill-favoured birds swirled above the fallen form. They perched upon it, stabbing eagerly downward with their sharp beaks.

It is a deer, Rygehil tried to tell himself. *It is a sheep that strayed from its pen.* But his heart did not believe that, and it flared within him. He drove his heels into his horse's sides and charged forward to the ragged crossroads, scattering crows in all directions so that they cursed him loud and raucously with their harsh cries.

When he saw it was a man that lay in the scuffed and scattered leaves, his first feeling was one of relief, for the corpse was not Rhian. But in the next moment he recognized the face, cold and grey in the faint light of dawn, and then he saw what had been done to it.

'Whitcomb,' he breathed, tears stinging his eyes. He dismounted and knelt beside his steward.

The mutilations were vile, obscene, and the true old man's blood was everywhere. The men behind him were saying their prayers. Someone retched. Above all the crows cawed, speaking to their comrades of their prize. Rygehil squeezed his eyes tightly shut as he crossed himself. Bitter gall filled his throat and his soul.

You deserved better, my friend. Better than me for a master, and a far, far better death than this was.

Slowly, Rygehil stood and looked about him. The men, who had remained on their ponies murmured uneasily to each other. The boys holding the reins simply looked scared.

Leaves and loam had been churned and kicked. Whitcomb's blood had spilled freely onto the exposed and muddy ground. That same mud held hoof prints that travelled in several directions, as did the prints of men's boots, and the smaller disturbances of a woman's feet.

He looked down to the road. The hoof prints continued north and east, already blurring and softening as dew and warmth worked on them.

Does he have you then, my child? Did Whitcomb offer up his life to try to buy off that fate I sold you to? Or are you free now and gone far away?

Gradually, Rygehil became aware that he was cold, and that behind him, ponies and mules stamped and snorted and men blew hard into cupped palms.

Hobden, a thin man with a wispy beard, coughed behind his rawboned hand. 'My lord,' he said. 'Shall we go on?'

Rygehil looked out at the crossroads again, but his mind seemed to have gone as numb and as cold as his naked hands.

'No,' he answered at last. 'We will take Whitcomb home with us.' He turned away.

'B – but my lord,' stammered Hobden. The man had turned pale, with fear or with anger, Rygehil could not tell which. 'Your daughter . . .'

'May God preserve her,' Rygehil said, bowing his head so that the men would not mark his shame at his own cowardice. 'For I no longer can.'

FOUR

It was almost dawn when Euberacon rode once more in sight of his habitation. To most eyes, the place he approached looked to be a single, crumbling tower, the remains of some fortress of the Romans, or perhaps of the Saxons and their failed war against Arthur. The bright rays of the rising sun touched on pale stone mottled green by moss. The whole structure listed to one side and any builder with half an eye would have said that it would collapse completely with one more winter.

To Euberacon, it was a palace like nothing else the length and breadth of the whole cold, crude isle. It was built of pure, white marble. Its four towers were topped with gilded roofs that flared with vibrant light as the morning touched them. Inside the single gate was a courtyard walled with cunningly painted tiles, so it seemed he rode into a fantastic garden of drooping trees laden with fruits of red and gold. A fountain spread its bowl in the centre of the yard, showing a mosaic of all the ocean's fishes swimming in sapphire waters. Another mosaic, this one depicting delicate, twining flowers, spread out beneath his horse's hooves.

This place could appear to be many things; a cottage, a

grove of trees, a single miraculous tower standing on its own rooftop. The spells that protected it and shifted its appearance were of ancient origin, and costly in time and material. They were, however, well worth the care he had taken with them. This was a small land, and for the time being, he must remain hidden.

During the day he was the master of this place and all its forms. At night, there was uncertainty, and there were shades that passed where his eyes could not see. But he had found his cure for that, and once she was done working her other mischief, he would bring her to him.

A boy of about ten years entered the tiled court, bowing respectfully. Euberacon passed the boy the horse's reins. With the competence of an experienced stablehand the boy caught hold of the animal's bridle to hold it steady as Euberacon dismounted and retrieved the saddlebags that held his trophies. If one looked steadily into the boy's eyes, it could be seen that he stared too much and did not blink quite enough. In his mind, the boy was still fostering in the hall of one of the island's many petty kings. He remained unaware that his foster mother had sold him for a potion to rekindle her straying husband's lust for her.

The few servants that kept Euberacon's house had been purchased for similar prices. The fact that he needed to descend to such barter for his most basic needs galled him, but he had schooled himself long ago to patience. Each day brought him closer to his victory.

A bird squawked overhead. A raven perched on the windowsill of the north-west tower. More of them circled over head. Kerra had returned, then. Good. He needed to speak with her about recent developments.

But first, he needed to confirm his suspicions.

The south-east tower was Euberacon's alone. No mortal servant, however completely enchanted, entered here. On the first floor was his sleeping chamber, its door bolted and barred with oak, ash and magic. The chamber immediately beneath the gilded roof held a small menagerie of caged animals: doves, ermine, foxes, crows, wrens, and their like. These he fed and cared for with his own hands, ensuring their health and wellbeing so they would be ready when he had need of them.

But at this time, no such sacrifice was needed. He climbed the spiralling stairs only to the second storey. Light and cold filtered in through the arrow slits in the outer walls. Warmth was the one thing with which he could not supply his dwelling. It was the constant reminder of where he truly was.

A silver key hung on a chain around his neck. Euberacon unlocked the ash-wood door in front of him and entered his private workroom.

The scents of herbs and rare essences overlaid the less savoury odours of old blood and decay. Euberacon uncovered the brass brazier by the door and dropped fuel onto the smouldering coals so that the flames sprang up, providing a flickering light. Despite this, the room remained densely shadowed. Bags and bundles hung from the ceiling. The shelves were crowded with mortars, alembics, braisers, along with sieves and bowls made from all manner of materials, both precious and base.

What the room did not contain was books. He had not been able to bring a single tome or scroll when he fled Theodora's assassins, and those that pretended to practise the high arts in this barbaric land did not see far enough ahead to write their learning down.

Euberacon had heard rumours that Merlin had several mystical volumes in his private chamber in Camelot, but no art or artifice had enabled him to see into that cunning man's sanctum. The extent of Merlin's knowledge remained his own secret.

Perhaps then, they are not so foolish, Euberacon admitted grudgingly to himself. *But they are yet not wise enough.*

First, he dealt with the trophies of his night's work, plunging them into pots of honey, setting aside the hand which needed to be cured in spirits of wine. When he was finished, he washed his own hands in a silver basin, letting the action calm and clear his mind even as it purified his flesh. He discarded his gory robe, covering himself with the clean garments he kept in a cedar chest for when they were needed. The rich black cloth was trimmed and lined with fur and did some good to keep out the eternal chill.

From under a square of white linen, the sorcerer drew a silvery mirror one palm in breadth. He had made it from the sword of a man who had come too close to his refuge. He had heated and pounded and polished the artefact, working the over-bold wanderer's blood into the reshaped steel. Around its rim, as prescribed, he had engraved the names of power – Latranoy, Iszarin, Bicol, Danmals, and the rest, with the name of Floron at the apex.

He laid the mirror on the smallest of his wooden tables and then turned to his work benches. In a clay bowl he mixed together equal proportions of milk, honey and wine, whisking them together with a brush of fine twigs. He shook the brush over the mirror in the manner of a priest anointing a body with holy waters.

'*Bismille arathe mem lismissa gassim gisim galisim,*' he intoned. '*Darrgosim samaiaosim ralim ausini taxarim zaloimi hyacabanoy illete.*'

The chant wound on, snaking through the room, reaching out to the shadows, thickening them, bringing them weight and substance, like cobwebs, like nightmares. It called, it compelled, it bound. It wound itself around the mirror, found its substance sympathetic to its purpose and sank within it, infusing and transforming it, making what had been a tool of reflection into a window onto other worlds. The steel of it misted over, swirling, first white, then red, then black.

Judging the time was right, Euberacon hardened his voice. 'Floron,' he spoke the demon's name as a command. 'Respond quickly in the mirror, as you are accustomed to appear.'

The black mist slowly took shape, forming itself into the likeness of a man riding a black stallion and carrying a black spear three ells long beneath his arm. The man had no face, not even eyes, only shadow, but all the same, Euberacon felt the figure's burning hatred of him and of the power he wielded over it.

Euberacon smiled. 'I would see the future days,' he said. 'Show me what is to come for the ones who dwell secure in Camelot.'

The black horse stamped one hoof soundlessly, and the demon lost its coherent shape, once again becoming the swirling mist of shadow. Slowly, that mist took on new form and fresh colour, and Euberacon looked deep, and the future became clear.

He saw the great hall of Camelot broken and in flames. He saw the famed cadre of the Round Table milling uselessly, their ranks broken for want of a leader. He saw Kerra laughing in the ruins, her ravens swirling overhead in a great and noisome cloud. He saw himself on the prow of a boat laden with treasure, standing beside the Saxon leaders. The ship's oars were out, and the barbarians rowed across the ocean, ready to gather more of their fellows, and he was ready with magic and sword to reclaim Constantinople, to set his man upon the throne and himself to the true rule. He saw fresh fires, but these rose from the Hippodrome and the great cathedral.

Last he saw a pair of black, black eyes staring at him,

woman's eyes, witch's eyes, seeking the past as he sought the future, and for a moment Euberacon's nerve quailed. He felt the power within that gaze. This, surely, was the fabled Theodora, looking hard for him.

She would not find him, not until it was too late.

The final vision faded, leaving only the reflection of his face. To his displeasure, Euberacon saw the sheen of sweat on his brow. He wiped it away. He should be well beyond such displays of emotion. What had he to fear from a woman's eyes? He had seen the future, and it was his.

Euberacon's lips twitched as a quiet admonition passed through his mind. Those who scried the future did well if they understood that what they saw was only one of many possibilities, and that nothing came to pass without effort and vigilance. But the possibility of his triumph was there, and it was stronger and more clear than it had been when last he sought the vision out. Euberacon's mouth bent into a smile of satisfaction as he once again covered his mirror and set it back in its place.

Now, to speak with Kerra.

Kerra watched from her solarium as Euberacon crossed the tiled court, the sleeves of his black robe flapping behind him in a poor but vigorous imitation of wings.

Kerra had always seen him more as a crow than as a raven. He did not hunt. He let others fight the battle while he watched. He sought no allegiance from those who were not strictly of his kind. Instead, he held his peace until all others believed the best was finished with, and then he stole what he wanted. He was cunning, yes, but not so wise as he fancied himself.

As soon as they returned from their night's watch, her companions had told her all that had occurred. Euberacon must be fuming that he had lost his little prize to Gawain.

She wondered if he would even think to mention it, or what lie he would tell to cover it.

What was not in question was that he would come to see her when he had finished with whatever working he had in hand. She wanted him disposed to talk, so Kerra readied her chamber for his comfort. She had already dismissed her companions. Euberacon found them distasteful. He preferred his slaves either human or incorporeal. She had closed and locked her four carved chests so he might think she kept something of worth there and waste his time ferreting out what it was. She checked the long-necked jar to make sure there was wine in it, but did not pour any out so it did not appear that she had thought too far ahead. Lastly, she made sure of her dress and appearance, repinning her hair beneath its veil and resettling the bronze circlet engraved with the likenesses of ravens with garnet eyes. She smoothed and straightened her skirts and sleeves. Her dress was russet cloth trimmed with silver, very fine, but not the best. When she ruled in Camelot, it would be scarlet and her crown would be gold.

She picked up her hand loom, set to work on the meaningless weaving, and waited for Euberacon. Sometimes she grew sick of all the time she wasted waiting for the eastern sorcerer. Unfortunately, neither she nor her true mistress were yet strong enough to topple Camelot without great risk, nor could they safely bring Merlin to heel. So they must wait and bide their time and use this foreigner to do as much of their work as he could. Eventually, her mistress would send her messengers across the sea to find this Theodora and offer him up.

A single knock sounded on the door.

'Enter,' said Kerra. Once the door had opened wide enough to reveal Euberacon's dour face, she hastily thrust her weaving into the basket beside her couch. Euberacon's eyes glittered briefly, thinking he had caught her at some secret work.

Kerra gave him her most radiant smile and rose in greeting.

'My lord.' She moved forward, her hands outstretched. As usual, he did not take those hands – Euberacon declined to touch her in any way – and as usual, she lowered them to her sides without comment. 'This is a pleasure.'

Euberacon did not answer what they both knew to be a false pleasantry. Instead he let his gaze wander about the chamber, taking in what had remained the same – the luxurious couch, the locked chests, the simple hangings, and what had changed – the basket, the wine jar.

Again, Kerra affected not to notice. Instead, she returned to her couch and sat gracefully down. 'Will you take your rest, my lord?' she asked, indicating the space beside her, and glancing from beneath her lashes as she did.

The look Euberacon returned her was cold and sour. 'You should know by now woman, I will not be one of your victims.'

'That would be sorry payment for all you have given me, my lord.'

'It would indeed.' The utter dryness of his voice made Kerra laugh. She reclined on the couch, allowing her skirts to fall so that the shapes of her legs could be discerned beneath the cloth. She did not expect this to inflame Euberacon, only to let him think that she relied on one particular sort of power. He thought her little more than a glorified whore. It suited her to let him continue in that belief.

'So, tell me, my lord, what of this pretty little thing you went to fetch? She did not come home with you?'

'She did not. Arthur's man Gawain intervened.'

Kerra arched her brows. 'Did he? That is poor luck indeed.'

Her light tone made him glower, as she had known it would. 'Did you know about this, woman?'

'I knew he was near that road, no more.' She gestured towards the window. She had removed its slatted screen to allow the ravens entrance and egress. 'My friends see much that is useful, but will tell only what they are asked. You did not ask me about Gawain.'

'It is dangerous to taunt me, Kerra.'

'And it is dangerous to forget me, my Lord Euberacon,' she answered sharply.

To her surprise, a smile flitted about his thin lips. 'Rest assured, Kerra, I know and respect your powers. I do not trifle with you. Your ends suit mine and this petty bickering does not become either one of us. Tell me what your friends have to say regarding Gawain.'

Mollified, but still wary, Kerra stretched out her hand. As she did, a gleaming black raven alighted on the window sill. It croaked once and then hopped obediently onto her wrist, its claws lightly pricking her flesh. She wore no glove to separate herself from the bird. She stared hard into the raven's dark eyes, seeking the slippery touch of its awareness. Pictures, colours, half-understood images flitted through her thoughts. Slowly, her mind began to make sense of what the bird had seen and add to it her own knowledge. 'They tell me the pair keep to the old Roman road. That they are seeking speed rather than stealth. This is to our advantage. Were they to take to the woods they might come across Harrik and his men. But 'ware, for they will stop at Pen Marhas.'

'Could Gawain turn the tide there?' muttered Euberacon. 'For all his prowess, he is but one man.'

'But where Gawain is, Arthur will be.' Kerra deposited the bird on the back of the sofa. It glared at Euberacon with one round eye and fussily began setting its feathers in order.

'That much is the truth.' Euberacon's eyes narrowed,

seeing something beyond the tower walls. 'Has Harrik enough men to take them? Is he that firmly your man he would fight against Gawain?'

'He would fight against God Most High if I asked him to now.' She smiled, remembering how that had come to pass. Most men turned clumsy in their desperation, but he had the controlled power of a warrior. There had been an unusual pleasure in making Harrik one of hers.

Her thoughts must have shown in her face, because the perpetual disdain of Euberacon's expression deepened.

Kerra laughed and waved that disdain away. 'In Harrik, my "husband" Wulfweard is secure and well advised. Harrik is in many ways the better man,' she mused, and made sure Euberacon saw exactly what she was thinking of. 'We should have begun with him.'

'We would have failed,' said Euberacon bluntly. 'Our task needs weakness, not strength.'

Kerra shrugged. 'It is well for you then, my lord, there are so many kinds of weakness.'

'Yes,' he murmured more to himself than to her. Kerra felt her own eyes narrow. Had he been scrying the future? What had he seen? One day she must find the way into his tower and his secrets. They would complement her own most sweetly.

'Have you use for my men?' she prompted. 'Or for me?' She gestured once more to her couch, moving her ankles just a little as if to make room for him.

Euberacon did not move. She had not truly believed he would. Still, one day he might. There were so many kinds of weakness.

'I need Gawain and the woman separated,' he said. 'I need them afraid. It is fear that will make them useful. The fear in their hearts that will give them to us.'

Kerra sat up, leaning close. 'What have you seen?'

Euberacon smiled. 'I have seen Arthur's fall, and I have seen mighty Constantinople. It burns, Kerra. If Gawain fails and Arthur falls, then all Byzantium is mine.'

Kerra smiled, pretending to share his glee. Underneath it, she felt only irritation. It seemed he saw little else for all his learned necromancy and dark mutterings. He could at least come up with a new lie.

Suddenly, she could no longer bear having him in front of her where she would have to smile and play the seductress.

'Then I had best begin my work, hadn't I, my lord?' She stood, inviting him by word and gesture to leave her room.

But Euberacon was not quite done with her yet. 'Go carefully. The girl is not without power, and Gawain is on the watch. It will not be so easy to take them from each other without rousing their suspicions.'

'You may rest assured, my lord, that I will keep myself and my purpose well hidden.' *It is, after all, something at which I am quite practised.*

That answer seemed to satisfy him and Euberacon left. When he shut the door, the raven perched on the couch let out a single derisive call and flew to her shoulder, running its beak familiarly through her hair until she reached up to stroke its feathers.

In response to its call, first one then another of the great black birds glided in through the window, settling themselves on chests and chairs, on the bedstead and the couch and any other surface where they might find room. Soon they were as thick as autumn leaves, filling the air with their raucous conversation, and filling her mind with their mischief and impressions.

'Yes,' she murmured to her friends, and to the man who had just departed. 'I have had much practice at keeping myself concealed.'

Euberacon knew little of her past and cared less, or so he

had said. She had told him her grandmother had been a slave in a sprawling villa when the Romans still ruled the island. For the great family, grandmother had been herbalist and bone-setter and had been well rewarded for her work. She had also been fair on the way to teaching her own daughter her arts.

When the last of the Romans fled back to their own hot land before the fast-approaching Saxons, grandmother had simply dressed herself and her daughter up in travelling clothes and set them on the road. They would walk until they found a village or other settlement. A healer's talents were always welcome, she reasoned, and would be well rewarded – perhaps with a cottage and some goats or pigs.

What Kerra had not told Euberacon was how badly grandmother's plan had failed. He believed Kerra had been raised in the bosom of a noble house and come honestly by her bearing and manners. But the truth was, the Saxons had raged across the country like a wildfire, taking what they wanted and burning the rest. It was only slowly that they began to think of staying in this rich new land. As grandmother walked on, she found great need for her skills, but none who could afford to keep her and her swiftly blossoming daughter, so they continued to walk.

In time, the daughter had a daughter of her own. By then, mother had grown to love the roving life, and gave no thought to settling down. She walked contentedly from place to place, plying her arts, taking whatever payment in coin or kind she was offered, and moving on again.

All might have gone well, but as Kerra grew, it soon became clear that all was not right with her. Voices no one else could hear whispered in her ears. She suffered violent headaches, and would sometimes fall to the ground, foaming at the mouth, her body writhing uncontrollably. At such times, she saw visions and uttered prophecy in strange tongues.

The attacks became more frequent and no amount of prayer or physic seemed to help them. Mother found herself less welcome in the villages. Here and there a voice muttered 'witch', and pointed at Kerra. Once, the people drove them out with stones and clubs, the priest leading the way, his cross held high.

After that, mother started telling Kerra to stay behind, to hide in the woods until she could determine if it was safe for Kerra to come inside the walls of the town or the limits of the croft. Sometimes, Kerra would be smuggled in after dark and hidden in a barn or pantry. Other times, she would be left in the woods, with mother venturing out to bring her food when she searched for the plants and herbs that were her cures. These times became more frequent and Kerra began to fear the day that mother would decide to walk on and leave her mad, bedevilled daughter to fend for herself.

The dreams only made it worse.

At night when she closed her eyes, Kerra began to see a black-haired woman. At least, sometimes she was a woman. Sometimes she was a flock of ravens, or a great, black mare. The woman promised Kerra she could take away the fits, and make it so the voices only came when Kerra wished for them. All Kerra had to do was help her.

At first, Kerra tried to block out the dreams. She prayed herself to sleep and made herself a cross to clutch through the night. But gradually, she began to listen to the dream woman. No one else had ever said they could help. The midwives and cunning men mother consulted had done little more than shake their heads. The priests had laid their hands on her head and raised their eyes to Heaven, and nothing had changed. This woman swore she could help, and all she wanted in return was a healer. Her infant son was ill with a fever in his lungs, she said. The sickness had spread to her. She was weak. He was dying. If Kerra helped them, saved their lives as her mother surely would had she but known, then Kerra would be taught to control the power that was within her.

Kerra could not long resist such a promise. It was harvest time. They were staying with a cluster of fishers on the ocean shore who agreed mother's 'half-wit' daughter could stay in the drying shed as long as mother played midwife for the two bearing women and healer for the men who worked with lines and nets.

At the dark of the moon, Kerra crept from her warm, stinking shelter and fled inland to where the woods began. There she found the woman who named herself Morgaine and the infant boy, her son, saved from drowning she said. His lungs were bad, and his fever was high, and his mother had little milk to give him. Kerra built them a shelter of branches such as she and her mother used when they were on the road. She brought them goat's milk, and fish and mussels she searched out from the tide pools. She brewed them strong teas using her mother's recipes and herbs she had filched from her mother's bags or ferreted out from the woods.

Slowly, the babe improved. His cough subsided and his limbs grew round and strong again. When it became clear that he would live, Morgaine began to keep her promise to Kerra.

Kerra, Morgaine said, was not cursed, but blessed. It was only because she was untutored that her natural powers threatened to run wild. She taught Kerra the rites that would summon the voices and the visions, and send them peaceably away. Her fits faded away to memory and all her dreams were of the normal kind. She learned how to call the ravens to her as friends, and how to work with bone and poison to achieve her ends when the healer's art was of no use. She learned the names of the powers that inhabited land and sea, their natures and which were to be avoided and which might be plied or pressed into service.

In time, she also learned manners, dress and bearing. She learned the ways of men and women and how they might be enhanced with her other arts. To all these studies and many more she applied herself willingly, until the day came when it was she who walked away. Leaving her mother to her roving, Kerra set herself firmly and finally to Morgaine's campaign against the king in Camelot and his helpmeet and fellow conspirator, Guinevere.

The voices of her companions roused Kerra from her bitter reveries. Their thoughts pushed against hers. They did not like this place. They wanted her to come with them, to fly, and to sport on the winds.

Kerra smiled at the great flock gathered around her.

'Yes, my friends,' she said. 'Yes, we will fly.'

Kerra retrieved her sewing basket. From under the meaningless pieces of fine work, she drew out a great black cloak. The basket itself was far too small to conceal such an object, but it came to her hand nonetheless. She shook it and the sunlight glinted on the rich black feathers borrowed from one thousand living ravens. Kerra settled the cloak over her shoulders, closed the bone clasp, drew the hood up over her hair and steeled herself against the pain.

Kerra's bones began to shrink. Her legs lengthened and her joints buckled, feet and toes split and splayed. Her body solidified and her neck thickened even as her face lengthened and bone split skin to form a sharp, black beak. Feathers sprouted from every pore and from the tip of each finger as her arms reshaped themselves to become her wings and all around her the ravens voiced their approval.

Then, one bird among many, she took to the air, beating her wings joyfully until she was able to catch the wind and soar with the rest of the flock over the tops of the trees and away out into the countryside.

*   *   *

As Euberacon watched, the ravens one by one left their perches on the roof and in the trees beyond the fortress walls, joining Kerra in her eyrie.

He knew she had her own plans that she kept carefully hidden from him. She thought she was using him, just as she thought it was his carelessness that led Gawain to take Rhian from him. She was wrong, but that did not mean she should not be treated with great caution. Even a barbarian could be dangerous. The pike and the axe could kill as thoroughly as the sword. It was as well to trust her no farther than absolutely necessary, and when he left these shores for Byzantium, it would be wise not to leave her alive.

For now, though, she was most useful. She would lay the traps that would drive Gawain and the girl apart. Her mischiefs would bedevil them and make peace of mind a stranger. It was likely she would fail, but the attempt would have the effect of making them cling more closely to each other, and that closeness would breed the weakness he needed for his own work.

Euberacon crossed his beautiful courtyard, returning to his tower and his carefully laid plans.

FIVE

The day was clear as crystal and at least as cold. Rhian was glad Sir Gawain kept the pace brisk, for although the wind stung her cheeks, Thetis's motion helped keep her warm and distracted her somewhat from the lack of food.

And she needed every distraction she could get. They were still in the wooded country, with the great trees gathering close to the road, waving their branches in salute to the morning's wind. This was not a well-travelled section of the road, and the ruts and holes had become puddles the size of young lakes. Twice they had to dismount and lead the horses through the trees to avoid burgeoning bogs. Sunlight and shadow shifted, spread and scattered like foam on the sea. The world filled with the rush and creak of the trees' song, a constant accompaniment to the calls of birds and the hundred nameless noises of the newly wakened forest dwellers, all of them seeking shelter somewhere away from the disturbance made by three horses and two human beings. It took all Rhian's strength to keep from starting at shadows ahead that might be a dark man with heavy-lidded eyes, or from turning constantly to see behind. Were the only hoof-beats she heard truly from the three horses of their party?

Or were there others? Their tracks were plain in the mud and the soft earth along many long stretches where the stones the Romans had laid down were broken and gone. Anyone, certainly any of father's men, would only have to look to know where they had passed. How much more would a sorcerer be able to do?

It did not help at all that the words from one dark ballad had begun to beat their time through her mind again and again and would not be shifted.

'Light down, light down, Lady Isobel,' said he,

'For we are come to the place where you are to die.'

That all ended well enough for the lady in that tale gave her no comfort. Her mind could not reach that far.

For we are come to the place where you are to die.

'I see my lady favours a bow.'

Rhian nearly jumped out of her skin. Thetis whickered and broke stride. Rhian had to pat the horse's neck and prod her to continue before she could look up at Gawain, whose face was all casual inquiry.

'I do, yes,' she answered, trying to warm to the idea of polite conversation. What was that in the trees? Was it only a bird?

'Do you hunt?' he went on.

'When I can.' How many sets of hooves drummed on the road? Mud muffled and confused sound, turning steady drumming into wet and uneven plodding. The way ahead rose steeply. They were leaving the lowlands for the hills, with their dells and valleys and deep folds in the land, where anyone might conceal themselves. She could see next to nothing. She could not hear properly.

'Lady Rhian.'

Again, Rhian jumped. Again Thetis complained of it and had to be soothed. When she was able to look up at Gawain, his fine face was all sympathy.

'Take heart, Lady Rhian,' he said. 'We are alone on this road.'

Rhian dropped her gaze. 'I know it, Sir,' she said. 'It's just that . . . if I . . . if. . .'

At her stammering, Gawain gave a small smile and Rhian felt a blush blossom across her entire face. 'Lady Rhian,' he said again, as gently as he had before. 'Last night I said you were under my protection. I will not permit any harm to come to you. If an oath is necessary to make you believe this, then I swear it.'

'Sir, please believe that I do not doubt your word. But if my father . . .'

'Your father is the king's man and needs must obey the king's word. Until the king himself appears, that word comes from me, and I say you are going to Camelot.'

Rhian looked away, trying not to scan the budding underbrush for movement. 'Would 'twer that simple.'

'It is that simple, Lady Rhian. It is law.'

He spoke the words so plainly. Did he not understand? Churlishness rose in Rhian and would not be dismissed. Before she could guard her tongue she said, 'You have slain dragons, my lord. The rest of us know rather less of such legendary battles.'

Sir Gawain stared at her blankly for a moment. 'God in Heaven,' he said at last. 'Is that what they say of me now?'

'Every year at the feast of Christ's Mass.' *I've told it myself,* she added in her mind, but decided not say so aloud.

A spasm crossed the knight's face, as if he was not certain whether he wished to laugh or curse.

Laughter won out. 'Well then, my lady, if you can believe I have slain dragons, it should be a matter of no moment to believe I can stand up to your father!'

Much to her surprise, an answering laugh bubbled out of Rhian. It felt surprisingly fine, like a spring morning, and Gawain's smile had returned in truth, turning his face again to that picture of a man's beauty she had seen so briefly before, even with the dark stubble dusting his chin.

After a moment, his face grew thoughtful again, studying hers. Rhian fixed her gaze on the rising narrow way ahead, on the shifting patterns of light and shadow from the branches waving in the spring wind. Thetis did not like uneven ground and was growing nervy, so that Rhian had to concentrate on keeping her seat and on guiding her mare, which was just as well. She needed to think of something else but Sir Gawain's eyes studying her so closely.

'It is good to see you smile, Lady Rhian.'

It is good to believe I will smile again, thought Rhian, but that was hardly a thing she could say to this man. She concentrated instead on keeping the reins loose in her fingers. It would not do to have Thetis betraying her moods.

Perhaps in my next flight into the wilderness I should go on foot.

Gawain was not content to let her keep her peace, however. 'May I ask your thought?'

'Oh, it is nothing of importance, Sir.'

At this, Gawain reined his palfrey back, bringing himself as close beside Thetis as the broken road permitted so that he could look her directly in the eyes. 'Lady, you asked this morning that I speak plainly to you. Grant me the courtesy of doing the same for me. We are not, after all, in your father's hall, nor my uncle's. Out here, I am only a knight errant and you are the daughter of a liegeman. Shall we then be Gawain and Rhian, you and I?'

Rhian felt her tongue freeze to the roof of her mouth. It was too presumptuous. She was not sure she could do such a thing. Yet, at the same time, she longed to.

Mother Mary, I'm becoming a stuttering fool. 'I will try.'

'I can ask for nothing better.' He was smiling again, that smile that lit and filled the world and suffocated sense and senses. Part of Rhian knew she had better take hold of those same senses, or she was in severe danger of making far worse than a fool out of herself, be this man ever so refined and politic in his manner. Part of her did not care and only wanted to see him smile again. During the few heartbeats she was basking in the light of that smile, she no longer had to be afraid of what followed her, and she felt no nightmares resting on her shoulders. She greatly yearned for that relief.

'So, Rhian,' he stressed her name and the smile flickered about his lips as he did so. 'If you will not tell me your thoughts, what shall we talk about instead?'

Curiosity itched at Rhian's mind, and she decided to dare his disapproval. 'Can mmm . . .' deeply ingrained habit made her tongue stumble. ' . . . you tell me what brought you to the borders of my father's land?'

Gawain looked at her carefully, weighing and judging some quality Rhian could not guess at, and he made his decision. 'The Saxons plan to start the wars again,' he said. 'I am carrying that warning to the High King.'

His words at once dropped fear into Rhian's heart, making it beat slow and heavy and filling her with the sharp and sudden longing for the stone walls of her father's hall. All her life, she had heard tales of the Saxon invaders, of the raids and rapes, sackings and burnings. She had also heard, and told, how High King Arthur had broken the invading forces, sending them scurrying back to Gaul, or leaving them clinging to the eastern coasts muttering to themselves in their dark fortresses behind wicker fences.

That they would come again . . . that they would be *here* . . . In the light of day it was comparatively easy to shake off the immediacy of magic and sorcerers, but the spear, the knife and the torch – those were far more solid things. In an instant, the trees were once again the home of terrors, and Rhian had to swallow hard against her fears.

'How close are they?' the words came before she had time to worry about discretion.

'Two days' ride.' Gawain looked to the distance. They had topped the rise and ahead the wood seemed to be thinning, but Rhian was no longer sure of her bearings, though Gawain seemed to be. *How much time has been lost already?* she could practically hear him thinking.

Rhian bit her lip. 'Is there any way to get word to my father? He should know.'

Gawain looked genuinely shocked. 'After what he has done to you, you would care?'

'Does my mother deserve to suffer for what my father has done?' snapped Rhian. 'The men and women of our holding?'

Gawain looked quickly away. 'Forgive me, that was an unworthy thing that I said.' The apology was smooth and courtly, as perfect as all his other manners, but there was something more underneath it, a trace of some old wound or faded nightmare of a memory. Whatever it was, Gawain shook it quickly off. 'It would not do to let the invaders know yet that we have word of their plans. As soon as I have taken counsel with the king, I am certain he will send out messengers to his liegemen to stand in readiness.'

But will that be soon enough? It was all Rhian could do not to look back down the twilit road again.

'I do not seem to be succeeding in reassuring you, Lady Rhian,' Gawain said wryly.

It was indeed lighter ahead. She should concentrate on that, see it as a sign, behave properly and forget her curiosity. 'If I want reassurance, perhaps I should simply stop asking questions.'

'I think that such silence would ill become you.' Was he simply being polite once more, or did he truly mean that? His face had softened, particularly around his eyes. 'It might make the road more smooth.'

That brought him out of reverie into philosophy. 'And where is the glory in the smooth road?'

I wonder, Sir, if you've forgotten who you are speaking with. 'I have been told glory is not for ladies.'

'I know of at least one lady who would argue that point.' Gawain's eyes took on a knowing glint.

Rhian drew her shoulders back and set her face in a fussy imitation of Aeldra. 'What lady might this be to say such an unladylike thing?'

'The High Queen, Guinevere,' replied Gawain matter-of-factly.

Rhian found she was not ready for that answer. She concentrated on keeping seat and hands steady while Thetis picked her careful way down the slope between the stones, gouges and damp drifts of leaves. The day had warmed and clouds of midges swarmed around Thetis's ears. Perspiration prickled Rhian's scalp under her veil and the lack of food was beginning to have an effect on her. She wondered if Gawain had any bread in his bags that they might stop and share. The last swallow of watered wine seemed a long time ago.

'What is she like, Queen Guinevere?' she asked instead, not wanting to complain or slow their progress. 'I have never been to court.'

Gawain smiled then, and for a single heartbeat, Rhian thought he looked more like a man thinking of his lady-love than one thinking of his aunt. But as he spoke, she told herself firmly that she was most mistaken.

'A more loyal and virtuous lady is not to be found. She is wise in her counsel both public and private, and generous to those in need. Her appearance is noble in all aspects, and her grey eyes are justly famous.'

> *Grey-eyed Guinevere, she*
> *who rode at the king's left hand*
> *the fairest flower of womanhood*
> *e'er seen in Christom's vasty lands.*

The words rang unbidden through Rhian's memory. She wondered if Gawain knew that particular poem. He certainly seemed ready to confirm its praises. She should have felt reassured by this. She was certainly in need, and she could think of nothing she had done to deserve what she had come to, but she could not bring herself to take heart.

'She is learned, as well,' Gawain was saying, warming to his theme. 'Schooled in Greek and Latin, and familiar with poets and writings in both languages. She is perfectly matched with her husband in this respect. Arthur seeks to rule with learning and follow the Roman traditions of laws and letters. It is a good way. It is a better way . . .' but his words trailed off and all at once, the road ahead seemed to take all his concentration. They had come to level ground again, and the trees here were younger and thinner. Patches of meadow grass sprang up between the gnarled trunks and the bird calls grew softer and at last, they broke the treeline, emerging, blinking into the sunlight of a marshy meadow land dotted with white and yellow flowers and smelling of damp grass and warmth.

Rhian opened her mouth to ask Gawain to continue, but then he reined his palfrey back, causing Gringolet to check his step. Rhian pulled Thetis up as well, and she followed Gawain's gaze. Ahead, where the trees began again, there rose a thick column of dark smoke, dispersing to a black mist on the faint breeze.

'What is it?' she asked, seeing how Gawain's face had grown suddenly grave.

'That smoke is too heavy for a camp or a charcoal burner,' he said. The palfrey danced impatiently under him, and Gawain patted it automatically, but he did not look away from the smoke. 'There is no village or town in that direction. I do not like it.'

Without another word, Gawain urged the palfrey forward,

leaving the road for the muddy meadow and taking his direction from the smoke plume. Gringolet lifted his hooves high and fastidiously to follow. Rhian and Thetis had little choice but to do the same.

The trees soon closed in around them once more, making it impossible to ride, and they both dismounted to lead their horses, pushing aside whip-like branches and directing their paths around decaying logs and pools of standing water. Rhian could not see the smoke now, but she could smell it, strong and acrid, and wrong somehow. It did not smell like a friendly hearthfire, nor did it carry the tang of the forge or the kiln. The birds overhead had all gone silent, and the only noise was the squelch and crackle of their passage.

No. Something else.

Rhian strained her ears, and heard a vague and distant crackling noise that should have been familiar, but that she could not make her mind identify.

They came to a narrow and rutted track, an offshoot of the main road, so little used that the forest plants were already beginning to sprout along its length. Gawain held up his hand, signalling her to halt. The scent of smoke had grown stronger, and the crackling, Rhian realized, must be the sound of the fire that made that smoke.

Gawain peered through the trees across the track. Rhian could see little through the greening branches, only some dark shapes that could have been anything from standing stones to an overgrown Roman fortress.

'Wait with the horses, lady.' Gawain did not look back at her as he spoke. He did, however, loosen his sword in its sheath.

With the smell of smoke and the sound of fire in the wind, and the knowledge that the Saxons were planning to begin their wars once again. Rhian did not want to walk forward to find out what was burned in these woods, but neither did she want to stand here alone.

She covered her fear in bravado. 'You urge me to follow the example of Queen Guinevere. Would she remain behind at such a time?'

He turned to stare at her. She made herself look determined, although inside she was beginning to feel ill.

But her countenance must have been strong enough. 'Agravain is ever reminding me to guard my tongue more closely,' Gawain muttered. 'Did you bring a spare bowstring?'

'I did.'

'Then restring your bow, Lady Rhian, and come.'

Quiver and bow slung over her shoulders, Rhian followed Gawain through the trees. They had left the horses tethered by the track. Gawain moved cautiously, like a man hunting, peering through the trees and scanning the ground before he took his next step, and she copied his gait and demeanour. The day was now far too warm, and far too quiet. The smoke took on the sweet smell of cooking meat, and the tang of fresh blood. Rhian's mouth went dry. Behind her, the trees seemed to whisper uneasily. Ahead, the fire crackled and hissed.

Gawain pushed back a final screen of brambles and froze. Through the leaves Rhian saw what made the foully-scented smoke.

It had been a croft. There were countless such on the fringes of the woods. Several families had raised pigs here, perhaps some sheep. They had cleared some little land to put under the plough. If they prospered, more families would join them and perhaps in time they would become a village.

Or they would have, if fate had blessed them. Instead here was a scene of havoc. The cots and outbuildings had collapsed into ash and char. Coals still glowed among the black and shattered timbers. A piebald sow lay sprawled on the churned ground, slit from throat to belly so that its entrails spilled out into the ash among the shards of smashed pots and buckets. There would be worse under the timbers, Rhian knew that in the pit of her heart.

Without a word, Gawain walked forward into the chaos. The cleared ground had been churned into a sea of mud. Lumps of char and streaks of ash and blood were trampled deeply into it. This had been the work of men with horses. The marks of hooves as well as sandals and boots showed clearly on the ravaged ground. Despite the sound of the smouldering fires, the place seemed strangely silent. There should be more noise, Rhian thought, absurdly. There should be echoes of the screaming that had surely happened here, of the shouting and the pleas. There should be something of the life, of the voices, to remain, not just silent patterns in the earth and wisps of smoke to be blown away on the wind.

Gawain picked his way through the smouldering ruin to the wreck that had once been a cottage. His back stiffened and he spoke quietly, but Rhian heard every word.

'They did not spare the children.'

Rhian crossed herself automatically. *Mother Mary pray for us . . .*

Gawain still cast about the ruins. Overhead a raven croaked. Fear took Rhian, although she could not say why. The horror here was done.

But movement flickered in the trees and the wind blew. Rhian's eyes stung as the fresh ash touched them and through the tears she saw a shape standing at the edge of the clearing, great and green, a giant man leaning on the haft of a battle-axe nearly as tall as Gawain's shoulder. She saw another man, this one pale as milk and bright as brass, carrying a sword smeared red and black from its work, and that man crept out of the ruined cottage, and slipped up behind Gawain and raised his blade high.

Gawain straightened up and the ghostly sword slashed at his torso. A second ghost fell, clutching its belly, and that ghost was Gawain.

Rhian's hand flew to her mouth, but the vision was gone, and there was only Gawain, and the noises of the forest. A bird whistled overhead. A coal fell from a roof-timber to the ground. Both the Green Man and the raven were gone.

Gawain was staring at her.

'I saw . . .' she croaked. 'I thought . . .'

'Rhian,' murmured Gawain. 'Get to the road and free the horses. Do not look back.'

Rhian nodded and tried to comply. Behind her, she heard the rasp as he pulled his sword from its sheath and fear shot through her. She did not look back, but concentrated on the way forward, trying to remember her woodcraft and slip through the trees, but her fright made her clumsy. She tried not to think of the Green Man. Why should she see him again? Why now in this ruin? What was that ghost that had felled Gawain? Was it a warning from the Holy Mother, or was it the work of the Devil?

Collect yourself Rhian, you're useless this way.

She reminded herself how to step softly, how to avoid branches rather than plough into them. It was then that she heard the bird call again, and this time she could hear it was not a true bird.

'Run!' shouted Gawain.

Rhian hiked up her skirts and obeyed. She crashed through the sea of branches and bracken, every twig becoming a claw clutching at sleeves and hems to hold her back. Behind her, the world exploded into noise such as only humans could make – the hoarse cries of men's voices among the crash of branches.

The clash of metal.

Rhian looked back without thinking. Three men burst from

the forest, short swords in their hands and caps of leather and bronze on their heads. One of them looked at her and his pale eyes glittered as he charged.

'Run!' bellowed Gawain again, and he flung himself against the marauders.

The Saxons were not expecting such a fierce attack. They fell back before Gawain's longer sword and reach. But that advantage would not last, not in the trees. Gawain slashed like a madman, driving the Saxons back before him, not truly landing any blows, just keeping them busy.

Keeping them busy so she could get away.

Get to the horses, get to the horses! she cried in her mind, demanding her feet to flee, despite what she saw. Gawain was fighting to keep her free, and if she stood there, she would not remain so. When he broke free (*and he will break free, he must break free*), she needed to have the horses untied and ready so they could outrun the surviving Saxons.

Unless . . .

Metal glinted through the trees ahead of her and the sound of a horse's angry scream cut through the air. Rhian's madly beating heart filled her throat.

Unless they had already found the horses.

Instinct took over all conscious thought, and Rhian measured her length in a patch of unfolding ferns. Sheltered by the bracken, she pressed her hands over her mouth, trying to stifle the harsh sound of her breathing. The noise of the battle behind gave her some cover as did the screaming and thrashing of a maddened horse before her. She stared out through the screen of delicate leaves and stems and tried to quell her rising panic.

The Saxons had found the horses, and had put three men to guard them. The guards were greedy though. Goods from the saddlebags were strewn on the ground. One of them also apparently had tried to ride or handle Gringolet, and now the charger was doing his best to bedevil them. He bucked and reared, flailing out with his hooves, while two of the men tried in vain to catch his swinging reins and a third shouted and cursed in their harsh tongue. He had his sword out and was staring into the trees, trying to see through to the melee near the croft, to see if the wrong person had broken free of it.

In that chaos, Rhian saw her chance. She unslung her bow and reached for an arrow. Moving slowly, she pushed herself up onto one knee. Her own soft noises were masked by Gringolet's outrage, the Saxon's cursing and the clash of metal and splintering of wood as she pulled an arrow from her quiver, and nocked it into her string.

The Saxon with his sword drawn stood near the treeline. She shifted a little to get a clear line of sight.

It is just like a deer. It is just like a quail. Breathe slowly.

It is a deer. It is not a man. I am not about to kill a man.

Rhian drew the string back to her ear. She sighted along the shaft. Thetis, answering Gringolet's distress, backed and swung her head, trying to free her reins from the branch where she was tethered. The palfrey whickered, the men shouted at one another. Gringolet reared again. In the woods, Gawain's voice rang out.

The Saxon turned broad towards her, and Rhian loosed her arrow. It flew straight and true, without a sound, and plunged into the Saxon's belly. He looked down, surprised to see this unnatural limb that had somehow sprouted from his body. Rhian, breathing now as if she had run a mile, drew another arrow. The Saxon she had shot toppled to the ground, screaming as the pain took him. Rhian nocked the fresh arrow. One of the remaining Saxons shouted to the other. Abandoning the harried and harrying Gringolet, he sprinted to his comrade's side. Rhian drew back her bowstring and waited. The Saxon's sword was in his hand and he turned his back to the trees, just for an instant, to shout to the other to leave the maddened horse and come to see. Rhian took her aim again, and again let go the string. She had meant the shot to take him between the shoulder blades, but as the arrow flew, he turned, and it was only luck that he was just a little too slow. The arrow drove itself through his arm and into his side. He dropped instantly, rolling and clawing at the wooden shaft. The third man saw his companion fall and stared at the woods. Gringolet reared again, pawing the air. The Saxon had wit enough to jump back. Rhian fitted a third arrow to the string.

She did not have a chance to fire. The man fled into the trees on the opposite side of the road, not even bothering to draw his sword. With the last Saxon gone, Gringolet calmed down, stamping and whickering but no longer so wide-eyed. His ears tipped forward again, alert, not laid back in fury. His calm eased Thetis and the palfrey and they quieted, easing their stamping and their calls.

At their feet, the men Rhian had shot screamed, their cries growing hoarse and choked with tears.

Rhian lowered her bow, letting the unshot arrow drop from the string. Her hands shook and despite the heat of the day, she felt cold. It was not until then that she realized the noise of the fight behind her had ceased, and footsteps now rustled leaves and undergrowth as they approached.

Rhian flattened herself against the ground again. She could not see clearly into the depth of the wood, she could not take aim, even if she could steady her hands again. The screams of the wounded men confused her mind. She could only huddle in the mud and pray for steadiness and silence. It would be Gawain, it must be Gawain, because if it wasn't Gawain, she was lost.

The footsteps broke through the bracken and settled into the mud. Rhian dared at last to lift her head. In front of her,

Gawain stepped from the woods to the track, his sword in his hand. He looked down at her handiwork, and with two swift strokes, brought the silence Rhian had craved but a moment before.

Rhian pressed her face against her sleeve, shuddering, until she could remember that what Gawain had just done was merciful. Those men were already dead; now they were out of pain.

When she could look up again, Gawain had turned, searching about him on all sides.

Rhian made herself pick up her bow and get to her feet. Gawain heard the noise clearly and swung around, sword coming up and ready.

'It's Rhian,' she called out as she made her way forward. 'Alone and free.'

Rhian pushed past the last of the trees to stand on the uneven track. Thetis snorted in greeting and nuzzled her shoulder. Sweat, blood and dirt streaked Gawain's face. More of the same decorated his hauberk and the blade of his sword. His damp hair hung in elflocks and ringlets around his shoulders.

'God and Christ be thanked,' Gawain said fervently, and with his free hand, there beside the victims of her archery and his blade, Gawain seized her around the waist and kissed her. It was not the kiss of peace or courtesy. His mouth pressed warm and sensual against hers, seeking to part her lips, to open her to him. Rhian felt hot, then cold. Her whole body seized up stiff as a board as his mouth moved, seeking . . . seeking what? The answer to that question flickered through her mind and her hands pushed against his hard, broad chest.

Gawain loosened his hold. Rhian pulled away, knowing herself to have gone pale as she looked at him, and saw how startled he was.

'Lady, forgive your servant,' he said, returning to courtly formality in his shock. 'He meant no . . .'

But Rhian could not stand there and listen. She turned on her heel and fled.

She could not have gone more than a handful of yards before she brought herself up short and dropped onto a fallen tree because she did not think she could stand up any longer. Rhian wrapped her arms around herself, trembling. Why had Gawain done that? Had she led him to believe somehow . . .? Was there something she had done that was too familiar, too wanton? Some look or turn of phrase? She tried to think, but could not. All she could think of was the crush of his lips against hers, and how it had been wet and warm, and how for a moment her breasts had pressed against his chest, and how for a heartbeat, she had wanted to remain there in his arms.

That thought caused her to tremble even harder.

It was not that Rhian was ignorant of the ways of men and women. It was not that she had never before been kissed in a way that was other than chaste. But she also knew that while milk maids and cowherds might do as they pleased, when they pleased and with whom, she was an outland lord's daughter. Lacking cows to keep herself, she must get married, and her maidenhead was part of her dowry. Without her father's blessing, it was indeed all the dower she had, and she did not know whether her father would ever give such a blessing, nor if she would ever wish to return to his hall to receive it.

And the king's nephew, the heir to Camelot, would not, could not marry the dowerless daughter of a minor liege-man. *It was only a kiss,* she tried to tell herself. *It was nothing more. Just a kiss for celebration and thanks. If it was more, it was only so in your mind, fool girl.*

Just a kiss, for joy and celebration and all the rest that she only suspected, given and taken among the dead men. The men she had slain. Rhian's stomach churned suddenly and for a moment she feared she might be sick.

'Lady Rhian?'

Rhian jerked her head up to see Gawain standing there.

'Lady, I truly am most sorry. I should not have presumed. It was a liberty and I ask that you forgive me.'

'Of course,' she said, ashamed at how weak her voice sounded. 'There is nothing to forgive. It was not . . . I didn't . . .' *Save that it was and I did, even with the dead lying at my feet. My dead.*

Gawain knelt beside her. 'Death has been too much with you these past days, has he not?'

Rhian nodded, grateful to be spared the necessity of speech.

'It is a hard thing to know that a man has died by your hands. It must be even harder when you never imagine you must do such a thing.'

'My father has high and low justice in his lands,' she murmured, although she didn't quite know why. 'He once sentenced a man who had murdered his wife. They hanged him from the oak on the green. His face went blue. Everyone cheered. There was no blood then.' She wondered why she wasn't crying. She felt too hollow for tears. 'They left him there.'

Gawain nodded in understanding. 'When I was a boy and still at home, the Pictish men attacked us. We weren't in the fortress at Din Eityn then, just one of the lesser halls. They're a dark people, with eyes like flint. They meant to loot and burn us, saying we had stolen their lands. I stood on the earthworks and watched the men ride out to meet them. Even then, I heard the noise of the screams and the clash, and saw the circling crows and smelled death . . .' He shook his head. 'I had to go off and be sick, and I hadn't even struck a blow. Battle is never easy, and glory only comes when you've cleaned hands and sword and had time to understand that you are still alive.'

He touched her shoulder. 'We are still alive, Lady Rhian, but we will not remain so if we do not hurry away.'

Rhian nodded again. His hand was warm on her shoulder, heavy and strong. It brought back memories of his kiss.

God and Mary, why could she not stop shaking?

'I will get the horses,' said Gawain. 'Come as quickly as you are able.'

He stood and left her there. She did not look back to see him go.

SIX

The congress of ravens flew north and east until well after noontime. Kerra flew with them, wholly as one of their own, enjoying the freedom of the wind and the sky. When they caught sight of a deer's ravaged corpse, she feasted as greedily as her companions and they gossiped together about the ways of the forest and the great changes wrought by spring's blossoming.

It was when she flew as a raven that she understood why her mother had kept to a wanderer's life. There were times she also wished to stay forever in motion and forever free.

But to do that would be a betrayal of the one who had saved her life, and her soul.

Sated, Kerra flapped her wings, and in her mind's eye saw herself flying alone on one of her strange errands, casting off what her companions considered her true shape, and walking the world as a human again. They protested, as they frequently did, but she also pictured herself bringing them dainties such as the forest could never provide. They shrieked their approval, and she rose alone to catch the winds.

Alone, it was easier to concentrate on her errand. No longer sporting, Kerra flew due north. There was not far to go. The hills rose steeply here, and fertile land grew scarce. The grey bones of the earth began to poke through its tattered green cloak.

Nestled deep within the folds of that threadbare cloak waited a lonesome hall. Kerra could have flown directly into one of its windows and been welcome, but that lacked respect. Instead, she lighted down just inside its wicker fence and in her raven's voice she spoke a certain word three times. Pain coursed through her as she grew long and human again, and her feathers once more became the feathered cape. If any witnessed the transformation, it did not matter. She had come home.

Unlike Euberacon's home, this place was what it seemed – a long and low house, its stone tightly mortared, its roof well thatched. If it needed to be otherwise, its mistress would make it so, but not until then. *The truth is stronger than any lie,* she said frequently to Kerra. *Use it whenever you can.*

Those who lived and served here did so willingly and well. Boys and old men tended herds of fat sheep and pigs. Young men sat around their fires in the yard, yarning with each other, repairing clothing or cooking in iron pots. The swirls and crosses tattooed on their skins marked them as following the true and ancient ways. They watched Kerra walk between them, but she felt no menace from them. She also served their mistress, and none would any more raise a hand against her than they would against a beloved sister.

Since the weather was fair, the hall doors stood open. White-haired Talan waited just inside, playing the porter, but not with the greatest diligence. Kerra found him digging his knife into a blue-veined cheese that smelled so strong she was surprised it didn't set his eyes watering. Her shadow fell across him where he sat and he leapt at once to his feet.

'Lady Kerra,' he said with a smile and a respectful bow.

'She said you'd be coming today. She's waiting in the hall for you.'

'Thank you, Talan.' She had thought she might talk with the old man about how things were here, but if their mistress was already waiting, there was no time for other news.

A second pair of stout doors, deeply carved with sigils for watchfulness and strength, led to the hall. It was no grand place, but its darkness was warm and if there was smoke, there was also an abundance of fires to welcome a traveller with the scents of boiling, brewing and baking. Strong-armed women, mates and matches for the men outside, moved between the fires. Their dark hair hung loose about their shoulders, with only one or two slender braids confining a few of their tresses. Their clothes were of the plainest stuffs, with simple embroidery. Nearly all of them had a nod and a warm smile for Kerra as she passed, but none tried to delay her with talk. They knew her time was precious.

At the far end of the hall sat another group of women, engaged in the endless task of making cloth. The oldest women supervised the youngest children, teasing burrs and chaff from the heaps of shorn wool. Others spun, or wove at the standing looms, drawing the shuttles back and forth between the weighted threads. Still others sewed the finished cloth with ivory needles.

One woman sat in a great, carved chair. Her hair was black, streaked with white. Beneath its cloud her face was strong and still beautiful, for all it was lined with care. She wore her simple cloud-grey dress as well as any queen could wear her finery. Her black eyes, ever-alert, darted back and forth, first watching the women working around her, next attending to the drop spindle and the pale thread twisting through her own long fingers, as fine and strong as a spider's spinning, then noting the activity in the rest of the great hall.

Kerra approached silently, and dropped into a deep curtsey.

'Daughter,' Morgaine smiled, and Kerra warmed to the approval of her voice. 'Rise. Let me see you.'

Kerra obeyed. Morgaine looked her up and down, not blinking, drinking in every detail. Kerra suddenly felt ashamed of the broad, burgundy cloth of her dress and the twisted silver of her trims and jewellery. Who was she to appear in this place dressed more finely than her mistress? These gauds were nothing. True nobility, true power came from within, and all her lusting after gold and scarlet cloth was sheerest vanity. She was certain Morgaine's eyes discerned this folly clearly, and she wanted to apologize at once. Even her cloak of feathers seemed a covering for empty pride. Her power was nothing. She had not learned one tenth of what Morgaine could have taught her. Before this woman she was scarcely a child.

But then Morgaine smiled at her, and the sun came out again. Kerra was a child, but she was a dutiful child. She served with her whole heart. Morgaine knew this and accepted her service, and that was all Kerra could ever ask.

Morgaine wound her thread and passed her spindle to one of the waiting women. 'Come, Kerra.' She rose. 'Walk a little with me and tell me what you have seen.'

There was no place to be alone in a hall such as this, but none would dare speak a word of anything they overheard from their mistress. Nonetheless, Morgaine led Kerra to the shadows, where they would be hidden from any who entered as well as from most of those who worked there, but none would be hidden from the mistress's bright, sharp gaze.

Morgaine listened attentively while Kerra told her all the news of Euberacon's doings, of his going to claim Rhian of the Morelands and of Gawain's intervention. Gawain's name made Morgaine frown with an old and bitter fury. Kerra cringed before that rage, although none of it was for her. Morgaine gestured impatiently for her to continue. Kerra did, but her tongue stammered and stuttered for a time before she could recover herself. She told Morgaine of the task Euberacon had set her to, and how she had seen only peaceful land between his fortress and Morgaine's hall, which told her that if Arthur suspected the Saxons were on the rise, he was not yet sure, for none of his men were massing or moving.

She fell silent, waiting to see how Morgaine received her news. Morgaine watched her hall for a time, noting the ebb and flow of its people, their smallest motions, to whom they spoke and who they passed by. No detail escaped her, even while she mulled over the full import of Kerra's message. Morgaine the Unsleeping, the men outside called her, and Morgaine the Goddess. No one here called her Morgan the Fae, and no one ever would.

Morgaine's restless gaze caught on a small, slender boy, and her face lit up in a smile such as even Kerra seldom saw. The child stood a solemn and polite distance away, waiting to be acknowledged. His hands were clutched across his chest, concealing something.

'Mordred,' said Morgaine, the name filled with a mother's pride. 'What is it you have there?'

The boy ran forward and opened his hands, displaying his treasure. It was a tiny rabbit, so small a man's fist could have closed around it.

'The dogs found its warren,' he said quietly, his eyes wide with what he had seen. Kerra could imagine the small bodies tossed into the air, and the blood on the hounds' muzzles.

Morgaine crouched beside her son. 'That is their duty,' she said quietly. She extended one finger and gently stroked the rabbit's fur. The tiny creature trembled, but its fear had removed the ability to struggle.

'I know.' Her son moved a little closer to her. 'But he's alone now, and he's so little . . .'

Morgaine nodded. 'Go to the dairy and soak a rag in milk for him, and then you may make a nest for him in the stables to keep him warm. You will have to feed him often. Speak with Ahern. He will be able to tell you much of what you need to know.'

Mordred nodded happily. 'Thank you, mother!' he said, and snuggled his new pet close against his chest again, making to run at once to the kitchens. But Morgaine caught his chin, and turned him firmly to face her again.

'He has come to you in need, Mordred,' she said. 'It is now your duty to care for him and not neglect him. Do you understand?'

The boy nodded, all solemnity again. 'Yes, mother.'

'Good boy.' She smiled again, ruffled his hair and gave him a push towards the hall door. The boy scampered happily away with his treasure. Morgaine looked after him, sighing and shaking her head. The shadow of anger crossed her face as she watched her son vanish into the daylight, and something of sorrow.

But whatever she was thinking, Morgaine kept it to herself. When she turned her attention again to Kerra, her thoughts were all on their business and the work yet to be done.

'You have done well,' said Morgaine. 'But he is a busy one, Euberacon, and he is making still more work for you.' She smiled almost apologetically at Kerra. 'I fear I must keep you from home awhile longer yet.'

'What would you have me do, mistress?' asked Kerra immediately.

'This Easterner plays too many games. There are too many reverses. He should learn the value of simplicity.' Her long fingers tapped restlessly against her thigh. 'I think you should do just as he has told you. Have your men capture this Rhian, separating her from Gawain.' Morgaine's gaze grew distant then, filling with memories and the deep, burning pain that never left her. 'But should they be a little too zealous and kill both her and Gawain, that can hardly be your fault.' She smiled a fresh smile then, one that made Kerra's heart quail within her.

It was a long moment before Kerra could make herself speak again. 'He clearly wants them alive, mistress,' she ventured. 'Should we not try to discover why that is?'

Morgaine considered this, her fingers still tapping out the rhythm of her thoughts. 'That much is quite plain. He wants Gawain and, by extension, Arthur, confused and weakened at a critical time, and if one wishes to weaken Gawain, one could do far worse than to play on his heart. As for the girl . . .' Morgaine's mouth tightened in disapproval, even as her eyes looked to the future. 'As a slave, such powers as hers could be useful in many circumstances. If he returns to Constantinople with her and claims she was bought in a slave market while he was abroad, who is to say differently? Certainly not she. No,' she sighed as a woman might seeing the number of chores that must be performed in a day. 'I think they are both better off dead. Gawain's death will strike Camelot at its core, and the girl's death will at same time weaken Euberacon and set back his plans, so that he must stay and shield our own work from prying eyes that much longer.'

'Then it shall be as you say, mistress.' Kerra bent her knee in reverence and in recognition that the audience was over.

Morgaine laid her hand on Kerra's head in approval and blessing. 'Take care, daughter. He is half blind, that sorcerer, but he is no fool. He will kill you as soon as he can.'

'Then he had best learn to sprout his own wings and quickly, mistress, or my friends will have something to say about it,' said Kerra with perhaps too much solemnity.

Her bold jest earned her one of Morgaine's rare laughs, and Kerra left the hall in high spirits. Night was coming, but there was perhaps an hour or two of light left. She could make some progress. There was no time to waste if she was to complete her work and return before Euberacon grew suspicious.

Kerra lifted the hood of her cloak and raised her eyes. A raven once more, she launched herself into the sky.

It was not even noon before the Saxons found Rhian and Gawain again.

It had been a cold night. They had kept to the track until the light and the horses were exhausted. No shelter offered itself, so they had been forced to sleep in the open, with only their cloaks and the horses for warmth. Dinner was crumbling and overripe cheese and hard bread. Breakfast was the same, livened by the eggs of a quail and their parent roasted overnight in the coals of a minuscule fire and washed down by the last of Gawain's watered wine. The only consolation was that the rains seemed to be staying away for the present.

Gawain looked tired, though hale. Rhian wondered how much of the night he had spent in watching over their small camp, but could find no way to ask. She wanted the world to begin again with the morning, and was content to leave the night and previous day behind. The visceral discomforts of a cold night and nagging hunger made it strangely easy for Rhian to set aside her discomforts of mind. Guessing how much farther it was to Pen Marhas – where there would be a much larger fire, and bowls of stew and roast meats and the day's fresh baking – pushed back memories of the dead, and unconsidered kisses.

She found herself humming under her breath as she shifted her weight back and forth on Thetis's back, trying to ease the pain from the constant riding. The tune gave a little vent to her feelings and her hungers. To her surprise, Gawain took up the words.

'Oh, waken Queen of Elfin, and hear your woman moan
Oh, mourn you for your meat? Oh, mourn you for your fee?
Oh, mourn you for the other bounties, Ladies are want to gi'e?'

He had a good voice, rough but pleasant, and it seemed he enjoyed the act of singing, or perhaps he just hoped to put her once more at ease. Rhian was more than willing to let him.

She added her voice to his, soft but true, and they worked their way through the story of the woman lured from her home by the Elvish queen.

'I mourn not for my meat, I mourn not for my fee.
Nor mourn I for the other bounties, Ladies are want to gi'e.
But mourn I for my young son, I left him four nights ago.'

The trees thinned, and the road dried, but the way grew steeper and more rocky, making riding more difficult and leaving little breath or mind for singing. As the forest fell behind them, so did the birdsong, leaving them alone with the wind and the distant call of hunting ravens. Rhian shivered at the sound.

Gawain turned from the rising hills and took them towards the slopes that led down again to the broadening valley. A grey and brown ribbon of road cut straight across the distant valley floor. The ground between them and that road was rough, and Thetis quickly began to complain at having to find a path between the holes and the stones. Rhian realized she would have to get off and walk before they reached level ground.

Gawain did not seem at all relieved to see the clear way below them. He was looking behind them, squinting towards the folds in the hills that towered over their backs as if he thought them eavesdropping. The palfrey he rode snorted and balked at his lack of attention, and even Gringolet pulled at the tether that tied him to the smaller horse. A raven croaked to the east, and another to the west. Stone clattered against stone, and a pebble rolled past Thetis's hooves, making her pull up and whinny in annoyance.

Rhian lifted a hand to pat the mare's neck, but as she did, a fist-sized stone tumbled through Thetis's shadow, followed fast by another. The mare shied, and Rhian was barely able to stay on her back.

Gawain shouted, but the clatter of stones drowned out his words. They skipped and bounced down the slopes – grey-green and brown, singly and in chattering streams, a whole scree of missiles aimed straight at the horses' hooves and ankles.

All the horses screamed, high, human sounds. Thetis reared back, throwing Rhian to the ground. The breath slammed out of her body and the world spun in a riot of colour. Hooves flailed overhead. A stone skipped against her side. Rhian threw her arms over her head, curling up into the tightest ball she could. The harsh roar of men's voices cut across the horses' screams. Fear uncurled Rhian and sent her scrambling up the slope. Her eyes focused more slowly than her hands and feet moved, so it took a moment for her to see the danger.

A dozen Saxons raced down the hill. Thetis galloped towards the valley floor in blind panic, bearing Rhian's bow away with her, leaving her with nothing but her bare hands against the wave of men racing towards her, their axes and short swords flashing in the sunlight, their cries mixing with the ravens' mocking calls. Nearby, the palfrey lay on its side, screaming in pain and panic as its body twisted and jerked grotesquely from Gringolet's frantic efforts to yank his tether free from the fallen horse. Gawain was struggling with Gringolet, dodging hooves and heavy head, his knife drawn, trying desperately to get hold of the tether so he could cut the charger loose.

Rhian tried to run, tried to get the maddened Gringolet between herself and the marauders, for the outraged horse was the only shelter there was. Gawain finally managed to slice through the tether. Gringolet reared and spun all in one fearful motion, tossing Gawain backward to land on a cluster of loose stones with a painful cry. The stallion leapt over him as if he were no more than a fallen log and raced down the slope.

The roar of warriors in full charge turned to raucous laughter. The Saxons ringed Rhian and Gawain, making a living fence of brown and bronze. Their noseguards had been worked into shapes like boars' snouts or the muzzles of hunting cats and wolves, lending them a bestial appearance. Their eyes glinted ice pale beneath their helms. Rhian's reeling mind threw out the memory of the pale ghost she had seen in the croft. That ghost could have been any one of these ferocious, grinning men.

Gawain struggled to rise, but his eyes were dazed and his elbow buckled as he tried to push himself up. His knife had flown from his grasp, and one of the Saxons scooped it up and stuck it in his belt.

Seeing there was no possible resistance left for their prey, the Saxons darted forward. Two grabbed Gawain and hauled him to his knees, ignoring his gasp of pain. Another slammed his heavy hand between Rhian's shoulders, forcing her down beside Gawain. He gripped the back of her neck with his gloved hand, digging his fingertips into her flesh so that she could not move without more pain.

One of the Saxons strolled over to the screaming palfrey. The man looked at the horse for a moment and then casually thrust his sword through the animal's throat. The palfrey sputtered, and died at once in a welter of blood and foam. The clean wind filled with the scent of sweat and death. Rhian felt something crumble inside her. Gawain just watched in grim silence.

Without appearing to notice the abundance of gore, the Saxon helped himself to the saddlebags and other gear, including Gawain's spear, sword and shield, and tossed them to his waiting fellows, doubtlessly to be shared out later.

The man holding Rhian squeezed her neck a little harder, in anticipation of the spoils. Rhian's stomach turned over.

The first of the ravens lighted on the dead horse. It dipped its beak down to feed, and Rhian tried to turn her head to look away. This only made her captor laugh and grip her neck all the harder. Rhian swallowed her gall and made herself remain still.

Then, one of the Saxons, whose helm was fashioned so he had the appearance of a wild boar, said something in their guttural tongue. Four of the dozen loped away down the hill, clearly on the track of the other horses.

His men dispatched, the boar's head – whom Rhian took to be the leader – turned towards the captives. As he did, he pulled off the helmet and wiped the sweat from his face and beard. His hand, she saw, was missing two fingers.

Gawain stared in open shock, and mouthed a single word.

In response, the man spat. A slow and deadly smile spread across his face.

'You did not think to see me again so soon, did you, my Lord Gawain?' he said. His accent was heavy, but his words were carefully measured so as to be understood.

'Harrik.'

You know this man? thought Rhian, stunned.

Gawain's face had gone paper white and he stared at the one he called Harrik. 'What are you doing?'

The feral grin spread even wider, but the heat of it did not reach his winter-blue eyes. 'Avenging my brothers slaughtered by your king and living as one of my blood should live.'

Gawain glanced to either side of Harrik. The other Saxons were watching, but they watched for movement of hands, watched for the return of their fellows with the horses, or watched the saddlebags, attempting to divine their contents. They were alert, but they did not behave like men listening to a conversation they comprehended.

'I do not believe it,' said Gawain evenly. Not one of the Saxons grunted or laughed, or gave any other sign they understood what had been said.

Harrik leaned close. He smelled sour and warm, like sweat and bad beer. 'Believe,' he said harshly, but his eyes were wide with some emotion Rhian could not readily name. For a heartbeat she thought it might be fear. Harrik straightened abruptly. His jaw worked itself soundlessly back and forth a few times. 'Or do not. You will be dead in a few moments, so it does not matter.'

'No!' Useless fear tightened all Rhian's muscles, thrashing her body against her captor's grasp. The man simply laughed and forced her forward so he could more easily grab her flailing wrist and yank it up hard behind her shoulders.

Tears of pain flooded her eyes, but Rhian made herself go still. *This is no good. You cannot escape like this.* She strained her gaze to see Gawain from the corner of her eye. Rage had hardened him face and limb. His guards held him close, their weapons out and ready.

Harrik turned his face towards the men who held Gawain. The ravens clustered on the palfrey's corpse lifted their heads as if in anticipation. Panic flooded Rhian, turning her thoughts into a gabble of prayer and pleading.

The Lord is my Shepherd, I shall not want ... Mother Mary, spare him, save us, don't let him die ... He prepareth me a table in the midst of my enemies . . . Mother Mary help us, help us . . .

'What of your son, Harrik?' cried Gawain, and the man froze. Gawain went on relentlessly. 'Do not think Arthur will shrink from doing what the law demands when he learns you have broken your word.'

'My son is a warrior of the true blood.' The words seemed to grate against the man's tongue as he spoke. His jaw was again working itself back and forth, chewing something unseen. 'It is better he die young than live as a chained dog.'

Behind Rhian, metal rasped against leather, and she knew a knife had been drawn. One of the men beside Gawain lifted his axe.

Harrik turned his back.

'Your son will not die on his feet Harrik,' said Gawain steadily. 'He will hang from the great oak, a coward's death, for his father the coward and traitor.'

Rhian closed her eyes, waiting for the heat of steel on her skin and found she could only pray the blade was sharp so death would be swift and the pain brief.

Harrik spoke one word. Overhead, a man answered, and Harrik barked an order. The edge of the knife did not touch her throat. Rhian dared to open her eyes.

Harrik stalked over to Gawain. 'Be very glad that none of my men speak your barbarian tongue or I would have to kill you myself.' His face filled with hate, but did his gaze glitter too brightly? Could those be tears shimmering in the eyes of this monster?

'Harrik, what has been done to you?' whispered Gawain.

But Harrik did not answer. Instead, he said, 'You know well the mind and habits of your uncle. This may buy you a few more hours.' His teeth clacked and chattered together, grotesquely chewing at tongue and cheek so that Rhian winced to see it. It was as if his body fought against his mind and would not let him speak.

Is he mad?

The ravens croaked from the hills above.

Or bewitched?

'I think you can tell me much that is useful before you die, and I think the woman will stand surety to make sure your tongue is loose and willing. There is so much worse we can do than slit her throat.'

Rhian felt the blood run from her heart and for a moment thought she might faint. Grim determination kept her upright. Death's delay had allowed her to collect herself somewhat. If she must be afraid, she at least would not give way to it before her enemies.

Harrik spoke again to his men, calling out his orders. One of the Saxons, the one with a cat's muzzle on his helm, said something in reply, a lazy, mocking question. Harrik's answer was low and dangerous. The man held his ground, stating his case plainly, gesturing first at the captives and then up the hills. One or two of the others muttered what Rhian took to be agreement, but most stood silent, looking to Harrik.

Beside her, Gawain was straining every muscle. The cords of his neck stood out plainly. His face was flushed with fury and fear, but his guards gripped him tightly. He shifted his shoulders, and one of them rapped out some harsh words, and laid the edge of his sword against Gawain's belly.

Rhian let her eyes flicker between the Saxons, looking to the way they stood and how they held themselves and their weapons, looking for some chance, any chance, to break away. But her captor did not loosen his grip at all, and there were still far, far too many of them for any plan that fluttered through Rhian's fevered mind.

Harrik was speaking again, his anger clearly mounting. Gawain was watching him. Did Gawain speak their tongue? What were they saying? Was Harrik changing his mind about delaying their execution? Panic threatened again, and again

Rhian fought it down. Panic would not save either of them.

A shout rose from the valley floor. The four men sent in pursuit of the horses had succeeded. One of them held the reins of a relatively docile Thetis and tried to keep her clear of Gringolet, for Gringolet was anything but docile. Again, and again, he reared and his hooves lashed out. Three Saxons held tight to his bridle, all but dragging the stallion between them. He tossed his head repeatedly, trying to shake them off, and more than once succeeded with one or another, causing them to have to dance about until they could catch a piece of harness and hang on again.

The men surrounding Rhian and Gawain laughed and bellowed what sounded like jests or bets until Harrik growled at them. Four left their posts as guards and headed down the hill to help their fellows.

But Gringolet had seen Gawain. The great horse renewed his struggles. The Saxons ringed him, trying to drive him and yet stay out of range of his flailing hooves. The ones who fought to hold his bridle cursed and shouted to their fellows, but none of the others were anxious to try to come close. The stallion's battle and all the scents of blood and death were finally too much for Thetis and she too lashed out, swinging her head this way and that. Kicking backward, she landed a hard blow on one of the Saxon's legs. The man toppled to the ground, grabbing his thigh and adding his own cries to the cacophony.

Harrik barked out an order to the remaining men. The one holding Rhian jerked her to her feet. He shifted his grip. One of the others brought out a strip of leather to bind her hands, to lead her away as if she were another captured mare. But there were only four of them now. Another Saxon near the horses cried out. Gringolet reared. His hoof caught the man on his helm, and the man dropped like a stone.

The ravens rose in a great, black cloud, croaking and shrieking their disapproval.

As if that were her sign, Rhian screamed. She poured all of her fear and desperation into the wordless sound. Startled, her captor's grip faltered. Rhian dived towards Gawain. She grasped the nearest sandalled foot and rolled, throwing all her weight into the move and bringing the Saxon down.

Gawain leapt, the suddenness of the movement breaking him free of his startled captor. He measured his length on the ground beside the fallen Saxon, and scrambled at once to his feet again, a long knife in his hand.

Rhian wasted no time. She rolled onto her knees, scooped up a rock in her hand and brought it down hard against the face of the fallen Saxon. The blow jarred her arm up to the shoulder and she heard bone and teeth break. She scuttled backward, yanking the hems of her dress out of the way with her free hand so she could get to her feet. Another Saxon bore down on her, and Rhian threw the stone without time to aim. The man ducked, giving Rhian time to catch up another stone and this time take a sighting before she hurled her missile. The stone caught the man in the eye, causing him to cry out and topple to his knees.

The world was a blur of screams and thunder. Gringolet had broken free and charged towards his master, bowling men to left and right. The Saxons rallied, knives and axes out, ready to kill the horses. Rhian fell to her knees again, scrabbling among the stones that had made their ambush, hurling them as quickly as she could grab hold of them, anything to keep the Saxons dodging and disorientated while Gawain mounted Gringolet.

He had neither spear nor sword, but it did not matter. Gringolet himself was a weapon, well honed and terrible. He had no fear of armed men and charged where his rider directed, breaking what little order the Saxons had managed to bring to their numbers, scattering them, knocking them flat to hit their heads against the unforgiving stones or to tumble comically down the slope.

Rhian forced herself to concentrate on reaching the pile of looted gear. As quickly as she could, she tossed Gawain's swordbelt over her shoulder, shoved the shield onto her arm and snatched up his spear. Clumsily, she ran for Thetis who circled and danced, looking for a clear direction to flee. One Saxon had presence of mind enough to dart between Rhian and the maddened mare, his axe out and ready. Rhian levelled the spear and charged, sending him reeling backward. Thetis reared again, and her hooves caught the man's shoulders, felling him. Rhian managed to catch Thetis's reins with her free hand. The sight and scent of her mistress enabled the mare to hold her place long enough for Rhian to switch the spear to her shield hand and half-climb onto her saddle. Another Saxon staggered to his feet and stumbled towards them. Rhian swung the shield outward. Fortunately, the man had little fight left and fell back quickly, allowing her to clamber up onto Thetis's back before the mare's remaining nerve gave way.

Gawain, weaponless on Gringolet, faced Harrik, who had his sword in his hand. Most of his men lay on the ground, dead, stunned or bleeding. The three who remained standing were motionless, waiting for their leader to make his move. Rhian thought to draw her bow, to finish off this traitor with an arrow in his throat, but to do so she'd have to drop Gawain's arms at the feet of their enemies.

Into the stillness, a raven called, and that call ushered the sound of thunder.

Not thunder. Hooves.

Harrik smiled, a pained and wild smile.

Gawain's gaze met Rhian's and without a word between them, they both wheeled their horses around towards the valley. Rhian drove her knees into Thetis's ribs and gave the mare her head, allowing her to find her own way down as fast as she was able. She had only one hand anyway. Gawain's weaponry was an unwieldy burden, and trying to keep hold of it was costing her her balance. If Thetis balked, she'd be thrown again. The thunder grew louder behind her. She risked a look back. A black and bronze wave poured over the hills, a troop of Saxons on squat and shaggy mountain-raised horses raced past their defeated fellows without pausing, all their intent to run down Rhian and Gawain.

Gawain let out a sharp curse and with some difficulty turned Gringolet across the hills. Rhian fought with Thetis to make her follow, and almost lost. She saw what the knight was doing. The footing was treacherous, but down on the level ground there was no shelter. The Saxons on their fresh mounts could simply run them down. Up here, if they could get out of sight, perhaps they could hide, perhaps they could get far enough ahead that they could vanish behind a ridge and find their way down unseen. Thetis could almost keep pace, but she would not be able to for long. Foam already flew from her mouth and her sides heaved hard from the force of her breath. Rhian leaned down close to her neck, doing nothing more than trying to stay on the mare's back and keep her eyes on Gawain.

Gringolet neared a rise and put on a fresh burst of speed. Wincing in apology, Rhian drove her knees again into Thetis's side. The mare squealed, outraged, but obeyed and they topped the hill and started down again, ahead of their pursuers and out of sight.

Racing dangerously downhill, Rhian clung to Thetis with all her strength, and prayed. Gawain shouted.

To the left was a tumble of great boulders. Gawain must have known this place. He turned Gringolet sharply so horse and rider vanished behind the giant stones. Rhian urged

Thetis to follow. By the time Thetis agreed, Gawain had dismounted. Rhian leaned down so he could take arms and shield from her. Gringolet trembled and sweated beside his master. Rhian threw herself from her saddle, and, without waiting to be told, grabbed her bow and quiver from her saddlebag. The horses could run no further. There was no other shelter.

'Make the shots count, Rhian,' said Gawain harshly as he pushed his shield up on his arm and freed his sword from the sheath.

Rhian fit arrow to string and drew. The hoofbeats drummed louder. She tried to think, to shoot horse or rider, which would be best? Could she bring herself to shoot the horses? Her mind was numb. There were too many of them coming. She did not have enough arrows for them all.

Overhead, she heard a deep chuckle. A raven, black as night and big as a hawk sat atop the tallest of the boulders. Memory of her vision seized her with a fear and compulsion so strong she did not pause to question or even breathe. She swung up the tip of her arrow and loosed. The arrow split the carrion bird's breast. It fell from the stone to the ground like a rotted fruit.

Gawain stared, stunned and disconcerted. Rhian ducked her head down again.

The riders thundered down the hillside, drowning out even Rhian's heartbeats as she nocked another arrow to the string.

Then the Saxons were atop them and Gawain went as taut as her bowstring. But Rhian did not loose, and Gawain did not leap forward, and the Saxons rode past in a blur of browns and golds, the breeze from their passing ruffling Rhian's hair. Belatedly and absurdly, she realized she had lost her veil.

And the riders were gone, and the world was quiet again. One by one, the honest birds began to sing.

Gawain listened. Rhian could feel the tension thrumming from him as he strained his ears. But there was nothing. He stood, his amber eyes looking left, then right. Still there was nothing.

'They will soon realize they've passed us by.'

He did not need to tell her to hurry. But habit turned Rhian aside for a moment to retrieve her arrow from the other side of the boulders, and to see, if for a heartbeat, her quarry. In the stone's shadow, her arrow, whole and complete, lay on the ground. Blood stained the tip. The bird's black corpse, though, was nowhere to be seen.

'Leave it, Rhian,' said Gawain. 'It has touched some evil thing. Let the clean earth have it.' He paused. 'How did you know?' he asked softly.

'I don't fully understand. I . . .' Rhian swallowed. 'I have seen strange things of late. Visions. I am no witch, I swear before God and Mary, I am not.'

'I believe you, Rhian,' his voice was soft and serious. 'Come.'

Her legs ached as she again swung herself into Thetis's saddle. Her hands shook as she took up the reins again and wisps of hair floated down before her eyes, tickling tears from her eyes and tremors from her skin. She wanted nothing more than to lie down on the grassy slope and sleep until her body forgot all that she had done and seen these past two days. But because she also wished to live to see the next morning, she shook the reins in her weakened hands and urged Thetis forward.

SEVEN

Gawain was ready to cry aloud in thanks when Pen Marhas at last came into view. Dusk was settling in. He had pushed the pace as much as the animals could stand, keeping them to the stony hillsides where they would leave fewer signs if the Saxons were tracking them, and where there was at least some shelter should they be found. Fire burned in his ribs when he breathed, and every step Gringolet took jarred his spine. The thought of another skirmish, this time with mounted men, worried him deeply. Rhian looked ready to fall from her saddle, and her mare was not going to last much longer. Gringolet himself was obedient but spiritless.

When pursuit did not come, Gawain tried to feel reassured, but he could not. A small raiding party, a group of bitter and adventurous men who burned a crofting and happened on a prize hostage, that was one thing and a fairly small thing at that. But a dozen mounted men? These were not raiders. This was a war party. This was what he had been hurrying back to Camelot ahead of, and now it seemed he had not been fast enough. Even if the pursuit was not immediately at their heels, they would not stay ahead of the Saxons for long. It might be they were watched even now, while Harrik determined their destination and decided if it was worth the men to pursue them. Or it might be he already knew where they must be going, and was advancing his own preparations.

Harrik, what has happened to you?

Gawain wished desperately he could go straight to Camelot with his warnings, and bring back a host of men at once. But as painful as it was to admit, he could not make the ride, not at speed, not with the chance of a cracked rib. Not even if he left Rhian behind him, an idea which twisted his tired heart.

Pen Marhas was a fortress town that had been rebuilt countless times across the years. Ancient, grass-covered earthworks were backed by new wooden palisades. The gates had not yet closed for the night and the workers ambling in from the freshly ploughed fields turned to stare as Gawain and Rhian rode past. Gawain made no concession to such curiosity, but took them straight to the gates.

Unkempt, gaunt, grim, with bad news in his purse and worse at his heels, this was not how he had imagined returning to this place.

'Halt, Stranger!' shouted the sentry from the palisades. 'Who are you? What is your errand?'

'I am Gawain, and my errand is from the High King Arthur!' Gringolet's head hung low and he was blowing and snorting from the pace to which he had been put. Rhian patted her shivering mare's neck constantly. She herself looked grey. Had she taken some hurt of which she had not spoken? 'I must speak with Thedu Bannain.

'At once, my lord! You there!' The sentry turned and the sense of the rest of his orders was lost to Gawain, but another man in a short leather jerkin and scuffed, metal-bound cap clambered down the nearest ladder. He saluted Gawain in the old Roman style that Arthur had adopted for use by his champions.

'Follow me, my lord.' Under the helmet, he was young, with his first growth of beard still jutting proudly from his long chin. He turned and ran smartly up the rude lane crying, 'Make way! Make way for the messenger of the High King!'

Pen Marhas was not a large place and it had never been subjected to the Romans' notions of order and uniformity, which meant it was crowded and chaotic. Wooden shacks and sheds stood alongside the more sturdy cottages and warehouses. People scrambled to get themselves, their goods and their herds of pigs, sheep and geese out of the way of Gringolet's hooves. Rhian followed, keeping Thetis admirably close.

Unbidden and unwelcome, the vision of the place set aflame by the Saxon raiders came to him. To make matters worse, his mind's eye showed him Rhian sprawled dead on the ground in the middle of those flames, an axe buried in her breast.

He kept his face forward so she would not see the anger that hardened his features. She did not need to be frightened with what had not yet happened.

Not that she would not bear that fear well. By God, she was ready to face anything! She kept her wits about her through death and black magics. If he were honest, he had to admit she had saved him twice now. Had she been a man, he would have sworn her to him as a brother and felt safe to sleep in the open with such a one at his side. As it was. . .

Sir, discipline your thoughts. Or perhaps you have forgotten this is not some hawking party?

Bannain's hall had been built on the gentle rise that passed for high ground in this valley. Its yards were surrounded by a second set of stout palisades. Their gates had been thrown open in greeting. The hall's wooden walls rose from stone foundations and were topped by a peaked roof. The front of it was long and narrow to accommodate the great hall, and it widened behind to make room for the living quarters, stores and workrooms.

As they rode up to the steps of the hall, they were met by a stout man surrounded by a cluster of boys to catch the horses' reins and help the riders dismount. He was a stranger to Gawain, but Gawain could tell by the way the man's knowing eyes widened at the sight of Gringolet that here was someone who understood horses and that the charger would be well housed while they remained here.

Bannain's steward, Clement, stood on the top step, dressed in a tunic of fine blue wool and a cloak trimmed in good furs set off by a silver belt and silver chain. The steward looked slightly dismayed as he saw Rhian dismount, for he had brought no woman to greet her, but that could not be helped. Clement recovered his countenance quickly and bowed.

'My master Bannain, son of Ban, welcomes the envoy of his liege lord, the High King Arthur, and bids you come before him without delay that he might hear your message.' His gaze slid sideways to Rhian, who only lifted her chin.

Gawain said nothing of this, but extended his arm that she might take it. If no other courtesy could be observed at this moment, he could at least see her properly escorted into the hall. She took his arm with slightly stiff dignity, as if trying to remember a movement from an unfamiliar dance. This only made Clement look ill at ease, but he kept his silence, and led them indoors.

The board was just being laid for evening meal. The high table had already been spread with a white cloth and the boys were setting the other boards and trestles in their places in front of the two long hearths. The air filled with the fragrant scents of wood smoke and of the roasting meats that the women were busily cutting from the spits. It was not a rich hall, but not poor either. There were three tapestries to decorate the carved walls, and half-a-dozen shields, and over the high seat, a battered ceremonial Saxon war-axe that Ban had captured at Mount Baddon.

Bannain stood as they entered his hall. He was a square man, his skin hardened to leather from all the time he spent out among the elements, patrolling his lands or aiding his neighbours in fending off their own thugs and raiders. He had the reputation of having little use for ceremony, but he knew courtesy, and in his own hall he dressed well in autumn-brown wool and creamy linen. He was only slightly more grey and lined than Gawain's memory of him. Cailin, his dark, slender wife, stood at his side, a gentle counter-point to the grim-faced warriors who filled out the table. Gawain remembered her well too from other times as a noble hostess and a fine lady. Her black hair was beautifully braided and coiled beneath a veil of finest linen. A collar of silver and turquoise adorned her throat. Gawain felt Rhian tense at his side, maiden's pride of appearance taking hold against her will. He wished he might make some gesture of re-assurance. She was fair as she was, and so noble Queen Guinevere would stand in awe when she heard all that Rhian had done.

'My Lord Gawain,' Bannain's voice boomed, echoing against the walls. 'Your return is most welcome in this hall, and this good lady is twice welcome for your sake.'

'My thanks, Thedu,' Gawain used the old title. Bannain himself was not opposed to Arthur's adoption of Latin titles and Roman stylings for his court and companions, but the rough and hard-eyed men at his side still saw that old empire as conquerors and thieves. 'This is the Lady Rhian, daughter of Rygehil, barown of the Morelands, who travels with me to Camelot so that she may act as messenger to the queen.'

'Then this night she may act as honoured guest in our hall.' Lady Cailin rounded the table and extended her hands to Rhian. 'Come, lady, let me take you to where you might be refreshed.'

Rhian released Gawain's arm, curtseying first to her hostess and then to him, as propriety dictated. Cailin took up Rhian's hand and escorted her out the back of the hall towards the private quarters, with an appraising glance back at Gawain.

He set that aside. There would be time for banter with the ladies after the coming battle, God willing.

'Bring the knight a chair,' Bannain ordered one of the boys. 'Sit with us, Sir, and tell us your news.'

Gawain stayed as he was. 'I will not sit until you send your men out to make sure your people are in from the fields and your gates are all shut fast.'

Bannain stared at him in blank surprise for a moment. Then, he nodded to the man who sat at his right hand and had a brown beard like a bird's nest. The man was on his feet in an instant, striding from the hall and bellowing for the steward.

Satisfied, Gawain took the chair the boy had drawn up to the table. He accepted the cup of watered wine set before him and drank gladly.

Bannain watched him drink, curiosity warring with courtesy in his face. But he did let Gawain set the cup down before he said, 'Now, Sir, tell me what matter breeds this urgency?'

'Thedu, we have come here bare hours ahead of a war band of Saxons. They are raiding the countryside and I believe they mean to attack Pen Marhas.'

Bannain's fist curled up tightly on the cloth. He struck the table once, hard, so that it rattled on its trestles and all the serving boys started.

'Damn them!' growled another of Bannain's men. Alun. Gawain remembered him by his nose which was so flattened by the blows it had taken that his breath came in wheezes and whistles. 'The High King showed them too much mercy. He should follow them to their dirty holes and slaughter them down to the least babe!'

Gawain held himself very still. 'The High King gave his word when the Saxons sued for peace that their homes would be left unmolested. Do you say now that he should have broken that word?'

At that, the hall went very quiet, as Gawain knew it would. He understood their kind very well. Among men such as these, honour was paramount. At court, there could be talk of the law, of treaty and compromise backed by goods and silver. But court was more than three score miles away. Such ideas would not touch these men's blood, and even under a steady hand such as Bannain's, their blood was what ruled them.

'No one here says the High King should break his word.' Bannain looked hard at his man. 'Nor would he if he wished to remain in my hall. Is that not right, Alun?'

Alun met his lord's eyes belligerently, but only until he saw how grim Bannain's face had become.

'I meant no such thing, Sir,' said Alun. He looked also at Gawain, who had not permitted himself to move a muscle. 'The High King is a man of the greatest honour and I would never say otherwise.'

Gawain nodded and took another sip of wine to show that the remark was forgiven.

'What is your counsel, my Lord Gawain?' asked Bannain. 'What are their numbers and from what direction will they come?'

'They will most likely come from the south, as we did, but it is also possible they will come from the east, if they know we have beaten them here. I saw a dozen on foot, and that many again mounted. I suspect they have at least three times that number waiting in the hills.' Less the men left dead on the ground, but now was not the time to speak of that.

'My counsel is this, keep your folk inside the walls and set your men to the defences. Send three riders out at once for Camelot. Let them take my ring as token. They can tell Arthur all that has occurred so that he may send reinforcements.'

Bannain nodded his head. 'What you say is sound. Do you have any word to add, my brothers?' He looked to his men. Alun shifted his weight, but held his peace.

'Should we not wait for day?' asked a man who had lived long enough that his beard and hair had gone iron grey. 'Three score cannot move as quickly as two alone. It may be we have time to send out scouts of our own and take note of all their numbers and arms.'

Gawain nodded. 'This is wise, father, but I ask you, if they are expecting a town open and helpless and come to a town closed and defended, might they not pass by altogether? It behooves us to close the doors and quickly, for the enemy may have scouts of his own, and our preparations are something they should see.'

The greybeard pursed his lips thoughtfully and said no more.

There was more talk then, of men and boys, of arms in the stores, of harness for men and horses, or at least ponies, of the town's defences and their repair. The news was not all that Gawain could have wished, but it was not as bad as he had feared. They would be able to mount a good defence and it was likely they could at least hold the Saxons off until they either gave up or the fresh men arrived from Camelot.

When matters of defence were settled, Gawain suffered himself to be led away to the round-walled bath chamber where he could be washed and dressed in fresh clothing, and where Bannain's healer could have a look at his ribs, which, to Gawain's relief, the man pronounced bruised but not broken. He applied tight bandages well soaked in some concoction of herbs and weeds that looked distinctly unwholesome and smelled worse. But the heat it generated was soothing and Gawain found he was able to breathe and walk with less pain than before.

Refreshed and ravenously hungry, Gawain was taken back to the hall. Bannain had left the seat at his right hand open and Gawain bowed to the thedu and took his place. They remained standing, however, for right behind Gawain came Cailin, and the hall's ladies.

Rhian walked beside her hostess. She too had been well attended. All trace of battle and hard travel had been washed from her face and hands. Her beautiful fall of hair had been rebraided with ivory-coloured ribbons to match the veil that had been laid over it. The fawn-coloured dress suited her well. A gold necklace hung about her throat and an emerald ring sparkled on her hand. She was every inch the lady, beautiful enough to inspire a poet's verses.

Then Gawain saw who walked behind her and his heart broke in two.

Lady Pacis had changed not one whit in the two years since he had last seen her. Her chestnut hair still shone with lights of red and gold. Her deep brown eyes were still shy and yet rich with woman's knowing. His fingertips at once remembered the silken touch of the skin at the hollow of her throat, now modestly hidden behind a string of garnets and freshwater pearls. Her form and carriage were still as refined and graceful as a swan's.

Had anyone told her he was here? She lifted her modestly

downcast eyes, and her gaze went through him like lightning. He saw in that instant that she did know he was in this
hall, and the revelation made her sorry. But was that sorrow
caused by his return, or by the fact she had sent him away?

The moment passed. Pacis looked down again at her hands.
Gawain was left to collect himself as best he could and bow
to Lady Cailin while her retinue took their places at the table.
Rhian was given pride of place beside Lady Cailin, while Pacis
was seated somewhere beyond Rhian, obscured by a number
of anonymous profiles, so that it was difficult to see even
which hands were hers.

It did not matter. He knew that she was there. He ate, but
did not taste the meat or bread. He answered his host's polite
questions, but had no idea of what he said. Memories
crowded his mind, threatening to overwhelm him.

Soon after Gawain had come to Camelot from Goddodin,
Arthur conceived the notion of sending him to the halls of
various liegemen – not for fostering, he was years too old
for that – but to learn the ways of the men and their people,
and to learn the lie and the languages of the land he would
one day rule. Without trust in their king, and their king's
honour, their loyalty would not hold, Arthur said. He was
right in this, as he was in so many things.

It had been high summer then, and Pacis had come to the
hall, newly married to a man named Oran, who was greasy
and fat and seemed content to put her in the weaving rooms
and never think on her again, as if she were a worn-out
garment to be stored in a chest. Gawain spoke with her at
dinners, at the hunts, and in the evenings when there was
music and poetry. He had soon found himself wondering
how any man could be insensible to her laugh, her smile,
the music of her voice.

Oh, he had fallen fool in love with her, older and married
as she was. He had gone out of his way to stand at her side,

to do her what small favours he could, to bring a little sunlight into the life that made her sigh so wistfully.

When she permitted him to kiss her, he thought he had understood what awaited man in Paradise.

Then what happened? he asked himself grimly, as he took another swallow of his ale, startled to realize he had drained the mug. *Remember that as well.*

From that first kiss, their meetings quickly became amours. Now she sighed in his arms from pleasure and his love soared to heights he was certain no poet had ever visited. When the day came for him to leave, he begged her to come with him.

'Your husband is no fit man. The High King can free you. We can be together as man and wife.'

She had looked into his eyes for an endless moment, and he had believed he read the whole future spreading before him, as paradisiacal as that first kiss had been.

Then, she laughed. Not a pleased or startled gasp, but a long and hearty sound, as at an excellent jest.

'Away with you,' she said, patting his arm as if he were no more than a boy on some minor errand.

'Pacis, I am in earnest.' He reached across the pallet that was their bed, taking her slim hand in both of his.

She withdrew it instantly. 'As am I. The house will be stirring soon.'

'Pacis, do not send me away. All will be well, I promise. My uncle . . .'

'You mistake me, Gawain. I do not mean to stand before your uncle except properly, at my husband Oran's side.'

Cold filled him to the rim. His hands began to tremble. So did his voice. 'You said you loved me.'

'Which will teach you not to believe what a woman says in her bed.' Her gaze had softened for a moment, and her fingers traced his cheek. He could still feel them. 'A devoted husband would soon break both himself and me, Gawain. Go, and understand that I am well content with what I have.'

Someone had refilled his mug. His host's face had gone a little grave, and Gawain wondered how long it had been since he had spoken, and what had been said in the meantime.

'Forgive me, Thedu Bannain,' he said, setting the mug down. 'I am a sorry guest. I must cry your patience and plead the fatigue of two days' hard ride.'

'It is I who must ask your forgiveness, Lord Gawain,' replied Bannain at once. 'A place has been prepared for your rest.' Clement was on his feet without Bannain having to say any more, along with the boy – what was his name? Calder – who had been assigned to wait on him. Gawain rose and bowed to the company. He caught Rhian's worried glance and wished he could reassure her. Pacis was looking down at the trencher before her, and he found he was glad. He did not know if he could keep his countenance if he had to look into her eyes at this moment.

Clement led him to the sleeping chamber for Bannain's captains. Chests and beds had been rearranged – no doubt hastily – to make room for the stout frame piled with feather beds and blankets of wool and fur. Gawain had slept in similar rooms most of his life and there was comfort in its familiar feel and its odours of leather and humanity.

The boy, Calder, waited on him with the nervous overcaution of a child anxious to do a good job. Gawain wished he had a coin to give him. He climbed into the bed and fatigue fell against him like a weight. His eyes closed at once, but his mind found a moment to wonder where Rhian was, and if she was comfortable in this house that was utterly strange to her.

Then, he wondered where Pacis was, and if she was still happy in her life.

Sleep dragged at him and he surrendered willingly, for oblivion was far preferable to the thoughts that filled him now.

Rhian watched Gawain depart, and bit her lip. Should she try to follow? She had never in her life been alone among total strangers before. She did not know what to do. The parts of her story she had chosen to tell had already been eagerly taken apart and examined by the hall's ladies. Her appetite was gone, leaving only the aches and formless fears of her time in the wilderness.

Thedu Bannain's wife, Lady Cailin came to her rescue. 'Lady Rhian, you must also be exhausted. Let me take you to rest.'

'Thank you, lady,' said Rhian, with honest relief. 'I would be glad of that.'

Cailin stood, taking Rhian's arm to raise her to her feet at the same time. 'Husband, you will excuse us.'

'Of course.' Bannain stood and politely bowed. Rhian curtsied in reply. Formalities seen to, she was able to follow Lady Cailin from the hall.

Rhian's weariness shamed her. Every other woman in the hall seemed swept up in the flurry of activity. Every available vessel was to be filled with water, in case of fire, or siege, or both. Stores had to be assessed, and rearranged, to make room for the people who would have to be housed within the hall in the event of attack. The kitchen fires would be lit all night, since as much as possible had to be baked, salted, or preserved in case of siege. The animals were already being herded within the walls. She could hear the squeals and bleatings.

Bedding and blankets must be prepared, and medicines and dressings for the sick and the wounded. The least of servants had to be given their tasks, not only because there were a thousand details to be attended to, but to keep them calm and reassure them that their lords would meet any assault that was to come.

'The Saxons will starve before we do,' said Lady Cailin grimly. 'My mother told me of their ways. They will not take my home.'

Coldly, she ordered the largest of the kettles to be hefted up to the palisades before the light failed. As soon as the dawn came, they would be filled with pitch and fires would be lit beneath them. She had a lash for a tongue, this gracious hostess, and her people moved as much in fear of it as they did in fear of the Saxons' arrival. Rhian could not help but think what her mother would do at such a time. She would have been in the thick of things, helping wherever a hand was wanting, Rhian was sure. Cailin, though, arranged and watched, and scolded.

An extra bed had been erected in the women's quarters, but except for Rhian and the girl Cailin directed to wait upon her, the room was empty. Cailin told her to sleep as long as she wished, and at once hurried away to supervise one of the thousand tasks she had set in motion.

At a loss, Rhian turned to look down at the girl who stood beside her. She had dirty-blonde hair and deep blue eyes. With a shock, Rhian realized that at least one of her parents must have been Saxon. The girl curtsied, spreading her skirts wide, and waited for Rhian to say something.

'Stand up,' was all she could think. 'What is your name?'

'Holda, my lady,' she said, keeping her gaze rigidly on the floor.

Take hold of yourself, Rhian, she ordered herself. *The child cannot help her parentage, or do you think this little one is going to stab you in your bed?*

To keep herself from mulling that over, she said, 'Will you help me unlace, Holda? I'm ready to fall asleep where I stand.'

But as Holda moved to obey, and Rhian schooled herself to the stillness required for the efficient removal of sleeves and bodice, a voice sounded softly from the doorway.

'Lady Rhian?'

Holda scuttled to the room's corner, seeking to vanish like a good servant. A willowy woman glided into the room.

'I came to see if you had need of anything,' said the lady.

'No, thank you . . .' Rhian groped for the woman's name. She had been introduced to so many people so quickly. Barely in time, she remembered. 'Lady Pacis.'

'I fear it is only a hasty welcome you have had from my aunt.'

To Rhian's dismay, she realized this woman meant to stay and make companionable conversation, and Rhian had no choice but to go along. If she were in any way impolite, it would reflect badly on Gawain as well as on herself. Her body ached. Her head felt like it was stuffed with uncarded wool.

'Lady Cailin is your aunt?' she said, hoping she did not sound like a half-wit.

Pacis nodded, sitting in one of the neatly made chairs that furnished the room between the beds and the chests. 'And you are kin to my Lord Gawain?'

Her gesture compelled Rhian also to sit, and nearby so that they might both comfortably continue their talk. Rhian's knees burned as she bent them. She wished desperately for her mother's unguent of mint and goose grease, and at the same time tried to remember what she had been asked.

Kin. 'No, lady. He . . .' How to explain at all, let alone quickly? Awake and rested she could not have performed such a feat. She had repeated this story several times already. Where had this woman been all the day?

'Your rescuer, perhaps?' the lady prodded.

Was there mockery in Pacis's words, or was it just that her exhaustion made Rhian foolish?

'He did rescue me, yes.' She tried to stiffen her spine, to bring some dignity to her words and her bearing, but she was a hollow reed, and could only bend.

Pacis was too set on her own purpose to see Rhian's weariness. 'The High King has no greater champion than Gawain,' she said, twisting her long, fine hands together. 'It is good to have him here again at such a time. It has been too long since I have seen him.'

What was happening here? Rhian felt a current under Pacis's words, but she could not make out where it came from. 'You know Lord Gawain?'

'Very well. He spent a summer in this hall not so long ago, when I was newly married. I have missed him.'

That pricked Rhian like a dart, and her mind began to clear as to the meaning of Lady Pacis's conversation. 'I can understand how one would.'

Pacis leaned forward. 'You know by now, I am sure, how fortunate you are in your protector.'

Oh, God and Mary, this woman cherished some passion for Gawain, and she was looking to Rhian to help her polish this heart's treasure. No. Hospitality and politeness could go hang. 'I have thanked Christ and the Virgin many times over for him.' With those words, Rhian stood.

Pacis blinked at the suddenness of the gesture. But then, she also stood. 'I am thoughtless. You must be exhausted.' But under the observation was something tart, almost prim. 'Holda, attend your mistress. God watch over you this night, lady.'

'God watch over us all.'

Pacis slipped from the room and Rhian stared after her, even as Holda began undoing her laces and removing the sleeves of her dress.

What had she done? What did Pacis think she meant by her gesture of dismissal?

Oh, no.

What if she thought Rhian did not want to speak of Gawain because they were lovers?

Rhian wanted to laugh. When would they have had *time* in the madness of the past few days?

In the woods, her wool-cloaked mind answered her. *By the fire, after the kiss . . .*

She tried to push all that aside. What did it matter if this woman loved Gawain from afar? There must be a hundred or more who did. And what matter that there would be rumours about Rhian and Gawain? She had known when she arrived escorted only by a single man that the gossips would be instantly busy. Compared to what waited outside these walls, it was nothing. God, Mary and Gawain knew the truth, and that would have to be enough.

Not that the High King's nephew would ever consider anything more than a dalliance with one such as she, and she had already made it plain that such a thing was not welcome to her.

Despite all her attempts to reassure herself, Rhian felt suddenly, horribly sad. She wanted to be at home, among her own things, with her mother setting the hall in order before bed, not surrounded by strangers in danger from within as well as without.

Mother, I pray you, have patience, have courage. I will send you word as soon as I am able. I miss you.

Mother would know what to say about Lady Pacis, and it

would probably not be complimentary. Would she know what to say about Gawain, though?

As soon as Holda had undressed Rhian down to her borrowed shift, Rhian burrowed under the bedcovers and took refuge in warm and blessed sleep.

EIGHT

The dawn brought the Saxons. They poured down out of the eastern pass in a river of light and darkness. Rhian, standing on the walls with the women of Pen Marhas, watched them come.

Rhian had heard mass with Lady Cailin in the darkness before dawn, and climbed up to the palisades as the day broke. She was dressed now in coarse wool that was spattered with the pitch she had helped pour into the kettles. Her emerald ring shone incongruously on her hand. It was a ludicrous gaud to be wearing at such a time, but she had come so close to losing it to the Saxons, she could not bear to leave it behind in the common sleeping room.

The stench of hot pitch mingled with that of offal and slop from the buckets waiting beside the kettles. With them were piles of stones and other refuse, anything that might be thrown down to wound, or at the least delay and confuse. Rhian had brought her bow, but she had only the one quiver-full of arrows. There were just four bows in the whole of Pen Marhas, counting hers, and the available arrows had to be shared out between them. The town did have a man who knew fletching, but he had used up all

151

his materials working through the night. Whatever arrows they had with them now were all they would have.

From here, it was easy to see Gawain. Gringolet's white hide shone like a beacon in the cold morning light. They had not spoken since he had left the table last night. She wondered if he had asked after her. She had not heard that he had.

A few other things on his mind perhaps, she suggested to herself as she watched him gesturing left and right to other riders. Thedu Bannain rode a chestnut gelding and clutched an axe in his gauntleted hand. Pen Marhas's lord had mustered ten other men on horseback to meet the Saxons.

The rest of the hall's able men waited behind the earthworks. At first light, they had been as busy as ants shoring up their defences. Now, with the pounding rush of the Saxons pouring over them, they crouched with their heads down, concealing their numbers, waiting for the Saxons to reach the valley floor. The horses' hooves shook the ground as they charged. The war cries shook the air. All at once, she heard Gawain's voice, clear as a hunter's horn above the Saxons' dreadful thunder, and saw him charge out from the break in the earthworks, with the wave of the men of Pen Marhas surging up behind him.

The two armies clashed together in an explosion of sound like a hundred blacksmiths beating madly on their anvils. Gringolet bobbed here and there like a cork in a whirlpool while Gawain laid about him with his sword. Rhian could not even see Bannain. She leaned forward as far as the palisades permitted, her hands gripping the wooden pickets until her palms began to hurt, trying to see if Gawain was hard pressed, trying to see if his enemies fell or rallied. There was no way to tell for there was no way to distinguish friend from foe. Around her the women hollered, cheering on their husbands and fathers, brothers and sons, and cursing the Saxons for their arrogance and blood thirst.

The day wore on. The noise ebbed and flowed with the tide of men. Half-a-dozen times the defenders retreated behind their earthen banks. Half-a-dozen times they rallied and charged again to break against the raiders, surge through them, mix with them, clash and crash, cry out and die, or live to rise with the battle's tide again. The cacophony beat against Rhian's ears until her head hurt as badly as her hands from holding bow and arrow ready. As badly as her eyes did from straining to follow Gawain's movements through the swarm of warriors.

Rhian did what she could from the walls with her bow, but could not tell what effect her arrows had, save for once when her shot, by luck more than skill, transfixed a brawny Saxon warrior in the throat. She imagined rather than heard his gurgling scream as he fell, and flinched away from the horror in his distant eyes, surprised to find that despite this her hands held steady as they reached for another arrow.

The sun crawled across the sky so slowly, Rhian felt certain it had stopped in its course. She was hot. She was thirsty. Pain pounded at hands, arms, eyes and head. The wind blew in from the battlefield, bearing all the smells of metal, blood and trampled earth. Her ears had gone numb from the noise and she wanted nothing more than to creep away somewhere quiet and hide.

This had gone on too long. It had to end soon. It had to.

But it did not. On the field, the warriors milled, separated and retreated, and came together again, raising once more the terrible riot of metal clashing against metal and the sound of voices raised in screams of pain or bloody triumph.

At long last, the sun did sink towards the horizon and dusk reached down from the hills. The men of Pen Marhas ran back behind their earthworks, and the Saxons loped and limped back up into the hills to wait for the morning, so they could descend again, so the battle could begin again.

Evening and quiet came together, broken only by the cries of the wounded. Those men who could still stand guarded the walls while the gates were opened just wide enough to allow the men to slip in and women to slip out to help retrieve the dead and hurt. Blood mixed with the salt sweat soaking Rhian's dress as she helped a youth with a deep gash in his arm up to the shelter of the inner walls and the stout hall. She had assisted her mother in nursing men who had been hurt by scythes during the harvest, and once with a man whose horse had rolled on him and crushed his pelvis. She had heard these screams before, and she had seen death.

But by the time she and her man entered the hall, there must have been a score of men already laid out with their women and children beside them, doing their best to bring ease with water and prayer. The physician and the skilled women moved among them, packing the wounds with wax and cobwebs, or grimly stitching the deeper wounds while the irons were heated to sear those hurts that could not be stitched. The ones who were still whole held the men down as they screamed around the biting stick. The stench of blood and waste was far worse in here than it had been on the field. Over the work and the prayer hung the knowledge that this was only the beginning. These sons and brothers and fathers were only the first to fall.

Rhian felt hatred blossom in her heart.

She worked with the others, fetching and carrying, hold-ing the hands of strong men while they screamed from the healer's attentions. The torches were long lit by the time the last man was tended and covered in a blanket to find what rest he could. There'd be fevers by morning and poisons of the blood. God would take some to him and leave others, and it was all in His hands now.

Suddenly, the heat and the stench, the weeping of the

wounded and the women, became too much. Rhian fled out into the night. She leaned against the wall doing nothing but breathing the fresh air. She could ignore the battle taint on the wind, for out here at least, it was cool, and quiet.

The clouds were thickening overhead. There would be rain before morning, but enough moonlight remained to allow her to separate shape and shadow. With wandering steps she circled the hall, stretching out the cramps in her legs and hand. Even though her eyes adjusted to the fading light of the moon, she kept them lowered. She did not want to see the sentries on the walls, nor yet the black bulk of the hills above them where the Saxons waited.

Ahead of her came the sound of someone sighing and splashing. Rhian halted in her tracks. She had come round to the stables, and ahead of her a group of men bent over one of the stone horse troughs. Their backs were bare and they scooped up the water in their hands, rinsing the day's battle off head and arms. One of them, straightened up and brushed his dark hair over his shoulders, causing the water to run in silver rivulets down his back, wetting the bandages that encircled his ribs, and Rhian realized it was Gawain.

She meant to speak, or to retreat, she was not certain which, but one of the men lifted his head and saw her. He paused in his crude libations, which immediately caused all the others to turn and look as well. Gawain faced her, and Rhian found she could not speak at all.

He was beautiful. Not perfect, for he was scarred. Two ragged lines ran down his chest, disappearing underneath the bandages, and he was bruised on both of his arms from the pounding he had taken yesterday and today. There was no blood on him, thank Christ. His sun-browned skin was whole and sound over the planes of his muscles, his wide shoulders, his trim waist.

You're staring, you fool.

She was, and she was not the only one who noticed. The other men, half-naked, bearded, bruised, covered in old scars and fresh cuts, also stared, at her.

'Well, here's a pretty little thing,' said one, wiping his beard.

'I think she's here for you, my lord,' laughed another, stepping back solicitously so Gawain could get by. Rhian felt herself blush deeply.

'See if she'll come back for me!' roared a third, which set all the men guffawing with sharp-edged mirth.

Gawain set his back to Rhian, his shoulders absolutely square and rigid. 'I did not hear that, Donyerth.' Although he spoke quietly, Rhian could clearly make out every word in the sudden silence. 'I trust the jest was not in reference to this lady.'

There was not enough light to see if the man blanched, but his apology was hasty, and sincere. 'No, no, my Lord Gawain, I was . . . it was someone else. Not the lady, of course not.'

Gawain donned his tunic and came to Rhian's side. 'Lady Rhian,' he bowed formally. 'May I escort you to the hall?'

'Thank you, Sir.' She took the arm he offered her. Though she knew the men would say nothing in Gawain's hearing, she still felt their gazes heavy on her shoulders as they walked away. They'd have plenty to say soon enough, and she could easily guess the sort of talk it would be.

The sounds of splashing resumed behind them, growing fainter as they walked the length of the hall. 'I'm sorry for that,' said Gawain.

Rhian found herself looking up at the sky. There was only the faintest sheen of moonlight left behind the clouds. What little illumination lit the yard came from the guards' torches on the walls. 'There's no avoiding it. I am a woman alone with a man who is no relation.'

Gawain halted, and faced her. 'They are men fresh from battle, glad to be alive and terrified that they will not be so when evening comes tomorrow.' He lowered his eyes, as if speaking reluctantly of something close to his heart, and perhaps he was. 'It produces in the soul a sort of drunkenness, a forgetfulness of courtesy. In normal times, Donyerth would have kept a civil tongue.'

'Do you know him?' she asked, remembering that Gawain had spent some time in this place before.

'A little. A good man, as most of them are, loyal to their lord and their land.' She thought he meant to add something more, about the men, about the hall, but he did not. Rhian rubbed her arms. It was growing cold. But that was not what Gawain saw. 'You are tired.'

She nodded towards the sheltering walls. 'I've never been to war before.'

Gawain shook his head. 'This is not war. This is a battle. When there are a dozen or so of these all clustered together, then it is war.'

'It sounds like the pox.'

That earned her a small laugh. 'But it will kill you far more quickly.' He ran both hands through his hair, and then slumped against the wall. In that posture, with his simple tunic and sandals, he looked more like a cowherd or farmer than the champion of Camelot.

'It is odd the things that come into a man's head in battle,' he said, looking towards the palisades with their flickering lights. 'I heard there was an archer on the walls, and I wondered if it was you, and when I did, I thought of a poem I had once heard, about the pagan god Apollo and a nymph – I've forgotten her name – but he was doomed to love her, it seems, and his love caused her to turn into a laurel tree.'

'*A filmy rind about her body grows,*' recited Rhian.

> *'Her hair to leaves, her arms extend to boughs:*
> *The nymph is all to laurel gone;*
> *The smoothness of her skin remains alone.*
> *Yet Phoebus loves her still.'*

'You are well versed.'

She spread her hands. 'Spinning and weaving are dull work. In our hall, someone would sing or recite to keep us all amused while we worked. Frequently, I was that one. I was said to have a pleasant voice and I did have a good memory for stories.' She hoped that did not sound too boastful, as she hoped she did not look too hag-like from her day's labours. She wondered why she should care, and then she could only hope the flickering torchlight would not show the blush creeping into her cheeks as she realized Gawain was studying her thoughtfully.

Fool, fool, fool. Go to bed. You are too tired. You are dreaming on your feet. You'll become as bad as Lady Pacis if you don't take hold of yourself.

'What happened to Phoebus after that?' Gawain asked.

Rhian dragged herself out of her thoughts with difficulty. It was growing cold. At first the cool air had been refreshing, but now it began to sink too deeply into her skin, chilling her blood. Despite that, she did not want to move indoors. She wanted to savour this moment. She was certain that when she lay down in the crowded room among the strangers her dreams would not be half so pleasant as standing beside Gawain and speaking of poetry. 'Phoebus declares the nymph, the laurel tree, will be his sigil from that time on. Then . . . he goes on being a god, I suppose. He does, I believe, fall in love many more times.'

'Ah,' said Gawain a little wistfully. 'But can there be true love again, once that first is taken from him?'

Which was not something Rhian had ever considered. 'I do not know.'

Gawain folded his arms against his chest. His hand brushed the hall's wooden wall, and it came to Rhian that perhaps he hoped to find something else there, a sleeve or a hand, rather than the hard and unresponsive timbers. 'A hard fate for a god,' he said.

So everyone says. 'I've always thought it was rather harder on the lady. She's the one who had to give up what she was and be rooted by the river forever, and even then he will not leave her be. He can go on to whatever loves await him, and she is trapped.'

That seemed to startle him. He bowed his head in polite acknowledgement of the declaration. 'You may be right.'

But Rhian could only hear her sour words ringing in her own ears, along with the reminder that despite his serf's garb, this was still Lord Gawain in front of her and that if the walls of Pen Marhas stood, she was still dependent on his good will. 'I'm sorry.'

'For what?'

'For speaking so plain. For ... ah, Mother Mary.' She turned her eyes up to the blank, black heavens. 'I do not know.'

'I do.' Gawain pushed himself away from the wall. 'You are sorry you are so tired that you cannot say what you wish and can only say what you mean.' He took her hand. 'Come. Let us return you to Lady Cailin. Your heart and hands will be needed come the dawn.'

They walked to the great doors in a silence that felt to Rhian surprisingly companionable. Weariness, the peace of night and a fresh wind that smelled for a change of nothing but the coming rain were hard to resist. Gawain's hand was warm, though roughened from his day's work.

What would he do if she turned to him now and took back that kiss he'd had from her? For an instant she thought, *what harm?* Her reputation here was already tarnished. If she was to face the penance, why should she not commit the sin?

Because she did not want to be the woman who would behave so, and she did not want Gawain to see her as that woman.

They'd reached the hall's steps. Gawain paused again, and Rhian felt rather than saw him looking at her. His face was lost in shadow, and she felt strangely glad. Her heart was beating slowly and heavily. She could feel his warmth, and he was standing strangely still, almost as if he was afraid to move. 'You were the archer on the walls today.'

'Yes.' She tried to speak plainly, simply, but again, she felt currents beneath the words, and between the two of them, with Gawain standing so close and so still.

'You did not have to go.' His words were little more than a whisper.

Rhian felt her mouth twist into a tight smile. 'If the Saxons break the gate, they will not stop to realize I am only a guest here.'

She had meant to make him laugh at that, or at least smile back there in his shadows, but he remained completely serious. 'You are wondrous brave, Rhian.'

No. Oh, no, she was not. She wanted so badly to run away. If death did not wait outside these walls in so many forms, she would have. 'I am only doing as I must.'

'No. It is more than that. I have seen necessity, and desperation both. Your actions spring from a courageous heart.'

Do something, say something. Turn away from this. If you don't you'll choke on your own breath. 'You need to sleep, Sir.'

'I know. But what appears as drunkenness in some men . . . in me, is restlessness.'

'You will make yourself ill, and then be no good to anyone.'

He stepped back and bowed with a courtly flourish. 'With

my lady's permission, I will walk a little yet, and then, I swear upon mine eyes, that I will seek my bed. I have no desire to topple onto a Saxon sword because I've fallen asleep in the saddle.'

Rhian found she could not even smile at that. She just returned his bow with a curtsey and a studiously grave face that she hoped would be taken for a dry jest in its own right. Turning, she gathered up her hems. To stay a moment longer would be to utter words she could not take back.

But Gawain's voice came again, freezing her in her place. 'Never be sorry for speaking openly with me, Rhian.'

'God be with you on the morrow, Gawain,' was all the answer she had. Then, because she could not bear to stay a moment longer, she hurried away.

It was dark in the women's quarters, forcing Rhian to pick her way to her bed with extreme caution. As it was, she prodded more than one sleeping body with her toes, only to be swatted at, or softly cursed. She did not even try to apologize.

At last, she reached that little island of wood and feather beds that was her own and crawled up onto it. The woollen dress was made for one who had no waiting women, so she was able to shuck it easily. The night's cold draughts moved across her skin.

She had thought to fall asleep as soon as she lay down, but instead, she felt more wakeful than ever. Perhaps something of Gawain's restlessness had infected her.

Or perhaps it was just something of Gawain.

Rhian stared out into the dark. How did people fall in love? How did one know it had happened? She did not feel faint or inclined to fall to her knees and beat her breast when she thought of him. Gawain had given her no token to swoon over. Nor had he sung her any poem, sent word by any messenger or lingered beneath her window, nor asked for her sleeve – not that she had one of her own to spare him – or done any of the things lovers in the epics did. Nor was she certain she could perform such miracles as, oh, wearing out three pairs of iron shoes walking the world in search of him, should he disappear.

But if this was not love in her, what was it?

She remembered sitting at her mother's feet while mother combed her hair, patiently picking out tangles with an ivory comb, tugging gently but almost never pulling.

'He will be a good man,' mother said. 'Of good family. Your father and I will see to it. And when he comes, you will open your heart to him, and learn what is good in him. From this, love will come.'

'Was that how it was with you and father?' she asked, leaning her head against mother's knee.

The comb paused, and mother laid her hand on Rhian's hair. 'No. When I saw your father . . . it was sudden. Like lightning.' She shifted, and the comb returned to its work, picking quickly, gently at a snarl. 'But lightning is no guarantee of happiness, my dear. Sometimes all it brings is a roll of darkening thunder. Life is a long journey and slow understanding is the surer road.'

It was a good thing to say, and meant lovingly, and now that Rhian knew so much more of the way things were between mother and father, she understood why it was said. Memory of home and her mother only brought fresh pangs to her bewildered heart.

Rhian rubbed her frigid hands together and tucked them under the blanket. They were growing chapped from her days out in the wind, too long holding Thetis's reins, too long working her bow. Lady Pacis had smooth hands that looked to work little more than threads for the finest tapestries. Come to that, she had not seen Lady Pacis on the walls today. She would have thought that was the best place for that fine lady to catch a glimpse of her hero.

Am I jealous now? Oh, God and Christ.

This was ludicrous. It was childish. A war band sat outside the walls waiting for their chance to swarm over the dykes, batter down the gates and take all they could carry, including Rhian and any other woman they could reach. They had a witch helping them, and she had a sorcerer waiting for her.

As if these weren't worries enough, she was wringing her hands because the thedu's wife's niece had an eye for the High King's nephew.

And what of Vernus? Rhian huddled in on herself. How long had it been since she had thought of him? She had let her heart get so out of order, she had forgotten that she meant to marry him, that he was going to speak to his father to speak to her father . . .

Would Vernus come to court to fetch her if she asked him to? The king could marry them. He might even be able to force father to pay her dower. It could all be done quickly, and that would be an end to her pining for Gawain.

Would it?

Rhian wrapped her arms around her knees and hugged them to her as if she were a small girl. She had to keep her mind on staying alive, on helping in the protection of her protectors and lying here mooning in the dark would only leave her more exhausted on the morrow.

But, Mother Mary, I'm so lonely.

She had never before been among so many strangers. When she was sent to Clywd for fostering, she was greeted by family and surrounded by cousins. Soon she had place and friendship. At her father's hall all the surrounding crofters and freemen knew her name, and if they did not know her face, they knew her at once by her dress and her manner, as she knew them. She knew who she was and how to act and what to do.

Here, she was no one. She had no kin, no ties to any, except Gawain, and those ties were suspect. She could see that plainly enough in the eyes of the other women. She was unknown and while not entirely unwelcome, not wholly welcome yet either, whatever their protestations. They did glance at her from the corner of their eyes, as if she were a servant who might be thieving. That was as far as it would go, at least while every hand was needed in Pen Marhas's defence, but it was there, and it would remain since not even battle could halt gossip.

It was nothing. It would pass. If she and Gawain lived, if tomorrow and the day after that came, they would leave, and they would go to court and she would tell her story to the queen, and then . . . and then . . .?

Rhian found she could not dream so far ahead. For a long time, she stared into the darkness while the women sighed and snored around her, but she saw nothing ahead save the night.

Outside, the rain began.

Gawain watched as Rhian vanished into the hall, swallowed more quickly by the night's darkness than by the solid doors.

He had lied. He would not seek his bed, not for hours yet. When the battle was done, he would sleep the night through again, but not until then. That was how God had made him, and he knew well enough by now there was nothing to be done about it. Normally, he would not have even come behind the inner walls, but Gringolet was favouring his fore-hoof and Gawain wanted to see to his charger personally and make doubly sure the stallion had proper shelter for the night. Now he was trapped in this small yard, with nothing to do but prowl its confines.

He climbed the palisades and visited the sentries, grizzled men and nervous boys, glad to see him and ready to be cheered by a small jest and a brave word from Arthur's man. They wanted to know about the messengers to Camelot, when he thought they would reach the court, and what response Arthur would send. Gawain answered as fairly as he could, although everyone within the sound of his voice knew that comforting guesses were all he had to give. The way through hill and wood was dangerous, even without the Saxons

Even without their witch, who had somehow caught up with Harrik, Gawain was now certain.

Perhaps Rhian killed her, he thought, looking out towards the hills, towards the faint stars of the Saxon campfires. *Perhaps that raven was the witch disguised, and with her death Harrik is free from whatever glamour has taken him, and he will come as soon as he can to help us.*

But in his heart, he knew that was a vain hope. Witches were not so easily defeated. They did not present themselves for a clean fight, no. They hid, they schemed, they sent their servants and their spells, and although a man might think he had at last rid himself and his family of the danger, yet they would come back.

The witch was still out there, as was Harrik, and in the distant darkness, Rhian's sorcerer.

Rhian.

He hoped sleep had found her. He hoped she knew some ease of heart in a bed that was, at least for this night, safe and warm. He wished . . . he wished so many things he thought heart and soul would overflow.

When the rain began, great, fat drops falling like pebbles into the dust of the yard, he sought shelter in the stable rather than the hall.

Gringolet had a stout stall, clean straw and a warm blanket

on his back. The place was full of the warm smells of leather and contented animals. The stallion's limp had proved to be nothing more than a small stone, easily remedied. He must have been exhausted, however, because neither Gawain's step nor his scent roused him from his sleep.

Overhead, men and boys snored in the hayloft. Above them, rain pattered on the thatched roof, making its straw rustle like a thousand small fingers searching through it, seeking . . . what?

Rhian would know. Some snatch of poem or song about rain and searching.

He had not been the least surprised when he found she had gone out on the walls. Furious, yes, but not surprised. If he'd had his way, she would have been behind the stoutest walls Pen Marhas had to offer, waiting for the end of the fighting and their rescue. Rhian, however, could no more hide and wait than he could sleep during battle. It was not in her nature.

But what is?

She was not like any woman he had known before, not even the queen. He would not have said it were possible for one woman to possess beauty, learning and nobility along with courage and quick-thinking that would do a Roman soldier proud. And the way she sometimes looked at him, as if there was much she would say, much she would do, if she dared, if modesty permitted.

If only she were of higher birth. If only her father were not a fool and a coward to have sold off his daughter's body and soul in a devil's bargain. Then they might be free, then. . .

Then, what? Gawain seemed to hear his brother's voice speaking from his mind. *She is what she is, and you are what you are. And for once this woman you're mooning over remembers that.*

Gawain sighed and bowed his head down until it rested

on the back of his arm. *God help me, it's happening again, isn't it?*

Love and Gawain were no strangers. Love came to him as often as the tide came to the shore. But not love he could have, not love that would grace his life until God himself chose to part him from it in death. His heart had no discretion and very little sense. It reached out to sadness, it reached out to need, and it did not care for marriage or rank, or any other of men's laws. It charged up to such walls time and again, only to break itself against their stones.

There was no comfort in the knowledge that he *would* marry one day, because he must. Arthur would pick the lady, and she would be good and probably beautiful. She would definitely be wealthy and of rank and connection. Would his heart cease to break itself over others once the betrothal was made? Could he finally harness that part of his nature and do his duty, and produce an heir? Some days he thought he could, but other days . . .

Other days, it seemed to Gawain as if God had decided the legitimate line of Goddodin must end. Agravain showed no interest in women. Which was just as well, as he was sour enough to turn sweet love to vinegar. Gareth was too bound up in his worship of Lancelot and the way of arms to give thought to the maidens who sighed so loudly over him from the fences by the practice yard. Geraint, now, stolid and unimaginative, Geraint, would marry who he was told and do his duty as he knew it. Perhaps the hope of heirs lay with him. If there was any hope.

If we are truly seeds of our father's tree, perhaps it would be better if there was no such hope.

The memory of a woman's screams filled Gawain's mind. Abruptly, he left Gringolet's stall and strode to the stable door, and out into the rain, so that he might run across the yard to escape those screams.

The great hall was a place of dim light and muffled sounds. Families slept on blankets beside their wounded men, who tossed and moaned in their pain and tried to find rest. The fires had been allowed to burn down to coals, but they had not been banked for the night, allowing the wounded some warmth. A woman tended one of the hearths now, adding another few sticks of wood to smoulder on the coals. She must have heard his footsteps, for she straightened to face him.

Pacis.

She looked grave and wan, as did all the people of Pen Marhas's hall after this day's battle. The fresh flame showed her face clearly enough for Gawain to know she was not in the least surprised to see him, that she had been waiting for him.

He collected his manners and bowed. 'Lady Pacis.'

'Lord Gawain,' she whispered his name and curtsied. Her dress, he noted, was clean and fine, laying lightly against her form, and her hair shone in the firelight as he remembered. All about her was as he remembered.

He found he did not dare take one step towards her. He had faced a sea of armed men from dawn to dusk, and this one woman left him paralysed. 'You are well?' he asked.

She sighed, looking at the freshening fire. 'As can be at such a time, yes.'

'Your husband?'

She said nothing.

'You should be asleep.' *You should not be here where I can see your sadness and remember the warmth of you in the afternoon when you would laugh and lean close to me so I could smell the sandalwood you used to perfume your hair. Do you still smell of sandalwood, Pacis?*

'What is one night, more or less?' He thought she would say something more, but she just looked back over her shoulder at the makeshift hospital the hall had become. She pulled a rush light from the basket near the hearth and kindled it in the fire. With only a glance at him, she strode swiftly towards the far end of the hall, towards the work-rooms and living chambers.

I do not have to follow, Gawain tried to tell himself. But he knew that he did. He had known such a moment must come ever since he saw Pacis enter Bannain's hall. Unless he himself had died in battle, Fate could not permit it to be otherwise. Neither, he was sure, could Pacis.

She led him to the spinning room. When he entered, she was carefully placing the rush light in a wall sconce. The soapy scent of its tallow mixed with the warm smell of the wool that waited in great piles, some of it cleaned and carded and waiting to be turned into thread, some of it still raw from the backs of the sheep. Spindles and looms lurked like fantastic monsters in the shadows among the chairs and stools that waited for the women to come and occupy them.

He remembered what Rhian told him about how dull the work of spinning was and wondered what stories had been told in this room, and who had told them, and what Pacis had said and heard here.

She faced him now, standing directly under the light. He stepped across the threshold, and did not close the door. Pacis waited for a moment, and when Gawain did not move, she reached for the latch.

'Don't,' he said, ashamed at how it sounded like a plea.

She did not listen. She closed the door firmly. 'I wished to speak to you without other ears to hear.'

Without other ears, without other eyes. Oh, Pacis, shadows were ever our home.

Remember, he counselled himself. *Remember what she said, what she did.* Memory returned some strength to him. 'Why would you wish for that?'

Her face tightened, as if she sought to close off part of herself. Her long hands twisted together. 'So that I could tell you how much I have repented what I did to you.'

Gawain found he had no answer to that, only more memories; of her eyes and voice and skin and scent. Of love filling his heart with courage and certainty. Of the last night, the last time, when she had laughed and turned him away. But there had been so much else, so many shared moments of love. Through the years that had followed, when he could bear to think on it, he had told himself some of those things must have been real to her as well as to him. It seemed he had been right.

Pacis sat on one of the stools, her hands in her lap. She would not look at him. 'What I did was cruel.'

'No, not cruel.' The words were out of Gawain's mouth before he could stop them. How could he say that? After all the pain, after all the times he tried and failed to reclaim what he had known with another woman in her place. But he could smell the sandalwood now, as if from a long-ago dream, and it told him there was so much more to remember besides that last night. What had come after, was that her fault? Didn't the blame lie with him?

What Pacis saw in his face, Gawain could not tell. He had moved closer to her, but he did not know when that had happened. She could reach out now and take his hand in hers. Her fingers were warm, the skin of her palms smooth and soft. Not as soft as the skin at the hollow of her throat. Gawain suddenly felt very tired. The act of standing seemed a great effort. He wanted to kneel, to lean close and rest his head against her, to feel her arms holding him close in safety and promise, as it had been once before.

It took all his strength to pull his hand from hers and step away. He had none left to form any conciliatory words.

'I knew you loved me, and I knew that love to be sincere, and I did what I did despite that.'

Do not look at her. Do not look into those deep eyes that were so merry, that shone so brightly as they teased the boy you were. Do not believe. Do not remember all the other nights, all the other shadows. 'There was a time I would have given all I had to hear those words from you, Pacis.'

'I was as raw as you, and far more frightened. I had never met my husband until the wedding day, and when he never came to me more than to consummate the vows . . .' Her voice caught hard in her throat, and despite himself, Gawain looked again at her to see she had bowed her head. 'You neither need nor want to know any of this, I am certain. I only wanted you to know that I am truly sorry.'

Do not go closer. Leave here. 'Thank you, Pacis.'

The silence fell so thick and so deep, Gawain could hear Pacis's breathing, low and urgent, as if she were trying not to cry.

A lock of hair slipped out from under her veil and fell across her cheek. She pushed it back impatiently. It was a small gesture, an everyday thing. It was not until he saw it that Gawain realized he'd seen her do that very thing a hundred times before, and remembered that he used to dote on it.

'Lady Rhian is very beautiful.'

To hear Rhian spoken of by Pacis wrenched Gawain's thoughts painfully from his memories. Pacis lifted her head, now looking at him closely, examining him for signs of what? Love? Falsehood?

'Is she your new love?'

Gawain said nothing, in part because he did not wish to speak of Rhian in front of Pacis. In part because in truth, he did not know.

But Pacis was not content to have silence as her answer. She stood and walked towards him, until she was close enough that he could feel the warmth from her skin and see how her hands trembled. 'Gawain, what am I to you now?'

Memory held him. Memory turned away his head. 'A dream.'

'To me you are a wish. A wish of what I could have done, had I been brave. Had I been of truer stuff than I am.'

She kissed him, and he smelled the scent of sandalwood in her hair. The caress of her mouth on his melted memory into desire. He tried to think of what she had done to him, tried to think of Rhian, tried to think of honour, but it was as if past and future and the whole wide world had fled, and there was nothing for him to do but wrap his arms around her and draw her close, answering her kiss with his own.

'Once, Gawain,' she said when they parted at last. 'That is all I ask. Let me dream the dream that is you one more time.'

Forgive me. Gawain could not have said whether the thought was to God, or Rhian or his younger self. He lowered his head to kiss Pacis again and fall into her dream.

NINE

Rygehil stood before his wife's door and wondered if he had the courage to go inside.

He had not seen Jocosa since returning from his ill-fated search for Rhian. She had stood in the yard, then, watching as he and the men approached with Whitcomb's desecrated body tied to one of the ponies. She had not even let him speak or explain. White as a ghost, she had simply retreated to her private chamber. Her ladies came and went, but they said she sat like a statue, speaking little and eating less.

She is distraught and has every right to be, Rygehil told himself sitting at board alone, drinking too much beer, as had become his sorry habit. *Her heart will resolve itself, given time.*

But it did not, not that day, or the next, or the next. At last, drink could no longer drown Rygehil's distress, nor cloud his mind to the fact that the whole of his hall went about with sad and frightened faces. Murder had been done, and no justice was sought, not even revenge. Rhian was gone, God alone knew where to, and no search, no inquiry followed. Their lady was sick and secluded. Their lord was dissipated. Those set to rule their land and lives were crumbling beneath the weight of their human failings, and there was nothing at all they could do. It was no wonder their hearts were growing dark with worry.

That, as much as anything drove him to his wife's door. He might have lost Jocosa's love (*God no, please no*), but he still had his duty. He had learned that much at his father's side. The barown had a duty to the land and to the people. His word was justice, so he must act justly. His nature and title were noble, so he must act as nobility demanded.

It had been easier once.

He knocked at the door. 'Jocosa,' he called. 'Will you let me in?'

There was a long silence. He knocked again. 'Jocosa, I would speak with you. Please, let me in.'

Slowly, the door opened. Aeldra, Rhian's woman, stood there. Aeldra had aged ten years in the past three days, and had not left Jocosa's side for more than a score of breaths.

'She says she does not wish to see you, my lord,' said Aeldra. Despite those words, she let the door swing open so that Rygehil could enter the chamber.

Jocosa sat by her embroidery frame, her other two ladies, ancient Una and dove-like Maia, standing helplessly behind her. Her hands held neither thread nor needle. Instead, they clutched an ivory comb carved with a fanciful image of a whale.

She had loved her daughter's red-gold hair. More times than he could count he had seen Rhian sitting at her mother's feet so Jocosa could lovingly tease out each tangle and snarl while Rhian sang or recited some piece of poetry. Rhian's wild rambles and love of hunting were a trial to Jocosa, but she always smiled as she helped set the girl's beautiful waterfall of tresses in order, never minding the time it took. On feast days, she always braided Rhian's hair herself, weaving in bright ribbons or silver threads, then setting it off with baubles of enamelled bronze, or sprigs of fresh flowers.

She knew he was there. She must, even though she gave no sign.

'Leave us,' he said to the women. He did not know what would follow, but whatever it might be, he did not want other ears to hear it.

The waiting women curtsied and did as they were told. He thought he saw relief on their faces, except for Una. In Una he saw words unspoken and anger long withheld. But she too knew place and duty, and left as silently as the others.

Alone with his wife for the first time in days, Rygehil groped for words. To his surprise, Jocosa spoke first.

'Rhian told me a story once,' she said. 'I don't know where she learned it. It was of a girl whose mother had died when she was born. The girl grew to be so like the mother that her father decided he would take her to wife, and he would not be gainsaid. The girl wept over her mother's grave, and her mother's ghost sent her a dress of deerskin. Thus disguised, she ran away and took service in the hall of a great chieftain. She did the dirtiest tasks and was the butt of all scorn. But when the feasting days came and the hall doors were opened, she secretly threw off her deerskins and appeared there, the fairest of all maidens, so that the chief's son fell sick with love of her.' Her words trailed away. 'Perhaps I should have died when Rhian was born so that I might have given her such a disguise to save her from her father.'

There was no answer he could make to that. He could only speak plainly. It was what he had come here to do. 'Jocosa, tell me what I must do to have you back again. I cannot bear this.'

She did not look up. She just stared at the comb, touching its carving as if it were a holy relic.

'You must come down to the table. It is not healthy for

you to stay shut up here.' He paused. 'She is not returning to us, Jocosa. We must let her go and pray God to keep her soul pure.'

Jocosa stirred a little at that, but it was only to turn her face away. 'Leave me, Rygehil. I do not want to hear you anymore.'

Those words, spoken in so rigid a tone, struck him a blow such as no man ever had. All strength of heart and will failed him and Rygehil fell to his knees. Still Jocosa did not look towards him. She stared at the tapestry covering the wall, the beautiful weaving of a merry summer's day. He knew she saw none of it.

Desperate, he snatched up her hand, holding it hard, although she struggled to pull free. *You* will *hear me!* cried his breaking heart. 'Jocosa will you not even try to understand? You were dying! Should I have let you? Should I have robbed us of our life together?'

Those words turned her gaze fully upon him, and he thought the weight of her grievous pain would crush the breath from his body. 'What was it you think you did instead?'

Rygehil stood, but he did not feel as if he willed himself to do so. He stood outside his own body and watched it, a faintly curious witness to how he traversed the floor and laid his hand on the door latch. Distantly, he heard himself say, 'My father was right. I should not have married you. Love is too inconstant a thing on which to build a life.'

'How strange,' said Jocosa icily. 'My mother said the same.'

'Will you come down, Jocosa?' he asked, as if it was a form of courtesy that had to be observed.

'No.'

Still outside himself, he drifted down the corridor and down the stairs. He could not see properly. Around him, the hall seemed to have turned shades of grey and red. All forms were indistinct and fragmented.

This is how it is within my heart, he mused. *It has cracked apart and now the whole world follows suit.*

'My lord, my lord.' Hobden hurried up to Rygehil, his wispy beard sticking out in every direction, as if some outside force had tried to pluck out each hair individually. Rygehil had appointed no new steward to replace Whitcomb. Hobden had been taking the duties upon himself, because the tasks stubbornly remained, not knowing there was no hand to complete them.

Rygehil turned his head, but did not seem to have breath or mindfulness to speak.

'A man is come to see you, my lord.' Hobden tugged at his beard, disordering it even further. 'He will not give his name, but neither will he depart until he has seen you. He says you know him, lord. He says you and he have unfinished business.'

I ought to know. Rygehil drifted towards the hall. *I ought to know what is happening.*

A man in black robes stood before Rygehil's carved chair, his dark eyes hooded, as if only moments had passed since Rygehil had stood before him in the ruins of the Roman fortress and bargained his life away. The world snapped back into place with painful swiftness. Rage burned through his blood, seizing up the pieces of his heart.

'You knew.' *You heard us, with your black arts, you demon. You heard my wife send me away.*

The sorcerer raised his dark brows. 'What is it you think I needed to know?'

Rygehil became aware of Hobden hovering at his elbow. He dismissed the man with a wave, and Hobden seemed glad to go.

Rygehil dropped himself into his seat and without any moment of reflection, reached for the pitcher of ale. He filled his cup without offering any to his guest. *To collect myself,* he thought as he drank. Then he said, 'That Rhian has fled. Well, your trip is wasted. I know not where she has gone.'

'But I do.'

Rygehil stared at Euberacon. The sorcerer's dark eyes reflected nothing. Even the firelight was absorbed into the black irises.

He drained his cup and filled it again. 'Then why do you come here?'

'Our bargain stipulated you would give her to me.' He spoke pleasantly, as if the matter concerned nothing more than a sow or a sheep. 'It is from your hands I will receive her, or your wife's life is mine.'

Rygehil looked back over his shoulder towards the staircase. Jocosa should be busy in the hall, attending to the thousand tasks that were the unending work of a true lady. Never once had his home lacked for comfort or care. Never were the sick left to fend for themselves. Never were his people left ragged or unheard. Despite the tragedy of two lost sons, despite a wild daughter and a drunkard husband, never did her will to do what was right and necessary flag within her. Never, despite all, was he left to doubt her love. From the first, she had loved him with heart's true love such as even Rhian's poets did not understand. It was he who had wasted it. He who had struck that love its killing blow.

'No,' he said. 'You may have me in her place.'

The sorcerer's eyes narrowed in scorn. 'You are no good to me. Your daughter or your wife. Choose.'

'No.' Rygehil set his cup down. He climbed to his feet and crossed the stones to stand before the sorcerer. There was no fear left in him, no rage, no pain. There was only duty, and the debt he owed his wife for a lifetime's worth of failure. 'If it is God's will Jocosa should die, then so be it, but I will have no more hand in this.'

'Have you learned some measure of courage then, in all

these years?' Euberacon pursed his lips, like a man might when judging the quality of goods he meant to barter for.

'God grant that I have.' Rygehil realized he meant that with all his wounded heart. 'Now, get you from my lands before I take you up and have you hanged for the murder of a good man.'

'Or perhaps you only have nothing left of value to lose.' The sorcerer went on as if Rygehil had not spoken. 'Perhaps I was mistaken. Perhaps you will be of use yet.'

Rygehil barked out a laugh, sharp and bitter. 'My dealings with you have cost me all that I love. What makes you think I would go on with them?'

'A son,' said Euberacon.

The world froze in place. There was no motion, no sound save for a strange ringing in his ears.

'What?' Rygehil was finally able to force the word out.

'You lost two sons to fever when they were babes, did you not? I can restore one to you.'

Rygehil turned away. His ears still rang. Much more than ale robbed him of his balance. He gripped the arms of his chair to keep his feet. 'You lie,' he said without looking back. He could not stand to look, not yet.

'You know better than that.'

Do not listen. You must not hear. Rygehil squeezed his eyes shut. 'You are the devil sent to tempt me. I will not heed you.'

'A son, Lord Rygehil. An heir. A future.'

In his private darkness, there was nothing else but the maelstrom of his thoughts, and the sorcerer's steady voice.

'What future can your daughter bring you now? She has already tainted her name by deserting her father's home. Shall I tell you what company she fell into? She travels alone with a man from the High King's court.'

His eyes snapped open. 'Not Rhian.'

'She is alone, without protector, without family. What future will she have left when that journey is done? You are not an innocent, Rygehil. You know the ways of men and the prices they demand for their good will. What do you think will happen?'

Rhian. Images filled his mind. Rhian sitting at her mother's feet, singing old songs. Rhian coming into the hall at Whitcomb's side, her eyes and cheeks bright with exercise, a brace of partridge on a string.

Rhian standing before him demanding to know why she was forbidden to marry.

'This is my fault,' Rygehil whispered.

'Perhaps. But the fault is not fatal. All you need do is fetch her back. Give her to me, and at the next full moon, you will find your son, an infant still, healthy and strong in the cradle you set out for him.'

Rygehil straightened. With a force of will and nerve he had never needed even while riding into battle, he made himself face the sorcerer. 'You say you know where she is.' His voice was hoarse. His mind was teetering on the edge of a precipice. 'Why do you not take her yourself?'

The knife-blade smile flickered across Euberacon's face. 'Ah, but then perhaps you change your mind, and you go to your king and you say, "My daughter was stolen from me". No.' He shook his head once. 'The king's champion will see you reclaim your daughter yourself.'

Rygehil had thought he was resolved. He had made his peace with God and was ready to die, ready to prove to Jocosa with that act that he was still worthy of love. He was done with this devil. But now . . . a son. He swayed on his feet. A future that had been lost, buried in an infant's grave, opened before him again. A little one to heal Jocosa's heart now that Rhian was lost. A miracle, such as God wrought for Sarah and Abraham when Sarah was too old to bear children . . .

What would Jocosa say? No. She was already broken. But this would be the healing of her, this last secret. He could give Jocosa another one she could love without reservation as she could no longer love him. In this, he could give her back her heart, and perhaps, just perhaps they could both live to see their love that had been cut down grow again.

Jocosa's love. It was all that he wanted. It was worth any bargain with any devil.

'Very well,' said Rygehil. The world ceased to sway and his body was once more steady and strong and under his command. He would have Jocosa's love again. Rhian had been lost as soon as she had chosen to run. 'Where is my daughter?'

Kerra was in the Saxon camp when the men returned from the second day of battle before the walls of Pen Marhas. They were exhausted and bedraggled, covered in mud and blood. The wounded groaned as they limped to the fires, leaning hard on the shoulders of their comrades. Some were tied to the backs of horses that were as weary and as gore-spattered as their masters. Even Wulfweard, to whom battle was a drug, trudged on heavy feet, his bonze helmet dangling from his hand. A long, ragged tear ran down one cheek. The blood dried darkly against skin and beard.

'My husband.' She knelt before him as a proper wife of his people would do, taking both his hands in hers. 'Let me tend your wounds.'

Wulfweard grunted and suffered her to lead him away. His eyes were dull with exhaustion and anger, and something else which she had not seen in him since she had made him one of hers – fear. Kerra held open the flap of his tent so that Wulfweard could enter easily. As she did, she caught sight of Harrik dropping himself down beside the fire and pulling at the straps on his helmet. He met her gaze and she saw the same stunned weariness in him, and fear as well. Not fear of what he had seen on the field, but fear that he would disappoint her.

Then let him stew in that fear awhile yet. She held her face still and blank as she followed Wulfweard into his tent.

The tent was fragrant with the special resins and incense she laid on the fire. She had anointed herself with the necessary perfumes for her work as well. Wulfweard threw himself onto his bed of sheepskins and breathed deeply as she took his helmet and began to wash and dress his wound. She doubted he was even aware that he smelled something exotic anymore.

'What happened, my husband?' she asked softly as she laid the wet cloth against the gash in his cheek.

'That damned whoreson from Camelot, that's what happened,' he growled, keeping his voice low, knowing as well as she that the whole of the camp was straining its ears to hear what their war leader said to his woman. 'Yesterday, he fights like one of their city men, careful, controlled, doing no more than is needed. He knows he's got the walls and we're sitting in the open. Time's on his side. Today, though. Today, he's gone mad as any berserker. Turned red butcher on us. No plan, no care for who was behind him or with him . . . I thought he was going to chase us all the way back to the hills on his own!'

His wound was bleeding freely now, and Kerra laid a clot of cobwebs and peat over it. 'What held him back? You could have had him.'

'Wotan himself knows, I do not,' muttered Wulfweard. 'We were running back, and I was thinking, "Come on up, you bastard, we'll give you the welcome you want," because I swear on my head, he was acting like a man who didn't want to see moonrise. But he turned back before I could put thought to deed.' Wulfweard closed his eyes. 'I tell you, wife, we lost fifteen good men today to Arthur's cubling out there. Another day of this, and we're done.'

'And the messengers to Camelot?' she asked, patting her medicines into place. It was a shallow cut. The scar would be a mere thread.

Wulfweard grunted again. 'I've had word we got two of them. The men think there may have been a third. They're still hunting him.'

Which meant there might be very little time indeed.

Kerra stood. 'There will not be another such day.' She kissed his craggy brow, and cradled his head close to her bosom so he might breathe in the perfumes that lulled his suspicions and raised his lusts. 'If you listen to my counsel, and bide by what I say, Pen Marhas falls before the next dawn.'

'Listen to your counsel,' repeated Wulfweard dully. 'Always. Always.'

'Yes, beloved,' she smoothed his hair down. 'Always.'

It was only a few moments before he was fast asleep and Kerra lowered him onto the skins. She had to hurry before he started to snore. She left the tent, and stepped up to Harrik's side. 'Your master would speak with you,' she said, softly enough to make it sound like a confidence, but loudly enough to make sure it was overheard. There was more than one set of suspicions to be lulled among these men.

Harrik followed her nervously, like a child who knows punishment is coming. Inside the tent, he dropped at once to his knee, head bowed. Kerra let the flap fall behind him, cutting off the daylight. When he heard no command to rise, Harrik risked a look up and saw his lord and master sprawled on a pile of sheep skins.

'He sleeps,' whispered Kerra in case it was not obvious, but then, a man in Harrik's state needed all the help that could be had. 'We need to speak, you and I.'

Harrik stood, his eyes wide. Any minute he would start shuffling his feet. If the matter had been any less urgent, Kerra would have laughed.

Instead, she hardened her face and put as much steel as she could into her whisper. 'I am most angry, Harrik.'

'We underestimated the woman. But she is trapped in Pen Marhas.'

Yes, the woman. You, at least know how to keep your mind on essentials. 'I know what happened today. Pen Marhas will not be cut off for long.'

'Your husband . . .' Harrik began heatedly.

Kerra raised her hand to silence him. She could not risk him getting so angry he raised his voice. 'Is my husband, Harrik,' she replied gently. 'And I may not speak against him,' she lowered her eyes, and let out a soft sigh. *Breathe deeply, Harrik, my own. Breathe deeply.* 'It does not matter that my heart lies elsewhere.'

Now Harrik knelt to her, pressing her hand to his lips. 'Gawain and his woman will die. We will take this place.'

She tilted his chin up so that he might look into her eyes. 'You will, if you will heed me.'

'Tell me what to do.'

Kerra smiled for him. 'Choose four of your best men. Tonight, when the moon sets, take them up to Pen Marhas's walls, to the place where you see the raven sitting. When that raven caws three times, scale the walls. You will be able to find your way through the streets, and open the gates.'

For a moment, Harrik's face clouded. The man inside, chained by her magics struggled against his bonds for a moment. 'It is witchcraft, Kerra.'

She leaned close, she spoke for him and no other. She belonged wholly to him. She was all his need and desire. There was nothing else in all the wide world. 'It is what must be done, Harrik,' she told him. 'You will do this for me, for our love. Once you have left the camp, the men will follow you down in twos and threes, and they will wait ready for the gate to open. Darkness will aid them, I can promise you.'

He caught her face in both hands, and kissed her long and desperately. She permitted the gesture for a time, and then pulled gently away, her hands capturing his wrists.

'It will be as you say, my heart,' he told her with all the force of a man taking a blood oath.

She touched his head in benediction and acknowledgement. Harrik rose and there was nothing more than obedience and smouldering desire in his eyes. The man was still once more.

Kerra smiled behind him as he left the tent. She would yet succeed in her aims. It had been humiliating to have to stand silent before Euberacon while he castigated her for failing to bring him Gawain and Rhian. It had been past comprehension to learn that they were still alive. Morgaine had warned her she believed too strongly in her own powers, and that she looked too little towards the possibility of failure. Again, her mistress was proved right. Euberacon had gone off without telling her where to take measures of his own to reclaim his little treasure. Probably he was going to bully the girl's father into handing her over.

But all was far from lost. Pen Marhas was more than vulnerable to Kerra and her friends. She had thought to open the gates by her own means, but the wood of those gates was banded with iron. There was no magic to which iron would yield. So, it would have to be Harrik, and after him, Wulfweard could do his work.

Kerra stared in the direction of Pen Marhas, as if she could see through the tent's skin walls. 'I would rather you had been killed on the hills, Gawain, but perhaps this is best. Now there can be no suspicion as to why and how you died.'

She smiled then. This must be what it was to be queen,

this unquestioning loyalty, this feeling of power in one's hands. The satisfaction of watching one's works set into motion. The knowledge that one ruled hearts as well as hands. Such things would wash away even the memory of hunger and hiding. She would enjoy her ascendancy to the great hall at Camelot. In Arthur's fall, she would pay all her debt to Morgaine, and in the power that came with sovereignty she would finally know true freedom.

Kerra reclined in the tent's one chair, and prepared to wait for darkness.

TEN

The mood in Bannain's hall that night was almost celebratory. Even the wounded men drank toast after toast to Gawain's boldness. Tomorrow would be time enough to worry that the fields outside, so newly ploughed and planted, were nothing but mud and blood. It would also be more than time enough to worry that the Saxons still nursed their wounds in the hills and that there had as yet been no word from Camelot. Today, Pen Marhas had dealt a telling blow to her attackers, and her people would cheer, even though the night's supper was nothing more than stew and bread. Tomorrow, Bannain promised at the top of his lungs, there would be roasts and pies to welcome home the victors after they had chased the Saxons back into the sea!

That speech earned another thunderous cheer, and another round of beer and wine. Rhian, seated at the high table, raised her cup with the rest, but kept her silence. She was sure of only two things. One was that on the field today, Gawain had been nearly out of his mind, and the other was that although darkness was settling in, he had not yet returned to the hall.

There was only one other at the table who seemed less

than triumphal, and that was Lady Pacis. She scowled down at her meat, stabbing restlessly at the stew with her knife, but eating nothing.

'Was that a sigh, Lady Rhian?' Lady Cailin asked over the rim of her own cup.

Rhian collected herself hurriedly. 'Forgive me, my hostess. I am tired.'

'I am not surprised,' put in Lady Pacis, each word as sharp as the knife she held. 'There will be themes sung on your courage as well as Gawain's.'

Rhian had to stop herself from asking where Pacis had spent her day. 'I only did what I could.' It did not seem to Rhian that there was anything particularly courageous about sitting out in the wind and the sun, holding an arrow ready until her fingers ached, and praying to God that Gawain did not decide to try to chase the Saxons all the way back to their hills single-handedly. It had taken Bannain's orders to stop him.

'As do we all.' Lady Cailin looked hard over Rhian's head at Pacis. Something akin to a silent scolding passed between them. Pacis, however, was undeterred.

'Oh no. Lady Rhian has done so much more than was needed. She is a heroine from ancient Rome, such as are spoken of inhabiting the imperial palaces. A woman of uncommon perseverance and endurance that all men may marvel at.'

Her words were pitched to carry, and the others at the table were beginning to look up from their feasting. Rhian felt her cheeks flame crimson with anger as well as embarrassment.

'Someone must work when there are wounded men. What use were you today?'

Pacis shot to her feet, and all at the table turned to stare.

Rhian waited to hear what remark Pacis would make now, her heart in her mouth, but Lady Cailin spoke first, and bluntly.

'Pacis, you are making a fool of yourself. Sit down.'

Pacis glowered at her aunt and then without another word, turned on her heel and whisked out of the hall.

Rhian swallowed, the knowledge that she was alone among strangers coming down hard over her again.

'Lady Cailin,' she said. 'Please believe me, I meant no offence against your niece, nor any . . .'

But Lady Cailin waved Rhian's words away. 'Pacis would be better served if she could keep better count of her days and her men,' she said tartly. 'Pay her no heed, Lady Rhian.'

Rhian picked up her goblet and took a long swallow of the small beer to keep from staring at her hostess. There was only one thing Lady Cailin could be inferring. God and Mary, if Pacis had cuckolded her husband, why did she need to try to embarrass *Rhian* in public?

Unwelcome reasons stirred in the back of Rhian's mind, agitated by the fact that Gawain was still nowhere to be seen. Bannain moved about his hall, speaking to his men, both the ones at board and the ones lying on their makeshift beds among their families. There would be another toast soon, and more cheer.

Does no one see this is not over yet?

As this thought came over her, she also saw that the ladies on the other side of Cailin were in a whispered conversation of their own. Rhian set her cup down, feeling suddenly ill.

Lady Cailin gave a small sigh and patted Rhian's hand. 'Perhaps you should retire, Lady Rhian. Water is being heated. You can wash if you wish.'

'Thank you, Lady Cailin.' Rhian stood, keeping her eyes modestly downcast so that she would not have to look at her hostess, or anyone else for that matter. Cailin's words were tolerant, underscored with impatience. It seemed to Rhian that she was saying, *if you are going to sin, you could at least be brave about it.*

Pray for patience, Rhian counselled herself. *And pray that tomorrow brings the victory everyone says it will so that we can leave here before the wings of rumour have a chance to fly ahead of us.*

She hoped the women's sleeping chamber would be empty so she could have a moment's peace to collect herself. The dim room was silent when she reached it, and she sighed in relief. It was not until she had closed the door behind herself and turned towards the fire that she saw the other woman standing as still and white as an alabaster statue.

Rhian opened her mouth, but Pacis stalked forward like a hunting cat. 'This is your fault! You drained the vitality from him!'

What on God's green earth is she talking about? 'Lady Pacis. . .' Rhian spread her hands, trying to find something to say that was both conciliatory and sensible in the face of the other woman's rage.

But Pacis grabbed her shoulders, shaking her hard. 'I need a son! What right have you to keep him from me!'

Even as understanding solidified, Rhian's patience shattered. She stepped back, striking sharply at the lady's wrists to break her hold. 'Lady Pacis,' she said evenly. 'I am sorry you are in distress, but it is no fault of mine.'

Rhian had heard of marriage contracts that were contingent on the wife bearing a son. If no male heir was forthcoming, the wife could be set aside. Pacis evidently had been written into such an agreement, and when God, her husband and her body had failed to keep the bargain, she had sought other help, in the form of Gawain.

And Gawain had turned her down, or had failed in some other way. Rhian did not want to know any of this. She most certainly did not want to be standing here.

'I will be turned out without even my portion, sent in disgrace back to my father's hall with three useless daughters in tow, because you have blushed and simpered your way into his heart!'

'Lady Pacis.' Rhian began again, trying to remain firm although she felt as if the very ground were shifting under her feet. 'I do not know what complaint you have against me, but I will not be insulted, nor will I be made to answer for the actions of another.'

It was a thing Lady Pacis was most unwilling to hear. She circled around Rhian, looking for an opening, a place she could stab with her hatred. Rhian did not turn to face her. She stood as she was, her eyes forward. *Be still. Be stone. She is nothing.*

'Listen to me, you little whey-faced Messalina,' Pacis sneered. 'You think you've won Gawain? He is fickle and faithless as the winds. He goes from woman to woman because he can't have what he wants. I own him. His heart is mine, and it is my will it obeys, do you hear me?'

Which was too much. Rhian pivoted on her toes and faced Pacis. Her beautiful face was creased in fury and for a moment Rhian thought she could see the bitter crone the woman was to become. Rhian spoke, and her voice was light and calm. 'I hear you and your words are perverse as they are poisonous,' her tone was almost pleasant. 'If you own Lord Gawain as you say, why are you wasting breath on me? Why are you not with him even now?'

In answer, Pacis drew back her hand and delivered Rhian a ringing slap. For a moment Rhian was stunned, and could only cover the place with her hand. Then, seeing the impotent fury in the other woman's eyes, Rhian very deliberately turned her head, offering up the other cheek.

For a moment she saw murder in Pacis's eyes, but she did not flinch. She had faced a black sorcerer and a Saxon raiding party. She could face this one heart-sick woman. Pacis raised her hand again, and Rhian remained as she was, waiting for the blow. Pacis's open hand balled into a fist and she pressed it against her mouth as she rushed from the room.

For a moment, Rhian stayed as she was, swaying on her feet. Then, she collapsed onto her narrow bed and pressed her face against her palms, Pacis's words ringing in her head louder than iron bells.

It means nothing, she told herself. *Nothing. She's a liar and a schemer and understands nothing beyond her own wishes. Such a one could never own Gawain's heart . . . There were no promises, no understandings. Only dreams. You knew you would have to wake when you reached Camelot. It is just a few days sooner. That's all.*

And it might all be lies start to finish.

But it might not.

Rhian lifted her head, and realized her face was wet. She wiped at it quickly. The place would soon be filling up with women. Pacis's shouts had most certainly carried. She was not ready to face the curious stares and polite, veiled inquiries as to the state of her mind, and yet she couldn't leave. Pacis might have gone anywhere.

No, not anywhere. There was one place in the hall where Rhian could seek the solace she needed and where Pacis in her current frame of mind was highly unlikely to venture.

Rhian hurried from the room, heading down the darkening corridors to the hall's chapel.

The chapel was small but beautiful. The walls were painted with bright images: the disciples kneeling at the feet of the solemn Christ, Mary holding her infant son, and rather more of the glories of Heaven than the punishments of Hell, an affectation Rhian heartily approved of.

It was also occupied by a broad-shouldered man kneeling at the altar rail.

Gawain.

He did not turn at the sound of her footsteps. His prayer

held all his attention as he bowed before the carved and painted crucifix, with the Lord's arms stretched out over him in suffering and benediction. His whispers filled the painted room like a soft wind.

'Give me strength,' he prayed. 'Father, take this thorn from my side.'

Rhian fled in silence, but there was nowhere left to go. Even God's house was closed to her. She could not stay under this roof. The honest and unguarded night was preferable to these stifling walls. Her breath was already coming in short gasps.

The kitchens had a door to the herb gardens and the animal pens. Ignoring the stares of the servants, Rhian ran out that way and down the narrow path, her heedless passage stirring up sleepy complaints from geese and chickens. The wind blew hard against her face, drying her sore cheeks, and loosening her breathing. Her footsteps slowed, and her vision cleared.

Mindful of what had happened the night before, she turned her path away from the stables, although she would have liked to visit Thetis, to take some comfort in a fellow creature. If there was any comfort to be had in this night where the stars shone down placidly on dangers without and within.

I'm so tired.

Perhaps she should not have run away. Perhaps this was all punishment for defying her father, and the fate God had set for her.

No. She could not believe God would be so cruel. Despair was a sin. This was a trial, a trial only. She could stand it. She must. There was no one else to stand it for her.

There in the yard, Rhian knelt. Surely the whole world was God's house. Surely a prayer could be heard anywhere. She bowed her head and clasped her hands.

'Our Father . . .' she began the pater noster fervently.

It was then Rhian heard a raven's harsh call.

Her tongue froze to the roof her mouth, and her skin prickled sharply.

No. Even the birds that feasted on the dead were sated and asleep in the ruined fields.

The call came again, faint but clear on the cold night wind.

God and Christ, I'm losing my mind.

But the call came again, down the gentle slope outside the hall's defences, to the west, she thought, although it was hard to tell. Rhian hesitated for a handful of heartbeats, and then, murmuring a far different set of prayers, ran back to the chapel.

Gawain was still there, and still kneeling before the altar.

She called his name and he turned on his knees as if he'd heard a sword being drawn.

'Rhian . . .' he went utterly pale at the sight of her. There was no time to let him speak another word, and Rhian found herself secretly glad.

'Gawain. I heard a raven out by the walls.'

The confusion on Gawain's face quickly cleared, and he leapt to his feet. 'Did you see anything?'

'No, but . . . I do not like it. Will you come with me?'

Rhian realized she was placing a trust in Gawain. They had both seen what they had seen, and knew that hidden arts and powers worked around them. He could deny it, though. It would be difficult to explain to Bannain why he was going out in the dark to chase a bird.

But Gawain wasted no time on questioning her eyes or intuition.

'I will get my arms. Fetch your bow and meet me at the hall doors.'

Rhian nodded and hurried down the corridor. She burst

into the sleeping room, sending a flock of women and ladies of the hall fluttering from her path.

'Where are you going, lady?' asked a sly, cultured voice as Rhian caught up her bow and quiver from under her bed.

'Hunting larks,' she answered sharply and left before any other query could follow.

Gawain stood ready by the hall steps, watching the darkness alertly. The sentries moved with steady strides around the inner palisades. Torches and rush lights flared, driving the dark back just a little.

As soon as Rhian descended the steps, Gawain nodded, and side by side they crossed the yard.

The guard on the portal beside the inner gate was clearly loath to let them leave, but was, fortunately, even more reluctant to closely question the lord-and-hero Gawain, and they were allowed out with only a minimal delay. Beyond the inner walls, night turned Pen Marhas into a maze. Although the moon was high, there was not enough light to pick out any more than the roughest of shapes. Rhian strained her ears. Random noises – the bleating of a sheep, a pig's grunt – drifted on the wind along with the smells of wood smoke, animal pens and, faintly, of the dead still unburied beyond the walls. It was as impossible to tell the direction of any one sound as it was the origin of any one scent. Rhian wished in vain that she had her hounds with her for this strange hunt.

Gawain matched her pace exactly, moving with caution and grace at her side, always taking care not to step in front of her and so always leaving a clear path for her to shoot the arrow she held ready in the string. She had only three left. They could not afford to waste even one chance for a shot at their prey.

The torches atop the outer walls grew closer, but only slowly. A man's voice called out. A dog barked. Nothing more or less than the sounds of a town's night.

'Did I dream?' muttered Rhian.

'We will make sure all is right at the outer walls,' answered Gawain. 'I'll take caution at even a dream of yours.'

Rhian concentrated on the sounds beyond the silver-tinged shadows. A baby's high, thin wail. A cow's lowing. A door. Footsteps stumbling on rutted dirt. A long, low creaking, as of something heavy being slowly moved.

Gawain stopped dead. 'God on High. The gate. Rhian, run, wake the hall!'

The gate. The Saxons were opening the gate. Rhian jammed her arrow into her quiver as she took off running, slipping and splashing in mud-rimmed puddles.

'The gate!' she shouted as she ran. 'The gate is open! The walls are breached!'

Voices raised around her, calling out from houses. Doors slammed open, and hastily kindled lights bobbed out into the night. Rhian did not slow or stop to make any answer. She just sent her warning as far ahead as she could

'The gate is open! The walls are breached!'

Behind her, the screams began, and the roar of maddened men. It was then she realized she was alone in her flight. Gawain had stayed behind.

As clear as day, her mind's eye saw him standing in the street, bellowing orders to the sentries, sword in hand, ready to meet the enemy's tide. Her voice choked off, but her speed redoubled.

The inner walls blocked the way in front of her. The light from blazing torches cascaded down.

'Who . . .!' began the sentry, his voice tight and uncertain.

'Lady Rhian!' she cried back before he could finish his question. 'Let me in! The Saxons have breached the gate!'

The sentry overhead did not move. He was only a frightened boy. But someone had some presence of mind; the little portal beside the gates was flung open and Rhian darted inside.

'Is the thedu awake?' she bawled at the man who stood nearest the door.

'He's been sent for . . .'

She did not wait to hear any more. She just ran for the stables, her breath tearing at her lungs like sobs. Around her, men ran as well, for the horses, for the walls, for their weapons or their wives. Their voices blended into an incomprehensible din. Firelight chased back the darkness. Over the walls, the sky began to glow, and a new, ominous roar began under the shouts and clatters.

A woman screamed.

The stable doors were wide open. Boys and men rushed past her, arms loaded with tack and saddles. Rhian waded between them to Thetis's box. Gringolet might throw her, but Thetis knew her touch from when she was a little girl, and when she was a little girl she had ridden in the oldest style of all. Rhian seized Thetis's mane, hauled herself up onto the mare's bare back and dug her knees into the horse's sides, sending her flying out into the yard. People flung themselves out of her way, and cried out what might have been curses. Rhian threw her weight backward to pull Thetis up short as they reached the wall.

The man was the same who had let her in, and he did not waste time asking what she thought she was doing

'My lady, the Saxons . . .!' he tried.

'Lord Gawain is out there alone!' she cut him off. 'Open that door and bring who you can behind me!'

Thankfully, the man obeyed. Rhian threw herself flat against Thetis's back and a lifetime of loyalty caused the mare to respond when Rhian, with rough heels and hands, ordered her through the narrow door and down the twisting street.

In the time it had taken for Rhian to run to the hall, the

night of Pen Marhas had changed completely. Now it was filled with noise and horror on all sides. Fire clawed at the sky from thatched roofs. Screams blossomed with the flames, women's and children's terror mixed together. Men's impotent shouts. Cruel laughter in answer. The stink of burning flesh and the mindless cries of animals. Bodies swarmed through the street, running in utter desperation for the hall and the inner walls, knowing that they might not make it in time, knowing that they might be trapped between the Saxons and the closed gates.

Thetis balked and bucked. Rhian had finally asked too much of her. She knotted her hands in the horse's mane, but there was no controlling her. She wheeled around, and Rhian felt herself begin to slip. It was either jump off or be thrown.

She landed on the rutted ground, stumbling before she found her balance. Relieved of her burden, Thetis bolted into the chaos, leaving Rhian to hope she found some kind of safety for herself.

She had no idea where she was. All the walls around her looked identical. Faceless forms ran past her, bumping and jostling. She made her way against their current. Gawain would have headed to the walls. His first priority would have been to try to get the gates closed.

Rhian's hand gripped her bow where it hung on her shoulder. It was useless in this flickering light, these uncertain shadows, but it gave her strength to keep going, hugging the shadows, trying to think clearly, trying to shut out the screams and the heat of the fires.

'Rhian!'

Rhian's head jerked up. Without warning, a man's hands seized her about the waist, jerking her off her feet, hurling her to the ground. Her head slammed against the dirt, and for a moment she saw the Saxon towering over her, firelight turning his knife and helm blood red. Rhian scrabbled at the ground for some weapon, any weapon, and the Saxon swooped down.

Then there was the flash of a blade, and a guttural scream, and the Saxon was gone, replaced by Gawain's silhouette. He grabbed Rhian by the arm, hauling her upright. Before she could find her feet, he dragged her through the nearest doorway.

The house had already known the attention of the raiders. The furniture was smashed, the folk fled, the fire flung from the hearth, its flames smouldering in the middle of the dirt floor. Gawain ground them out with the heel of his boot.

'What were you thinking?' he demanded, stamping out the last of the fledgling fires.

That you were out here alone. But he knew that. How could he not know? She kept her silence and tried to find her breath again. Gawain stared for a moment at the ashes, and then turned to her. His heart was all in his eyes, and Rhian felt her own reach out in answer. All that they had not said, all that they had tried to keep from each other, passed between them now with nothing more than that look, while Hell opened all around them. They could not lie now, to each other or themselves, as they might have tried to once.

'Forgive me,' he whispered.

Rhian swallowed. 'There is nothing to forgive.'

'There is. I would tell you if there was time. We need to head for the outer walls. If we stay here, the fire will take us, even if the Saxons don't.'

She thought about the mad scramble at the hall for men and weapons. 'Bannain . . .?'

'We cannot help them if we're burning with his town. The outer gates are still open.'

Fresh screams rose from the chaos. Gawain grabbed Rhian's

arm, pulling her through the doorway. The screams grew closer, accompanied by the sounds of weeping, and of laughter.

It was a cluster of women and children surrounded by Saxons who drove them with kicks and axe hafts against their backs. One had a woman by her hair, dragging her behind him so that she had to run to keep from falling. Her captor ignored her screams, or perhaps he enjoyed them. Gawain let go of Rhian's arm at once, and stood before them.

He was going to say something, offer some challenge, for he was a captain and a champion, or perhaps because he couldn't see straight yet from the smoke. Rhian snatched up a piece of wood, some post from a broken fence, and charged like a mad woman for the nearest raider, screaming at the top of her lungs.

Caught off guard, the raider swung around too late and Rhian drove her fence post into his belly, knocking him off his feet. The women screamed and scattered. Gawain swung his sword, parrying another raider's axe, thrusting at throat and belly. Rhian whirled around in time to see a raider with his knife out bearing down on her, but in the next heartbeat he saw she was not standing alone. There had been no time to tie the women, and they were not going to simply flee. They came back, with sticks and rocks, with bare hands and screams and flaming brands. The raiders fell before them, tumbling into the mud to be kicked and beaten, or driven back between the burning homes. The children cried and screamed, the youngest huddling behind the oldest. A few picked up stones and threw them after the fleeing Saxons.

Gawain dispatched his man and turned to look for more, but saw only women and children, and Rhian standing there, clutching her makeshift weapon, and breathing lungfuls of smoke until each breath was a cough.

'Rhian, take them out of here!' he shouted to be heard above the roar.

'There's no shelter out there!'

'There's less in here! Get the children away!'

Come with me! she wanted to cry to him, or *I won't leave you!* but she did not. He was armed with steel and she with a stick of wood. Her bow was useless in this hideous light and the shifting winds the fires created. He could do far more in here than she. The poets could fill in the grand gestures later.

'Hold onto each other!' She caught up the hand of the nearest woman. 'Keep close! We're going to the gates!'

They came by ones and twos, mothers carrying babies, clusters of children, old men hoisting their grandchildren onto their bent backs. They clutched at sleeves and hands, stumbling through the inferno their home had become, coughing and retching. Rhian tried not to look at any of them, she tried only to see the way out. Her right hand curled tightly around her ridiculous stick, but it was all she had.

At last, the gates of Pen Marhas opened before them like the gates of Paradise itself. A gout of clean, cold wind caught Rhian in the face and she thought she would faint from the giddy delight of it. She slogged forward with her charges. There was no one left on the earthworks. There was no one left in the field. The Saxons had all gone in to sack the town. The soldiers had all gone in to defend it.

And here they were, this ragged band, to watch it burn.

'We should get up above it,' said Rhian. Smoke and emotion turned her voice hoarse.

Numbly they followed her, across the valley and up the hillside. One of the women knew where there was a spring, and she led them into the gully where the water ran clean and cold as ice, chattering to itself as if nothing were happening. They all drank. The women washed their children's faces, and soaked their burns in the icy water, wrapping them in pieces of sleeve and skirt that one of the men cut free with his knife.

Then, because there was nothing else to do, they sat on the hillside, huddled close for what little warmth there was to be had from each other, and watched Pen Marhas burn. Children crawled into their mothers' and grandfathers' laps, or leaned their heads against their knees. Those who had no parent with them crowded together beside their neighbours. Rhian wrapped her arms around herself and shivered. She tried to be grateful for her life, for the lives of those around her, for the small blessing that they were upwind from the town, so they did not have to breathe the stench of it into their ravaged lungs. Her skin stung in a dozen places, as if she had been in a swarm of bees, and her throat was raw with smoke and shouting. Despite the heat of the other bodies around her, she was cold.

Down below, fire leapt to the sky, but it had not yet reached the centre of the stronghold. The hall itself did not burn, she thought, she hoped, she prayed. She could make herself believe while the hall still stood that there was some haven for Gawain to retreat to. That there was some chance for him.

It took Rhian a long moment to realize it was not just fire that lit the sky. White sunlight turned the horizon pale. Dawn was coming.

'Look there.' The woman whispered, as if afraid of being overheard.

And maybe she was. A stream of bodies was fleeing Pen Marhas. Caught between fire and dawn light, all were black silhouettes. It was impossible to tell who they were, or whether some chased others or they all fled the fires in camaraderie. Rhian leapt to her feet, straining her eyes and ears for some sign. Then she heard the shouts of triumph from below. They bounced off the hills, harsh, incomprehensible.

Saxon.

Despair clamped onto Rhian's heart. What was she to do now? Where were they to go? Had the Saxons taken the hall or were they just fleeing with their loot? Even so, they'd be combing the hills for the survivors. There was no place to go, and here she was caught with the women and children, and only a handful of arrows, to be pressed into slavery or worse . . .

She turned to them. They looked at her, some wide-eyed, some sceptical. They knew her rank, but would they listen? Would they help? They had to flee. They had to try. *Oh, Gawain.*

Before she could open her mouth, a new sound wafted over the hills, so unexpected it took a moment for Rhian to understand what it was. The notes of a hunting horn, bright and brave, rose to meet the dawn. It blew again, its notes winging over the sound of fire and the raiders' cheers.

Once more, a river poured over the eastern hills and down the broad road, a cascade of men and horses, flashing all the colours of the rainbow and more: brown and white, green and blue, silver and gold, riding close in tight discipline. A red and gold banner led them all. The Pendragon, broad and bright, unfurled beneath the bloody light of the rising sun. The messengers had reached Camelot, and Camelot had answered.

'Camelot!' cried Rhian. 'The king! The king!'

The exhausted women took up the cry, their jubilation ringing out like the notes of the horn that led the charge. They lifted their children high so that they could see their salvation racing towards Pen Marhas.

For now it was the Saxons who would be trapped. If the hall had held out. If the inner gates had stayed shut. If Gawain had been able to hold the men together . . .

If Gawain was still alive.

The fresh cascade broke against Pen Marhas. Some turned to follow the now-fleeing Saxons, riding them down easily. Men on horseback took up positions outside the earthworks, guarding the way out. Others dismounted, leaving their horses in the charge of their fellows and went into the town on foot to deal with what they found there. The clash of steel, shouts of command and shouts of fear overpowered the sounds of the fire and looting.

'Should we go down?' murmured a woman behind her. 'Can we go home?'

'Nay, wait,' answered an old man. 'There's work for the knights awhile yet.'

The sun climbed up over the hills. Every so often, a cluster of men ran out from the gates, to be taken up or cut down by the sentries. Rhian's hands itched for her bow. Her feet wanted to run down, to search the fires and the ashes for Gawain. At the same time, she wanted nothing more than to sink into sleep. Her eyes seemed to have forgotten how to blink. The whole of her body ached with exhaustion, cold and long waiting.

The day warmed. It seemed it had been a long time since any raiders had tried to break free of the town. The fires grew old, sinking back into themselves, their rage softening to sighs. Rhian noticed something odd. She had not seen one raven the whole long morning. Not a single bird circled the battlefield.

A lone man emerged from the encircling walls. One of the sentries approached him. They stood together for a time, gesturing in various directions. Then, the man mounted one of the waiting horses, and turned its head towards the hills. Towards them.

Rhian could not have held back those with her, even if she had wanted to. They ran past her, leaving her to stagger in their wake. Within moments they surrounded the rider, a lean, weather-beaten man with a scar on his forehead and ancient blue tattoos on his cheeks, shouting a hundred questions. The rider held up both hands.

'Pen Marhas is saved!' he called out. 'By grace of God, your enemies are fled and the king's men hold your streets!'

This was the answer to all questions, and it raised a cheer from every throat, including Rhian's.

'Which of you is the lady Rhian?' he asked.

Rhian pushed her way to the front of the crowd. 'I am she!'

The rider bowed in his saddle. 'My Lord Bannain bids you and your charges return to Pen Marhas.'

My Lord Bannain. Rhian's heart sank.

'What of my Lord Gawain?' she blurted out.

'I have not seen him,' said the messenger. 'Come, my lady. Come home, all. Every hand is needed.'

I have not seen him. That was all that he had said. It meant nothing. Gawain was one man; even if he had been at the hall, it must be crowded with every survivor from the town. He might not even be there. He might be on the walls, or chasing the Saxons back to their camps.

With the rest of the women, Rhian followed their messenger back down to Pen Marhas. They cheered the sentries waiting by the earthworks, and were waved on and cheered in return.

The cries of celebration died the moment they entered the charred and pitted gates. The smoke still hung heavy in the air. If Rhian had thought the remains of the burnt-out croft in the woods were foul, the corpse of Pen Marhas was a thousand times worse. Children sat in the mud and howled. Men wailed over the bodies of wives, wives over husbands. Animals lay everywhere, dead or dying. Fences, sheds, whole houses had been smashed like eggs by fire and axe. The stench was abominable. Rhian clapped her sleeve over mouth and nose.

Her 'charges' evaporated, running every which way into the streets to find what remained of home and family without a backward glance, their wails and cries fading into the cloud of mourning. Soon, there was only Rhian to follow the messenger and trudge through the destruction, trying not to see any of it, because there was nothing at all she could do. All the strength had drained from her hands and mind. It was all she could do to keep walking and try not to choke on her own breath.

But the further they went, the less damage appeared. Houses, even a few of the warehouses, stood whole, except for some singed straw and planking. Animals bellowed, but it was in confusion rather than pain, and the ashen wind grew a little clearer.

The inner walls lifted themselves ahead, and the gates stood open, still stout and strong. The yard behind them was filled with horses and men in mail, talking with each other or taking care of their beasts.

On the steps of the hall stood Bannain, and beside him, covered in soot and grime, waited Gawain.

Before any thought of propriety or restraint could enter into her mind, Rhian ran up the steps and threw her arms around him. He returned her embrace at once, lifting her up onto her toes and burying his face in her hair so that she felt his breath against her neck, felt his mouth move as he said, 'Thank Christ, thank Christ,' over and over.

'Gawain.'

The sound of that voice stiffened Gawain's back. He set Rhian down on her feet and straightened. The man behind them had Gawain's amber eyes and his rich, black hair, but he was more slender, and time had hardened his face into a look of permanent disapproval. He turned the whole of that disapproval towards Rhian.

Gawain sighed and stepped away, taking Rhian's hand in a belated gesture of propriety.

'Lady Rhian, daughter of Lord Rygehil, barown of the Morelands, may I present to you my brother, Agravain.'

ELEVEN

'Who is she Gawain?'

Gawain stared at his brother for a moment, slow to understand what he was talking about. He had been at the hall, breaking his fast with Bannain and some of his captains, although it was nearer noon than dawn, when a boy had come running to tell him Agravain needed him out at the walls. Gawain had thought it was to discuss the ordering of further patrols to track any of the raiders who might be escaping back into Saxon lands.

Instead his younger brother stood under a sky grey and heavy with rain clouds with his arms folded, surveying the battlefield as if it were a badly rendered painting. A few men were out wading in the mud, with hoes and shovels, looking to see if there was anything of the new planting that could be saved. Around them, fearless gore crows picked through the mire, looking for food, and looking so like ravens from this distance, that Gawain had to suppress a shudder. He would find this witch who plagued them, and she would pay for all her damning mischief.

But that was not the 'she' of whom Agravain spoke.

And you did not want any at the hall to hear this conversation.

Discreet of you, brother. Gawain sighed. 'Her name is Rhian of the Morelands. She's the daughter of that barown. She's beset by a sorcerer and needs protection.'

Agravain raised one eyebrow. 'A sorcerer this time, is it? Well, at least their stories are getting more entertaining.'

Gawain's jaw clenched. 'I saw his powers, brother. The lady does not invent or dissemble.'

'Surely not,' said Agravain blandly. 'Have you bedded her yet?'

'Agravain!'

Agravain did not blink. 'Have you?'

'It is beneath you to ask that question, Agravain.'

Another man would have looked away. Another man would have sighed, or made some other gesture to show he was tired, or that he did not relish this conversation. Agravain made no such concession. 'I only want to know how far you mean to carry this one.'

Gawain forced himself to hold his temper. 'She comes with us to Camelot. She means to ask for the protection of the queen.'

'And this was her notion, this daughter of an outland barown?'

'What is your meaning, brother?'

Agravain's face twisted as it did when he was trying not to speak. Anger clenched his fists. He set his foot on the bank of the earthworks, resting his arms on his thigh and scowling out at the workers and the crows. 'Our uncle sends you out on a mission of delicacy, to find out what dangers threaten the peace of our lands,' he said to the world at large. 'Does Gawain go swiftly and return swiftly as he is instructed? Oh, no. Gawain must stop and find a pretty little liegeman's daughter to rescue so he can bask in the glow of her gratitude and relieve her of her maidenhead . . .'

'Agravain, if you do not stop this . . .'

'I hope she's deep in love, Gawain.' Agravain paced back towards the palisade. 'Because we do not need her father at the great hall claiming his rights with his daughter beside him, her belly full of your bastard and her eyes full of tears.'

'Agravain . . .'

'What?' His brother whirled around. 'What, brother? How dare I? How dare I speak the truth to the valiant, stainless Gawain, champion of the Round Table and of women wherever he finds them?' Rage shook Agravain's frame. 'I swear to you, brother, our uncle has more to fear from you than from any of these barbarians clamouring at his gates. If you stuck to milkmaids it would be no great matter, but you *insist* on taking your privileges with wives and maidens of rank.'

Gawain took a deep breath, unclenching the muscles of his jaw and arms one by one. 'Agravain, you do not understand.'

'Then explain it to me Gawain.' Agravain threw his arms out wide. 'I am here, we have the time. *Explain* it to me.'

Gawain met his brother's angry eyes. Did he dare speak the truth? To say the words out loud, now, to Agravain in his anger?

But Agravain saw his hesitation and only groaned. 'God's teeth,' he swore. 'If you have the gall to tell me you are in love, I swear, I will knock you flat.'

A different spark lit in Gawain at those words and his voice grew low and dangerous. 'Then you had better do it on the first blow, because you will not have the chance to strike a second.'

They stared at each other, two warriors on the edge of the broken and trampled field of battle with the crows calling insults overhead. It occurred to Gawain that anyone who looked down from the palisades could easily have taken them for enemies rather than brothers. Conscience pricked at him, deflating his anger just a little.

'Come, Agravain,' he said. 'This is beneath us both. Such a quarrel can bring no honour to any.'

'Honour.' Agravain turned the word into a sneer. 'Always it comes down to that with you. What is honour? Does it win battles? Does it settle disputes or put money into coffers? Does it undo an ill-conceived dalliance?'

'No,' said Gawain. 'It merely wins hearts. That is a lesson you would do well to learn from our uncle.'

With those words, Gawain turned and marched through the gates into a town that was still filled with the smell of smoke. He strode between the ruined houses, ignoring those who called out his name and hoping vaguely that they thought him on some important errand. Folk were out with rakes and with barrows to try to clear the ruins. Bannain was going to spend much of the coming weeks sorting out the ownership of cows and pigs that had survived the fire, but strayed from the wreckage of their pens. Most of those still here were women and children. The men had gone to the forest to cut new timber to rebuild the wooden walls. Arthur, ever mindful, had sent Agravain with a full purse and word that new seed would be sent from the High King's granaries as soon as Bannain asked. News of these provisions had spread quickly, and as a result the mood of Pen Marhas was more hopeful than otherwise. Its folk were ready to believe they could remake their homes and lives. He could even hear the sound of singing over the clamour of shifting timbers and neighbours calling to one another for help.

Damn Agravain! At a time like this, how could he be speaking as he had? Gawain ran his hand through his hair. There were more important things to think about. Why had Harrik turned again? Had he survived the assault, and where had he gone? What were they planning in the southlands, and what were their movements, and how far gone were what plans they had? Damn Agravain.

Damn him for being even a little right.

Agravain would have taken Rhian to the convent as she asked. He would not have seen a lovely face and been unable to let her go. Without her, Gawain would have been able to make all speed back to Camelot and warn the king that the Saxons had help from a witch, and were no longer licking the wounds dealt them at Badon.

And Pen Marhas would have fallen, and perhaps the raven spy would have led its masters to him on the road.

But it was not in Agravain's nature to think of such things, nor to listen to them, especially when it was Gawain who spoke. Agravain was a worthy knight, and when he had come to Camelot to learn the duties of a ruler from Arthur rather than their father, Gawain had been delighted. He soon found, however, that life had made Agravain cold. Sir Kai had once quipped that Agravain's head was so hard the armourers declared he had no need of a helmet. Gawain sometimes wondered if his heart were not even harder than his head. It was certain he had no time for ladies and their charms. He could not be distracted by childish fancies, he said. When the time came for him, he would choose a wife carefully and for the proper reasons.

Which was right. Agravain also was heir to a throne. One day he would return to Goddodin and Din Eityn and take up their father's rule. He would need the alliances a good marriage would make.

The time *was* wrong for concerns of the heart. Agravain was right about that as well. The High King might soon have to ride to war again. All his champions must be ready and not in any way distracted, and first among them must be the sons of Lot.

Gawain shook his head towards the wind, as if its breath blowing through his hair could bear away unwanted thoughts like autumn leaves. Did he truly wish for a heart as hard as Agravain's? Did he wish to be so safe, so right in matters of responsibility, not even duty, but responsibility?

Did he want the life of his heart to end as it began, in Pacis's game?

Yet Arthur himself loved deeply and was loved in return by his queen. Agravain might accuse him of being blind and boyish in his loyalties, but Gawain could not believe that if Arthur did a thing it was incompatible with kingship.

Gawain remembered when he first arrived at Camelot. He'd been little more than a boy, gangly and awkward. He came alone, on a broken-winded pony with a woollen blanket around his shoulders instead of a cloak against the weather. Arthur was going to send for him in a year or two, but Gawain could no longer wait. He had witnessed his father's barbarity for the last time and he would not stay at Din Eityn any longer. The morning was grey with rain and fog. Gawain was coughing worse than his enfeebled mount and his head felt flushed with fever. Worst of all, he was lost. Cursing himself, cursing his pony, the weather, his father, Agravain who had let him leave alone, and anything else he could think of, Gawain bowed his head under the misting rain and tried to urge the exhausted pony a little further.

Then, he heard hoofbeats, and like a spectre or a dream, the dark shape of a man on horseback formed out of the fog, bearing down fast on Gawain. Gawain had barely time to see him, let alone to goad his pony to action, but the horseman must have been an expert, for he swung his great mount to the right, close enough that the breeze of his passing flapped the edges of Gawain's sodden blanket-cloak.

The horseman wheeled around and came trotting back. Gawain saw a man with a neatly trimmed beard, a thick cloak and kind eyes.

'Are you all right, lad?' the man asked.

Gawain promptly fainted.

When he woke again, it was to warmth that had nothing to do with fever, but belonged instead to the pallet bed underneath him and the thick blankets of fur piled over him. Around him were the snowy walls of a fine pavilion. A fire burned cheerily at its centre, filling the air with the scent of applewood.

Gawain struggled to sit up, appalled at how weak he felt.

'Steady, young man,' said a soft voice, while soft hands pushed him forward so that he might sit. 'You've been ill these past seven days.'

The speaker moved into his field of vision. It was a grey-eyed woman in a simple green dress. Gawain stared, no, he gaped, for he had never seen anyone so fair in his whole life, and then she smiled and her beauty doubled. It was a long moment before he realized the gleam of gold at her throat was from a torque made in the shape of a swan with its long neck curved around her neck.

Torque. The old symbol of kingship. Gawain's befuddled brain started and stumbled like a reluctant horse. He was closer to Camelot than he had hoped, or feared.

'Your Majesty,' he tried to bow and clutch the furs to him at the same time, for, he belatedly realized, he was naked.

Queen Guinevere accepted the gesture with a regal nod, as if he had been properly attired and armed and in the great hall, instead of on a cot shivering with the effort of sitting up.

'Please, Majesty, I need to speak with the High King. I have come from Goddodin to see him.'

The queen held up her hand. 'He is already on his way. He asked to be sent for when you woke.' She gestured to a maid who had been in the pavilion's shadows. The girl came forward with a tunic of soft, white wool for Gawain to slip

over his shoulders. The queen herself piled furs and pillows
behind his shoulders so that he might sit without strain. She
directed her woman to hold a cup of warm wine and herbs
for him to sip.

More awake, it occurred to Gawain that he had not told
the queen his name. She knew nothing of his rank or person,
and yet she did all this, and she had nursed him to health.
A kind of giddiness seized him and Gawain suddenly felt that
he would slay lions with his bare hands if this woman asked
him to.

A moment later, the flap that served the pavilion as a door
was pushed back. Maid and queen alike curtsied as two men
entered the tent. First came the horseman. This time Gawain
saw that he too wore a golden torque. His bore the long,
lithe shape of a dragon with ruby eyes. Gawain had never
before seen his uncle, but no one else would dare wear the
dragon in this country. Seven days ago, he had almost got
himself killed by High King Arthur.

Behind the king came a lean man dressed in black, who
was a good handspan taller than the king, despite the fact
that he leaned heavily on a crutch to support a thin and
crooked leg.

'What's this?' said the lame man, looking Gawain up and
down. 'Surely it's a fish that needs to be dropped back into
its pond.'

'Leave off, Kai,' said Arthur Pendragon amiably. 'I'll wager
the boy's had enough bad luck without adding the rough
side of your tongue to his misfortunes.' His right eye closed
to Gawain in a half-wink. 'Now then, lad, what brought you
out in such weather to the king's maying?'

Maying? It was May Day? He'd been on the road a full
month, wandering south and west. 'I'm sorry, Majesty,'
Gawain stammered. 'I didn't know. I was looking for
Camelot.'

'And instead Camelot found you.' The man, Kai's, eyebrows rose. 'How propitious for the fishes.'

'Kai.' This time there was a note of warning in the king's voice. 'What is your business at Camelot then?'

Gawain hung his head. He was going about this completely wrong. He had spent a month on pony-back rehearsing his speech for when he met the king and queen. He had pictured himself kneeling, straight-backed, in the great hall of Camelot, pledging his fealty. Now he was propped up on a cot, forcing the queen herself to take pity on his weakness and he couldn't even get the right words out of his mouth.

'Come lad,' said Arthur Pendragon. 'Whatever your worries, set them aside for the time being. You have my protection here, and my attention. Tell me who you are and what it is you want.'

Gawain looked up into the king's blue eyes and saw that he was absolutely serious. He did not know who this was before him, but it did not matter. Whatever Gawain had to say would be heard and closely considered. He saw wisdom there, and patience, honour and reason. Things he had never seen in his father's eyes.

'My name is Gawain,' he heard himself say. 'And I want to be your champion, Sire.'

All these years later, and Gawain still remembered how he felt when he spoke those words. It had been more than a boy's wish or an attempt at courtly rhetoric. He had given his heart with those words, and never once regretted it. He had thrown himself into learning all he could of martial matters, of riding and using sword and spear. He studied the old Roman ways of leading men into battle and conducting the fight once it was joined. But it had been much more than that. Arthur had given him over to tonsured monks who forced Latin and a whole range of more vulgar languages into his reluctant mind until he could read and write them,

and speak without tripping over his own tongue. Each
challenge, each hurdle his uncle placed before him, had deepened Gawain's love for the man. For in those tasks, even the
ones that involved nothing but parchment and ink, Arthur
said that he trusted Gawain to keep his promises, that he
felt Gawain worthy of his place, that Gawain could be more
than a barbarian chieftain whose pride was even more
important than the lives of his children. Gawain could be a
champion and worthy of the name.

Someone whom one day a woman noble and beautiful
like Queen Guinevere would look on with love.

Time and again he thought he had found such a woman,
but time and again, he found that he had been deceived, or
that he had deceived himself. Gawain knew he had wept as
often as he had been wept over.

But now there was Rhian, and Gawain allowed himself
to hope that this once there was no deception. If he tried to
explain to Agravain that this time, this lady, was different
and above all the others, his brother would only laugh. But
no other lady had ever come to his aid, none had put themselves in more than lover's danger for him. Rhian had risked
not just her precious reputation but her life, for him.

Even Agravain must in time see that was a true sign of
heart's love.

'My Lord Gawain!' a voice startled him out of his reverie.
'My lord! Your attention, please!'

A small boy that Gawain recognized as one of the servants
in Bannain's hall came running up to him. Gawain stared
around himself, uncertain of where in the ruins of Pen
Marhas he was, or how long he had been wandering.

'Sir, you're needed at the hall,' panted the boy.

Gawain nodded for the boy to lead on. It was time to stop
this maundering. He needed to speak with Rhian. He had
not seen her since yesterday, for she needed rest as badly as

he did. He must take counsel with Bannain and afterwards get back on the road to Camelot as soon as possible. When he and Rhian were alone again and out from under Agravain's disapproving glare, he could make the fullness of his heart known to her.

The boy turned at once and ran back the way he'd come, only belatedly remembering to stop and wait for the man he was supposed to bring to catch him up.

The boy led him back into the hall. There, Bannain and Agravain stood at the foot of the dais with a third man. They all turned as Gawain entered. The stranger was haggard. His clothing was of good quality – his tunic trimmed with ribbons, his boots whole and his cloak clasped with bronze – but he had a hunted look about him. His beard and hair were untrimmed and wild. His eyes were shot with blood and sunken with exhaustion, and something else.

The boy bowed to Bannain and ran off as soon as he received his lord's nod.

'Thedu?' said Gawain. 'Agravain? What is the matter here?'

Bannain opened his mouth, but before he could speak, Rhian entered from the back of the hall. She saw Gawain first, and her brow furrowed. Then she turned to the dais and began to make her curtsey, but her gaze lit upon the stranger before she could complete the gesture.

'Father,' she whispered. It was a statement, not a greeting.

'Rhian.' The man's voice was rough and flat, his face without expression.

'What is this?' demanded Gawain of Agravain.

'Lady Rhian ran away from her father's hall. He has come to fetch her back again,' said Agravain as if remarking on the weather. 'As is his right.'

Rhian did not go forward to greet her father, she stayed

where she was, straight and tall, and absolutely alone. 'Is that what you mean to do?' she asked the harried man.

Rygehil of the Morelands, drew his shoulders in, as if he felt some invisible blow fall on his back. 'Did you think you could run away from this . . . from me? I *warned* you, Rhian.' His voice shook with fury as he spoke.

Gawain heard his own blood roaring in his ears. He wanted to grab this man and hurl him to the ground, to break his back and body for daring to come here, for daring to take the light from Rhian's eyes, but he could not move. Law and honour held him, even though his heart cried out for shame.

'Does mother know you've come?' inquired Rhian. She sounded calm, almost careless, but Gawain knew she was struck to her core. He could see it in her wide eyes, in the set of her jaw and the way her hands clutched at her skirts.

'Your mother has taken to her bed. Would you spare her more pain?' Something like hope crossed Rygehil's face. 'Come home.'

'Father.' The word was spoken on the edge of tears, but Rhian stopped and swallowed her sorrow. 'How can you ask that of me?'

Rygehil just shook his head. 'You do not know the damage you have done. But you will do your duty, by God, you will.'

Gawain saw his opening. He stepped forward, his hands made into fists and pressed against his sides lest he forget himself and strike this man down. 'Sir. If you or yours is in distress, come with me to the king. He will . . .'

'The king,' sneered Rygehil. 'Do not speak to me of the king. If I had not been so eager to throw myself at the feet of this king, my wife would not have fallen ill. If there had been no child . . .'

'You blame *me* for this?' Rhian stared at her father. 'Mother Mary preserve us, father, you've gone mad.'

'If you will not make the journey to Camelot, then speak to me,' urged Gawain. 'I stand here for the king.'

'Not in this hall,' snapped Agravain. 'You overreach yourself, Gawain.'

Agravain you are lucky we are in another man's hall. 'Thedu Bannain?'

Bannain turned to Rhian. 'Is this man your father?'

Rhian's mouth moved, shaping words no one could hear. 'Yes,' she said.

'Have you signed a contract of betrothal?'

Rhian lifted her chin. Would she lie? It would be a simple enough lie, and take time to verify, for such a document would have to be searched for. It would give Bannain room to make a different ruling.

But that was not Rhian's way. 'No,' she said.

Bannain shook his head. 'I'm sorry, lady. I cannot bid you stay if your father bids you go.'

'Rhian.' Rygehil spoke the name as an order. It said, 'Come here.'

As if she were a dog. Two spots of colour appeared on Rhian's deathly white cheeks. She did not move.

'I will ask you one thing, in front of these witnesses,' she said, biting off her words. 'Who told you where I was?'

'No one told me,' replied Lord Rygehil heatedly. 'I followed you.'

Without taking her gaze from her father's, Rhian slowly shook her head. 'We were not moving quickly. If you had followed me, you would have caught up with us on the road. I ask again, father. Who told you where I was?'

The man's eyes widened, as if he were on the verge of panic. 'Do not disgrace our name any further, Rhian. You are to come with me now, as you are, and return to your home.'

It was too much. There were old, old laws of host and

guest at work that rank could not overrule, but Gawain could no longer stand to one side. He circled the man, to stand before the dais, before Rhian and even the hall's master, so that Rygehil must look at him. 'She goes to Camelot to plead her case before the High King.'

But Rygehil only drew himself up straight, and to Gawain's shock he recognized Rhian in the gesture. He had not thought to find anything of her in this man. 'She is my daughter! She goes or she stays at *my* pleasure and none of yours. Will you spill my blood here in this hall before its master? Because that is what you will have to do.'

'No blood will be shed here,' said Bannain and his words were solid as stone. He knew his rights in his hall. It would be breaking the oldest laws for Gawain to challenge Rygehil now that Bannain had forbidden it, and Arthur would never excuse him if he tried.

Gawain felt Agravain's eyes boring into his back, but he did not turn. He could not relent. He could not abandon Rhian to this man who against all laws of nature would risk her death and damnation.

'Come before the High King with us,' he said. This man was a lord in his own land under Arthur's rule. There must be some respect for law and sanity in him, or Arthur would never have permitted him to keep his lands. 'If your case is just, he will pass judgement in your favour.'

'There is no case.' Rygehil spat the word. 'She is *mine*, by law and by right. Unless you can produce the priest that married you, my Lord Gawain, you have no claim on her.'

The memory of screams filled Gawain, of pain and barbarity and helpless, helpless rage at needless, useless death. Not again. Not ever again. Not to this woman most of all. Gawain faced her. 'Rhian, you do not have to do this.'

'But she does,' said Agravain, each word a cut with a knife. 'She belongs to her father, and he has spoken. If she is so impious and wanton as to disobey, then it is his judgement she must face and none of yours.'

Rhian rounded on Agravain, her hands clenched at her side, and for a moment Gawain thought she might strike him. 'No more shame, Rhian,' said her father wearily. 'You will come with me now.'

Rhian looked to Bannain, who only shook his head. He had rendered his judgement. It would stand.

Gawain reached out and touched her sleeve. 'I will take you from this place,' he said.

She knew what he did with those words, what old faith between liege and lord he betrayed before witnesses.

She wanted to say yes. He saw that in her as surely as if he saw through to her soul. She reached out and took his hand, and gently removed it from her sleeve. It fell to his side like a dead thing.

'Thank you, Gawain,' she whispered so softly that even he could barely hear. 'God bless you.'

Without looking back, her head held high and proud, Rhian walked to her father's side. He jerked his head, indicating she should precede him from the hall, and she obeyed. Rygehil followed without even a bow in parting.

Gawain did not move. He could not. Rage burned like madness in his blood and if he moved, it would be to reach for a weapon, to strike Rygehil dead, if he had to claw his way through Bannain and Agravain to do it.

Then, she was gone. Gone. Rhian who rode and sang and fought at his side. Who was proud and beautiful and noble of heart and form. How did God permit this? How was such a daughter allowed to have such a father?

He had been clenching his fists so hard for so long, his hands had begun to ache. 'You, Agravain,' he heard himself say. 'You of all men, encouraged that to happen.'

But in Agravain's answer there was no regret. 'To do

otherwise would be for Arthur to lose a liegeman and perhaps start another small war. He does not need such weakness now.'

'Her father sold her to a sorcerer!' *How can you be blind to this? How can you not care?*

'It is his right,' replied Agravain evenly.

'No, Agravain. No.' Gawain's head wagged back and forth, as if he had turned to an old woman. Perhaps he had. He felt that weak.

Agravain grasped his brother's arm. *A moment ago you would have lost that hand, brother.* 'I did not say it *is* right Gawain, but it is *his* right. Let it go. Do you want to help the woman? Finish this nonsense quickly and help drive the Saxons and their friends back into their holes. Then you may ransom her for whatever she's worth.'

Gawain stared at his brother. No. Not even Agravain's heart could be as hard as that. But Agravain did not flinch under his gaze, nor did he offer any other solution. He only said, 'You are not a fool, Gawain. You see how much may hang in the balance here.'

Resolve took hold inside Gawain. 'Oh yes, Agravain. Yes, I do see.'

Gawain turned to his host and bowed. Bannain had not spoken. What could he say? He had ruled as he must, according to the law. He was a good man, but duty could be harsh.

'You will excuse me, thedu,' he said. 'There is much to be done.'

Before even his brother could say another word, Gawain left the hall, heading towards the barracks. There were things he needed to collect, matters to arrange before anything could be forbidden or turned into rumour. It would be a long, long time before he stood under this roof again.

As he passed the women's quarters, a flicker of movement caught his eye and he looked up involuntarily to see Pacis standing in the doorway. Her eyes were red with weeping, and she seemed faded with the weight of her weariness. And even then, he remembered the touch of her, the scent of her, his sheer, unfathomable need for her that had let him fall back into her arms even knowing that she had broken every promise to him she had sworn came from her heart.

'Gawain,' she murmured. 'Do not leave me. Not now.'

Gawain stopped and stood. Pacis reached towards him and he looked at her fine, white hand.

'I'm sorry, my lady,' he said. 'I cannot do as you ask.'

He bowed, and he left her there. Rhian needed him and there could be no more delay.

Kerra was trembling with fury and fear when she returned to Morgaine's hall. All during her flight, her companions had called anxiously after her, dismayed at her anger and her silence. It was only with the sharpest of orders that they stayed outside the hall, clinging to the eaves and creeling like chicks.

She had been a fool. She had depended too much on her army and had not attended to what must be done herself. She knew better and now she would take her punishment. She deserved it richly.

She did not even acknowledge Talan as she strode past. It did not matter that she had left Wolfget weeping and ready to throw himself on his sword. It didn't matter that Harrik lay dead on the field and that her friends had feasted upon him for his failure. What mattered was that failure, which was hers so much more than theirs, for she ruled over them.

But not well enough.

Morgaine sat in her great, carved chair. Her eyes glittered in the dim light of the hall. The women drew back and whispered as Kerra passed. She did not care. She knew that Morgaine had already seen the truth of what had happened.

There was nothing left to do but what she did now, kneel at her mistress's feet.

'I failed, mistress.' The words fell like tears. 'I did not look. I did not see.'

There was no answer. She closed her eyes so she would not try to read her future in the patterns of the straw strewn over the hard stones. She would be turned away, cast out, and it would be only just.

But she felt Morgaine's fingertips touch her shoulder. Hope leapt inside her.

'It would have done no good. I know now the girl was not fated to die in Pen Marhas. She has been given help for those sharp eyes of hers and is too well protected.'

Kerra dared to lift her eyes. She could see no anger in Morgaine, only mild regret. It did not matter. She was angry enough for both of them. 'I should have snapped Gawain's neck with my own hands rather than leave him for those barbarians.'

Morgaine shook her head. 'I do not speak of Gawain.'

'Who then?' *What else have I missed?*

'The Green Man,' her mistress answered in a tone akin to wonder.

As well she might. The Green Man, Jack-in-the-Green, was one of the oldest and most elusive of all the ancient gods. He had always been, he always would be, the most secret, most changeable heart of the isle. Stunned, Kerra forgot discretion. 'Why would such a one as he aid a child who is no one and nothing?'

'Foolish question.' For the first time, Morgaine sounded annoyed. Kerra hastily bowed her head in apology. 'Have I taught you no better? He is a power and a wild one. He does so because it is his wish, because he knows what we cannot and walks where we may not go. Such a one as he needs no other reason and may not be gainsaid.' She spoke the last words with a flat finality. 'We are done with this. Leave your Easterner. If he is so foolish as to walk in the Green Man's footsteps, let him be.'

Her words sank in. As they did, a shout rose in the back of Kerra's mind. *No!* her thoughts screamed. *We have come too far, done too much! We cannot lose to a fading and hidden god, neglected and forgotten by all men. How can you let this difficulty cut you off from your triumph?*

It was unthinkable that she should say any of this, especially before the anger smouldering behind her mistress's eyes. Morgaine did not wish to be diverted from their course, but she was cautious. She cared about those who followed her and would not move unless she was certain the move would succeed. Perhaps, just perhaps, this was the time for a bolder strike.

'Even the Green Man must obey the laws, mistress. There are ways that he may be approached and times when promises may be exacted.'

Slowly, Morgaine left behind the anger into which she was sinking. She frowned down at her student. Kerra did not know how she found the strength to hold her head up before that frown, but she did.

'Kerra, what have I taught you about the old powers?'

Honour them, but do not treat with them. The oldest games are not for mortal players. 'Yes, mistress, I know, but this is not seeking to harness one to do our work. Our plans . . . your plans . . . are in jeopardy. If he cannot be countered, there may be no other chance. Arthur will only solidify his hold here and abroad.'

Morgaine did not answer immediately. 'It is bad that the Green Man walks with the girl,' she acknowledged at last.

'It is almost Beltane, mistress,' said Kerra eagerly. 'That is a time when a boon may be exacted. Let me do this.'

Morgaine laid a hand on Kerra's shoulder and looked into

her eyes for a long time. Kerra held herself straight and still under her mistress's gaze, though she felt as if the secrets of her soul must surely be laid bare. It was of no matter. Morgaine would see how well she served. Morgaine would know her true strength at last, and there would be no more waiting. They would destroy Merlin, they would take Camelot, and Morgaine would have her vengeance, and Kerra would have her freedom.

'Very well,' said Morgaine slowly. 'But if you seek to bind or barter with Jack-in-the-Green you must do it with the greatest care. One wrong word can skew a bargain with such a power. A missed courtesy or an ill-conceived phrase can put you into his power rather than he in yours, and that must not be.' Her voice softened such as Kerra had never heard before. 'I cannot do without you, Kerra.'

Kerra bowed her head. 'Gawain will lose his Rhian, and Arthur will lose Gawain, and the Easterner will be blamed for all. I will see this done. I swear it. All will be as you desire.'

'Yes,' Morgaine said with her knowing smile, laying her hand atop Kerra's head. 'It will.'

TWELVE

Father had meant it when he said she was to leave at once, as she was. With him at her heels, she was not permitted to turn aside to take any sort of leave of her hostess nor to reclaim her possessions. Bow, jewellery, clothes, all were to be left behind. Even Thetis, steady loyal Thetis, who had made her way straight back to the hall's stable after she fled in the fire, was to be left behind. Two brown horses, one with white fetlocks, one with a forehead blaze, stood before the hall in their harness. Father did not even speak to the boys who held the reins. He just swung himself up into the saddle and looked down at Rhian, waiting for her to do the same.

Perhaps he was waiting for her to demur, to threaten, to beg. She did none of these. She allowed the nearest boy to help her onto the second horse and met her father's gaze. Relief was written plainly on his features. But it was equally plain he did not trust her any further. He reached over and twitched the reins out of her hands.

'I will not run,' she said stonily.

Father did not answer. With a quick dig of his heels, he urged his horse to motion, leading her mount down the gentle slope, out through the gates and across the devastation that had been the fields of Pen Marhas.

Father did not look back. It seemed clear to Rhian that he would ride the whole way in silence if he had his choice. She was not ready to bestow that mercy upon him. He would not deliver her like a sack of wheat. 'What did mother say when you told her you were coming here?' asked Rhian, raising her voice to cross the distance he kept between them.

'She does not know,' he answered without turning around. 'I told you, she has taken to her bed.'

Those words cut through Rhian's anger. 'She is ill?'

'God willing, that's all it is.'

Rhian bowed her head. What had happened in the past weeks could make the strongest woman take to her bed. The idea of mother languishing in sickness made her want to drive her heels into this dispirited horse's ribs and gallop home with all speed. But what would that do? She would not be allowed to stay and nurse her mother. She would not be allowed to do anything but be the sacrifice her father was determined to make her.

Do not lose sight of what is truly happening. Do not permit him to work on your heart.

'Who told you where I was, father?' she repeated the question he would not answer before Bannain. 'There are at least three halls in these hills where I could have been. You did not have time to visit each of them.'

'I tried to let you go, Rhian.' She had to strain to hear the words he spoke so softly. 'I did try. But your mother fell ill and the sorcerer came. What would you have me do?' He raised his head and Rhian wondered if he was asking her, or God.

God had no immediate answer, so it was up to Rhian. 'Go to the High King, speak with his cunning man Merlin,' she said as adamantly, as persuasively as she could. 'Let them be your liege lords as they are sworn, and come to your aid.'

'And your mother dies.'

Rhian's heart ached with that thought. Father's dull, certain repetition of it chilled her to the bone. 'At least it will not be you that kills her.'

Her father made no reply and Rhian watched what little of his face she could see. She saw shame there, and determination and fear. She imagined regret, a great crushing load of that. What she did not see was any sign that he would change his mind. There was help. Why would he not see that? Why would he not try? And why, *why* would he not ask mother what she wanted? Why did he not consult her?

Guilt settled itself on Rhian's back. She imagined her mother lying still and pale in her bed with ancient Una trying to spoon broth and beer into her mouth. Sorcerers had all manner of means of casting a curse from a distance. This one with his snake's eyes that would make such a bargain as father had told her of, would not shrink from keeping it.

The correct thing, the dutiful thing, was to commend herself to God and do as she was told. Would not prayer and faith keep her safe, or at least assure her a place in Heaven when all was over? If she prayed hard enough, God might even grant her a miracle as he did his saints. A flock of doves, or some such, to bear her away from the sorcerer's clutches.

But Rhian knew she was no saint, and she knew in all honesty she lacked the heart to become a martyr. Did father count on her piety to save her? Did he believe that much?

Rhian looked at him again. He must have felt her gaze on him, because he glanced sideways at her and flinched, directing his eyes immediately forward again.

In that moment, Rhian saw the truth and it cut through her like the blade of a sword.

'You're not doing this for mother,' she whispered. 'You're doing this because you're afraid he'll kill you as well.'

'No.' The word came out low and harsh.

You're lying. 'Yes. You're thinking to yourself, "I'm still young enough. I can marry again. I can still father other children, if only I live."' They were hard words, horrible words. No daughter should speak so.

No father should act so.

'No,' he said again. The horse danced under him as his agitation became clear.

But Rhian could not stop. Once, just once, the truth would be told before God, if it never was again. If she would die, it would be knowing the whole of what had happened. 'Who put those thoughts in your head? Was it him? Was it the sorcerer that turned you into such a coward?'

His horse whickered and Rhian's answered, breaking its stride and protesting at being led. 'You will be quiet!'

'I will not!' She knotted her hands in her horse's mane. If it was going to balk, she would keep her seat. She would not be shaken off. 'You wanted me with you, father. Now you have me. If I were going to submit meekly to my doom, I would never have run this far.'

'God's wounds, Rhian!' Father turned his horse so that he could face her. Her own mount snorted uneasily, and there was little she could do to comfort the animal as it champed at its bit. 'Why are you so anxious to condemn your mother to death? Or damnation? Have you thought of that? Have you thought what happens to her soul if this sorcerer kills her without a priest to give her grace?'

'Have you sent for a priest?' She saw from his shocked face that he had not. 'All these fears, all these protests that I must do my duty and you have not even done that for her!'

Father was silent for a moment, and she watched his face flush with the anger burning beneath his skin. 'Do you want the truth, Rhian? Do you?' He threw down the reins he had clutched so tightly. A new steel edged his voice and he urged his horse forward so that they were side by side. Rhian saw not very far beneath his eyes a wildness that she had never known in him before, not even when he was at his worst for drink. 'Very well, I will tell you. What will I gain from giving my wilful, heedless, undutiful child to this man? I gain my wife's life, my own, and my son.'

'*What?*'

Father smiled, and even in the burning of Pen Marhas Rhian had never seen anything so grim and terrible. 'Your brother, Rhian, who was taken from us while still in his swaddling bands. He will be given back to us once you are with Euberacon. I will have a son again.'

'Oh, father, no.'

But this time he made no answer. He turned his head forwards and set his jaw.

If Rhian felt cut to the heart before, now she felt as if flayed and laid bare upon the butcher's table.

'This is a devil's bargain, father. God will not forgive.'

'Then so be it.' He pulled his horse's head roughly around to turn the beast, ignoring its sharp whicker of protest. 'I will have my wife's love again, and I will have my son.' He took up her reins again and Rhian watched him. She realized she could have taken them up herself, could have ridden away, but she had been too shocked to move, and now it was too late.

This was madness. This was damnation, and father would drag them all down with him, because of his obsession. A devil's bargain? The devil had no need to bargain with him anymore. The devil had him. The devil had gained him years ago, and had only now decided to claim him.

What could she do? There had to be something. But where could she go? She did not know the way to Camelot. She did not even know the extent of Lord Bannain's lands, and if she were caught anywhere in them, his judgement had already been passed and she would simply be returned to father. At home? With mother ill and Whitcomb dead? Aeldra would help, but there would be no time to plan or to act. The sorcerer might even be waiting.

She had failed. Failed. For all her defiance, for all her arrogance and bravado, she was lost.

Rhian's father rode ahead, and never once looked back while his daughter's heart broke in two.

The day wore on. Rhian rode in a daze, with nothing to do but keep her seat on the slow-stepping horse. The light brightened and faded as clouds scudded across the sky. The wind smelled of rain. They came again to the forest, and it was shady and cool. The road began to rise beneath them. They were leaving the valley.

All of this Rhian was aware of only distantly. The whole of her mind was consumed with her own sorrow. She could not even muster anger anymore. Her very heart felt too tired to try. She thought of escape. She thought of suicide. They seemed one and the same. She could not move. She could not decide. She could not even weep.

Her horse checked its stride, snorting its consternation. Rhian looked up, more from reflex than interest.

A man on horseback blocked the road. He had a short sword drawn. At first all she saw was the Saxon's helm, its guard chased and moulded to the shape of a bear's maw, and the leather jerkin and the shaggy horse. Terror brought mind and heart back to life with one painful lurch.

Then she saw the man beneath, and the green trappings on the horse's reins, and she knew who it was.

'Stand off, Rhian.' Father drew his knife. Rhian did not move.

'I know you, Lord Gawain!' father cried. 'You have no right here!'

But Gawain, in his clumsy Saxon's disguise only put his heels to the horse's sides and charged.

It was over in a moment. He barrelled past father, and dealt him a blow, not with the sword, but rather with the side of his fist. Father sprawled on the stones of the road. Gawain swung the balky horse around, and caught up Rhian's horse's reins. Before father could get to his feet, her mount was trotting obediently after Gawain.

Rhian looked back and saw her father, alone and wretched in the middle of the road. He shrank smaller and darker until she could not bear to look anymore, and faced forwards again, letting the tears flow unhindered down her cheeks.

Although no hoofbeats or shouts followed them, Gawain did not halt, nor did he turn to speak, until they had left two hills behind them and were surrounded again by stones rather than by trees. A shepherd leaned against one of the green-flecked boulders, one eye on their approach, one eye on his flock. Gawain reined his borrowed horse up before the man, who unfolded himself slowly. He vanished into a fodder shed, and emerged again with Gringolet on one side of him and Thetis on the other. More used to sheep than horses, he did not hold the charger's bridle tightly enough, and Gringolet swung his head casually to jerk himself free and trotted up to his master. Gawain tossed a coin to the shepherd that glinted silver. The man caught it out of the air with one hand and inclined his head.

Gawain helped Rhian down from her horse. He gave the animal a smack on its flank. It snorted at the insult and gladly trotted away, heading for whatever stable it called home, or perhaps towards whatever new master was lucky enough to catch it. Rhian stayed where she was, caught somewhere between not quite believing what had happened and not quite understanding it. Thetis nuzzled her ear. Rhian pushed her away absently. Gawain held the mare's bridle and Rhian mounted mechanically. Thetis stamped and whickered but Rhian could not seem to remember what the reins she held were for. Thetis, though, was content to follow Gringolet, and Rhian was content to let her and they rode once more into the hills, heading north and east again, avoiding the valley and keeping to the hills. The clouds overhead thickened, the wind grew brisk and the sounds of the birds and the trees grew restless.

Then, the horses' hooves found the stones of the highway again. Gawain reined his horse up short, bringing them all to a halt. He dismounted and came to Thetis's side. He held up his hands. Rhian let herself be helped from the saddle. She stood before him, feeling the clean wind, wondering when the rain would come, and understanding that something important had happened, but she could not think what it might be.

'It is over, Rhian,' said Gawain softly. 'It is done. You are safe.'

'Safe,' she said dully. She looked up at him, at his beautiful face, and felt nothing. Nothing at all.

'Rhian, what did he do to you?'

'Nothing.' She shook her head violently, trying to shake loose the truth, trying to shake life and sense back into herself. 'Nothing new, in truth.' She pressed her palms against her eyes. Her heart felt heavy as lead, her mind's confusion would not clear. 'But he wouldn't . . . he didn't . . . Ah, God help me, I can't, I won't . . .'

Gawain took hold of both her shoulders. She stared up at him, startled by the gesture. 'I know, Rhian,' he said, looking into her eyes. 'You must believe me, I do understand. If you cannot shield yourself with anger, then mourn him. Mourn him for the father you once loved. It is all you can do for him now.'

Those words broke the malaise that held her, and Rhian began to cry, as she had when she first saw him. Gawain wrapped his arms around her and drew her close, holding her safe from falling while she cried for her father, for the good man who had once resided in his heart and been murdered by Euberacon's black promises and his own weakness. After a time, she grew quiet, and still Gawain held her, enveloping her in warmth of body and soul, and drained dry of grief she found in that warmth the thing she desired above all else – peace.

'Is my lady well?'

'No,' she admitted. 'But I will be. My . . . Gawain, I owe you . . .'

He shook his head, cutting off her words. 'Let there be no talk of debt between us, Rhian.'

She felt herself smile. 'What talk shall there be then?'

She had meant it as a joke, but his face remained solemn. Carefully, he reached out and touched the line of her jaw. His touch was exceedingly gentle, and the warmth of it went at once to her blood.

'Shall I say it, then? Does my lady permit her servant to speak his heart before her?'

Rhian found her mouth had gone dry. Her heart pounded so that she could feel its pulse in her throat. But she nodded. This once, no matter what happened next, this once, she would hear him say what she longed to hear.

'Then let me speak of love, Rhian. If I were granted a poet's tongue I would fashion you a song that would last down the ages and sear the souls of all who heard it. But as I am, I can only speak in the plainest words. I love you. I

love your courage and your noble heart. I love your song
and story. I love your face and form, and I shall never cease
to love the whole of you as long as God may grant me life.'

Rhian had no words to answer him. What words could
there be? There was no verse, no vow that could be enough
for what she felt. Instead, she kissed him. He was startled
for a heartbeat, and then returned the kiss, with passion,
with longing, with deepest love.

This, then, was what the poets told of. This was how one
knew. One knew because the whole soul sang of it, because
even the broken heart rejoiced.

Both an instant and an age passed before they parted.
Rhian found herself breathless and strangely light, as if she
might fly up into the air at any moment. Gawain, however,
seemed to become more solid, as if his declaration of love
had given him roots much more than wings.

'Come, Rhian,' he said, taking her hand. Even that simple
gesture now was filled with his warmth. 'Let me get you safe
away from here to where there are stout walls and strong
friends around us.'

But there was one thing. One last thing before she began
this journey afresh. 'Gawain, do you think . . . will Queen
Guinevere send for my mother if I ask it? She cannot stay
in my father's hall, not with . . .'

Gawain did not require that she finish. 'I am sure that the
queen will do so, as soon as she knows the full story. It may
be that Merlin himself will ride out to fetch your mother for
you.'

'Thank you.'

Gawain's eyes sparkled as he bowed. Then, sweeping his
short Saxon cloak back with a flourish, he knelt on the road
and cupped his hands for her step up. Rhian lifted her nose
haughtily to her stepping-stool and permitted him to help
her back onto her horse. He stood and bowed humbly, and

when he dared to lift his eyes to her again, Rhian could no longer keep her countenance and they laughed, long and loud and freely.

When at last their laughter had spent itself, Gawain mounted his riding horse and turned the animal so it faced the way they must travel.

A thought came to Rhian. 'Your brother will not be pleased.'

But Gawain only smiled. 'Agravain will not be pleased when God Almighty raises him from the dust on the last day. It is far more than mortal man can accomplish.'

Side by side they set themselves on the road to Camelot.

Walking the streets of Caer Ludien, Euberacon saw the ruins of greatness on every side. The temple of Mithras crumbled in on itself, the roads were buckled and potholed, even the bridge had begun to list to one side. There were some great houses that still looked habitable, even well appointed, but most had fallen down, leaving heaps of rubble to be over-grown by encroaching greensward, or shored up by mud and thatch hovels with wicker fences. Some efforts had been made to repair the wall, at least. Even a Saxon could see the need for defence.

The market was still there. It was a sea of mud, and the tiny warehouses looked as if they could barely hold enough cargo for one of the natives' little coracles to carry. But there were ships berthed at the broad river's edge. Fat valley sheep milled about in their pens. Tall, blooded horses from Andalucia gazed about with scorn. Men sat at rickety tables, examining samples of metals or artisan work, hunched over their cups, speaking the universal language of barter.

He had heard that in the days of the Romans this place had been bustling, its ports crammed with ships come for wool, enamel, tin, silver, lead and slaves. Arthur was working to restore the Britons' trade, but so far the results had been meagre indeed. The Saxon overlord who held this place was both arrogant and greedy. Arthur had flattered and traded, and bribed and bullied, and had some measure of success. At least now his people could walk here unmolested.

The air by the river was somewhat fresher than in the warren of the ruinous city streets, with fewer smoky fires and stinking animals wandering free. Little dark men had set up tables, or just stacked up crockery jugs, to sell the black beer and fiery liquor the Saxons were learning to relish along with their native mead. They squatted in the mud or on chunks of broken stone, trading lies and drinks, growing more raucous and unsteady with each round. There would be fights before long, and the traders would have to look to their tents and their sheep.

In the middle of this display of barbarity was a small island of civility. A clean-shaven man with his black hair swept back from a high, intelligent forehead, wearing a dark blue cloak, surveyed the ruffians over the top of a clay liquor cup. He wore a short sword at his hip, and held himself as if he knew how to use it, but his real protection clearly came from the two square men who flanked him with their axes in their hands and their knives in their belts. He conversed with another man who looked to be from Greece, or perhaps Crete. Both were sun-browned and clean, well barbered and unafraid. Envy gnawed at Euberacon's heart as he strode forwards.

The man in the blue cloak saw the magus approach and touched his companion's elbow, saying something softly. He set the liquor cup on the rickety table without any sign of having touched its contents and came forward, his hand outstretched.

'Magister,' he said as they clasped each other's arms. 'God!

How do you bear it here? It's no wonder the Romans fled this place.'

'I prefer life to death, Quintus,' Euberacon replied blandly. It felt good to speak his native language again. The patterns rolled comfortably off his tongue. 'But come, give me the news.'

Quintus looked around him, but the only man who might possibly understand what they spoke of stood over by the Andalucian horses, and he was already deep in conversation with their keeper. Even so, Euberacon moved them away from the liquor-sellers to stand by a fragment of brick wall that had somehow remained standing. Quintus's body guards followed, repositioning themselves to better keep up their watch. 'The news is good. Justinian has ideas about tax collection that have upset many.'

Euberacon snorted. 'That is to say he means to collect them.'

'The fog has not entirely dampened your mind,' said Quintus with a nod. 'Yes, that's it exactly and both the Greens and the Blues are making noises that something needs to be done about it.'

The idea of those two parties uniting should have been laughable, but an emperor who actually meant to enforce the tax laws might just drive the rivals together. 'Have any of them a plan?'

'Not yet, but they do have a man, or a boy at any rate.'

'Who?'

'Hypatius. He's a nephew of old Anastasius.'

Anastasius had been emperor when Euberacon's father was a boy. Content with having enough in the treasury to fill the Hippodrome with chariot teams and exotic animal acts, he had never bothered anyone for more than that. Just the sort the richest citizens of Constantinople would prefer to have wearing the purple.

'Has he any strength of character about him?'

Quintus shrugged. 'Not that I've seen, but that may be all to the good. Justinian has strength of character and to spare.'

Quintus was a smuggler. Euberacon had in the past bought a number of jewels and poisons from the man that should not have been sold. If Justinian meant to enforce the tax laws, what else did he mean to enforce and who would he empower to do that enforcement? It was hideously expensive to bribe honest men.

'And Justinian's woman?'

'You had best learn to call her empress,' said Quintus, leaning against the broken wall. 'They are to be married.'

No. Euberacon felt his spine straighten one joint at a time. 'Impossible. The law forbids a patrician to marry an . . . actress.'

'Justinian is changing the law.'

Euberacon pressed his hand against the wall. The rough bricks scraped his palm. Theodora, the daughter of a whore and a dead bear-keeper. Theodora was to be *empress*? It could not be. It could not! If she wore the purple . . . if she were legitimized . . . he was trapped here in this place of mud and cold. He could never go home. He was lost.

'It will not happen,' he said through clenched teeth. 'I will not permit it.'

'Magister,' said Quintus carefully. 'You'll need money to buy your way back in. You are a joke in the city now, the great magus chased out by Justinian's whore.'

Euberacon ignored that. 'Before two more winters have passed, I will have enough wealth even for Byzantium, and then we will make Justinian regret his choice of wife.'

Quintus's face wrinkled as he looked over Euberacon's shoulder at the crumbling city. 'I don't want to doubt you, magister, but . . . how are you going to find that much gold out here?'

Euberacon smiled. 'Even the barbarians have their gilded idols. The one they call the High King, Arthur, has a treasury stuffed with wealth his father raided from the Romans as they fled.'

'You're going to bring down a barbarian king to bring down an emperor to bring down a woman?' Quintus looked as if he did not know whether to be impressed, or appalled.

Euberacon only smiled. 'You will tell the ones who should know in the city that men and treasure will be coming to their aid?'

Now Quintus just looked sceptical, but he shrugged again. He knew Euberacon well enough to know he did not make promises he could not keep. 'They will be glad to hear it.'

They spoke of politics awhile longer, of who was heading up the Blues and who the Greens, and of who had decided to throw their lot in with Justinian, and what shape those shifting loyalties were taking, of who was yet living and who had suddenly died. The men of this island thought themselves fierce because they would kill each other over a handful of cows? They knew nothing. In Constantinople, a man could be murdered for training animals too well, or for keeping the horses for the wrong chariot team, and no one would think of it twice, as long as the proper bribes had been paid.

Almost no one.

It took awhile, but at last, Quintus's store of news and gossip was emptied. Regretfully, Euberacon held out his hand again. 'I must bid you farewell, Quintus. I have business to attend to here, and then I must go see that an item I have need of has been acquired.'

They clasped arms again. Whatever Quintus thought of Euberacon's chances of success here, he kept it to himself. It didn't matter, as long as he told those who needed to know that Euberacon would return, as long as he came back next year to bring the news and to remind Euberacon of the world beyond these shores.

The world to which I will soon return, Euberacon told himself as he walked away from the trader and the river, heading back into Caer Ludien's smoke and shadows. *Where I will take my rightful place, and make Theodora wish she had kept hers.*

Euberacon had been meant for a clerk. His father had paid a decent bribe to get him apprenticed to a secretary in the imperial warehouses. It was a good enough position from which he could rise to a reasonable level of prominence, but not so close to the imperial palace that he would have to be made a eunuch to gain an appointment, nor that politics would get in his way, if he were quiet and kept his head down.

That was his father's ideal. Work hard, take what you were given. Stay quiet and uninvolved, and you could live a good life. He had no ambition, no courage, no ability to understand why his son might be plagued with discontent.

But Euberacon saw a world around him that made no sense, a world of wealth he could never have, of secrets and powers he would never know. So much that was forever shut off, so much that was shifted without warning and yet could not be made to shift by the likes of him. Why? Be content and trust in God, his father said. But how could one trust in a God that was so far away, and who tormented even his chosen people?

He might have learned contentment eventually. He might have become the private secretary for some prominent citizen and found his place in intrigues enough to believe he was actually shaping the world around him in some fundamental way. Instead, however, his master, Lucius, decided to give Euberacon access to his library. Lucius, and his father,

and his grandfather, it seemed, had all drilled their appren-
tices by having them make copies of books and public
documents, and then keeping those copies for themselves.
Euberacon had never seen so many books in one man's hands
before. He spent all of his free time in that bright room with
its high windows. He pestered Lucius to teach him Greek
and Arabic as well as Latin so he could decipher some of the
older texts.

It was in that room, late one night, by the yellow light
of an oil lamp, that he found the book on necromancy.

At first he thought he was reading some fable, but it quickly
became clear they were recipes – for love, for divination, for
finding what was lost, for guarding, for poison. It explained
the nature of several of the various demons and of angels,
and when they might be summoned, and what they might
be called on to do. It explained that any man, be he pure of
body and of learning and intelligence, could have this mastery
over the invisible.

Such promises were made in the market every day. This
unguent would bring beauty. That amulet wealth. Euberacon
shut the volume and returned it to its place, but he came back
to it time and again, reading over the mysteries, wondering if
he had been wrong. What if God was not distant after all.
What if the divine and the ethereal were close beside him?

'Could it really be reached out and touched so simply?'

'Not so simply.'

Master Lucius stood in the library doorway. Euberacon
made some feeble attempt to hide the book, but soon realized it was pointless. His master already knew what it was
he read, and what was more, he was pleased.

'Much of what that book says is pure foolishness.' Lucius
was a tall man, and he crossed the library in three strides,
lifting the slim, red volume out of Euberacon's hands. 'But
there is enough of truth in it to begin with.' He smiled and

ran his hand across the leather binding. 'You have the talent, Euberacon. I saw it in you. You can learn the high arts, if you want.'

Euberacon did not hesitate for so much as a heartbeat. 'Yes, master. I do.'

That night, Euberacon had dared the curfew and crept out to the city walls. He had sat on the warm stones beneath the sky's million stars and he'd thought about what the book said, about the angels and how each ruled a day and an hour, about the devils and their ranks and orders. It seemed to him that all that was solid had become soft, like clay, and that it could be moulded and worked, and if one could speak to the hands that moulded it, if one could tell them what to do . . . then anything was possible. Even for a clerk with a mouse for a father.

It was no wonder the Father Church forbade such studies. It was a dangerous route he undertook. The church disapproved, and while they were willing to tolerate a number of heresies in Constantinople, this was not one of them. If he were caught in its practice, he would die, publicly and painfully. The church, hand-in-hand with the imperial powers, traded on the ignorance of the people and would permit only those they blessed to look into esoteric matters. Master Lucius assured him that if he went into the church, it would be one way he could continue study in safety. But Euberacon did not mean to cloak his studies in a cleric's robe. He would take the other route.

In Constantinople, wealth bought power. Power, in turn, brought safety, and safety brought peace. With enough wealth, he could buy the peace he needed to practise the highest arts. He could study without fear, and he could understand all the greatest secrets, of angels or of devils, of the workings of the universe and how they could be made to turn or not, as *he* chose.

A few of the smallest miracles, and men began to come to him. A chariot race won unexpectedly. A successful prediction, a caught spy, a dead thief. They came with documents to be copied, or to have letters written, and they left with cures and charms, potions and prophecy, and Euberacon's house grew rich with books and fat with secrets. He was able to purchase the dragon's blood and gems, and even poisons needed for the most subtle and complex of summonings. He was able to bribe the proper officials to keep their eyes averted.

Then, a fat and sweaty man calling himself Octavius had come to Euberacon, sodden with drink. He wanted a girl. A girl he had seen that day in the Hippodrome. He would pay to have her, but it could not be done the ordinary way. Her father had worked with the animals, been a bear-keeper or some such. He might still have friends. But he would pay for a love potion so the girl would come to him willingly.

Euberacon had sent him away, staggering even more badly than when he had come. But the fool had returned. He would have his girl. He would pay for her to come to him willingly.

By this time, Euberacon had heard something of the story. Apparently it had been a small and sordid drama. A woman, the wife of the Greens' bear trainer, had stood up in the Hippodrome, before the emperor and all the public, with her two daughters beside her and exhorted, cried, shamed and begged for the pension owing her so that she and those same two daughters would not starve.

'Why not buy the one you want from her, if she's short of money?' Euberacon had asked.

'No, no,' the fat fool had insisted. 'She must come to me. She must be willing. She must love me.'

It was as unsavoury as anything Euberacon had yet done. In addition, it was a complex spell involving a particularly difficult sacrifice. He named an enormous sum. 'Octavius' brought it soon thereafter. Apparently the mother had been only partly successful with her public plea for help and had been forced to put the girls on stage to help earn their keep. He had seen her. She was marvellous. He could not sleep for wanting her.

'Why do this?' Euberacon remembered asking, although he normally cared little what his clientele were doing, unless it might be something of use to know later. 'An actress can be purchased for one-tenth what you give me.'

'No!' cried the fat man, shrinking backward. Beads of sweat rolled down his cheeks. 'She must want me, as I want her! An actress . . . with other men . . . no, no. She must be all mine!'

Euberacon shrugged. He took a white dove and made the sacrifice. He drew the required picture and anointed it with the blood as prescribed. He wrote the necessary runes and said the incantations, and at last added the girl's name. Comito. One look at Octavius while he had the parchment about his person and she would fall madly in love. She would burn for him and forsake everything she had to be at his side.

Euberacon took his payment. Octavius went happily to the theatre. Euberacon continued to back his men, do their favours and pursue his studies in safety.

So he had thought.

No divination, however powerful, could have told him that the other sister, the one he had heard had been reduced to acting and wool-spinning for her keep, would catch the eye of Justinian, Emperor Justin's heir, that she would help guide him through the maze that was politics in Constantinople, where a friend could as easily poison one as a foe, and be raised up herself in return. Any true man would have discarded her, but Justinian did not, and as soon as it became clear power was within her grasp, men began to die.

It seemed her father had not just died. He had been murdered. For money or favour, there were those who would right such wrongs. Theodora now had both, and she was going to find the men who robbed her of her father, and of her sister. Comito, it seemed, had never returned to her family, or anywhere else.

The men who had killed her father went first. 'Octavius' followed shortly thereafter. Euberacon was supposed to have been next.

How she found out it had been him, he did not know. Presumably, if she had assassins in her pay, a magus would not have been too much for her indelicate sensibilities. Or her men could have simply wrung it out of Octavius's fat throat. It didn't matter. What mattered was that she had paid her men enough that they had been willing to chase him up the coast all the way to Gaul and had only given up when he had crossed the sea to this God-forsaken place.

And now this woman was to be empress in Constantinople. Well, let her wear the purple. Let her rule Justinian and the empire for as long as they could stand her. It would be sweet indeed to watch her fall from that highest of all places.

But now there were different men to visit. The Saxons who held this place and the surrounding lands needed to be pricked and pushed. Things were not going well in Pen Marhas, and these men, their southern brothers, had to know of it. These were not men who wanted to believe they were weak, that those farther north and inland were better men than they. Some of them were even intelligent enough to realize that while Arthur's cadre was out poking about in the western lands, his eastern border might be vulnerable for a very little while. These were men who were used to moving quickly, to seizing their opportunities, and Euberacon's business now was to show them what those opportunities were, without them knowing it was he who had done so. There were ways to alter appearance, to make men forget where or how they had heard a thing.

Euberacon smiled at the distant Hippodrome some Roman overlord or the other had built. He'd see the real thing soon enough. The end was already in sight.

But if he was to accomplish anything, he had to work quickly. He wanted to summon his steed and be back in his fortress before the island's night came with its mutterings and mysteries. Still, he would have that under control soon as well. All things were moving at his direction. This was his day, his hour and here he ruled. And if Arthur, Gawain and Theodora did not know that now, they would very, very soon.

Darkness came again. Jocosa's women moved around her, lighting rushes and two good tallow candles. Una came in bearing a bowl that smelled of meat and pepper. Loyal Una. She had used some of the hall's small fortune of spices to tempt her mistress's appetite. She should try to eat. It would be a sin to waste such broth.

'My Lord Rygehil has returned.' Una offered up the news like the bowl of broth, as if one or the other might quicken Jocosa's melancholic spirits.

Jocosa looked at the wooden screen that blocked the window now that night had come. A draught curled around the casements, further seasoning the scent of the broth with the hint of yet more rain. Rygehil had gone to find Rhian. It was her ladies who told her this, not her husband. There was too little left between them that he should think to mention such a thing to her.

But if he was back . . . Slowly, Jocosa's mind put the two facts together, and understood what was being said.

Trembling, she turned towards her waiting woman.

'Is Rhian with him?'

Una dropped her gaze towards the steaming bowl she held, as if aware her efforts were about to be for naught. 'No, mistress.'

'Oh.' There was in truth nothing to be said. Nothing to be done. She had let her daughter go. That was all there was. Everything else had been done long ago.

She remembered her wedding day. She remembered how happy she'd been. Not even her mother's frowns could touch her. 'At least he's blooded,' mother had groused. 'You could have gone and set your heart on some goose boy I suppose.' But nothing had mattered, nothing but Rygehil smiling at her, holding out his hand, speaking his vows clearly and without hesitation, kneeling beside him so they could take communion together, to let God witness that they two were now one person.

One person, one soul, one heart, and that soul was failing and that heart had grown cold.

'Mistress,' began Una tentatively.

She's going to try to make me eat again. Jocosa sighed. The peppery scent was beginning to make her feel ill. She hated to disappoint the woman, but there was nothing to be done about that either.

'Mistress, I heard him say . . . I heard him say . . .'

'Yes?' *If you must speak, Una, please do so and be done.*

'I heard him call her ungrateful, mistress. He'd found her and she ran away again, yesterday on the road from Pen Marhas, she'd gone with . . .'

Run away? Rhian is free? 'But he's given her . . .'

'No, my lady, she's with Gawain of the Round Table.'

One muscle at a time, Jocosa straightened up. 'Rhian is with a champion of the Round Table?'

'Yes, mistress.'

'And her father calls her ungrateful?' He'd had beautiful eyes, once. Eyes full of laughter and wisdom and love. Where had those eyes strayed?

'He says she does not care whether you die or live. He says she could save you if she did as she was told.'

'He has said so before.'

'I beg you my lady, speak with him. It is some madness that seizes him. You are the only one who might bring him to his senses again.'

Rhian's comb lay on the table. Jocosa stared at it. She wanted to reach for it, to hold it close because she could not hold her girl, but her hands seemed to have lost the will for movement. 'I have tried Una.'

'You must try again.'

But she remembered his face as he turned away from her that last time, and heard again his voice. *My father was right . . . Love is too inconstant a thing on which to build a life.* They had laughed at such words once, in their innocence, their ignorance of the payment God would exact for that laughter. 'I cannot. There is nothing left.'

'There is always something.'

'No. You do not know what he has done.' Outside, the rain began to fall in slow, fat drops, smacking against the window screen, making a sound like fingers tapping to get in. 'Leave me now.'

Una was not defeated yet. 'You will want to get ready for bed.'

'I said leave.' *Perhaps I will be able to apologize one day for this anger.* 'If I wish to go to bed, I will call for you.'

'Yes, my lady,' said Una.

'Yes, my lady,' said Aeldra, sounding even more tired than Una.

The door opened, and the door closed, and Jocosa was alone.

Will you come to me again, my husband? she wondered. *What will you say if you do?*

With slow and clumsy fingers, Jocosa undid the catches on the window screen and folded it back. Then, gripping the stone casement tightly, she thrust her upturned face out into the rain, letting the drops trickle down her cheeks, making use of the sky's tears, for her own had been long ago drained dry.

When at last the cold became too much, she drew herself inside again, face, throat, hair, veil and dress all soaked through. To her surprise, she heard a new sound. The flapping of heavy wings.

A raven, fighting hard against the rain, landed on the sill. It shook itself, flipped its wings onto its back and cawed three times.

Jocosa blinked at the bird for a moment, and then turned away, leaving small puddles of rain behind her. 'Well, come in if you wish, Mistress Raven, though there is small comfort to be had here.'

'Thank you,' said a voice behind her. 'I will.'

A woman stood before the window. She was tall and golden, half hidden by a cloak made entirely of black feathers. She stood still, letting Jocosa stare until comprehension finally came to her, accompanied, Jocosa found herself surprised to note, by nothing so much as relief.

For did not the angel of death have black wings?

'Have you come for me?' she asked the golden woman.

She inclined her head. 'Yes.'

A very little fear fluttered in Jocosa's throat. 'Will it be quick?'

'If you do not struggle.'

Jocosa sighed. She wiped the last of the water from her face and smoothed her dress down fussily. Odd to wish to look one's best at such a time. 'I do not want to be a danger to my daughter any more, you see. She may weaken. She may try to return.'

'She will be in no more danger from you, I promise.'

'May I say my prayers?'

'Of course.'

Jocosa knelt, crossing herself and bowing her head. The woman waited with all signs of patience.

After the final amen, Jocosa lowered her hands from their attitude of prayer, but remained on her knees. 'I am ready.'

'Very well.' The woman knelt before her, leaning close, as if she meant to give Jocosa the kiss of peace. Instead, she inhaled deeply, taking in all of Jocosa's breath as Jocosa expelled it. Jocosa felt a great lightness infuse her blood. All her memories poured through her, a river of pain and beauty, love, wonder and fear. She saw Rygehil as he was when he filled her heart with delight and desire. She saw Rhian in all her aspects – infant, sturdy girl, and beautiful young woman. Her heart filled with the music of their voices, and her mind with all the scents and songs of her life.

But those all ran quickly from her, as the rain had run down her cheeks, and they left behind only peace, only the night full of stars, and Jocosa let them go.

Jocosa's body swayed and fell forwards. Kerra caught her gently and laid her out on the floor. After a moment's thought, she folded the dead woman's hands and closed her eyes.

The lady's soul was sweet with its seasoning of sorrow, full and heavy, like the taste of summer's cream, and rich with experience and memory. Kerra felt a melancholy unusual for her. Perhaps because she had never before been welcomed when she came on death's wings. What a strange, sorry thing, to want to die, although she had known the feeling. How sad it was that Jocosa had no one to come and save her as Morgaine had saved Kerra.

'For myself, lady, I would have let you live. Perhaps you would have found your way again. But Euberacon was determined to make your man pay for his failure, and I and my friends must have strength for what is to come. So you see, your life was needed by us all.'

Shaking her head, Kerra left the corpse where it lay, and flew out into the night.

THIRTEEN

As Gawain and Rhian approached Camelot, the road grew ever more crowded, even as it ran through the deep woods. Carters and folk carrying their bundles on their backs moved off the wide highway to let their procession pass, but no one cursed. Instead, heads were raised and hoods were doffed. Cheers went up at the sight of the knights and soldiers, accompanied by cries of 'God bless Lord Gawain! God bless Lord Agravain!'

Agravain just nodded, his face growing ever more pinched. Gawain responded always with his magnificent smile and a wave of his hand to all who called out. Rhian felt her head lift and her shoulders pull back as she looked this way and that at the people thronging the side of the road. She felt a great lady on her horse beside her lord with all the town come out to see them pass by.

Agravain had not only been displeased when Gawain caught up with the party returning to Arthur, he had been livid. The brothers had gone down the road, out of earshot, but Rhian and the dozen men, and all the boys and squires who waited on them, could easily see them gesturing broadly and angrily to each other as they spoke. When they at last returned, Agravain was still flushed with his fury. Gawain, however, looked completely at ease as he mounted his riding horse and gave a reassuring smile to Rhian.

Agravain had not spoken another word to his brother, at least none that any could hear. Even when they stopped for the night at the monastery of St Joseph, Agravain remained as silent as one of the monks who served them their plain supper of soup and bread.

Gawain was also distant, but not from anger. As soon as they had joined Agravain's men, he became his most courtly and correct, treating her with rigid deference and respect. She knew he did it for her sake, so that the other men would follow his example, regardless of Agravain's distaste for her presence. Still, it made her wish they had travelled alone, so they could have talked, and sung, and enjoyed themselves as lovers for a little longer, before they reached the court, and all things would have to change again.

Still, sometimes Gawain would glance at her, and she would see the delight that shimmered just beneath his gaze, and be content.

Ahead of the party, the encroaching trees pulled back to make way for sown fields, and Rhian saw Camelot.

It was built on a hill, as she had heard, with Arthur's great hall at its crown. But none had spoken of how the town spilled down the sides of that hill, flaring out like a woman's skirt, the roofs of the good stone houses all black and red with slate and tile. Stout walls and banks of earth protected the city. The gates were all guarded by men in leather jerkins emblazoned with Arthur's red dragon. They cheered as heartily as the folk on the road and lifted up their spears and pikes in salute to the victorious company.

Past the earthworks and the outer walls, Gawain took the lead with Agravain. With Agravain's squires riding beside them to carry shields and banners, there was no room for

Rhian. She found herself surrounded by strange men on tall
horses. They cast sideways glances at her, despite the fact
that they had had two full days to become used to her. She
felt they would have liked to stare openly, but some of the
courtesy Gawain had attempted to instil prevented that.
Worse than the strangers' curious glances, though, were the
walls. She had never been in a city where the buildings
crowded around her shoulders and rose higher than her head
on horseback. The shutters on the upper storeys flung themselves open so that men, women and children could lean
out and cheer. There were strangers above and beside, and
even below. Passers-by were forced into doorways and
narrow lanes by their passage, and children darted perilously
close to the horses' hooves to snatch up the occasional penny
the knights directed their squires to drop.

Rhian patted Thetis's neck constantly, but she wasn't sure
if she was trying to calm her horse or herself. Bolting did
not seem such a poor idea right now, back to the woods and
fields she knew. She glanced ahead to Gawain, but saw only
his back. He was waving and accepting the greetings that
were his. Rhian's throat tightened.

Despite all, Rhian managed to keep Thetis and herself with
the procession, although far at the back. The streets broad-
ened as they rose, which was a mercy, but the press of noise
grew worse. Word had apparently flown ahead of them, and
the folk of Camelot were determined to cheer them all the
way to the gates of Arthur's hall.

Those gates were the strongest Rhian had ever seen. Set
in walls that had been old when the Romans came, they
were black and grey and grim. Rhian, already unnerved,
wished she could hesitate and collect her wits, but she was
given no time. Gawain at last had seen how far behind she
had fallen and raised his hand. The whole of the procession
halted. Amid the sound of too many voices, the stamping of

hooves and the snorting of the ponies and mules, Gawain turned his horse and rode back to where Rhian waited.

'Come,' he said. He could not extend his hand, but his gaze sparkled with welcome and assurance as he smiled. 'There is room enough for us to ride through together. I wish certain persons to meet you.'

Rhian smiled in return and lifted her chin. Taking a better hold of Thetis's reins, she urged her mare into step beside him. The guards hoisted their pikes and axes in salute as she passed through the gates of the Great Hall of Camelot at the side of their champion.

Arthur's hall was finer than any building she had ever seen. Made all of stone with a roof of red tiles, it could have held five times a hundred souls. Its entrance was carved with granite pillars, warriors, twining vines and fabulous beasts. Before it all spread broad steps of white marble and an apron of bright mosaic tiles.

Before all this grandeur stood those who held its rule.

There was no mistaking them. Circlets of gold adorned their brows and torques of gold encircled their throats. Cloaks lined and trimmed with sable protected them from the brisk wind. High King Arthur was no longer a young man. Silver lightened his bark-brown hair and neatly trimmed beard. Lines had etched themselves into a face gone permanently brown from wind and weather. His body, though, was powerful beneath its clothing of fine linen, all in shades of blue that rippled in the breeze and made him appear to be wearing cloth made of water.

Beside him, Queen Guinevere stood straight, slender and fair as a birch tree in summer, clothed all in white, trimmed and clasped with silver. A great ring of keys hung from the belt at her slim waist. Her rich chestnut hair had been braided and bound with threads of silver that sparkled in the sun and found answering lights in her wide, grey eyes. It was those

eyes of hers that were said to have captured the heart of the
man who would become the High King of all the Britons,
and seeing her now, Rhian could well believe it.

Beside the king stood a tall, wiry man with black hair
and tawny eyes. Some old battle or accident had broken
and twisted his right leg so that he was forced to lean on
a crutch. His rich, black tunic was ornamented with a chain
of gold and silver with each link made in the shape of a
pair of crossed keys. This then must be Sir Kai, King Arthur's
seneschal and foster brother. Beside Kai stood a man who
at first glance seemed he must be moulded of bronze, so
fair and strong was he, with lapis eyes and a square jaw.
His cloak was madder red and his coat of silver rings was
trimmed with bright brass. The sword he wore at his side
had a golden pommel. This could only be Lancelot du Lac,
come across from Brittany to join King Arthur's champions when he heard the tales told of the battle of Mount
Badon.

The ladies beside Queen Guinevere were no less impres-
sive than Arthur's champions, in bright clothing of all the
colours the summer had to offer, each ornamented with
jewellery of enamelled silver, copper and bronze, all
cunningly worked into the shapes of flowers and animals,
or knotted into complex patterns to circle waist and brow.

But even amidst that beauty and wealth, the High King
and queen shone forth. Looking at the pair of them, regal
and proud in the sun, knowing all they had done and all
that they stood for, Rhian felt she now understood the true
meaning of majesty. Awe filled her. At the same time, terror
parched her throat and turned her hands to ice. If she had
felt uncouth and bashful entering Bannain's hall, she now
felt that anything would be preferable to meeting these two,
with her chapped hands and her hair fit only for birds to
nest in, her poor clothes stained and creased by travel, and

manners that could barely pass muster in a smoky outlandish hall.

Let me spend the night in a scullery, or the sty, I wouldn't care. Do not bring me before these.

A small army of grooms and pages swarmed out to surround them, so Rhian could go neither forward nor back. The reins were taken expertly from her hands and a step was placed for her feet. She looked desperately at Gawain, but he seemed to have forgotten what he knew of mercy. He swung himself out of his saddle and held up his hand for her. Rhian tried to swallow, but her dry throat would not permit it. Gawain was smiling, confident, almost jubilant. He was home, after all, and he came home victorious. His kin and comrades formed up behind him. Rhian was uncertain whether she wanted to curse him soundly, or simply pray to God for the ground to open up and swallow her.

As neither thing was going to happen, Rhian gave Gawain her hand and let him help her down from Thetis. Still holding her hand, he led her up the marble steps with Agravain walking on the other side of him. Here at least, Rhian knew what to do. She stopped beside him, two steps below the royal party and knelt, her head bowed and her gaze properly and firmly fixed on the ground.

From the corner of her eye, she saw the king's boots and hems descend the steps to raise up Gawain to give him the kiss of peace. He then did the same for Agravain.

'Welcome home to the sons of Lot!' The High King's voice rang out over the crowd. 'They bring with them the praise of the lord and people of Pen Marhas which stands safe and strong because of these men and all their brave comrades!'

A mighty cheer rose up. Surely hoods were tossed into the air and the banners snapped in the breeze and Gawain smiled his dazzling smile. At these thoughts, Rhian found she was able to feel something other than bashful. For one thing, the sharp edge of the marble step was beginning to bite into her shins.

'And a warm welcome to you as well, lady.'

Rhian lifted her head. Queen Guinevere stood before her, holding out both hands. She smiled in honest and open welcome. A knowing look shone in her grey eyes that said she understood all that Rhian felt. Struck mute, Rhian took the queen's strong hands and stood. Queen Guinevere gave her the kiss of peace. The queen smelled of amber and incense and Rhian knew she smelled of sweat and horses, but for that moment it didn't matter.

Gawain came to Rhian's side. 'My queen, may I make known to you Lady Rhian of the Morelands, daughter of the barown Lord Rygehil. She is in sore need of your grace's protection, and I will stand surety for her honesty and the truth of her plight.'

Queen Guinevere cocked her head, frankly curious at these words. Rhian had the feeling they were not what she had expected.

'If she has need of protection, she shall have it.' The queen turned her attention back to Rhian and squeezed her hands. 'You will tell me your story and we will judge what is best to do. But first,' her glance at Gawain took on an edge. 'We will get you to a place where you can rest and refresh yourself. Gawain forgets that not everyone is as restored by a public procession and the acknowledgement of glory as he.'

Gawain bowed deeply at these words, but Rhian had no time to see if this sign of humility was real or sham, because Queen Guinevere took her arm and steered Rhian into the company of her ladies. 'Arianwen, Sioned, Idelle, go down to the champions and give them our praise and greetings. Assure all we will let them know the full measure of our thanks at board tonight. This poor lady is ready to faint from all this commotion.'

Perhaps the queen believed this, but she herself seemed
unready to make any concession to Rhian's supposed faint-
ness. She stretched her legs out in a stride Rhian's mother
would have termed unladylike and whisked Rhian through
the great open doors into the hall of kings. Rhian had the
impression of carved stone, of banners and tapestries, of
painted statues of wood and stone, and through one arched
doorway she thought she caught a glimpse of a great, curved
table that took up most of the chamber. Men and women
made polite obeisance as they passed, but the queen did not
slow down to give her time to take in any details.

After a turn into the western wing of the great hall,
Guinevere led Rhian to a door flanked by a pair of soldiers
carrying spears hung with green banners. There must have
been some signal, because as the queen approached, the door
was opened by a lady in an ochre gown who stood back and
curtsied to her mistress.

The chamber beyond opened like a lush meadow in the
forest. More candles than Rhian had ever seen in her life
burned in branched sconces of iron that stood as tall as her
head. A hearth allowed a fire to burn without filling the
room with smoke. Tapestries depicting the virtues and the
seasons covered the walls. The floor, rather than being of
plain stone, was a sparkling mosaic depicting a flock of swans
on a broad lake.

The furnishings fit the chamber for elegance. An alcove
held a bed curtained in emerald green and carved with swans
and dragons chasing each other around the posts. All about
the room were chests, instruments of music and embroidery
frames. There was even a desk, inlaid with ivory and laid out
with quills, parchments, and a leather-bound book as wide
as Rhian's forearm and two fingers thick. The chairs and stools
were all of polished and well-fitted wood. The ladies who
would occupy them were out greeting the returning knights,

but there remained no fewer than four well-dressed maids. All had the round cheeks and bright eyes that indicated good treatment and plentiful food.

If Rhian had not already been breathless, the sight of such wealth would have taken that breath from her.

But to Queen Guinevere, it was simply her room, which she entered. Her servants, all of whom were on their feet, dropped deep curtsies. The queen barely paused to acknowledge the gesture before she began giving instructions.

'Elowyn, this lady has travelled hard from sore trial. She is in need of fresh bread and whatever is hot on the hearth. Tressa, get to the wardrobe and bring out the grey wool with the blue trims and a clean shift. Roseen, hot water, towels and brushes. Jana, a good chair and then go see that a chamber is made ready for this lady.'

The servants leapt at once to their tasks, scurrying this way and that. One, Jana, brought a carved chair forward and laid a cushion down on it.

'Sit,' said the queen, and Rhian did so at once.

Queen Guinevere reached for her ring of keys, selected a tiny one of brass, and unlocked a casket that waited on a small table beside a pair of silver goblets. Inside lay a bottle of green glass. With careful, practised motion, she poured out a measure of tawny liquid into one of the goblets.

'Sip that slowly, lady,' she instructed as she handed the goblet to Rhian. 'It is a great restorative, but it is strong if you are unused to it.'

Under the queen's watchful eye, Rhian sipped. Warmth and a rich, autumnal taste rolled down her throat, loosening the tightness in her chest and stomach. The queen nodded approvingly.

'Now, then, let's have a look at that hair of yours.'

'Majesty,' said Rhian, timidly. This was not a woman, this

was a force of nature. She felt as if she were trying to interrupt a summer gale. 'If you please, I must tell you . . .'

Queen Guinevere waved her words away. 'When you are clean and fed, Lady Rhian, you may be sure you will tell me all. But I will not permit a guest in this hall to be left with the strains and stains of travel still on them while I satisfy my curiosity. So, drink, and let me have a look at this hair of yours.'

Rhian held her tongue, and sipped her drink. With deft hands, Queen Guinevere unpinned her stained and wrinkled veil and passed it to one of the maids. Her braid, trailing all its wisps and loose locks swung free down the back of the chair. The queen pursed her lips and nodded.

'Beautiful, Lady Rhian,' she said matter-of-factly. 'And of necessity, long neglected. Never mind, we will take care of that.'

The maid Roseen arrived with the hot water, brushes and towels. Rhian was relieved of her dress and helped to wash face, throat, hands and feet. She was dressed again in a gown of pearl-grey wool so fine it felt as light as linen, trimmed and girdled with sapphire ribbons embroidered with white apple blossoms. Bread, a portion of roasted capon and a mug of last year's cider were brought in by the second maid, Elowyn, and placed before her. While Rhian ate, two maids unbound her hair, spread it out across their laps and subjected it to the ministrations of ivory combs and actual bristle brushes such as Rhian had never had a chance to use before. The queen supervised all. Rhian felt a little like a gown being shaken out and looked over for moth holes and worn hems. The food, however, did much to ease her remaining discomfort. The capon was fresh and sweet, flavoured with sage and thyme, and a sprinkling of precious pepper. The bread was a pale, nutty brown – there had been no chaff in the fine flour that went into its making. She had to work to

remember not to lick her fingers and to take small bites so
the gravy she sopped did not spill down her chin. She took
the cider as slowly as she had the queen's 'restorative'. It
would not do to grow dizzy now.

'I've a mind to let our bard Dilwyn in to see this,' mused
Queen Guinevere, smoothing out a lock of Rhian's hair. 'He
would love to compose a poem in honour of such waves of
red-gold.'

Rhian blushed and swallowed her mouthful. 'Your Majesty
is too kind.'

'Never in life,' laughed Guinevere. 'I am a grey-eyed witch
who enchanted the king and I have a flint where my heart
should be.' Rhian's head jerked up, her mouth open to protest,
but she saw the queen was smiling, her eyes alight with the
tart jest. Guinevere took Rhian's chin firmly between her
fingers and directed it downward so that she faced her food,
and the maids were able to continue their work unhindered.

Rhian was far from the queen's only business. Other ladies
came and went, consulting Queen Guinevere in soft voices.
She would nod and make reply, occasionally handing out a
key with the instruction. Twice she left in the company of
one of her ladies to take care of some pressing matter. Rhian
wondered at the woman's energy. There were days her
mother's feet had scarce seemed to touch the ground she
was so busy flitting between this task and that. How much
more must be required of the mistress of Camelot?

At last, the maids divided Rhian's hair into portions for
braiding and bound it up with ribbons the colour of those
that trimmed her dress. They veiled her again with trans-
lucent cloth. Rhian felt full, clean and pampered. For a
moment, all feeling of being an oafish country girl dissolved
in a glow of wellbeing. In fact, if she were permitted to sit
here much longer before the blaze of the fire, she knew she
would fall sound asleep.

Queen Guinevere returned once more, accompanied this time by a boy page bearing a tray with clean noggins, a pitcher and a plate of honey cakes. The pitcher proved to contain simple watered wine which he served without spilling a drop on the white cloth he carried over his arm. The boy was golden, with eyes of cornflower blue. There was no mistaking it. He was Saxon, and a full-blood at that.

Even before Rhian had heard Gawain utter his dire threats to the man Harrik, she had known that one way Arthur maintained his peace was to require each of the Saxon chiefs who sued for peace after Badon to send one son to Camelot as surety for their good behaviour. This child, though, was too young for that to have been his fate. Unlike beleaguered Holda in Bannain's hall, he looked vastly content, almost cocky.

'Thank you, Orval,' said Queen Guinevere as she accepted wine and cake. 'You take note of our golden boy here, I see, Lady Rhian.'

'Your pardon, Majesty, I was only . . .'

'Curious.' The queen finished for her. 'Not all the Saxon chiefs desire to stay barbarians. Some have sent their sons willingly to learn what we have to teach. If he proves himself, one day Orval here will be picked to squire one of the Round Table's champions. Is that not so, Orval?'

'Yes, Your Majesty,' answered the boy and his whole face lit up at the prospect. The queen smiled and the boy bowed and took himself smartly out of the room.

'Thus is peace not only maintained, but increased.' Queen Guinevere sighed as the door closed behind the page. 'And that is what those who attacked Pen Marhas would shatter.' A spasm of anger passed across the queen's fair face, turning her eyes dark as thunderheads. 'I was born in the high country, Lady Rhian. I barely knew my father, he was so much at war, first with this neighbour, then with that. He bargained me away to Arthur because he saw that Arthur was the strongest of the kings of Briton, a true *dux bellorum* as the Romans would have styled him. So, for the price of my hand, my father would have an ally that would allow him not just to fight off his neighbours, but to conquer.'

Rhian stared at the pale wine in her cup, uncertain of what to say. Here she was in the place of songs, and those songs spoke of the great love between king and queen. If that was not true . . .

But Guinevere laughed kindly. 'Oh, fear not, lady. It was a bargain I entered into willingly. You see, by then I knew far more of Arthur than my father did. I knew his honour and his dreams of peace.' Her eyes were distant and full of things she was not going to say. 'So, I was glad to bring him the Round Table and the scabbard for Excaliber, as well as my own self.' Her attention focused on the room again and her smile became an expression for things present. 'Now then, Lady Rhian. I promised you would be made to tell me all, and I must not break my word. Help yourself to what is at hand, and tell me the whole of your tale.' The queen leaned forwards, her face open, her whole attitude saying how ready she was to listen.

Rhian sipped her wine. Perhaps it was lack of sleep or sheer comfort that loosened her tongue. 'I feel as if I have done nothing else these past days. Everyone wants to know who I am and why on earth I'm alone on the road with the nephew of the High King.'

'But now you tell it to me,' said Queen Guinevere. 'And you know that is a different thing.'

Rhian nodded and began what had become her recitation, but the Queen listened in such patient silence that she soon began to speak of things she had not yet told anyone else. She spoke of the blood, of Whitcomb's blood on his chest, of the blood of the Saxons she had shot so she and Gawain could escape. She spoke of Euberacon's eyes and how they had held her paralysed until they drew her forward from the fog her thoughts had become. She spoke of the heartbreak when her father came to Pen Marhas with no word of love or understanding, but only to force her back home to wait for the sorcerer he had sold her to. Of the fear that harm had come to her mother, as he said it would.

When at last, the words ran out she realized there were tears in her eyes and her hands trembled. Gently, the queen took the cup from between her fingers and placed it on the table.

'If you would weep, Lady Rhian, it would ease your heart,' she said.

But Rhian shook her head. 'I don't want to weep anymore, Majesty. I am sick of my own tears.'

'What do you want?'

'I want to go home,' said Rhian, ashamed at how plaintive she sounded. 'I want to sit with my mother, and go hunting with my hounds.' Words tumbled out of her mouth faster than the thoughts formed in her head. 'I want to speak Latin with my father and ride out with Whitcomb and scold Aeldra and run about bareheaded with my cousins in summer. I want to sew my dower cloths and doctor the servants and gossip with the women in the hall and marry . . .' Just in time she was able to remember where she was and force the correct name from her mouth. 'Vernus.' It felt strange to say his name. How many days had it been since she had even thought of him? Since she had imagined taking shelter in his father's hall?

She had thought so much of her heart of late, but had spared scarcely one of those thoughts for him.

'I want to know my mother is safe and well,' she finished weakly.

If the queen noticed the stumble, she said nothing. She

only took Rhian's hands. 'Rhian, I cannot give you back your home. That is not in my power. But I can offer you a new one.'

Rhian lifted her head, hope shyly creeping into her heart.

The queen nodded. 'I'm certain Gawain said as much to you, am I right? But you did not know what to place your faith in then?' The flicker of Rhian's smile was all the queen needed for her answer. 'Well, let your heart be at ease about this much. You are now under my protection. None now may dispose of your person without gaining my permission first. Your mother will be sent for as soon as it can be arranged.'

'But . . .'

'But?' Queen Guinevere's eyebrows arched.

Rhian felt over-bold bringing up this fact in the face of that single, severe word. 'He is my father.'

'And he is subject to the word of the High King, as are you,' she pointed one long finger at Rhian. 'And equally you are subject to my word, unless my Lord Arthur should decide to contradict me and I can promise you before God and Mother Mary that in this he will not.'

Rhian fell onto her knees. 'Thank you, Your Majesty. I don't . . .'

'Get up, lady.' The queen tapped her lightly on the head, as if scolding a silly child. 'There is no need for such gestures at this time.'

Rhian only raised her head. The speed with which her fate had been decided left her more light-headed than the wine had and she was not sure she had the strength to obey. 'But I don't know how to thank you.'

'If you would thank me, serve God and heal, Lady Rhian. I think there will be calls enough upon your strength and your heart in the coming days that you will need both to be whole.'

Rhian swallowed, and the queen did not fail to mark it. She laid her hand on Rhian's shoulder. 'You are safe, lady. Lay aside your fears.'

Safe. At the word of this woman. As easy as that. Rhian turned her face aside.

'Speak your thought,' said Guinevere.

'I was thinking it must be very simple to be queen.'

'For a queen some things are indeed very simple. Other things . . . they are less so. Come.' Guinevere raised her up. 'Let Jana show you to your chamber. I think you need not endure board in the great hall tonight. There is to be a feast tomorrow night, for victory and May Day, and that will be pomp enough to formally welcome you to Camelot. Jana.' The queen beckoned to the black-haired maid in the ochre dress. 'I charge you especially to look after Lady Rhian with all diligence, until we can find her a suitable servant of her own.'

The maid curtseyed. 'Majesty.' Then she turned to Rhian. 'If my lady will follow me?'

Rhian also curtseyed to the queen, holding the pose of respect and reverence as she would if she were in a great hall with all the world looking on. This time the queen accepted the gesture with a nod of her head and a seriousness in her gaze that told Rhian she knew the fullness of Rhian's heart.

Jana led Rhian up a staircase to a corridor where slits high in the outer wall would let the summer sunlight enter in sharp, broad shafts. But it must have been late, for those slits now showed only shadow and dimming sky. Despite her recent refreshment, a wave of tiredness struck Rhian.

Jana opened a plain door set in the left-hand wall. On the other side waited a chamber that was simple in comparison with the queen's but to Rhian looked to be the very essence of comfort. This room too had a hearth. Two stout wooden chairs covered in tapestry sat before the gently crackling fire, along with an inlaid table where refreshment might be placed. Fresh rushes strewed the floor, and there was even a small knotted carpet beside the stout bed which was curtained and canopied with sage green. A tapestry of knotted ribbons and roses completed the decoration.

'Is it to your liking, my lady?' inquired Jana.

'Yes, yes, it's beautiful.' Rhian stepped in hastily. 'I wonder . . . if I might lie down for just a few minutes. I know the queen excused me from board, but, just in case . . .'

'Of course, my lady. I would suggest we remove your dress, so it will not wrinkle.'

Jana was an efficient maid and the laces were soon undone at bodice and sleeve and Rhian was able to slip beneath covers of fur in her shift and sink down onto clean beds of eiderdown so soft she felt as if she were being cradled by the wings of angels.

Oh, Mother Mary thank you for these blessings. Thank you for . . .

But Rhian fell asleep before she could finish her prayer.

From the place where he stood beside the king, Gawain saw Queen Guinevere take Rhian by the hands and lead her into the hall. His heart found room to contain a little more gladness. Now Rhian would learn what a proper welcome was. Agravain still wore his displeasure plain on his face, even when their uncle presented him to the crowd as 'the great champion', and 'hero of Pen Marhas'. Gawain, to his shame, did spare a glance at Lancelot. The knight of Brittany did not look at all pleased at having been left behind from a chance at honour and glory.

Well, if the signs were right, there would be plenty more chances like Pen Marhas before the snows fell in winter.

The ladies and their attendants glided among the champions, graceful as deer every one, welcoming them home with cups of wine and fair words. Gawain accepted a silver cup from Lady Kelyn, who arched her brows as he took a welcome drink of the sweet wine. She was longing to ask about Rhian, he was sure, but, thankfully, was too courteous to do so.

The High King raised his hand once more to the cheering crowd and then with a nod to Gawain and Agravain, swept back into the hall. Gawain gave Lady Kelyn a parting shrug, handed the cup back and followed his uncle and brother inside.

Gawain turned to Arthur, but the High King did not wait for him to speak. 'As soon as you have refreshed yourselves, Gawain, I will see you and Agravain in the war council chamber.'

They both bowed deeply and the king gave them leave to depart. Agravain strode down the corridor at Gawain's side, his eyes pointed straight ahead and his mouth clamped tightly shut.

'Agravain,' Gawain began.

But Agravain just quickened his pace and drew ahead. Gawain sighed and let him go.

Gawain shared a room with his brother Geraint. Agravain preferred to be closer to Kai and the secretaries, while Gareth was required to live in the dormitories with the rest of the squires. So Gawain was a little surprised to find his youngest brother sitting on his bed when he opened the door to his chamber.

'Gareth.' He embraced the young man warmly.

'Brother.' Gareth was grinning and relaxed, taking a moment to enjoy being off-duty and among family. If he was worried about what he had surely already heard, he did not show it. 'You're looking well after your travels.' He paused, and then added with an over-abundance of casualness. 'They're saying you've brought a lady home.'

Gawain rolled his eyes as he stripped off his boots and travel-stained tunic. 'I'm sure they are. She's a witness to some important events that the king will need to hear of.' Gareth, diligent squire that he was, had filled the wash basin and laid out a fresh towel. There was also beer and bread on a plate. Gawain had to give Lancelot this, he was training the boy well in more than fighting.

'They're saying the Saxons are practising witchcraft,' Gareth went on, clearly fishing for news.

'There's not a horse in the world can run so fast as people's tongues.' Gawain frowned at his younger brother in overly stern disapproval. 'I hope my Lord Lancelot is not teaching you the art of listening behind doors. No, wait.' He held up his hands to stop the boy's coming protest. 'What more *could* you be taught of such art?'

Gareth threw a sandal at him. Gawain ducked it easily and grinned at his youngest brother.

'My Lord Lancelot says the Saxons can't even practise swordcraft correctly, how skilled can their witches be?' Gareth chuckled, savouring his mentor's joke. 'He says . . .'

'Where's Geraint disappeared to?' Once Gareth warmed to the theme of Lancelot's sayings, he could talk for hours.

'The High King has him down by the walls with Sir Bedivere reviewing defences and the men's readiness. I said it was impossible the Saxons would attack here, because you and Agravain would stop them at Pen Marhas. But Lancelot said that it is necessary to check all defences when an enemy threatens.'

Unusually sagacious of him. Gawain scooped up the clean water Gareth had provided and scrubbed the dirt from his face.

'Do you think we will go to war, Gawain?'

Gawain turned and regarded his brother. Gareth perched on the edge of the bed, torn between eagerness and apprehension at this idea. He was too young to remember the last uprising of the Pictish men at home in Din Eityn. What he knew of war he had heard from glory-seekers, like Lancelot, and hard, old men, like Grimore.

'I hope not Gareth, but I fear we may have no choice.'

Gareth nodded, his seriousness making him look older than his years, but then he added 'My Lord Lancelot says. . .'

Gawain threw his dirty tunic, catching his brother square in the face.

Washed, dressed in clean linen and an autumn-brown over-tunic, Gawain hurried to the war council.

It was strange to see the chamber that held the Round Table so empty. Usually, there were at least the ten champions, Arthur's war leaders and advisers. The place seemed echoingly silent with only the High King and his servants there.

The Round Table itself dominated the room. Made of ingeniously fitted and inlaid woods, it was hollow at the centre so that chairs might be placed around both the inner and outer rims. Two hinged flaps could be lifted to allow the cadre or their servitors access to the centre. The object had become so much a part of his world, Gawain had almost ceased to think of it any differently from any other table at which he sat, but seeing it now, broad and empty, it brought back the first day he had taken his place there, all the pride, and all the fear, and how his voice had shaken when his uncle had turned and asked him his thoughts.

Arthur stood beside one of the room's other tables. It was a far smaller, far plainer circle. Its ornamentation was the beautifully drawn and painted map stretched out across its surface. Carved wooden markers in the shape of horses and coloured tokens were scattered here and there across the kingdoms, indicating the position of ready forces and the levies that could be quickly called into action. The small army

of secretaries and servitors who were the constant train of
kingship had retired a polite distance and Arthur stood in
relative isolation with his thoughts.

Gawain knelt before his uncle, who raised him up with
an absent gesture while he studied the map. Agravain arrived
a moment later, to make the same obeisance, and receive
the same leave to stand.

They waited in silence until Arthur had finished his
contemplation of the lands represented before him and beckoned to the crowd of servitors, who came forward at once
with chairs for them. Arthur sat, inviting his nephews to do
the same.

'Now, Gawain.' Arthur laced his fingers together. 'Tell us
what has happened, and begin with your meeting with
Harrik.'

'I think perhaps I should hear these counsels as well.'

The doors had opened soundlessly on their well-tended
hinges, and Merlin entered the room. He moved slowly, with
an old man's gait, leaning heavily on his wooden staff. It was
a deceiving appearance, Gawain knew. In dire moments, he
had seen Merlin move with a speed that a man in his prime
would have been hard pressed to match.

'Merlin,' Arthur hailed him. 'What news have you?'

'My own, my Lord King.' Merlin was the only councillor
who would even think to give Arthur such an answer. It was
one of the many reasons why it had taken Gawain so long
to trust the sorcerer when he had first come to Camelot.
'May I sit with you?'

'Always.' Arthur indicated that another chair should be
brought and Merlin lowered himself carefully into it. The
High King nodded to his nephew, and Gawain began his
tale. He tried not to look too much at his brother as he
spoke. Agravain was still frowning deeply. Even making
allowances for his brother's essential nature, Agravain's

constant disdain was beginning to grate on Gawain.

When Gawain had finished Arthur made no comment, but turned to Agravain. 'And what is your news?'

Agravain's account was shorter, in part because he had less to tell, in part because he was always more sparing with his words. He told of the ride to Pen Marhas, of the battle and how it became a rout. He handed across the letter from Lord Bannain detailing those needs of the ruined town that had not yet been accounted for. Arthur handed the document to one of the waiting secretaries who retired to hold it for his lord's later attention.

Agravain went on, speaking of the councils he had held with Thedu Bannain, how his men would set their patrols through the hills and send word of what had happened to his neighbours as quickly as they could. If the Saxons were minded to continue their assaults, they would find they had lost the element of surprise on which, according to Harrik, they had counted.

Which raised a question that had been long simmering in the back of Gawain's mind.

'Majesty,' he began carefully. 'Harrik's son . . .'

Arthur's demeanour was stern. Without intervention, the boy was forfeit to the king, and the laws of that forfeit were ancient and harsh. 'Do you truly believe that Harrik was coerced?'

Gawain spoke as steadily as he was able. 'I saw his eyes as he stood before me, Sir. It may well be he was bewitched.'

'Merlin?' The High King kept his gaze on Gawain.

The sorcerer tapped his fingers against his staff for a moment. 'There is much of that kind abroad this day. Harrik could well have fallen victim to the powers.'

Arthur nodded. 'Then it shall be so judged. The boy will be given the choice to remain or return to his people.' Gawain was not surprised to hear the lightest trace of relief in his uncle's voice. There were duties of kingship Gawain did not relish the thought of assuming.

'Tomorrow I will convene the Round Table,' Arthur went on. 'Then we will hold the celebrations for May Day and have a last moment of joy and peace with our ladies before we must turn our hands to war.'

Gawain made to kneel, but Agravain was not ready for their business to be concluded. 'Sir,' he said, and Gawain found himself groaning inwardly. There was only one thing Agravain could be bringing up at this time. 'The Lady Rhian . . .'

'I have not forgotten,' said Arthur patiently. 'The queen will hear her story and we may trust her judgement.'

This was not enough to content Agravain, however. 'Sir . . . the law has been broken.'

To Gawain's surprise, it was Merlin who answered. 'There is more here than a simple matter of law, my Lord Agravain.'

'At the very least, it is clear to me that further investigation must be made.' Arthur stood, causing the rest of them to get hastily to their feet. 'Be at peace, Agravain. The law will be observed in this matter. Thank you both for your news. We will speak further on these matters tomorrow. Merlin, stay here with me awhile yet. There are points I would discuss with you.'

'Yes, Majesty.'

'Yes, Majesty.'

Gawain knelt with his brother and rose to take his leave as Arthur and Merlin returned to the map table.

Out in the corridor, Gawain grabbed his brother's shoulder, forcing him to turn. 'Agravain, there is no need for this.'

Agravain's cheek twitched, an expression of controlled anger Gawain had not seen on him in years. 'You will have this your own way, Gawain, let that be enough.'

'No, brother, it is not enough. Why are you doing this? Even for you this conduct is outrageous.'

Agravain barked out a harsh laugh. 'My conduct is outrageous? You are the one who will choose to indulge himself regardless of the rights and privileges of others. My God, Gawain, you had better hope the men of this country have short memories or their women clever lies. To steal the woman out from before her father . . .'

'You heard what was said in council and you still think this is because I . . .' Gawain found he could not even finish the phrase. 'You think me some prating coxcomb then?'

'No, brother.' Agravain sighed. 'I think you nothing more than one of God's great fools. For it is a fool who cannot learn the fire is hot after his hand is burnt.'

With that, Agravain stalked away. Gawain did not even try to follow him.

You are wrong, brother, he said in his mind. *You do not understand. You never did. There never has been another fire like this. Not in my life, not in the life of any man. In time, you will see that.*

But the silence Agravain left him with began to ring in his ears, and Gawain strode down the corridor to escape it. He must find his way to rest. Tomorrow would be a very long day.

FOURTEEN

Rhian did not see Gawain for much of the next day. Arthur had called all his cadre to council. Several of the wiser ladies whispered the word 'war'. It seemed certain that Arthur would not leave those who supported such treachery unpunished. But all must be done carefully, and with sober judgement, for there were treaties in place that could not be broken without a great price.

Even though she slept so late her mother would have declared it sloth, no one could say Rhian's morning was spent in idleness. Queen Guinevere commanded her presence in the royal wardrobe.

'There is the May Eve feast this night, Lady Rhian, and the hunting of the white stag on the morrow,' she said, as Rhian stared in unabashed amazement at the rich cloth that surrounded her. 'We must find you something fitting to wear.'

The queen brushed aside Rhian's attempts to select from among the simplest dresses. When she saw that her guest truly had no idea where to begin, she held up gown after gown against Rhian, and discarded them all as not doing her justice, until she at last settled on a pair that she said 'would do admirably'.

She was about to turn her attention to the matter of a veil and jewels, when one of the waiting women opened the door to allow in a page boy wearing the scarlet dragon emblazoned on his over-tunic.

The boy knelt before the queen. 'His Majesty the High King Arthur bids the Lady Rhian of the Morelands attend him now and give her witness.'

Rhian, her mind already awhirl from spending the morning amid more luxury than she had ever dreamt of, felt her knees buckle at the idea of speaking before the High King and all his council, whether Gawain was one of their number or no.

'You have information your king requires,' said the queen, guessing Rhian's thought, and fear. 'Speak the truth. These men have all known many wonders and terrors in their time. I promise, all there will hear you with respect and sound judgement.'

You will not be called a hysterical woman, she meant. *You will not be called a witch.*

Rhian had hoped Queen Guinevere would accompany her on this task, but she realized that was selfish to the point of outrageousness. Her Majesty had already spent hours on Rhian this morning. Rhian followed the page down the bright, broad corridors, and was followed in turn by the maid Jana. She was grateful for the fine grey dress. It helped her remember she was a daughter of rank, and one well taught at that, and that she knew her manners and her duty. She had faced her enemies, she had faced her own heart, she could face her liege lord.

But it was not only her lord she must face. The guards opened the doors to the war council chamber, and all within turned to look at Rhian.

It was a large room, and it needed to be to hold all the men within it. The cadre of the Round Table numbered one hundred and ten, and it seemed that every one of them was there today, plus their squires and servants and a host of guards with pikes and polearms to line the walls. Over their heads hung the bright banners which would tell her exactly which of the cadre was in attendance if she knew all their signs. She saw the royal dragon first, and picked out Gawain's star amid the garden of birds and beasts, swords and crosses. There were as many colours on these walls as in the wardrobe.

The men to whom those banners belonged crowded the outer and inner rims of the Round Table. They ranged in age from little more than a boy to an ancient, white-haired sage who looked as though he could not have lifted a feather, let alone a sword, but who watched her keenly as she followed the page into the room.

King Arthur sat in a carved chair on the outer rim of his table. Gawain sat at his right hand, and golden Lancelot on his left. Rhian knelt before the High King and bowed her head.

'Rise, lady.'

Rhian did as she was told, and stood with her hands neatly folded and her eyes modestly downcast. God alone knew what these men had heard of her. Rumour flew far faster than fact, even here. If nothing else, she would show them she knew decorum.

'Now. Lord Gawain tells us you were witness to certain events that have a bearing on this council. Speak, Lady Rhian, and tell us the whole of what you have seen.'

Rhian looked at the hundred faces, all of them studying her intently. They were dark and they were fair, broad and lean, some as handsome as Gawain and Lancelot, others scarred, battered and even maimed from their adventures. These were the survivors of Badon and dozens of other battles she had never heard of. These were the protectors of her land and her king.

That thought gave her the courage she needed and Rhian told them of Euberacon Magus and her father's old bargain. She told them of the Saxons' ambush, and saw Gawain nod in agreement. She even told them of how the raven spy had vanished after its death, and how the raven's cry had alerted her in the night to treachery at Pen Marhas.

'Did you see anything unnatural about these birds?'

The question came from the corner of the chamber, not from the Round Table. A man she had not before noticed rose from a chair. He wore robes like a monk, although they were black rather than brown, and belted with silver. A close-fitting cap embroidered with silver thread covered his head so that only a few wisps of white hair showed at the edges. His white beard covered his chest and he leaned on a long staff of pale wood.

Merlin the Magus. Merlin the Cunning Man. Arthur's closest councillor, and, some darkly whispered, the true power of Camelot. Rhian swallowed hard, for when she looked at him, she could not help but see Euberacon.

He was waiting for her answer. 'No, Sir.' She had no idea what his real title was or how it was proper to address such a person. 'They appeared as natural birds.'

He nodded, coming closer until he stood before her. He was hunched over with age or care, perhaps both. His eyes were bright blue and seemed to glitter as they looked at her from under heavy lids.

'You have seen other marvels, I think, lady.'

Rhian dropped her gaze quickly. She did not like those eyes. They could take the breath from her, take the will from her limbs. She gripped her skirt to keep her hands from trembling. 'Yes, Sir.'

'I would be grateful if you would tell me of them some time.' He spoke gently, even pleasantly. What was it that filled her with such trepidation? 'But I will not take up any more of this council's time with an old man's curiosity.'

Merlin returned to his corner seat. The further he withdrew, the easier Rhian's breathing became, and the fear washed from her blood so quickly she wondered if she had even truly felt it at all.

Which is the illusion? The fear or the calm? Rhian found herself wishing she had not thought of that.

'You have our thanks, Lady Rhian,' said the king. 'You may depart while we give our careful consideration to your words.'

Rhian knelt again, and took her leave, but as she turned, she managed to catch a glimpse of Gawain. He was smiling, and gave her a quick nod. She had done well then. Assurance brimmed warmly in her heart, and Rhian returned to the women's chambers with a light step and head held high.

Her new-won confidence buoyed her all the rest of the day, even as Jana readied her for the feast under Guinevere's strict supervision. The queen had selected for her a gown of dark ruby red, trimmed and laced with silver and garnets. Garnets served as the centres of the lilies that made up the girdle, the golden necklace at her throat, and the circlet that was laid over the tissue of gold veil that covered her hair. The queen had determined she would wear it loose tonight, as was the fashion for a maiden of her rank at the court, so out came the combs and brushes again, and her hair was worked over until it seemed to shine with its own inner light. It hung down her back and shoulders like a luxurious cloak. When the queen stood Rhian in front of the polished bronze mirror in her chamber, Rhian had to touch her own face to determine that the image was real. The emerald ring on her hand was the only thing she recognized.

'Yes, my dear,' said the queen when she saw the stunned expression on Rhian's face. 'That is you, in truth. God has given you great beauty. Rejoice in it.'

'Is that not pride, Majesty?'

The queen's smile turned mischievous. 'Perhaps. But perhaps it is only displaying appropriate appreciation of all the gifts Our Father has seen fit to bestow upon us.'

Rhian found herself wondering what Camelot's bishop thought of the queen's theological interpretations.

Guinevere herself wore scarlet, a shimmering fabric so light it did not seem possible that human hands had woven it. The ladies said it had been brought from Constantinople, but the art of its makings originated even farther to the east. Gold trimmed the sleeves that were long enough to brush the floor, as well as the hems and the collar. Her girdle was a chain of golden roses. In addition to her torque, the queen wore a crown in her sigil shape crusted with pearls.

Before Rhian had a chance to grow nervous again, one of the waiting women entered the queen's chamber and curtsied. 'Your Majesty, the High King sends his compliments and requests your presence at his board.'

'You may tell His Majesty we are most pleased to attend him and will arrive presently,' answered the queen with the same mischievous spirit she had displayed before. Clearly such formalities were something of a jest between her and her husband, and one she enjoyed.

'Come, my women.' She slipped her arm companionably through Rhian's. 'Let us see what has been prepared for us.'

The remaining ladies assembled according to their ranks and all of them proceeded down the corridor, the sounds of merriment and anticipation wafting around them.

The doors to the great hall had been thrown open wide. Torches and candles flared, turning the room as bright as day. Musicians played, filling the air with the sound of flutes and harps. The singer was holding forth with a poem of Persephone and Ceres, and Rhian would have loved to listen, but there was so much else to take her attention.

Long tables covered with cloths of white and green stretched the length of the hall. It seemed no one could have been denied a place, be they ever so humble. The cadre of the Round Table, of course, sat nearest the dais, and the champions occupied the high table with their king. Also there was Merlin, and a man in bright robes who must have been the bishop.

As the queen and her ladies entered, all stood and cheered. Arthur himself, dressed in gold and scarlet to match his queen, stepped down from the dais, and Guinevere released Rhian's arm to go forward to meet him. To Rhian's utter surprise, the king knelt at his wife's feet, and she laid her hands on his head as if in blessing. Then, he stood and kissed her soundly, raising another cheer that seemed as if it must shake the tiles from the roof.

Then the champions left the high table and came down to the floor, each of them to take a lady's hand and lead her to the table. Gawain presented himself before Rhian, and bowed.

He looked more like a figure from legend than any living man had a right. His curling black hair flowed across his shoulders, his chin had been shaved completely smooth, and his hands washed clean of all signs of battle and hard riding. He wore a tunic of brilliant emerald green that had been slit at the sides to show the snow-white undertunic beneath it. A belt of golden stars circled his waist and a chain of stars hung across his shoulders, only partly covered by a summer-green cloak embroidered with trees that had yet more stars caught in their branches.

But his eyes and smile were his own, and both shone for Rhian alone as he took her hand and led her to her place at the table.

The feast was worthy of a song of its own. Each course was accompanied by jugglers, acrobats, poets or dancers. Mummers masked as goats and outraged Saxons chased each other about the hall, causing Rhian to laugh until she wept with merriment.

Then there was the food. Rhian could only taste a little of what was set before her and she was still more full than she had ever been in her life. There were dainty pastries, light as clouds, whole salmon roasted in butter, geese and peacocks cooked in golden crusts accompanied by eggs in aspic, last year's apples stewed with raisins, cinnamon and cloves and served with fresh cream, roasted pork flavoured by a foreign herb called garlic which set Rhian's eyes to watering afresh. To accompany it all there were endless jugs of beer and half-a-dozen precious wines brought from across the Christian world and even past its bounds for the delight of the king and his lady.

There were speeches, of course. Time and again, one of the cadre or the champions stood and told some tale of the valour of himself or a companion, or spoke of the love and beauty of their ladies. The ladies themselves were not silent. At the queen's order, one or another would sing, or speak a piece of some epic. But as the feasting continued, Rhian felt a sense of anticipation rising from the high table, as if all were waiting for some overdue event. Even Agravain seemed to feel it, a thin smile playing about his pinched mouth.

Then, it came.

Kai the seneschal, who sat between Gawain and Lancelot, smiled expansively at Rhian and turned to Gawain, raising his wine cup.

'A beauty you've brought to us, Gawain. A rare treasure. It never ceases to amaze, Lord Agravain,' he went on conversationally, 'just what your brother finds by the roadside.'

A chuckle rose from many at the table, but not from Agravain. 'It is a talent that seems to have possessed him since he came to the south,' he said in perfect soberness.

'The first of many things to possess him, so I hear.' Kai pursed his lips. 'It is a wonder that you do not send for a priest that he might be exorcised.'

'If I thought that would help with what ails him, I would.'

'Perhaps it is only too much feasting. A luxurious diet can cause such heartburn.'

Rhian felt her cheeks begin to heat up. Gawain carefully set his cup down as if he were afraid it would spill. Arthur only sighed, and Guinevere gave Rhian a look that seemed to advise patience.

Agravain eyed Rhian as he stabbed his knife into a piece of pork. 'I would not say his diet is too rich.' He popped the dainty into his mouth. 'Too poor, perhaps.'

'Ah!' Kai raised one long finger. 'But what one man finds worthless, is priceless to another, and who can say how well he sees?'

'It is said God knows all things,' replied Agravain.

'Yes, but does one have to be God to know the price of a roadside treasure, or only Gawain?'

That earned a round of full-fledged laughter. Clearly the court felt Kai was in rare form, and it was more than Rhian could stand in silence.

'Tell me, my Lord Kai, in all the treasures you have known, is courtesy among them?'

That raised yet another laugh, and even Arthur chuckled.

Kai looked rather less pleased and Rhian began to fear that in answering she had made a grave mistake. 'Your lady is most well spoken, Gawain,' said Kai, apparently oblivious to the mounting anger in Gawain's expression. 'Clearly they instruct their ladies well in the outlands.'

'Not so well as in Pen Marhas,' added Agravain. Gawain's fist curled on the cloth.

'I had thought myself learned indeed,' said Rhian, forcing

pleasantry into her voice. 'But there is no poet's verse that speaks the truth of my Lord Kai's matchless wit.'

'Indeed?' Queen Guinevere leaned forwards. Rhian also noted she pulled Gawain's fisted hand from the table as she did. 'And what do the rhymes say of our brother Kai?'

'Why, Majesty, they call him tailor, for each guest in Camelot is measured up by my lord, and then cut down to size.'

Laughter and a smattering of applause went up. 'Tailor Kai!' cried one of the champions, and that cry was taken up by the others. Rhian faced the seneschal sunnily, feeling she might actually have scored some small victory.

But Kai had gone suddenly and completely serious. 'There are many cuts to be made and taken, my lady, and not all enemies are Saxons.'

Arthur raised his brows. 'Do you say this lady is an enemy, Kai?'

'Never in life, Majesty. Gawain would not knowingly bring such a one to this hall.'

'And Heaven knows it is his sagaciousness my brother is renowned for,' added Agravain.

'As my brother is known for his merry moods and generous disposition.' The jest of Gawain's words was completely drowned by the hard warning in them.

Kai leaned across to Rhian, whispering elaborately behind his hand. 'As we speak of poetry, my lady, here, I believe is where you clasp your bosom and cry "Alas! That I should be the cause of strife between brothers!"'

Rhian's back stiffened. 'I think I am ill-suited for that role, Sir,' she replied warily.

'Then what part shall you play, lady?' Kai leaned his elbow on the table and his chin on his hand. 'The blushing bride, perhaps?'

The ladies shrieked in delight at that thought, and the men

waggled their fingers at Gawain. 'My part shall be as it pleases God,' was all Rhian could think to say.

And it was exactly the wrong thing. Kai's eyes glowed and he smiled a long, sly smile. 'And which part shall be found so pleasant, I do wonder?'

The cheers this time were loud and ribald, and finally too much. Gawain shot to his feet.

'Nephew,' said Arthur, pleasantly but the warning was clear in his eyes.

Gawain did not sit down. Rhian turned quickly to Guinevere.

'Excuse me, Majesty,' she said. 'I find I am not well. I beg your leave to retire.'

'Of course, Lady Rhian.' Guinevere glowered at Kai. 'Lady Marie and Jana will take you back to your room. I will be up shortly to see you are well.'

She looked to Gawain, trying to plead with her eyes, *Leave it. Let me go.* He gave her a small nod, but she had no idea what that might mean.

What she did know was that her dream was over and reality returned. However welcoming the queen might be, whatever she and Gawain might feel in their hearts, there was no place for her here, and no other place for him.

For the second time in as many days, Gawain watched Rhian be led away to the care of Guinevere's ladies. This time though, he felt no relief as he had before. The whole of the high table watched him, waiting for him to sit down. From the look on Kai's face, he had some new jest brewing.

It was not a blow Gawain was prepared to let fall. 'A word, my uncle.'

'Gawain . . .' Arthur sighed.

'A word, if it please you.'

'Very well.' Arthur set his cup down and kissed Guinevere's

hand. 'My wife, will you see these ruffians remember their manners as well as their wits?'

'It shall be as you say, my husband.' She was looking daggers at Kai. The coming clash between these two would be the talk of the court for months, Gawain was sure. He would have been worried had he not known his aunt more than capable of holding her own against the seneschal.

The king stood and the whole of the hall with him. A train of whispers and murmurs swept behind him and Gawain as they left. Oh, there would be a gossips' feast to follow this one, that was certain.

And I will give them a fine dainty to chew over.

Arthur's private chamber was warm and richly furnished, and seldom empty. When they entered, it was populated by two secretaries, three servitors and two pages. Arthur dismissed them all, an unusual gesture. As Gawain faced his uncle in absolute privacy, he was not sure whether to be worried or hopeful.

Arthur folded his arms. He did not sit down. 'Your word, Gawain?'

When the king was in this mood, it was best not to embroider or explain, not even on such a matter as Gawain brought to him now. 'I wish to marry the Lady Rhian.'

Arthur sighed and hung his head. Gawain had the distinct feeling he was not in the least surprised. 'Gawain, your gallantry has always done you credit, but if we were moved to marry every lady Kai made public sport of, we should each of us have more wives than the kings of Arabia.'

But Gawain was ready for that, and had his counter in place. 'Uncle this has nothing to do with Sir Kai and his barbs. It has to do with my heart. I would take Rhian of the Morelands to wife. I am asking for your permission and blessing for that undertaking.'

Arthur was silent for a long moment. He studied his

nephew. Gawain knew he was turning over the words in his mind, weighing and judging how they were spoken, measuring them against what he knew of the speaker. Gawain had watched his uncle do this same thing many times in court, but seldom had he stood himself before such scrutiny. He suddenly felt as nervous as a new-made squire whose master was inspecting his work in the stables.

Arthur turned away from him then and folded his hands behind him, gazing out of the narrow slit of the window. The screen had not yet been folded into place. Night's cold crept in, brushing against his throat and the backs of his hands.

'I committed grave sins while founding Camelot, Gawain,' the king said. 'The blood of innocents is on my hands. It is under the stones of my great hall.'

This startled Gawain, it was so far from any answer he'd imagined. 'So may all warriors say.'

'Perhaps.' The word lacked any conviction. 'I have prayed to God for forgiveness, for some sign of mercy, if not for me, then for Camelot itself, for the Britons. I pray that He not let my weakness, my pride be the shifting sand that brings all that is good here down to rubble.' He faced Gawain again. 'I walk the halls at night, taken by the fear that we will become but a confection of words and distorted deeds to be told on a winter's night to drive away the dark.'

Gawain swallowed. 'Only God can know the future.'

'That is the simple truth. When I look at you, though, Gawain, I feel as if I can glimpse that future, and it is good and stalwart, strong and honest.' Arthur laid his hand on Gawain's shoulder, and Gawain felt himself reflexively straighten. 'Men such as you and I must think beyond our pleasures, our simple needs. We must look always to the future, to the good of the realm and the maintenance of its peace.'

'Yes, uncle.'

'This woman, Rhian, she is fair and mannered and she comports herself with dignity, but is she true of heart? Is she wise as well as brave? Any woman you marry will stand beside you one day as queen. Can you tell me truly that she would be a worthy successor to Guinevere?'

Gawain met Arthur's gaze unflinchingly. 'I will do more than tell it, I will swear it, on my honour, and on my love of God and Your Majesty. The only question in my heart is whether I am worthy of her.'

Arthur peered at him searchingly. *Believe I know what I am saying, uncle. Believe that there is none who will be better than she. You know about Pen Marhas. You know how she conducted herself there, and not even Agravain can contradict that. Believe that I have thought of all the lost chances for alliance and treaty because of what I do now. Believe that my love and my lady are true.*

What Arthur saw in his eyes, Gawain did not know, but slowly, he nodded, and a smile spread itself from his mouth to his eyes. He too knew love, this man. It was he and Guinevere who had taught Gawain what it truly was to be husband and wife.

'Very well, Gawain. We will make the betrothal.'

Relief fell heavily against Gawain and he knelt, in thanks and fealty, and because for a moment he was not sure he could remain standing. He seized his uncle's hand, his love and pride shining in his eyes, and saw the king return it all. There was no need for words.

At last, Gawain said, 'With your permission, Majesty, may I . . .'

Arthur cuffed him on the shoulder. 'Go to it, lad, if Guinevere will let you past that is. She too has taken a liking to the lady.'

Gawain leapt to his feet. He bowed hastily. Arthur laughed, turned him around and pushed him to the door. Once out

in the corridor under the eyes of the waiting guards and
servitors, Gawain remembered his dignity and slowed his
pace to a quick walk, forcing himself to take the stairs up to
the guesting quarters one at a time.

As Arthur had predicted, Gawain met the queen and a
small covey of ladies in the hall.

'Gawain,' said Guinevere sternly. 'Where are you going?'

Gawain hesitated, trying to direct his attention towards
the queen, as courtesy dictated, but his gaze drifted, looking
over her shoulder and down the rush-lit corridor, where he
knew Rhian waited behind a closed door, and God alone
knew what she was thinking. 'I need to speak with the Lady
Rhian,' he said.

The queen set her jaw sternly. 'It's late, Gawain. Between
Kai and Agravain, the lady has been through enough this
night.'

Gawain bowed, acknowledging the truth of what was said.
'But I have good news for her, Majesty. Such as she will be
glad to hear.'

Guinevere studied his eyes for a long moment, observing,
Gawain knew, the impatience there, and, although it was
painful to admit it, the fear. He thought he knew Rhian's
heart, but did he in truth? He had seen her hurt this night.
What was in her mind now? Would she be disposed to hear
his suit, or even to see him?

But Guinevere smiled and Gawain realized she saw
precisely what news he meant to carry to Rhian. She gave
a short sigh. 'Be sure you *ask* her, Gawain. Let it be her
choice. Try to tell her what her future must be and you
may find that although you gain her hand, you will lose
her true heart, where you might easily have won her
completely.'

Gawain thought to answer the remark with a small jest,
but then he saw the flash of steel in the queen's grey eyes

and realized that for all her light tone she spoke the weightiest counsel.

He bowed his head humbly. 'As ever, Majesty, your words are most wise. I shall do exactly as you say.'

'Then I wish that the blessings of Lady Venus may attend you on this errand, Sir.' Guinevere stepped aside, drawing in her skirts with exaggerated care so that he might pass easily.

'Madame.' Gawain bowed. Then, as quickly as courtesy allowed, he hurried down the corridor. He was certain the queen's soft laughter followed behind him.

Rhian was ready to proclaim that of all the luxuries of Camelot, the best was to have a fire in one's own room. Still in her borrowed finery, she sat before the gentle blaze, delighting in the warmth, and, she had to admit to herself, the feeling of the elegant clothes she wore. The queen had come to assure herself as to the state of Rhian's spirits, and Rhian had been able to satisfy her that she was little more than tired and overwhelmed. She had sent Lady Marie and Jana away to enjoy the last of the feasting, saying she wished to sit up for awhile. In truth, she was determined to drink this night to the dregs, for the morning would surely bring something quite different.

Rhian closed her eyes and swallowed, trying to drive away the memory of Kai's pointed jibes and Agravain's smirks. Gawain had been unfailingly courteous, of course, and Their Majesties had treated her like an honoured guest, and she had looked well, she saw that in the eyes of the knights and nobles. It meant little, however. Gawain would have to turn from her now that he was home and must again be Arthur's nephew and heir, rather than a simple knight errant who might dally with a lady and speak pretty words to her. Still, whatever was to come, she could remember their days together and the heat of their kiss beside the highway. She would have the memory of love to keep her warm, however cold the days would be without him.

She would learn to love again, in some measure, at least. She would. She must.

A tear escaped her eye and traced a cool line down her cheek. After a time, she reached up and brushed at it. Her hand fell back into her lap as if the life were gone from it.

Think on the feast, on the smiles and the kindness. Think on the music and the light in Gawain's eyes, all for you, if only for this moment. Do not think on the morrow. It is not yet come. When it does, you will find your heart again.

Despite all this wise advice, another tear followed the trail of the first.

A soft knock sounded on the door. *Jana.* Rhian wiped the fresh tear quickly away. She did not wish the maid to find her sitting and weeping like a foolish child.

'Come in.'

'Lady Rhian.'

The sound of the man's soft voice froze Rhian's heart. Trembling, she rose and turned. There stood Gawain, his amber eyes shining gently in the firelight as they regarded her with all the great tenderness she knew him capable of.

She swallowed, trying to find her voice. She had not expected to see him before the dreaded morning. To have him here now robbed her of what little composure she had held on to.

'My Lord Gawain,' she managed to stammer out his name and remember to curtsey. 'I . . . I'm sorry . . . I . . .' she could not think of what to say and fell silent, her cheeks heating up from shame.

Gawain closed the door behind him and bowed low to her. 'Lady. Of your courtesy, I would speak with you.'

The blush burned Rhian's cheeks. *You could not wait? You*

could not give me the whole of the night before you must tell me
Arthur has reminded you of your duty and how I must be given to
someone of more appropriate rank and station?

Those thoughts must have showed themselves plainly in
her face. Gawain looked stunned, as if he had been struck
a blow.

'Oh, Rhian, no.' He crossed the room swiftly and took her
hand, which had gone cold. She could feel the warmth of
his skin, the strength of his touch. 'Do you think I come
with sorrowful news?'

Emotion closed Rhian's throat. When she was finally able
to speak, she could only note that at least her weary voice
stayed steady and clear. 'What else could it be, Gawain? You
must take up your duties again. I have no rightful claim to
make on you.'

Gawain reached out and with his fingertips traced the line
of her cheek down which her tears had fallen. 'That is not
true. You have the strongest of all claims on me, Lady Rhian,
for you may lay claim to my heart.'

With those words, he lowered himself onto one knee, holding her hand between both of his. 'Will you marry me, Rhian?
Will you be my second self and the wife of my heart?'

She stared at him, feeling his palm warm and rough against
hers. Her mind was suddenly unable to understand what was
happening. 'Gawain, we cannot marry.'

'Rhian.' Gawain's gaze was steady. The dark amber of his
eyes was as warm as all of summer. 'Do not think of what
can and cannot be. Tell me now, what is the wish of your
heart? If you had the whole of the world before you and
you could choose your destiny from all of it, what would be
your choice?'

The world Gawain spoke of seemed to have gone utterly
still. Even the fire fell silent, its flames seeming as steady as
sunbeams. Rhian reached out. Her fingers brushed Gawain's

cheek and touched, for just a heartbeat, the straight line of his jaw. His eyes closed, as if he wanted to concentrate completely on her touch, and his hand pressed hers, oh-so-gently, but with a warmth that went instantly to Rhian's heart and opened it wide.

'If I could choose?' Now it was her voice that trembled. 'Gawain, I would choose to be at your side and never leave you. I would choose to give myself and all I have freely to you, and think nothing of it.'

His eyes opened and they shone with joy. 'Then choose that, Rhian. Let me be your champion, your lover, your husband for as long as life is in me.'

'Gawain, we cannot be . . . The king . . .'

He stood, pulling her hand close to his breast. Her heart hammered hard in the base of her throat. 'My uncle Arthur has already given his consent, Rhian. There is no bar between us.'

'But Euberacon, my father . . . what of this curse on me?'

Now Gawain smiled, and his whole attitude filled with the confidence she had seen in him when he stood before Bannain in his hall and issued his orders. 'I have slain dragons, remember, Rhian? I am the champion of the Round Table and there is no knight here who has not fallen before my spear, not even that braggart Lancelot. Arthur and Merlin are my kin and my brave friends. No sorcerer, no matter if they come from the farthest shores of Hell, can touch you now, for whatever answer you give me, I have sworn you shall not be harmed.

'Rhian, my lady, I love you above all others and I shall strive with all my strength to make you happy. It is only the thought you might refuse that makes me weak. I beg of you, give me your answer. Will you be my wife?'

She could not speak, for she could not hear herself think. Her blood was singing too loudly in her ears. She could only stare up at Gawain's beloved face, at his wide eyes and red mouth. His black hair gleamed in the flickering light of the fire. She had never seen a man so fair. She never would again. But it was not the sight of his fine face that robbed her of her wits. It was the sure and sudden knowledge that all he said, all he had ever said, was true. His love was true. His question was honest, as were his promise and all his gentle words. He loved her. Gawain loved her.

At that same moment, she knew that she had been lying to herself. There would be no other love for her. There could only be Gawain for as long as she drew breath in the world.

With that, all fear left her. Voice and limbs grew strong again, her sight and mind became clear.

'Then, Gawain,' she said, her voice firm with purpose and filled with love. 'This is my choice. I choose to marry you. If God so wills, I will stand beside you for the rest of my life.'

He kissed her then. She knew he would, but that knowledge robbed the act of none of its sweetness. His strong arms pulled her close, pressing her against his chest. His mouth opened against hers and drank her in, leaving her dizzy with a passion she had never before known.

He lifted his head at last, giving her just room enough to breathe and the air was filled with his warmth and his scent. Slowly, she became once more aware that there was a world beyond him, a room with a fire and flickering tapers, and that someone was knocking at the door.

Slowly, smiling, his eyes shining with a light that came only from within him, Gawain let go of her and stepped backward far enough that propriety was observed once more. But he did not take his gaze from her, and his gaze seared.

The knocking continued.

'Come in.' Rhian was amazed at how calm she sounded. The air felt chill against her skin now that Gawain's warmth no longer enveloped her. She could no more look away from him than she could have taken Atlas's burden from his shoulders.

From the corner of her eye, she saw the door open. Jana stepped into the room.

'My lady,' Jana began, and then she saw Gawain, and stopped. 'My lord.' Jana curtsied deeply. Her eyes flickered from Rhian to Gawain, and back again. 'I came to see what my lady might require.' There was a note in her voice that was offended, as if she was annoyed that she had not been informed of this rendezvous.

'Ah.' Gawain did not move. His gaze did not falter. 'Is there anything you require of your servant, Lady Rhian?'

He was giving her another choice, she realized. This one too was hers, to accept or reject. His eyes told her what he wished, and what he understood. With one word, she could send him away, and he would go gallantly and wait patiently. With another word though, she could bid him stay.

'No,' she said. 'There is nothing I require, Jana. You may go.'

She saw the maid hesitate. Rhian watched thoughts of propriety, of her duty to Rhian, and to the queen, cross through Jana's mind. The maid had doubtless seen Gawain with other ladies, had perhaps even witnessed such a scene before. Perhaps she even thought to warn Rhian – whom she surely saw as an innocent from the outlands – of the reputation of the man who stood in front of her.

The man who filled her heart with such love. The man who would be her champion, her husband, her lover.

Her lover.

'You may go, Jana,' she repeated.

Jana reached her own decision. She curtsied and turned away. The door opened and closed again, and Rhian was alone with Gawain.

He walked towards her, his smallest movement filled with grace and strength. He stood before her, and once again she could breathe in the scents of earth and smoke, spice and warmth, that hung all about him. She could not move. Her heart fluttered in her breast, torn between wonder and fear. Her whole being was taut as a harp string, waiting for what might come.

Gawain lifted his hands to the sides of her head and gently removed the gold and garnet band that circled her brow. He laid it on the small table beside the chair. One by one, he removed the pearl-and-silver pins that held her veil in place over her hair. He drew the glimmering tissue away, and she stood bare-headed before him, her hair flowing freely down her shoulders. Still she did not move. It seemed to be all she could do to remember to breathe and each breath drew more of Gawain into her blood.

He was smiling and his mouth was wide and perfect. The light in his gaze had grown deep and smouldered within the dark amber of his eyes.

'Rhian.'

And she was in his arms, kissing him again, and there was no hesitation, no fear, no sadness in the whole world. There was only Gawain and the love they brought to each other, and that was all there ever would be.

FIFTEEN

The night the ancient priests named Beltane found Kerra in the depths of the oldest forest the isle had ever grown. The trees towered overhead higher than the arch of any king's hall, their trunks making crooked pillars three and four times the width of a man's body.

She had wanted to come alone, but Euberacon was not in a mood to humour such a request. That worried her. If she were straining his trust, things could go badly. There was enough that must be done tonight without having to prove herself over again to the one who thought he was her master.

The trees here were so old that their branches had long ago laced together to form a solid canopy. No moonlight could penetrate to the forest floor. Shadows hung all about them like curtains of sable. The lantern in her hand bobbed like a will o' the wisp, illuminating an area that was barely large enough to stand in.

It did not matter. It was not her eyes that led her. It was the host of other senses Morgaine had taught her of, it was heart and mind, the pricking of her skin and soul.

Eyes gleamed yellow and green, watching their passage. An owl hooted overhead. In the distance, a wolf howled, and another answered. The wind blew hard and cold, carrying the scents of fresh greening and dew. Old leaves and pine needles rustled beneath their feet. Euberacon drew closer and Kerra smiled to herself. Could it be the mighty eastern sorcerer was afraid of this untamed forest? Perhaps he was not such a fool after all.

In the centre of this ancient forest rose a mound, a round hill covered with moss and leaves. No tree grew there, no track of any beast disturbed its skin. A springlet trickled down its side, as bright and clear as a river of moonlight. Kerra's dry throat itched to drink that pure water, but she knew better. That water might be a gift to the beasts who lived in these woods, but the giver would not take kindly to such as her helping themselves.

'What now?' inquired Euberacon.

'We wait. When the time comes, the master of this place will show himself.'

Euberacon grunted wordlessly. This was not something he understood easily. That did not matter, as long as he stayed, and stayed quiet. Kerra blew out the light.

Darkness descended around them so completely, Kerra could not see the lantern in her hand, let alone the mound before them. Fear, unexpected and distasteful, speeded up her heartbeat.

Patience, patience. It is only darkness.

Darkness in the wild, where they were the intruders, where wolf or bear might come upon them, and they would be dead with the swiftness of thought, and her companions would feast on her remains and wonder where Kerra had gone. This was not her place. She belonged in the stone halls, huddled by her fire, not in the greenwood, not among the beasts who saw her as nothing more than their prey.

'Old power indeed,' murmured Euberacon. 'With very old tricks to call upon.'

Kerra swallowed, and tried not to feel how grateful she was for that reminder.

It seemed the darkness lightened a little. She could make out the curve of the mound, the rough shape of the nearest tree. She wondered if her eyes had finally begun to detect the faintest sliver of moonlight, but no. The master of the Green Temple had arrived.

Where he was, it was daylight. Where he was, it was summer and warm. He was as tall, as strong as the trees that surrounded him. Oak leaves crowned his flowing, green locks. Leaves and vines draped his body, reminding Kerra of her own cloak of feathers. In his hand he held the living branch of a hawthorn tree bright with white blossoms. He looked at them with eyes that were all the shades of green the wildwood could hold, and Kerra felt suddenly as small and fragile as a mayfly.

She knelt. Beside her, reluctantly, Euberacon did the same.

'So. You are come before me, little woman, little man. Come to invoke the ancient laws and beg a boon of Jack-in-the-Green?'

Kerra kept her eyes on the patchwork carpet of leaves spreading at her feet. It did not do to look too long into the eyes of such as stood before her now.

'Not to beg, my lord, but to honour.'

'Honour?' The word sounded over Kerra's head at once as soft as the rustle of leaves and as loud as thunder. There was humour in it, but there was danger as well. 'What honour would you do me?'

Do not look up. Do not seek his eyes. You will lose yourself in a heartbeat if you do. 'The ones who rule this land now have forgotten you, my lord. They disdain the true ways and worship a foreign god. It is a disgrace that all of the true blood must feel. When I am queen in Camelot, you shall have shrines again. Great stone circles will be raised for you and your praise shall again be sung across the land.'

'Do you seek to win my aid by bribery?' The humour and the danger both grew more marked. 'Little woman, you will need to find another trick.'

'It does not anger you to see this foreign worship displace you? When your followers are all converted, what will become of you?'

The Green Man laughed. The sound poured over Kerra like a flood, rocking her backward, almost, almost bringing her head up.

'You believe it concerns me whose name is cried out in prayer?' He laughed again, a wondrous, terrible noise. 'Jove came, Mithras came, now the White Christ comes, and the one his followers call Wotan. Let them come, it is of no moment. My place is the stone and the forest, the green grass and the deep places. There is no usurper who can lift me from them, no matter how loudly their priests chant to the heavens. Those whose blood and bones are old and of this earth will always know me, whether they know a name to call me by or not.'

Shaken by the force of the old god's laughter, Kerra could not find her tongue. It was Euberacon who spoke.

'If you cannot be persuaded, you may yet be forced.'

Silence, as terrible and as disorientating as the laughter had been, fell, and for a moment Kerra feared they were both dead.

'Little man, I know you,' said the Green Man softly. 'Your summonings crowd the night with their noises. All with you is binding and imprisoning. All your thoughts are vengeance. Beware, lest you look so far to your goal you fail to see the step that takes you into your grave.'

'Angels come to earth at my command. It is you that must beware.'

Kerra closed her eyes, struggling to find her wits again.

'Little man, you come close to angering me. Let your woman lead you away. Your doom is closer than you think.'

Kerra touched Euberacon's arm. Her hand had gone ice cold. *Be quiet, be quiet, you fool.* 'We have not yet begged our boon,' she said.

Did the growl come from the Green Man or from some wolf drawing near? Was that rustle overhead a raven's wing, coming not in friendship but in anticipation of a kill?

'It is your right according to the old bargains between your kind and mine. Speak then.'

'There is a man, Gawain. He must bind himself to us, or die without any seeing our hand in his downfall.'

'Must?' The very earth seemed to tremble beneath Kerra's knees. 'You are very free with that word.'

It is your right. It is the law. Do not let go of that. 'That is the boon we seek. You said yourself, lord, that you must hear. Gawain hides behind a shield of tarnished honour. Were his hypocrisy exposed, he would be helpless before it.'

'You say Lot's son Gawain is a false man?' The humour had returned, and something of curiosity. Kerra began to breathe more easily.

'In his heart he is. I have seen it.'

Does he smile? Does he frown? Her skin crawled with his nearness and her mind filled with the heady scents of summer, but also with the scent of blood that came with birth, and with death. 'Then, woman, you will have an opportunity to prove it. With you, I'll make a bargain, as you are of this land.' His disdain flickered towards Euberacon, and she heard the uncomfortable rustle of cloth. 'I feel your roots deep within, I feel your lust for the powers and the secrets that are this land's to give. I will bring Gawain to you. If you can prove him in any way false or cowardly, by my hand he will die.'

'And if she cannot?' asked Euberacon. She had known him daring and disrespectful, but she had not known the strength of either aspect until this moment.

'Then Gawain goes his way unhindered, and she,' this time she clearly heard the smile in his words and imagined his emerald teeth shimmering in the light that surrounded him, 'Comes to me.'

'Kerra?'

'Gawain will come to me. I am in no danger.'

'I do not like this,' muttered Euberacon. Kerra glanced at the sorcerer. He too had directed his gaze downward, proving that he was not entirely a fool. His face was tight with anger, and other things she could not put a name to, but fear was most definitely among them. 'It is dangerous to bargain thus with spirits. One must bind, or agree to be bound.'

Impatience tightened Kerra's hands. The presence of the Green Man was a weight on mind and body. She would not be able to bear up beneath it forever. The longer they stayed here, the greater the chance of some fatal mistake. Morgaine had been correct when she warned that the smallest slip could ruin all. 'It is a risk. I know that well, but it will be worth it when we win.'

'When *we* win,' sneered Euberacon. 'I am glad that you risk my victory for yours.'

'As you have done to me many times, my lord.' She spoke fast, trying to keep breath and thought under her own control. 'Do we play this game, or find another? The barbarians you ordered me to set upon Camelot have failed us. That plan is unveiled. How many days do we have before Arthur and Merlin come for battle and find us alone in your ruin?'

Perhaps he had an answer for that, but she did not give him time to voice it. 'It is a bargain, my lord,' she said to the Green Man. 'Bring me Gawain and I will show you how easily he breaks faith.'

'What do you give to bind this bargain?'

Without looking up, Kerra drew one of the long pins from

her hair. She drove the pin into her finger until a drop of shining red blood welled up. The Green Man held out his hand. The scarlet drop fell onto his palm and his fist curled around it.

'Done,' he said and his smile was wide, and despite all her certainties Kerra felt her heart shudder.

Rhian woke with the sun, feeling whole and well for the first time in what seemed an eternity. Gawain had left her a while ago, with a long kiss that was both promise and reminder. The touch of it lingered with her still.

A loud knock sounded on the door. 'My lady?' called Jana's voice, and that too was louder than necessary.

'Come in.' It occurred to Rhian to wonder where the maid had spent the night. It would be usual for her to sleep in the room with Rhian . . . she would have to apologize and arrange for some gift as soon as she was able.

Jana did seem put out, but perhaps not irretrievably so. She went about the tasks of getting Rhian presentable with efficiency and care, but with rather more sighs and harumphs than Rhian recalled from the previous day, especially when she once again had to comb out Rhian's hair. Rhian was to join the hunt for the white hart, the queen had been quite clear on the matter. As it was impossible for Rhian to ride with her hair unbound, Jana tied it into a braid, wound and pinned it tight and looped it into a netting trimmed with freshwater pearls. For a gown, Rhian wore the last of the queen's gifts; a dark green dress trimmed and girded with blue in a square pattern favoured, it was said, by the ancient Romans. A simple white veil topped with a garland of fresh cherry blossoms – apparently a tradition for this hunt – completed her wardrobe. Her profuse thanks seemed to loosen the tight moue Jana had held her mouth in for most of the morning. She picked up the hooded cloak with which

Rhian had been supplied in the most likely event that the weather turned foul, and followed along behind without a single audible sigh.

Outside the great hall, the morning was bright with sun and nearly as warm as summer. Riders and horses were already assembling. Despite the crowd, Rhian easily made out Gawain speaking to a younger man and holding the reins of a glossy black charger almost as large as Gringolet. He saw her and bowed, acknowledging her presence, but it was Queen Guinevere who came up to her first.

She did not even give Rhian time to kneel, but took her hands and gave her the kiss of peace.

'God be with you, this morning, Lady Rhian,' she said, her eyes shining, and Rhian saw at once that the queen knew all that had passed between her and Gawain, and moreover, she approved. 'Welcome to our spring rite.'

She was dressed in green, as were most of the others, lords and ladies both garlanded with flowers, and even a few early ferns and leaves. All did seem merry indeed and there was much teasing and laughter, along with exchanges of ribbons and similar tokens for kisses bestowed on hand, or on mouth.

A new pair of figures strode from the hall. The first was the bishop, all in white and gold, an elaborately curling crook in his hand. A priest in plain robes followed, clutching a leather-bound Bible to him that was so large Rhian was surprised there was only one man to carry it.

Queen Guinevere sighed. 'Forgive me. I must go mollify our bishop. He thinks this all a devilish and pagan ritual and frowns darkly upon it. We needs must all be blessed and sprinkled with holy water.'

The queen breezed away, leaving Rhian a bit breathless. She found herself looking around for another familiar face. Gawain was still among the lords and knights, deep in conversation with Kai and another she recognized as his brother

Gareth. She did not feel up to facing Kai so held her place. Then she saw a wiry boy back among the ladies' mounts holding Thetis's reins. Her mare had been given a new green saddle-blanket and new harness hung with green ribbons. She looked uneasy in the great crowd, and Rhian was glad to hurry to her side. The mare whickered in greeting, nuzzled Rhian's face and ears, and began searching her sleeves for treats.

'How thoughtless of me, I've brought you nothing, poor neglected animal.' In truth, Thetis looked in excellent health and had been as well groomed by the stablehands as Rhian had by the waiting ladies.

A shadow fell across her. Rhian turned and her good humour sank away. Agravain on horseback towered over her. The look on his face left her no doubt that he had heard of Gawain's proposal to her, as well as the king's approval of it.

She took refuge behind manners. 'My Lord Agravain.' She curtsied politely.

'Lady Rhian.' He returned a small bow from the saddle. They stared at each other for a moment, Agravain's fingers twining restlessly in the horse's reins. 'It is my understanding you are to be betrothed to my brother.'

'It is so.' *Did you think your brother a liar?* Rhian could not believe Gawain had left it to anyone else to tell Agravain what he meant to do.

'I suppose, then, you expect my congratulations.'

Rhian chose her words carefully, hoping formality might provide an acceptable cloak for honesty. 'I expect nothing, Sir. I only hope that one day you and I may greet each other in peace and felicity as brother and sister.'

Rhian was completely unprepared for the look of utter poison that formed on Agravain's face. For a moment it seemed his venom struck him dumb. At last though, he said,

'My brother will have surely told you, lady, I lack the capacity for felicity.' Then he wheeled his horse about and returned to the head of the procession.

Mother Mary, grant him patience, and grant the same to me, thought Rhian as she watched him depart. The circumstances of the betrothal were highly unusual to say the least. Seen philosophically, it reflected well on Agravain that he was concerned at his brother's choice of wife. It was only discourtesy, and that could be borne.

Gawain looked towards her over the heads of the assembly, his mouth set in a frown. Rhian lifted her hand to him, letting him know she was well. He nodded his acquiescence and continued his business.

If this is how we begin, by the time our first babe is born we will not need words at all. That seemed a delightful prospect to Rhian, to be always beside one with whom she could communicate heart to heart.

She thought wistfully of her mother then, wishing she could see that all was now well with her daughter. She would know soon. The queen's messenger would reach her in another two days.

Around Rhian, the noise was fading. Arthur and Guinevere, hand-in-hand, mounted the steps to stand before the bishop. King and queen, followed by their entire assembly, knelt to receive the blessing, which was delivered in a voice loud enough to carry all the way to Heaven, and there was rather more holy water than Rhian herself would have thought necessary. Slightly damp, but beaming to each other for all that, Arthur and Guinevere mounted their horses, which gave leave to the rest of them to do the same. The procession was formed according to rank, with the knights immediately behind the king and queen, and the ladies making a colourful train behind them. Banners, ribbons, servitors, guards and leashed hounds flanked them. Arthur blew a long, curling note on his horn, and all the court rode out through the great gates.

The whole of Camelot had given itself over to celebration of the feast day. Flowers and greening branches decorated every door and a goodly number of the people. The drink was already flowing and toasts were raised with the cheers as the procession from the great hall rode past. Arthur frequently clasped his queen's hand and raised it high, and whenever he did so the joyous clamour redoubled. By the time they reached the city walls, Rhian's ears were fairly ringing.

Outside Camelot's walls, the procession became much less formal, lords and ladies mingling freely. Laughter and gaity sounded on all sides. Even the animals seemed in a merry mood. The dogs strained at their leashes with their gambolling and nosing about, despite the efforts of their masters. Aging Thetis, egged on by the presence of the younger, lighter horses, stepped high and held her head erect and proud.

With all we've come through together, you should be proud. Rhian patted her mount's neck and grinned. In truth, setting aside her conversation with Agravain, the only blemish to the morning was that returning to the saddle revealed she was still tired and sore from all that had occurred before she arrived in Camelot.

That discomfort could not keep her from smiling and enjoying the green and peaceful land spreading around her. Ahead waited the fringes of the wood, which would be littered with broad meadows broken by clusters of young trees. Perfect country for deer, even a mystical white hart.

Gawain was not slow to take advantage of the abandonment of formality and reined in his horse until Rhian caught up with him.

'My lady seems in a festive mood,' he remarked, putting his steed into step beside Thetis.

'And who would not be on such a day?' She gestured expansively at the blue sky. The clouds were huge and white, but seemed inclined to wander individually about rather than clustering together to make a storm.

Gawain squinted at the sky, and then at Rhian. 'Ah, is that the cause? I thought perhaps my lady had received some piece of good news.'

Rhian blinked. 'Nothing in particular that I can recall, my lord. Have you heard of something?'

'No, not I, lady, but then, I pay no attention to gossip.'

'A wise policy.' Rhian nodded soberly.

They looked long and steadily at each other, almost daring one another to smile, until Rhian could bear it no longer and broke into a fit of giggles. Gawain joined her in a long, hearty laugh. The horses whickered, as if finding their own enjoyment in the joke, which only made their riders laugh harder.

When she could speak again, Rhian asked, 'How is the white hart hunted?'

'Largely as you see.' Gawain gestured at the relaxed and festive riders around them. 'We will ride, we will enjoy the sun, which has kindly agreed to show itself, and then we will return to the hall for the feasting.'

'A pleasant prospect.'

'Will you ride to the hunt with us?'

She thought about merrily racing Thetis through the woods and meadowlands, trying to keep pace with Arthur's cadre and such ladies as felt bold enough to join the race. Even with the thought that she would be beside Gawain the whole time, it was all she could do to keep from wincing. 'I would, my lord, but I fear the exercise would bring glory neither to myself, nor my poor horse.'

Gawain nodded, his face creased in sympathy. 'It is my intent to dare the jibes of my foster uncle Kai and return early to the company of the ladies. I trust this will not displease you.'

'On the contrary, my lord, I shall look forward to it.'

'And there is where you may take your ease to anticipate this and many another happy event.'

An entire flock of snowy pavilions seemed to have landed in the middle of the meadow. The servitors hurried forwards with steps for those who wished to dismount, and wine cups for those who intended to ride to the hounds. Rhian dismounted and allowed a groom to take Thetis's reins.

She turned to take her leave of Gawain. 'I have no sleeve or ribbon to give you for luck, my lord.'

'Well, then I fear you must give me a kiss, my lady.' Gawain leaned down. With serious decorum, Rhian kissed him on the cheek. Around them rose guffaws of laughter although by the time Gawain turned to glower, all faces were perfectly serious.

Oh, he will claim payment for this later. Rhian smiled as she dropped her eyes and folded her hands to make herself into the image of maidenly modesty.

When she risked a glimpse up, Gawain bowed solemnly to her, and winked. Then, he turned his horse and trotted to the head of the procession to take his place beside the king and queen. She felt, rather than saw Agravain staring at her and sighed. They said time was a great healer. She could only hope that would prove true between the two brothers.

'Lady Rhian.' Lady Marie strolled up beside her, apparently having seen she stood alone. 'Are you joining us while these others tear their clothing and the countryside to pieces?'

'If I am welcome, Lady Marie.' Memories of the scathing looks and whispers in Pen Marhas followed hard by the fresh recollection of the treatment she had received from Kai and

Agravain the previous day made her suddenly regret her choice. The other ladies already clustered on blankets in the shade of the trees as the pavilions were made ready for the midday meal and the return of the hunters.

'You are most welcome.' Marie sounded both friendly and sympathetic. Rhian hooked her arm through the lady's and let herself be led to join the feminine company.

The hunting party rode out and everyone cheered. As they vanished into the greenwood, the ladies turned to each other for amusement. Dainties, both sweet and savoury were set out with wine and small beer. Fine needlework was unpacked, and in short order, rather to her surprise, Rhian found she began to enjoy herself. Oh, there was gossip enough around her, but little of it was mean-spirited. There was talk of the Saxons as well, but it was sensible, rather than terrified or blood-thirsty. Rhian herself was questioned, as she expected, but the ladies took their cue from Marie and appeared content with her somewhat short answers, even when she only turned her gaze downward and blushed at the hintings at her betrothal. The king would make that announcement, and it was clear the court already knew most of the tale without her confirmation.

'Shall we have some entertainment?' suggested Lady Marie, seeing Rhian was determined not to elaborate on the subject of her relationship with Gawain. 'It grows dull in the heat.' It was an unusually warm day for the first of May, and more than the delicate pastries were beginning to droop as noon approached. 'Lady Rhian, would you be willing to oblige?'

At first, Rhian was relieved, but then unnerved. What could she know that would entertain these polite and sophisticated ladies? They surely knew the epics better than she did. It was equally certain they would turn up their noses at an outlandish country song. *Or would they?* Emboldened

by the delightful morning and her friendly reception, Rhian
smoothed her skirts out and began:

> 'An outlandish knight come from the Northland,
> He come a-wooing of me.
> He promised to take me into the Northland,
> And there his bride I should be.'

From the laughs of delight and the clapping, it was a good
choice, not least because Gawain himself was from the north.
She would live a long time among these ladies. Let that life
begin with laughter.

> 'And so he's turned his back around,
> And viewed the wold with great glee.
> She's grabbed him around the middle so small,
> And kelted him into the sea, the sea, and kelted him
>   into the sea . . .'

There were small cries then, in mock-horror at this blood-
thirsty deed, along with some remarks passed back and forth
about why Gawain should take care not to turn his back on
Rhian that would have caused some of the younger men to
blush had they been there to hear. Rhian herself was hard
pressed to keep her countenance.

> 'Lie there, lie there, you false-hearted man,
> Lie there instead of me . . .'

Something dark fell onto her skirt. Rhian brushed at it,
thinking it was a twig, but as her hand moved she saw instead
that it was a feather, long and glossy black.

She had no time to do anything but look up. They rained
down like leaves from the trees, talons extended, beaks open

and shrieking their triumph. Rhian heard shouts, heard screams. She threw up her hands, beating at pricking feathers and soft bodies, but they were too many. They blotted out the sun. She covered her eyes, crying out wordlessly. She felt the talons and stabbing beaks. They were everywhere. There was no part of her they did not touch. Then, impossibly, she felt the ground rush away from beneath her in a roar of beating wings and laughing birds. The terror was too much for her, and Rhian's mind went dark.

SIXTEEN

Rhian woke to nothing more alarming than a bare room and a thin straw mattress on a plain bedstead. She sat up at once. Her hands were slashed and bleeding from the ravens' attack. She wrapped her sleeves around them to staunch the still-oozing blood. The air around her felt slightly damp, as if she were in a cellar. A single sunbeam streamed into the room from an arched opening near the ceiling, but it was blocked by a bulky shadow. Rhian craned her neck, and saw a black bird sitting on the sill.

Unreasoning terror seized her. She screamed, throwing herself backward so hard she slammed against the wall. The raven chuckled, and flew away.

Rhian buried her head in her wounded hands. Shudders ran through her entire frame. She clenched her jaw to stop the screams.

I will not weep. I will not.

When she was able to look up again, the light streamed unbroken through the minuscule window. Rhian forced herself off the bed and went to try the plain wooden door. Several futile pushes told her it was barred from the outside. She stood on tip-toe to try to see out of the window and made out the edge of a tiled yard and the curving base of what might have been a fountain or a well. She saw no signs of anyone coming or going. She heard no sound but her own harsh breathing.

She lowered herself onto her heels and clutched her sleeves, trying to think. Before she could calm her storm-tossed thoughts, she heard the sound of scraping wood and whirled around.

The door opened and a slim woman in an ochre gown entered. She was fair enough to be Saxon. Her golden hair hung to her waist and her blue eyes regarded Rhian critically.

This was the witch. Harrik's witch. She must be. She was just as Gawain had described her.

'Well, let's have a look at you.' The woman crossed the room in two strides and caught Rhian's chin in her hand. Rhian swatted at her, but she simply seized Rhian's wrists in her free hand, twisting painfully. 'Now, none of that. Hmm.' She turned Rhian's face left and right. Then she let go and stood back, leaving Rhian burning with humiliation and anger. 'Pretty enough to snare a blind man like Gawain, but no real knowledge there. No learning or craft. There could be, though.'

'Who are you, and what do you want with me?' demanded Rhian.

To her surprise, the witch smiled. 'I want to be your ally, if you'll let me. You must listen quickly, for the magister does not want us meeting yet, not until he's sure his is the hand that holds your leash.'

The magister. There was only one person that could be. He'd done it. He had taken her. Rhian fought against the rising fear, carried by clinging tightly to her anger. 'Who brought me here? Was it you?'

'There's some spirit there too.' The witch nodded approvingly. 'Perhaps I will be able to work with you yet.'

Hope unlooked for surfaced in Rhian. 'Can you get me out of this place?'

But the witch only raised her brows. 'And what good would that do you?'

'I would be free!'

'You would not. Euberacon would only hunt you down again and bring you back. You may believe me when I say his wrath would not be a pleasant thing to face. You are better off where you are for the present, where you may learn the reality of things, and work towards a true freedom.'

Rhian steeled herself. The witch had left the door open. If she ran, if she were fast enough . . .

'You cannot be fast enough, not in this place.' The witch stepped closer. She smelled of mint and incense. Her breath was warm and sweet. Was this what enchanted Harrik? Was this what fed the ravens? 'Listen to me, little girl,' she murmured, and despite herself Rhian did listen. 'Euberacon thinks he understands. He thinks he can control you. He thinks he knows what women want, but even he has limitations. No sorcerer can see all possibilities and every spell has its weak point, for every sorcerer has his. Euberacon does not understand the choices of others. He believes that only he is in control, and that his choice is final. This is his weakness. Remember that, and you will have the whip hand over him.'

Rhian retreated. The cell did not afford much room for movement, but she could back away a few paces and find room to breathe, to think. What is it every woman wants? Where had she heard that question before?

'Why would you tell me this about your master?'

The witch's blue eyes glinted. 'Because he is not the one I serve.'

'Who then?'

'Not yet, Rhian.' *Yes,* her smile said. *I even know your name.*

What else do I know? 'I too must be certain of loyalty before I reveal so much truth.'

Rhian paced sideways, thinking to circle the witch, to bring herself closer to the door, but all at once a hurricane wind blew from nowhere at all, raising a gout of dust and noise. Rhian threw up her hands and fell back. The wind died as quickly as it rose, and she was able to see again. The witch was gone. The door was closed, and – Rhian rushed to it – barred.

She sat on the edge of the bed. There was nowhere else to go. Her hands hurt. Pinpricks of pain touched her cheeks, but nothing felt inflamed. There was nothing to do but wait for the one who had brought her here to reveal himself, and to try to keep her courage up.

Arthur and Merlin are my kin and my brave friends, Gawain had said.

Gawain would be searching for her. He would require Merlin to bend his arts to her aid. She must hold tight to that, no matter what happened. She was not abandoned. She never would be, not while Gawain lived. She knew that.

No sorcerer, no matter if they come from the farthest shores of Hell, can touch you now.

Rhian closed her eyes. *No. This is not his fault, not your fault. You must not think that way. Say your prayers Rhian. Stay ready. There will be a way. There must be a way.*

God and Mary help me, there must be a way out of this.

It was almost full dark when Gawain returned to Camelot. The groomsmen and boys came out with lanterns and torches to meet the horses and their riders. Gawain dismounted, ignoring them all. He heard Geraint calling him, but he did not look back. He strode ahead into the gathering darkness, across the yard and grounds, past the animal pens, the forge, the weaver's shed and the pottery, down to the low cottage where Merlin carried out his works.

The place had been built as solidly as any church, with stone walls and a roof of slate. It was said the hinges of the ashwood door had silver pins. Gawain pounded on that fabled door with his fist and stood back, breathing hard. His whole body ached from riding, dismounting and futilely searching, only to mount and ride again. Fatigue was beginning to wrap around him, but he could not, he would not, think of rest. Euberacon had taken Rhian. Gawain would find her. He must. It was only Geraint and Gareth's absolute refusal to go any further without more men and fresh horses that had brought him back here at all.

Over the harsh sound of his own breathing, Gawain heard a man's voice within the cottage. A second man answered it, and the first spoke again.

'Merlin!' shouted Gawain. 'I would speak with you, Merlin!'

Both voices fell silent for a long moment and Gawain heard the shuffling sounds of movement. The door eased open, revealing nothing but shadow, and Merlin standing in its heart.

Despite his intentions, there was something in the old sorcerer's face that made Gawain hesitate.

'Well,' said Merlin. 'If you are so determined, you had best come in.'

Gawain strode inside. It was one of the few places in Camelot where he had never actually stood. He had only dared peer through the windows once, as a young squire. Gareth, he knew, had once accepted a dare to come inside this place and steal something to prove he had done it. He had never said what happened, but Gareth had never taken such a dare again.

There was only one candle lit, so Gawain could see next

to nothing of the room he had entered. He had a vague impression of tables and other furnishings, but the rest was nothing but mysteries, except for the low and curving stone walls of a great well in the centre of the floor. Gawain blinked. For a moment it seemed to him a faint silver glow emanated from that well, but by the time his eyes adjusted to it, it was gone.

Merlin was lifting the well's cover and sliding it across the top. The cover was heavy, and the old man moved slowly. Gawain almost offered to help, but his skin crawled unaccountably at the thought of approaching that well and what he might see in its depths.

Wood grated against stone, and Merlin fitted the cover back into place. Some of the chill ebbed from Gawain. The sorcerer turned and lifted an iron wand, and with it performed the very ordinary action of poking up the fire.

Now Gawain could see him clearly, the bent old man who had been at Arthur's side since Gawain had come to Camelot. The fear faded and both will and wit returned.

'What have you found?' he asked at once. 'Did you see her? Do you know where she is?'

But Merlin only shook his head. Gawain's chest seized tight.

'Gawain.'

Gawain opened his eyes. He had not realized he had closed them. Nor that he had moved. He stood beside the wall now, and his fist had struck the stone. Were it not for his leather gloves, he would have split his skin from the unconscious blow.

Merlin laid a gnarled hand on his wrist, gently pressing down so that Gawain lowered it back to his side. Gawain's eyes swam with tears of pain and anger.

'Help me, Merlin. I must find her.'

'I know.' In the firelight, Gawain saw nothing more

mysterious than a room hung with bundles of herbs that gave forth fresh and pungent scents. Clay vessels sat on wooden shelves and locked chests stood against the walls. Merlin seemed little more than an old man in a robe of black wool as he sat in a finely made wooden chair before his fire. 'I have turned all my art to this matter, but I am defied.' He scowled at the flames. 'I can see that your way will be shown, and soon, but not how, or by what means, nor can I see what lies at its end. The waters are deep here, Gawain, and there is more than one power beneath them. Your Rhian has not been fortunate in her enemies.'

'But you have seen that I will find her? You can tell that much?'

'I have seen you will be shown the path, that is all.' Merlin shook his head and frowned harder. 'Go to the hall. They are still at board. Eat. Try to rest. I will see what answers I can bring with the dawn.'

Gawain wanted to argue. He wanted to shout, to grab the old man by the shoulders and shake him, demanding that he know at once where Rhian was. But for all his fear and fury, Gawain was a grown man, not a ranting boy. He knew Merlin had never played Arthur false, and would not do so with him. This was knowledge hard won, but it held now, and he was able to turn and walk away back into the night. What he could not do was speak. With words would come a flood of feeling he could not yet release. When he held Rhian again, that would be the time. When he looked again into her eyes and felt her breath warm against his cheek, her hands against his breast and her mouth against his. Then. Only then.

The great hall was full but subdued when Gawain arrived there and knelt before the king. Arthur stood immediately from the high table and came down to him, raising him up and giving him the kiss of peace. Gawain found he could not meet his uncle's eyes or make any polite greeting. Arthur seemed to understand. He put his arm about Gawain's shoulders. Had it been any other man, Gawain would have shaken him off. He was not in the mood to receive such sympathies. As it was, he must add shame to his other emotions. He had come into the great hall with the dust of the road still on him, reeking of horse and sweat, his sword still hanging from his hip.

Arthur, of course, said nothing of this. He simply steered Gawain to his place at the high table. Geraint watched him as he passed, but held his peace. Meat and wine were placed in front of Gawain. It was plain from the solemnity on every face that Geraint and Gareth had already told the tale of their failure. It was as well. He found he had no words in him for that either.

Only Agravain looked satisfied with himself as he watched Gawain over the rim of his wine cup. Gawain stared back stolidly.

One word, brother, one word and I swear I will not be responsible for the consequences.

But the only challenge Agravain made was his silence. Even Kai seemed disinclined to jest, and Gawain wondered if Arthur had said something to him. It didn't matter. Nothing here mattered. He stared at the steaming trencher before him. The meat looked tenderly done and its fragrance was rich with wine and pepper, but he could not eat. He could not seem to make himself move.

'Gawain,' came the queen's soft voice. 'You will do her no good if you have no strength.'

Which was, of course, the merest truth. He tore off a piece of good fresh bread, soaked it in the peppery gravy and managed to choke it down without tasting it. What fare did Rhian enjoy tonight? What roof sheltered her head? Did she call his name? Did she curse it?

Old memories, memories of screams and of deeds he could not prevent and a life he'd failed to protect, filled his mind, mixed horribly with the memory of Rhian's smile, and Gawain abruptly stood.

All voices ceased their conversation. All faces turned to regard him with curiosity and surprise, waiting for him to speak.

Gawain's throat was dry. He wanted nothing more than to fling the table aside and charge from the hall, naked sword in his hand, challenging the night itself to bring Rhian back to him.

'I . . .' he began.

The doors banged open, sparing him the necessity of finding another word. The porter, white-faced, ran into the hall. Arthur was on his feet at once beside Gawain.

'What is it, man?' cried the king.

The porter seemed unable to find his tongue. It would have been comic to watch him choke and point like a clown in a mummer's play, were it not for the terror in his eyes.

They all heard the noise then – the clop of hooves against stone. The porter fell back, and horse and rider entered the great doors.

He was green as summer, green as ivy and young wheat and a standing pond beneath the trees. He was the living essence of what the court had turned into a tame pageant on the hunt. He was huge, a giant who would have towered over every man in the hall, even were he not mounted on a steed the size of the mightiest cart horse that was as green as he. He was garbed in the old style, in tunic and breeches all belted and trimmed with green. A green torque twisted like tree roots around his neck. His green beard was as wild as tangled moss, and his long green hair was braided. In his hand he carried a mighty battle-axe with a haft as thick around as Gawain's wrist and a keen edge that glittered as it caught the torchlight.

Women screamed and started backward, knocking over chairs and benches. All the men in the hall leapt up, but not one of them was armed. Only Gawain still had his sword, and he grasped the hilt at once to draw it out, but Arthur's hand clamped down on his wrist like iron.

'Greetings to you good men!' The green rider's voice boomed like merry thunder. 'And my duty to your good ladies! I seek Arthur, who is called by men the High King.'

Gawain's hand shook to draw his sword, but his uncle held him fast and Arthur's voice rang out through the hall, as strong as steel and steady as stone. 'I am Arthur, and I am called High King. Who might you be, Sir, who comes so bold before this assembly?'

'As you see, King Arthur, I am the *Equite Caeruleus* – the Green Knight!' He spread his arms wide, inviting all to admire his magnificence. His grin, too, spread wide, displaying straight, even teeth that were as green as the rest of him.

Gawain saw one muscle twitch high in Arthur's cheek, but that was the only sign of concern he gave for this extraordinary vision that appeared before him. At Arthur's left hand, Guinevere sat as still as a statue. All the ladies at the high table tried to huddle behind her, but she herself made no move to show what fear she felt, if any at all.

'And for what reason do you come here, Sir Knight?' asked Arthur.

'For the only reason warriors should meet. For a challenge!' He was grinning from ear to ear now. He planted the haft of his axe against his stirrup and his other fist against his hip. 'It would be a sorry May Day to pass without some sport.'

The Green Knight had turned his gaze to Gawain. Gawain felt it before he saw it. It was as if a hand had touched his shoulder. 'I am told Gawain, son of Lot Luwddoc, is a merry gamester and well suited to accept a challenge from a fellow warrior,' said the knight.

Arthur tightened his grip in warning, but Gawain could not keep his silence this time. He pressed against his uncle's hand so that Arthur would feel his hand moving away from his sword. Arthur reluctantly let him go.

Gawain pulled his shoulders up straight. 'I am Gawain. How is it you know my name, Sir?'

The Green Knight raised his eyebrows archly. 'How not?' he barked the words like a sharp laugh. 'That name is cried from one end of this land to the other. Cried in the night by weeping women who are carried far from home and are seeking succour, cried in the day by men with dark eyes and dark hearts who cherish their victories over the bold and the valiant.'

Gawain felt the blood drain from his face. His hand shook as he struggled to keep it from reaching again for his sword.

'Uncle,' he murmured, not taking his gaze from the gigantic apparition waiting so cheerfully in the centre of the hall. Around it stood the whole of Arthur's cadre and their ladies; some frozen halfway to their feet, some clasping hands anxiously to bosom or side, seeking weapons that were not there. 'Let me take up this challenge. He speaks of Rhian. He must. This is some magician's apparition, surely sent by Euberacon to bedevil m . . . us.'

But Arthur did not waiver. 'Peace, Gawain. We know nothing of his nature or his challenge. Merlin will be here within moments. Do nothing.'

But this thing, this giant, knew of Rhian, and of Euberacon. There could be no other explanation for its words, not so soon after her disappearance. Whatever his challenge, it did not matter. Gawain would best it, and he would wring what it knew out of it with his bare hands if he must. 'Sir, I beg you.'

'I said peace, Gawain.' Though barely spoken above a whisper, the words were filled with command. In front of all the court, Gawain had no choice but to obey.

'Sir Knight,' Arthur again addressed the giant. Gawain had seen Arthur on the battlefield, facing a line of the enemy, he had seen him in single combat stepping back to give a strong foe room to rise, but he had never seen him display more courage than so calmly facing this giant that rode into his own hall. 'You cannot expect me to release my best knight on a challenge before I hear what it is. I must judge whether it is fitting to his merits and his honour.'

'Hear, hear,' muttered Kai, for how could Kai keep himself silent even under such circumstances? 'Simply facing down a giant would not be enough for the glory of our Gawain.' But Gawain heard how tightly he spoke and saw how his fist clenched around his crutch which rested where his sword should have hung.

The Green Knight pursed his lips and nodded sagaciously, but none of the merriment left his eyes. 'Fairly spoken,' he acknowledged. 'Very well. What I propose is a game of blows. The knight who challenges me may strike me one blow with this axe.' He brandished the great weapon he carried with him. It was four, no five, times the size of the weapon a man might wield. 'If I fail to rise from that blow, he will have of me one boon. Whatsoever he may ask will I grant. But should I rise, he must come to the Green Temple and accept one blow with the same weapon from my hand.'

One boon. Whatsoever he may ask. This stank so strongly of magic, Gawain felt sick in the pit of his stomach. But what magic promised, magic must bring. Even Gawain knew that was the way of it. With one blow he could find Euberacon and free Rhian. He was near to striding forwards and wrenching the axe from the giant, and he was sure his uncle knew it.

''Tis a strange game you propose, Sir.'

Merlin stood in the threshold. Gawain had not even seen him arrive. He was as Gawain had seen him before, in his black robe and cap with his white staff in his gnarled hands, but some trick of light or perception, or perhaps a trick of Merlin's art, made him seem as tall and imperious in presence as the Green Knight on his warhorse, and Gawain felt again the boyish fear he had felt in the shadows of the cottage. What the Green Knight felt as he turned to see Merlin stalk into the great hall, Gawain could not even fathom.

It did not, however, seem to be fear. 'Ah!' the Green Knight cried, as if he had caught sight of some long-absent friend. 'I wondered when you would appear.'

'You know me then?' inquired the magician.

The Green Knight nodded once. 'I know you, Merlin, No Man's Son. But do you know me?'

Merlin stood before him for a long time, staring into the eyes as rich and green as the forest at high summer. It seemed to Gawain that for a moment the old sorcerer paled and his hands clenched his staff a little more tightly, and Merlin's stature seemed to dwindle, though not his shrewd presence.

'It is a cold and a dangerous game you propose, Sir.' Merlin addressed the words to the Green Knight, but his gaze was on Gawain. 'And a great risk to ask of a man for the pleasure of sport.'

'The easy road does not lead to glory.'

Gawain started to hear words he had spoken to Rhian so nearly matched. Surely, surely, this creature knew what had happened to her. It was Euberacon's creature, some demon summoned to do his will. He would have it and its boon if he had to renounce his position in Arthur's hall to do it.

'It's a trap, Gawain.'

When had Agravain moved? Gawain had not even felt his brother come up behind him, any more than he had seen

Merlin arrive at the doors of the hall. All his attention had been focused on the Green Knight.

'It already has your wits ensnared,' whispered Agravain urgently. 'Do not do this. Let Arthur deal with it, and Merlin. This once, Gawain, keep your head.'

There was truth in the words his brother spoke, but it did not matter. This might be his only chance to find out where Rhian had been taken, and he could not brush it aside.

He faced Arthur. 'Uncle, for my honour, and that of yourself and your court, let me answer this challenge.'

Gawain watched his uncle's face shift. He was on the verge of refusal. Gawain's spirits plummeted. Could he really renounce liege and loyalty for the love of Rhian? If Arthur refused him permission, that was what he would have to do. Then even when he found her, he would be a beggar, perhaps without even his horse or sword. Arthur was a man of mercy, but he was also a man of laws, and he would not permit his nephew's return once Gawain chose of his own will to leave in defiance.

'Merlin said that my way would be shown to me, and soon,' said Gawain, and he heard the desperation in his own words. 'And now this . . . creature has come. Please, uncle. Even if it has naught to do with Rhian, we know the Saxons are using magics of their own against you. We cannot leave this matter unquestioned, and is there anyone else in this hall aside from you and myself who has a chance in striking a telling blow against this monster?' He hoped Lancelot had not heard. Now was not the time for the voluble Gaul to start arguing points of honour. If Gawain failed, there would be work enough for Lancelot to do.

Arthur looked across to Merlin and to Gawain's relief, Merlin nodded.

'Do as you must and may God be with you.' Arthur stood aside.

Gawain felt Agravain move towards him, but he did not look back. He walked down the dais steps, his gaze straight ahead.

Gawain felt himself dwindling to the stature of a boy as he approached the Green Knight. Even when the giant leapt nimbly from the back of his gigantic horse, it still seemed his head all but brushed the vaulting roof beams.

'Here is a true man!' the giant boomed. 'Do you accept my challenge then, Sir Gawain?'

'If I strike you a blow with your axe from which you cannot rise, then I will win from you a boon of my own choosing, and nothing is excluded from this.'

'So I have spoken,' said the Green Knight firmly.

Gawain's mouth had gone completely dry, but he made himself speak on. 'And if that blow should kill you, Sir? What then?'

Again the Green Knight laughed and the thunder of it seemed to shake the very stones beneath Gawain's feet. 'Even then you shall have your prize, Sir Gawain. Even then, I swear on my own head!' He grew serious, then, and Gawain's heart quailed within him. 'But should I rise from that blow, you will follow me to the Green Temple and there accept my blow with my same axe.'

It was a dreadful and perilous gamble. Gawain had never heard of the Green Temple and had no idea where it lay, and if he had to go on such a quest, he would have to abandon Rhian to her fate. What if this were a game to *keep* him from her? If he was wrong, if he failed . . . but he could not think of that. He had gone too far now to turn back.

'I swear it,' said Gawain.

'And you, King Arthur,' a sly note crept into the Green Knight's voice, 'you will stand surety for your man here?'

Trap! Gawain's mind and soul screamed Agravain's warning at him. *It is a trap and it closes on Arthur as well as on you!*

But Gawain did not move, nor did he speak.

God and Mary forgive me, he prayed earnestly. *I don't know what else to do.*

'I will,' said Arthur, and there was no trace of hesitation or doubt in those words.

Asking forgiveness now was useless. His choices were all made. He could not fail. Grim finality settled over Gawain like a mantle.

'Then, Sir,' the Green Knight held his weapon out to Gawain. 'Do you take the axe and strike your blow, and let us see how it shall land.'

Gawain grasped the axe with both hands. The sheer weight of it caught him off guard and he almost staggered as the Green Knight let go. He stood there for a moment, hefting it in his hands, letting his arms and his body get a feel for for the balance and weight of the massive weapon. The metal of its blade was neither iron nor steel, but gleamed both green and silver, the colour of frost on the grass. It's edge was keen, though, that much he could tell simply by look-ing. The green haft curved smoothly against his palms. It was too big for him by far, but he could still close his fingers around it. It was a good axe, beautifully forged and deadly. He could never wield such a thing in battle, but one blow . . . one blow he could deal out.

He took the measure of the giant before him. One blow from which this monster could not rise. His heart went cold and still as he made his calculations. He had a thousand times made such decisions in hot blood on the field – where is the weak-ness, where is the opening? But never before on a man who simply stood with his feet planted firm and square, and smiled.

Think of Rhian, snatched away by a witch's brood. Think of Rhian calling your name so far away you cannot hear. Think of Arthur falling before the Saxon magics and the ravens holding court in this hall.

Think of Rhian and strike as you know you must.

Gawain raised the axe. Sliding his hands together along the haft, he swung it back. With a wordless cry that shook the whole of his being, he brought it round, aiming the edge straight and true for the giant's neck.

He felt the blow strike home, felt flesh and sinew and bone part cleanly for the blade's keen edge. With barely any loss of momentum the swing continued, carrying Gawain around in a warrior's pirouette. The grisly thing, the head of the Green Knight cut clean from its body, rolled across the stones, coming to a halt at the foot of the dais.

But the Green Knight's torso did not fall.

The strength left Gawain's hands at once, and the axe thudded to the floor. Before the dais, the Green Knight's eyes opened wide and his thick lips whistled once. The torso did not waiver, nor did it hesitate. It strode over to its head and retrieved it, tucking it neatly under its arm. Then it picked up its axe while Gawain stood amazed past the point of movement.

Thus encumbered, the Green Knight leapt onto the back of his horse, landing neatly in the saddle.

'A fine blow, Sir Gawain,' said the knight's head. 'I look forward to meeting you at the Green Temple to return the courtesy!'

The body touched its heels to the horse's sides and the animal trotted obediently from the great hall, and was gone.

Gawain stared. There was not even blood on the stones to mark what had passed. He felt as if he must be in the midst of some strange dream. The court milled about him, murmuring, wailing, thundering, wringing hands and shaking heads, but he could only stare at the doors, and hear over and again his own promises, and the final words of the Green Knight ringing in his ears.

'Come, lad,' said a soft voice. It was Merlin. He laid a hand on Gawain's arm and began to lead him away. He lacked the presence of mind to resist, or even to see where he was being taken.

By the time he was able to rouse himself, he was in Arthur's private chamber. Chairs were drawn up before the hearth where the coals were banked. A single candle had been lit, but it was easy enough to see the care dragging at his uncle's features.

'So I must go,' Gawain said simply.

'Yes,' replied Arthur. 'I'm afraid you must. It is a dangerous thing to try to renege on a promise made to magic.'

'I do not know where I am bound.'

'The way will find you,' said Merlin. 'You may depend on it.'

'And then I am to die.'

Neither man spoke.

That silence focused all of Gawain's mind onto a single point. He raised his head. 'Uncle, swear to me you will not stop looking for Rhian. Swear to me you will not abandon her.'

'You know that I will not.'

'Thank you.'

Arthur stood. Long habit pulled Gawain to his feet as well. 'Go to bed, Gawain. Get some rest. You have a mighty journey before you.'

Gawain bowed his head. There was nothing to do then, but seek his chamber, to try to bide the long night to come, in prayer if sleep deserted him. Then to die. To abandon Rhian and to die.

He stared at the door before him. The distance to it seemed somehow impossibly far. *Are you angry with me uncle? Are you sorry? Perhaps now you think me too much of a heartsore fool to take your place and that you are well rid of me. But I did it for Rhian. I could do no other.*

'Have you any more prophecy for me, Merlin?' he asked, surprised at the lightness of his own voice.

'Only to stay true, Gawain. Remember your honour as well as your love. It is the truth of your heart that will aid you best now.'

Too bitter to speak, too weary to think, Gawain left his uncle and went to his bed, and prepared to wait for the morning when he must ride forth and seek his doom.

Shortly after both the Green Knight and Gawain departed the hall, knights and ladies as well left in threes and fours, some to seek their arms in case Camelot should come under attack, some to seek their beds and familiar surroundings so they might think, or cower under the bedclothes, whatever was their nature.

Agravain had thought to go to his room and wait for his other two brothers. The only two he would have soon. He thought he might sit with lighted candle and write down what he had seen, perhaps to try to understand it. To understand that Gawain would, must, do this thing. To try to understand why.

But when he reached his chamber, he could not seem to think what he had meant to do. He stood in the middle of the sparse furnishings, utterly at a loss.

Someone knocked on the door he had left open behind him. Agravain turned, to see Kai limp heavily into the room.

'No jibes, uncle, I beg you. I am not in the mood.'

'No jibes, nephew. I am here only to give sympathy.' Kai eased himself into one of the chairs before the fire, stretching his crooked leg out in front of him and resting his hands on his crutch.

'Sympathy?' Agravain spat. 'I don't have the stomach for such pity either.'

'Did I say pity? Do you think I do not understand what

it is to love the one who must ever be the hero?'

Agravain stared.

'You love your brother, Agravain, and I know it well. Such love brings pain to the one with fewer ideals and more practicality. How many times over the years do you think I have railed against my own brother? And how many times, for his sake, do you think I have done so in private, and then turned my face to the world to assist him as much as my crippled form can manage?'

Agravain bowed his head.

'There are times, Agravain, when the likes of you and I must trust that the heroes are doing their best, and we must stand beside them as they do it.'

'And if we know they are wrong?'

Kai shrugged. 'If we can save them, we must. But we must ask ourselves, what will we ruin by that salvation? If we break them in our attempt to rescue them, is it worth it?'

Agravain threw himself onto the stool in front of the writing desk. The desk was bare and ready for work. What work? What next? He could not think beyond the next heartbeat. 'What do you advise me?'

'Stand beside him or go home to your father's hall and take your place there early. But remember, if you leave, he loses your help for all time, and if he marries the woman, he will be in desperate need of all the help he can get.'

Agravain's mouth opened and closed. He could not seem to find the breath to ask the next question. 'Do you think he will return?'

'I think he has as good a chance as any man save Arthur.'

Agravain looked up and saw tears shining in his uncle's eyes. 'How can you bear it, uncle?'

Kai's smile was small and sad, and Agravain could not ever recall seeing such an expression on the man's face before. Nor did he think he was ever likely to again. 'Why do you think my tongue is so sharp, nephew? It eases some sorts of pain wondrous well. But you in your own way know this.' With a jerky but practised motion, Kai shifted his crutch and used it to push himself up until he stood as straight as he was able before Agravain. 'Honour demands much of us, Agravain, and the love of our brothers even more. Use your judgement, use it hard and harshly as you must, but do not give way to pride or jealousy. Let men say you have done anything else before they can say you have done that.'

Agravain watched his uncle's departure but said nothing. Then he turned back to the window and struck the sill with his naked fist, telling himself it was the pain that wrung the tears from his eyes.

SEVENTEEN

To her surprise, Rhian slept for a time. When she woke, the light coming through her tiny window had faded. Evening then, or late afternoon. To her embarrassment, hunger cramped her stomach. In the face of the danger that trapped her here, something as mundane as hunger seemed out of place.

But that danger did not seem inclined to come for her. Rhian rose and paced her cell, touching the stones to satisfy herself that they were solid and not merely some illusion of Euberacon's. They felt cool and rough and heartbreakingly solid beneath her fingertips. No one moved in the dimming courtyard. No sound issued from any direction. Boredom, fear and frustration flooded through her, and Rhian kicked at the wooden door.

Slowly, the portal swung open on silent hinges.

Rhian remained frozen where she was for several loud heartbeats. The door had been barred when the witch left her. When had it been opened? Who had opened it?

Does it matter? Rhian snatched up her skirts and ran.

The corridor outside was dark and straight, well lined with stones and smelling only faintly of damp. There might have been other doors along its length, but Rhian did not stop to examine the shadows. To her left waited a cramped staircase leading upwards. The remains of the daylight illuminated an arched doorway at its top.

Rhian flew up the uneven stairs and through the door. No one appeared to stop her. No voice cried out. She was in a dim corridor. Another doorway opened just in front of her to show a beautiful courtyard. A marble fountain splashed in the centre. It was this that she had seen from her cell. The walls and ground were tiled in many different colours, turning them into tapestries. In the left-hand wall, she could see the double portal of a great gate.

Every fibre in her moved to run, but caution gripped Rhian and she hesitated in the shadows. The gate looked to be closed for evening. In any other hall, it would also be locked. She had no reason to believe it would be otherwise here. Even if it were as unbarred as her door had been, to run across that broad and open court would mean being seen by whatever eyes lurked about this beautiful, silent place. She needed to find another way, a scullery leading to the work yard, a pantry with a small window, perhaps a place she could hide until her absence was noticed and she could creep out of the gates after all had gone in pursuit of her.

If there is anyone here.

The silence was beginning to unnerve her. The halls she knew were bustling places, always filled to the brim with people, not to mention with the noise of every sort of creature from children down to dogs and chickens. She had never been in a place built by human hand so full of stillness.

But was it human hands that built this place?

Rhian bit her lip. This was no good. Whatever this place was, she needed to be free of it, and freedom would not come if she just stood here. Gripping her skirts tightly, Rhian slipped down the shadowed corridors behind the courtyard walls, flitting past doorways as quickly as she could, blessing the soft boots Guinevere had given her. She strained her ears hard for any sound, any sound at all. But there was only her breath and her heartbeat.

On her left hand, doorways opened onto the fantastically tiled court, on her right, they opened onto rooms. She had vague impressions of complexly woven carpets and wall hangings and furniture carved of wood so dark it was almost black. There was nothing that appeared to be a kitchen or workroom.

She turned a corner. Ahead waited more doorways on left and right, but this time, in the first doorway that opened on the right, she saw a flicker of light. With it, she caught a bright and delicate scent she had smelled only once before in her life, but had remembered always. Lemons.

'Lady Rhian.'

Euberacon.

Run! she screamed to herself, but in the next heartbeat she asked. *Where?*

'You may enter, lady,' the sorcerer continued. His voice came from the lighted room. He sounded calm, even content. She could see nothing, not from where she stood.

The gate was closed. She could not scale a marble wall. She had no glimpse of outside light coming from any of the rooms she had passed. Would she return to her cell and try to barricade herself inside?

Mother Mary protect me. Rhian knotted her fingers into the cloth of her skirt, and forced her reluctant feet to move forward.

Through the doorway lay a dining hall lit by white candles that filled the air with the clean scent of beeswax. That was the least of the fragrances that filled the bright room, for on its long table had been laid such a banquet as she had never seen. Not even the May Day feast at Camelot could compare.

There were towers of fruit, both fresh and sparkling with sugar. Plump pastries had been arranged on dishes as white as marble. Savoury stewed meats and whole silver fishes lay on beds of rice the colour of gold. There were dishes of figs in honey, bowls heaped with all varieties of nuts, jellies and gelatins in all the colours of summer. Her empty stomach roiled painfully as she breathed in the warm air, for all the dishes were fresh and steaming, and everywhere was the scent of spices – pepper, cinnamon, cloves, nutmeg, and others for which Rhian had no name.

At the head of the table, almost obscured by the fairy landscape of food, sat Euberacon Magus. He was cutting into a scarlet fruit with a silver knife.

'I had wondered when you would appear.' The sorcerer sounded mildly affronted, like a lover kept waiting. 'Sit with me.' With his knife, he pointed at an empty chair by his right hand.

Rhian stayed where she was.

Hands grabbed her arms and shoulders. She could see no form, but she felt the press of palms and fingers and long nails. They held her more tightly than any human could have. She could not even struggle as she was propelled forwards, and forced into the chair. Those same hands pressed her arms against the chair arms.

Euberacon spoke a word she did not know, and the touch of the invisible hands lifted away. Rhian raised her wrists to stare at the place she had been held. Her skin, already scabbed and scraped from the ravens that had swarmed to bring her here, was now marked with a half-score of tiny red crescent moons where the unseen talons had pressed.

Fear shook her, and anger, but she struggled to keep her face still.

'You have questions,' said the sorcerer. He finished cutting at the fruit and split it open to reveal sparse white flesh filled to bursting with seeds coated in blood-red pulp. 'Speak.' With tapered fingers, he pulled free several of the seeds and placed them in his mouth, sucking them dry.

Rhian's first thought was to remain stubbornly silent, but there was one question that had followed her through all the days since she had learned of her father's bargain, and here might be her only chance to find the answer.

'Why?'

Euberacon spat out the seeds, now white and dry into a separate dish. 'Why?'

'Yes. Why do you want me? Why destroy my father, my family, to get to me?'

'Because you are what I require. Because you have the eyes that can see, and I have need of them.' He took three more seeds into his mouth.

Strained and unreasoning hope rushed into Rhian's mind. 'And if I do what you want? Then will you release me?'

Again, he spat out the seeds. Rhian could not rid herself of the image of the life being sucked away, blood being drained dry. 'You believe there is release for you? An ending? Oh, no, Lady Rhian. You are mine. You serve me. That service may be pleasant, and may bestow upon you a measure of power, or it may be vilest slavery. That is the only choice you have left to you.'

Rhian made no answer to that. The sorcerer's smile was sly and thin. 'You do not believe me, do you, little girl? You think you will find the way to free yourself. Or,' he paused and made a great show of pointing into the air with his red-stained finger, as if he stabbed some piece of truth there. 'Perhaps you believe your Gawain, your gilded knight, will come for you. You believe his love to be true and that he is a gallant of unstained honour and pure intent.'

Rhian held her peace. She would not be so trapped. Even an ordinary being could twist words to create doubt where none should exist; how much more could a sorcerer do?

'Would you know the truth, lady?' he said. 'Would you know what manner of man your Gawain is behind his pretty words and fair face?'

Rhian remained silent, and had the cold pleasure of seeing the sorcerer's confident smile flicker.

'No matter. You are a child, and like any child you must be taken in hand for your own good.' His hand shot out and grabbed her by the upper arm. He propelled her from the hall and across the tiled courtyard. She gazed with longing at the heavy gate. She could struggle. She could bite. As he pulled her up the winding staircase of the south-east tower she could throw her weight backward and take them both down the stairs, but what then? This place had only one egress that she knew of yet, and she was not Sampson that she could break down the walls surrounding her.

Still holding her fast, Euberacon stopped on the second floor of the tower. He reached inside his black robe and drew out a silver key that hung on a silver chain. Euberacon unlocked the door and opened it. The breeze it made carried scents of herbs and rare essences, along with the tang of rot and blood. Rhian's throat tightened and she forced herself to swallow. Euberacon pushed her into the darkness ahead of him.

The room had no windows. The door closed, cutting off all light, so that although the sorcerer let her go, Rhian did not dare move. Behind her, she heard the clanking of delicate metals. A moment later light flared, making shadows blossom on the bare walls before her. Euberacon had uncovered the brass brazier by the door and dropped fuel into the smouldering coals so that the flames sprang up providing a flickering light. This was without question the sorcerer's workroom. Bags and bundles hung from the ceiling. The shelves were crowded with bowls, jars, caskets and strange devices of bronze and steel that she could not give any name to.

A black cloth lay on a round table of inlaid wood. Euberacon pulled it away to reveal a silver mirror as clear as a pool of water. It drew the eye almost irresistibly, promising to show any who looked in it a clearer image than they had ever before seen. Before she was even aware of what she did, she took a step towards it.

'Look, Lady Rhian.' The sorcerer held the brazier high, casting a wide circle of golden light over the mirror. 'I have readied it for you. Look and see.'

Rhian turned her face away, staring resolutely at the wall.

Which was not something Euberacon was prepared to tolerate. Before she could move, he grabbed the back of her neck, forcing her head around however much she might resist.

'You will look.' His voice rasped in her ear. 'And you will see. Close your eyes and I will forget that I need you alive and snap your neck.' His fingers dug into the soft flesh of her neck until Rhian had to bite her tongue to keep from crying out at the pain.

Before her, the surface of the mirror had clouded, as if a haze passed over it. But that haze gradually took on colour – scarlet, black, emerald and sapphire. Those colours broke apart and settled into the image of a hall with stone walls and great wooden beams gone black with smoke from years of fires. Leather shields with strange devices hung on the walls between tapestries of golden lions, ivory unicorns and green crosses. In a heavy chair draped with scarlet and silver sat a bear of a man, his grizzled black hair and beard sticking out in all directions, and his blue eyes burning with an anger such as Rhian had never seen.

Before this great bear stood Gawain. But not the graceful, hardened knight Rhian knew. This was Gawain as a stripling boy, tall and thin, his hands too big and his neck too long for the rest of him. The boy, however, had Gawain's earnest face, its expression shifting to one Rhian had never seen him wear – that of fear.

As she looked, Rhian lost all awareness of where she stood. All sensation of pain or her own fear left her. She was wholly in this other place, a silent spirit beside this young Gawain.

The man shot to his feet. 'Who did this?' he bellowed. 'What man defiled my daughter?'

Gawain held up both hands, trying to placate the man. 'Father, calm yourself. It's not . . .'

Father? This wild man was King Lot Luwddoc? And what was this of a daughter? Gawain had never spoken of a sister.

'You bid me be calm, boy, when my name, my honour, are so disgraced!' The man reared up before Gawain. His heavy hand lashed out and came down on the boy's ear. Gawain must have been well used to such blows, because he barely flinched. 'Who did this! You tell me who or by God's teeth I'll break you in half.'

Gawain held his ground. 'I promised her you would be fair. I told her if he was a man of name especially you would bless the marriage.'

'Her marriage is made! I have given my word to Cinuit of Strathclyde that she is his. Does she say he did this?'

'She does not say, Sir, and she will not until you promise . . .'

'Until I promise!' bellowed Lot. 'Until *I* promise!' He shoved Gawain aside so hard the young man staggered and almost fell. Without waiting to see what he had done, King Lot strode from the hall, his face crimson with his fury.

As soon as Gawain recovered himself, he sprinted after his father, but as he dashed for the threshold, he knocked against another youth with black hair and a long nose.

'Gawain, what . . . ?'

'Later, Agravain.' Gawain ran ahead, not looking back to
see that Agravain had turned to follow him.

'Tania!' bellowed Lot as he stormed down the narrow
wooden hall. 'Tania!'

Gawain stretched his thin legs, trying to catch up with
him. 'No, father, do not do this. If you will stop a moment. . .'

But Lot did not stop. He barrelled down the corridor that
he seemed to fill with his wrath. At last, he burst through a
pitted door.

There was a workroom on the other side, filled with ladies
of all ages engaged in tasks of spinning and sewing. Tapestry
frames and looms decorated the well-lit chamber. As the king
barrelled in, all the dozen or so of them gasped and leapt to
their feet, too startled to make any sort of curtsey.

All did so, except one. She had pale skin and raven-black
hair, just like Gawain. She held herself proudly where she sat
on a stool with a drop spindle and a cloud of carded wool in
her hands. The bright blue eyes in the delicate face that gazed
cold and hard at the enraged king were a match for Gawain's.

'Whore!' shouted Lot, levelling a dirty and calloused finger
at the slender lady. 'Who is your man! Name him or go to
the devil!'

But it was not Lot the lady answered. Her gaze flickered
to the young Gawain who appeared, pale and out of breath
in the doorway behind his father.

'You told him,' she said, her voice flat and weary. 'After
I begged you not to, you told him.'

'Tania, I could not . . .'

'You will speak to me, slut!' Lot took two steps closer to
her, his hands clenched into fists. They were large hands,
Rhian saw, strong and hardened by work and war. 'Do you
deny you carry a bastard child in your belly?'

Tania set down her work on the table beside her, taking
care that the thread should not tangle. She stood and came

forward so that she stood less than an arm's length from her enraged father. *No!* Rhian wanted to scream as she saw the sinews bulge in Lot's neck. *Don't go near him!*

'Yes, gentle father. I am with child.'

The blow caught Tania on her face and knocked her sprawling onto the floor. She did not cry out, she only lay there, panting as a great red welt spread across her cheek.

'Who! Who is the father of your bastard! Name him!'

Slowly, shaking her head to clear it, Tania pushed herself up onto her hands. The ladies stood by, aghast, but not one of them dared to come to her aid. 'And if I do name him? What then?'

'Then he will die for this deed, you whore!'

'Promise of such a great reward will surely make me speak.' The woman was ice. Where did such courage spring from? Or was she simply past caring? She knew that blow would come and she went to meet it.

It was Gawain who stepped between her and their father. 'Sir, it does our name no honour for you to threaten Tania like this. Come to the hall with me. Let me call your chiefs. Cinuit of Strathclyde can be given some other prize.'

'Boy, if you do not get out of my way, I will break your head on the stones.'

Tania managed to get to her feet. The whole right half of her face was scarlet and swollen. 'Stand aside, Gawain. You've already done enough.' The words held both sorrow and anger. Gawain blanched white and turned to face her.

'Tania, I swear, I only thought to help. You cannot . . .'

But he was not allowed to finish. Lot flung him aside so hard that his head cracked hard against the wall, then dived forwards and snatched Tania's wrists and bent them back, driving her down onto her knees. That finally made the young woman gasp in pain, but her eyes remained defiant as she glowered up at him.

'Name your brat's father!' screamed Lot. 'Name him!'

'No, father . . .' Gawain was holding his head. Blood trickled in a thin thread from his brow.

'No, father.' Tania echoed his words steadily. 'You may not command so much of me.'

'I may command anything of you! You are mine! Mine! You will marry a swineherd if I order it!'

'No.'

Lot gave a wordless roar that seemed to shake the stone walls. He seized Tania by her dark hair and hauled her to her feet. She gasped, unable to hold in a cry of pain.

'Will you blacken my name?' cried Lot, striding forward, forcing Tania to stumble behind him or be dragged along like a sack of flour. 'Will you mother whoreson bastards? Make my word a joke among men? You will learn the price! You will learn!'

The nightmarish procession stormed along the corridor. Gawain stared after them. So did Agravain from his place by the door.

'What are you doing?' Agravain demanded of his older brother. 'Stop him!'

'He won't do it,' murmured Gawain. 'He wouldn't. Not his daughter.'

'You're a fool, Gawain.' Agravain sprinted down the corridor after his father.

Gawain stared for a moment at the place where his brother had been, then stumbled into a run to follow.

Rhian wished she could look away. With all her heart she willed herself not to see, but the spell of the mirror held her even more firmly than the sorcerer's grip and no matter how much she yearned to, she could do nothing but watch helplessly.

Gawain tried to race down the corridor, but the blows he had taken made him unsteady and he stumbled repeatedly.

Ahead of him, Lot dragged Tania through an arched door out
into the grey morning. Wind from over the stone battlements
lashed his wild hair. He did not break stride, but turned for
the narrow stairs that led up to the top of the fortifications.

'God, no,' Agravain exclaimed. 'Father! No! I know who
it is!'

But the wind snatched his words away and Lot climbed
the stairs. Tania's cold demeanour had shattered, and she
struggled, trying to break her father's grip. Tears of pain
streamed down her battered face.

'Stop, please!' begged Agravain, racing after them, with
Gawain bringing up the rear. 'Father, I know who the man
is! I know!'

Lot turned on the narrow stairs, dragging Tania perilously
close to the edge. 'Who is it then?' he demanded.

'No, Agravain, don't,' called Gawain, hurrying up the
stairs behind his younger brother. 'It's not for you to say
this.'

'Speak Agravain and I will curse your name to the end of
my days,' said Tania through clenched teeth.

'Tania . . .' said Agravain desperately.

'He knows nothing!' she cried. 'He just wants to try to
cool your blood.'

'Speak, Agravain,' grated Lot. It was a terrible tableau –
the enraged bull of a man, the perilous stairs, the woman
on her knees, halfway between the sky and the stones, the
two thin boys, each trying to bargain for their sister's life.
'Say who is to die for this defilement.'

'Agravain!' cried Tania, so many kinds of pain filling her
voice.

'Agravain, don't. You'll take away her only chance,' said
Gawain.

'Owein,' said Agravain and as he spoke the name, Rhian
heard the superiority that would come to be such a marked

trait in him. 'It is King Owein of North Rheged. I saw them together.'

His gaze met his sister's for a heartbeat, and in his eyes, Rhian could see he said, 'Forgive me.' And in hers, she said, 'I cannot.'

Then, Tania laughed. It was a high, incongruous sound made hysterical and horrible by her being on her knees, trying to hold her own hair to ease the pain of her father's terrible grip.

'Owein! You thought I was with Owein! Oh, Agravain, you are a blind old woman!'

This time Lot did not cry out, as Rhian expected. He just turned up the stairs and marched his daughter towards the top of the fortifications, as remorseless and relentless as the black clouds that bring the hail and thunder.

'No, father!' shouted Agravain. 'She's lying! She's trying to save him! Tell him, Tania! No man who leaves you thus is worth so much!'

Gawain's strength had rallied by this time, and he ran up the stairs behind his brother. The walkway of the fortifications was as narrow and treacherous as the stairs had been. Lot bent his daughter across the parapet, clinging still to her long hair, and showing her the whole, horrendous drop below. A wave of dizziness passed over Rhian. This was no high wall on a hill. This hall had been built atop a great rock and a jagged, black cliff fell away beneath it, hundreds of ells to the green valley floor.

'Who is it, Tania?' Lot's voice was soft and cold as death. 'For the last time, who is your whore master?'

Tania's face was white as she looked down to the distant valley floor. The wind blew across her face, touching the red weal her father had left. The parapet pressed against her belly, crowding the child she carried there, making it impossible to breathe.

'No,' she whispered, but what she was saying no to now, Rhian could not tell.

'Father, please,' begged Gawain. 'It does not have to be this way. A price can be negotiated to settle all sides. Tania did what she did for the love that weakens a woman's heart. I came to you with a son's love of father and sister. Your name is safe if you forgive. If there is shame, it is in what you do here and now.'

'Stop, Gawain.' Agravain seized his brother's shoulder. 'You'll make it worse. You know who it was as well as I do. Tell the truth.'

But Gawain did not stop. 'Father, I beg you,' Gawain went down on his knee. There was scarce room on the narrow walkway. 'A great king knows mercy and justice. He lets wisdom rule and does not let anger stain his honour.'

Listen to him, begged Rhian in her heart. *Mother Mary, make him listen!*

But as Gawain spoke his fine words, his father's face only darkened. 'You say I am the one who stains my own honour?' he spat the words. 'You say this is *my* doing?' The mad light brightened in his eyes.

'Gawain . . .' wailed Tania.

'You would save the slut?' Lot almost laughed and Rhian's blood froze. *Move, Gawain, move!*

The knight would have moved, would have taken advantage of the man's hesitation, but the boy did not know enough. He still wanted to believe in his father, still needed to believe.

'Then you go after her.'

And Lot pushed Tania forward. She hung on the edge of the parapet, scrabbling at the stone. Gawain dived for her, seeking to snatch at her sleeves and skirt where they fluttered in the breeze, but his fingertips only brushed the cloth and she fell, screaming long and high, as Gawain leaned over the parapet, calling her name again and again, until the scream was gone. There was no sound that reached them from the valley where her body was broken on the unforgiving earth. Neither did Lot make any sound as he turned from his sons and descended the stairs.

'There,' murmured the sorcerer into Rhian's ear. 'There is the stock from which your noble Gawain sprang. There is the flawless knight who could not even save his sister. Does he love you? Does he love Rhian? Or does he love another helpless girl whose father is too harsh? When will his pity be turned towards another wronged innocent? And when will his heart follow?'

Rhian couldn't breathe. Her throat had closed down and would not respond to the need of her body. Her bosom heaved, but no air filled her lungs.

'It's a lie,' she managed to whisper. 'You lie.'

'Perhaps. But the mirror does not. The high arts show only the truth. That is your first lesson.'

Now she could close her eyes and she did. She wished desperately for what she had seen to be a lie, but she knew it was not. It explained far too much of things Gawain had said, and had not said. It also explained the poison in Agravain's eyes when she had spoken to him of becoming brother and sister.

Gawain, I'm sorry. I'm so sorry.

It changed nothing, she told herself. It had nothing to do with whether Gawain would come or not. It had nothing to do with his love.

'Of course not,' said Euberacon as if he read her thoughts clearly. That idea sent a fresh chill through Rhian, but she steadied herself against it. Her thoughts showed in her face. That was all.

'After all,' he went on, with icy pleasantry. 'Even if Gawain should fail you, you still have your mother's love to shield you.' He smiled, a death's head grin, and in that moment, a new and terrible certainty came to Rhian's heart.

No. No!

'But yes, she too is gone. Your disobedience to me cost your mother her life, as you were warned.'

Inside her mind, Rhian screamed. She raged. She wept to Heaven, crying out to God and Mary to give her mother back, that it was not her fault, it was not right, it was not just! It took all the strength remaining in her body to hold herself still. She could do nothing, not here, not now. She would not let Euberacon see her break against the walls he had erected like a bird breaking its wings against the bars of its cage.

'You may have time to consider what you have seen and heard,' said the sorcerer. 'We will return to the board now.' Beneath his words, Rhian heard, *You may walk or be dragged.*

Rhian descended the stairs by her own will, and as she did a new emotion struck her. Shame. Shame that she was not fighting every inch of the way. Shame that she was not forcing him to hurt her, and hurt her badly, before he could have even this much from her.

No. Patience. Having your body broken will not serve. You must find your chance, and you must be ready to take it. For your mother's sake, if for no other.

She tried to imagine Gawain's voice speaking those words to her, but it would not come.

In the dining hall, nothing seemed to have moved since they had left it. The candles had dropped no wax. The dishes had not cooled at all. Euberacon returned to his place at the head of the table and sat almost primly.

'You will eat,' he told her. 'Refuse, and you will starve until your body wastes to the point when no more refusal is possible. I will not warn you again.'

Rhian sat. She took figs in honey, and nuts, and dates.

She took a slice of fish and lemons and a ladleful of the
golden rice. She did not look at the sorcerer. She swallowed
her shame with each elegant and flavourful bite. She sliced
off more of the fish, and a leg of a tiny fowl that might have
been a quail, but had the taste of a duck roasted in a sweet
sauce such as she had never tasted before. It was like honey
and lemons, but it was not either.

Euberacon filled his own plate time and again. She
watched him out of the corner of her eye, filling his plate
and emptying it again as if he were a starving man. Why
would he eat so eagerly? He was a sorcerer, he could have
such food with a word.

Or did it take more than that? Rhian had never before
considered that magic might take effort. The tales spoke of
magic having a cost, of payments and bargains made in return
for power . . . perhaps such a banquet was too expensive to
conjure on a whim. It was something to remember. If everything he did had a price, perhaps there was a way to make
the cost of her keep too dear.

Rhian sliced a piece of breast from the roasted fowl,
finished it, laid her hands in her lap for a moment, and then,
as if after careful consideration, took one of the pastries and
bit into it, finding it full of nuts and honey. She finished it
off slowly for it was too rich to eat quickly.

Then she returned her hands to her lap, and bowed her
eyes in modesty, waiting, her sleeves draped over her
wounded hands.

'Good.' Euberacon sounded genuinely pleased. 'It is obedience to my word that brings all rewards to you now. That
is your next lesson. My other servants will take you back to
your cell. You will wait in patience until I send for you again.'

She felt them beside her, left and right, invisible presences,
brushing her skin like cobwebs, ready to grab hold of her
with their taloned hands. He was showing her his power,

showing up her helplessness. Rhian turned without a word and walked back into the corridor, following it around the dimming courtyard and back down the stairs. All the while, she felt the invisible ones beside her, in the breeze that fluttered against her cheeks, in the pricking of the hairs on the back of her neck.

But none of them grabbed her hands. None of them pulled at her sleeves. They were doing just what they had been told. They were taking her back to her cell, and as long as she went that way, they would do nothing else.

They would not take from her the knife she had removed from the dining table and that she held now in her modestly folded hands, concealed by the flowing sleeve of her festival gown.

You can never be fast enough, the witch's voice spoke calmly from memory.

So you say, Rhian answered that memory fiercely. *Let me show you what I can do if I must.*

Rhian let herself be returned to her cell. She had been given no candle, nor any other way to make a light. The door was closed behind her, and this time she was sure that if she tried it, it would be barred.

With shuffling steps, Rhian found the bed, and lay down upon it. Alone in the silent darkness, she curled around her hidden knife.

Do you say Gawain will not come for me? That he is weak, and weakness makes him false? You may be right, but his are not the only hands that can strike a blow against you.

Then there was nothing to do but wait for day and mourn.

Oh, my mother, I will avenge you. I will.

The rain began soon after Gawain left Camelot. Light, cold, relentless spring showers soaked his clothing and skin within minutes. They turned the roads first to mud and then to streams running down to join the becks forming in every gully and crevice. He tried to hurry, hoping speed would give him a sense of purpose. Even a false certainty would be better than the bewilderment he felt now.

He travelled almost exactly as he had when he first found Rhian, riding the black gelding Pol in place of the palfrey, and leading Gringolet. He did not know what he would come to. He did not know but there might be a battle or some matter of honour and he would be sorry not to have the steady, trained animal with him, and he wanted Rhian to recognize him at once. She'd told him she'd seen the sigil on his shield and knew he was the answer to her prayer. He displayed that shield now, and he prayed to the one whose sign it was to intercede, to let him find her, to have mercy. To understand that he loved her.

Pol was less patient with the conditions of travel and whickered and whinnied almost constantly to let his master know the state of his displeasure.

Gawain had left the high road long ago, and the trails he followed north were mud up to the ankles. Frequently he had to get off the horse and pick his way across the worst of the holes and small swamps. Still the rain came down.

It was close enough to Camelot that his name and face were well known, and folk were generous when he paused at house or cot, with warm soup for him and dry blankets for the horses, but when he asked of the Green Temple, none had heard its name, not even the oldest greybeards in their corner by the fire.

Gawain rode on.

Twilight thickened and worked with the rain to turn the world into a blur of grey. Pol and Gringolet hung their heads and struggled to pull their hooves free from the slopping mud. Stands of trees began to merge with one another to become true forest. Their branches provided some shelter from the rain, but fat drops collected on leaves and fell off, splashing on head and hands, constantly startling the horses until Pol began to balk.

Feeling he would choke on his impatience, Gawain turned the horses, doubling back to a rickety hut he had before passed by in the hope that the rain would clear. The place smelled of old hay and new rot, but these odours were soon overlaid with the scent of steaming horses as Gawain unharnessed the animals and rubbed them dry. By the time he was finished there was barely enough light left to make a fire by. After many curses, he finally managed to make a small and smoky blaze by which to eat a rude meal of bread and smoked fish. Rain dripped through the roof, making pools of mud on the floor. Gawain shivered, and bowed his head.

This, then, is my punishment for arrogance. I accept it. I accept it. But Dear God, send me some sign it is not my doing that makes Rhian suffer. Let me know that she will be found and brought safe home. If not by me, then by Arthur. Please, dear Father. Do as you will with me, but do not desert her.

Gawain huddled by his fire, drawing what warmth he could from the flames and prepared to wait out the night. He tried to imagine some pleasant vision of the future, but could not, and in the end sank into a fitful dreaming in which Rhian ran in and out of his vision, calling his name, but each time he turned towards her, there was only emptiness. Through it all Tania screamed, and screamed again, until he could not tell her voice from Rhian's.

Morning dawned heavy and grey. The woods were as full of dank mist as they had before been full of rain. Gawain readied the horses with stiff hands and an aching head. He knew it to be cold, but he felt hot. Perspiration mixed with the beads of fog on his face.

Between the mist and the mud, the way was even more difficult than it had been before. There was no way to take his bearings, so Gawain had no choice but to follow the river of muck that in drier times was a narrow, rutted track. Pol seemed no fresher for his night's rest and even Gringolet walked with his head hung low, his breath blowing out in silver clouds to add to the dense mist that surrounded them. It clung in drops to his hair and face, as wet and cold as the rain had been. His ears had begun to ring and his tongue felt heavy and swollen. The pain in his ribs flared and reached up to join with the pain in his head. He rubbed his eyes repeatedly trying to clear them. The forest was shifting behind the mist, the trees rearranging themselves into more pleasing patterns, skittering across the path to gossip with each other more comfortably. The birds called out, saying that a guest was coming, that he brought news and gifts, and all the world watched him pass by with great interest. Pol shifted uneasily and Gawain slumped forward, barely catching himself before he slid from the saddle. He tried to straighten, but his back had no strength, and he fell forward across the horse's neck. Pol balked, and Gawain fell groaning into the mud.

He struggled to rise, but his head was too heavy and his arms were too weak.

I have been here before. I have done this before. I have come home then as now.

At last, Gawain pushed himself onto his knees. Up ahead, he heard the sounds of hooves, and the mist curtains parted to let through a horse and rider. Gawain blinked up at him, struggling to rise, but the trees were moving again, leaning close to hear what he had to say, raising their branches so the birds and the beasts might have a better look at this comical stranger covered in dirt and calling a woman's name.

Oblivion rose, and Gawain fell forward, and for a long time he knew nothing more.

EIGHTEEN

Gawain started awake, clammy from his own sweat. Stone walls illuminated by pale rush light surrounded him. Furs covered his nakedness and thick feather pillows raised his head.

He struggled to sit and after a time managed to do so. He was weak as a kitten, but at least his eyes were clear, and if his head throbbed, it was an easier pain than he had known before.

He was on a wooden bed in a small windowless room. Rushes and more furs covered the floor. His clothes lay on a carved chest with his boots, sword, shield and saddlebags beside them. There was a chair and table, and little else besides. Past the foot of the bed was a plain wooden door, tightly closed.

Gawain swung his feet over the side of the bed, ignoring the sudden wave of dizziness that washed through him. He planted them on the floor, but they seemed to grow further away as he stared at them.

The door opened. A fair-haired woman carrying a wooden tray took two steps into the room, and stopped, apparently surprised at seeing a naked man attempting to climb from his bed and not quite remembering the required motions.

Gawain did, however, remember something of modesty and pulled himself back under the bed coverings.

'I am glad to see you awake.' She set the tray down on the small table. It held a basin of steaming water, a clean towel and a wooden noggin. 'We were . . .'

Although it was poor manners, Gawain interrupted. 'How long have I been . . . ?'

'One night only. Rest, my lord. You are not well.' She held out the noggin.

Thirst itched in Gawain's throat. He drank. It proved to be nothing more than water with just enough wine to make it palatable. 'I cannot rest. I have . . . I must . . .'

'You cannot,' said the woman firmly, paying back his interruption with another. 'Your horse is lame and you are ill. Stay where you are, or you will do one of us an injury.'

The fact that she was able to push him back onto the pillows so easily, much more than her words, convinced Gawain to do as she said.

His head began to swim again. He drained the noggin and felt somewhat better. 'My horse is lame?'

'The black. The white is merely . . . perturbed.' Seeing Gawain's alarm, she held up both hands. 'Do not fear, my lord, our men are expert with horses. They are both well cared for. The black only needs a poultice. Our stablemaster will see him to rights.'

Relief rallied Gawain's wits. 'I thank you, my lady. It is certain you have saved my life. Will you do me the courtesy of telling me. . .'

Before he could finish the question, the door slammed open and a bluff, dark man sailed into the room like a hearty thundercloud

'So!' He planted his fists on his hips. 'This is the young eagle who has fallen from the nest and set all the ladies' hearts aflutter with tender feelings!' He laughed heartily.

Gawain saw the blue tattoos on his hands, complex knots faded with time and overgrown with hair.

He was, in fact, one of the hairiest men Gawain had ever seen. A rich brown thatch sprouted from his head and over-ran most of his face and neck.

And they call Arthur 'the bear', he thought, and then reminded himself that he had already known this man's hospitality and had better show his manners.

The man, however, spoke first. 'Well, my lord, I am Belinus and this is my hall and my woman here who nurses you so diligently is called Ailla. That is who we are. Who might you be, and what is so important you must seek it in my lands in the rain and dark?'

Gawain gave his name and titles. Belinus did not look impressed. Gawain added, 'As to what I seek, I seek the Green Temple, or any man who can tell me where it might be found.'

Belinus pursed his thick lips. 'The Green Temple? A strange name. Is it something you've heard of, my wife, with all your women's lore?'

Ailla just looked at her hands in her lap. 'If my lord has not heard of it, then I most surely have not.'

'There you are, I fear, my Lord Gawain. But now, the morning has turned fair and I must be away to the hunt with my men. You rest here as long as you please. Speak with my wife. Perhaps something will jog that lazy memory of hers, and I will ask after this Green Temple of yours among those of my lands. I promise to give you whatever I gain when I return, if you will do the same for me, eh?'

It was an odd request, but from the way the man was looking at him, Gawain realized his host expected an answer. 'Surely, my Lord Host.'

'Well then.' He slapped his hands together, satisfied. 'To the hunt! Take good care of our young eagle, Ailla. Rest well, Gawain.'

As swiftly as he came, Belinus departed, letting the door slam shut behind him. Ailla winced and Gawain's face creased in sympathy. That was a harsh man to be paired with so delicate a lady.

As soon as Belinus left, Ailla rose to her feet. She filled a basin with water and took up a cloth. Quickly, lightly, she began to dab his face. It was most refreshing. 'Why do you ask of the . . . this Green Temple, my Lord Gawain?'

How to explain? 'I have an errand there that must be completed, a matter of honour.'

'I wish you success then.' Ailla took up her basin and turned from him, but as she did, he thought he saw some deep sorrow on her face.

'Lady?' She looked back over her shoulder at him. Her face was blank, but her eyes were haunted.

She does know of this place. She does. 'You will consider the name, will you not? To see if you can remember what you might have heard of it?'

'I know nothing that my lord does not, Sir,' she repeated. 'I must let you rest now.'

She closed the door behind her and Gawain was alone.

Gawain slammed his fist against the bedcovers, and that sudden movement seemed to drain away all the strength his arm had left. He was still feverish, damn it, damn him, damn the Green Knight and Euberacon Magus and Rygehil of the Morelands all. He fell back on the pillows.

But, he was in a place where the Green Temple was known, if he could convince the lady to speak of it.

But why should I? Why am I not out seeking Rhian instead? There is time enough to die after she is found and safe.

Because he had made a bargain with the fantastic, and such must always be kept, even if Arthur had not stood surety for him before so many witnesses. If he did not keep to his word . . . he might curse Rhian so that she could never be found, he might break the very treasure he sought to cherish.

And perhaps, just perhaps, there would yet be a way through this thing. The Green Knight knew of Rhian, he was sure. He had taunted Gawain deliberately. Perhaps there was some way for him to survive this challenge, and then he and the Green Knight might have a more even contest, and he could compel his answers . . .

Kindling his hope in his heart, Gawain drifted awhile into a light sleep. He thought he heard the rush of the wind in the trees, and felt the rocking of a horse's gait beneath him. Ahead, he saw the hunched back of a black boar, crashing madly through the trees. Soon it would turn, soon it would fight. Soon there would be blood and death and life and promise and all would begin again . . .

Gawain started awake. The door to his room was opening, the wood scraping over the rushes, and Ailla was coming in with a tray holding a bowl, a cup and a lump of bread. Still befuddled by his dream, it seemed for a moment the sides of the bowl ran bright red with blood, but he blinked hard, and the vision was gone.

'My Lord Gawain?' She set the tray down swiftly and laid her hand on his head. 'You are white. Do you feel worse?'

'No, no, my lady. It was a dream, a dream only.' Her hand was cool against his brow, and she smelled of something sweet . . . at first he thought it might be sandalwood, but it was not. Something sweet and smoky.

'Your fever is gone,' she announced with satisfaction as she straightened up. 'You will feel weak for awhile yet. Broth and bread will help strengthen you.' She deposited the tray on his lap. 'Tomorrow you should be able to walk without help.'

'Tomorrow I must continue with my quest.' The broth was

rich and flavourful and smelled of sweet venison and onions. Gawain drank it gratefully.

Lady Ailla shook her head. 'If you do, you will do so without your horse. He will not be fit to travel for another day at least. If he is ridden too soon, the swelling will start again, so says our man. You must compose yourself to patience, my lord.'

Gawain dipped the good bread in the broth and chewed on it to keep his aggravation silent. Patience was not what he wished for right now, but he could not complete his quest for the Green Temple, or for Rhian, on foot.

'I will leave you to your rest.' Ailla dipped him a small curtsey and moved towards the door.

'Stay awhile, lady, if it please you,' said Gawain quickly. 'I have some questions I would ask, if you will permit.'

An odd look flickered across her face, as if she were both concerned and relieved at the same time. 'I will answer as I can, Sir.' She took the chair beside the bed, folding her hands, waiting politely for the questions.

Gawain sopped some more broth, looking in the bottom of the bowl for a place to start. 'I fear my fever took my sense of direction from me. I do not even know where I am.'

'You are in Caer Ceri. Two days ride north and you will come to Calchfynedd.'

He had come that far? Gawain found it suddenly difficult to swallow his bread. He must have been fevered longer than he knew.

He collected himself. 'Lord Belinus is not a name I have heard of before.'

'No.' It was a soft statement, almost a sigh.

Gawain cocked his head as if it might help him see her better. 'He calls the High King his liege, though.'

But Ailla just looked away. 'Who my lord calls liege is a delicate question.'

'I see.'

'No, my lord, you cannot.' She bowed her head quickly, biting her lip. 'I should not have said that.'

Gently, gently, Gawain. This one is a fragile spirit. Press too hard and she will only break. 'I cry you mercy, lady. I am being hopelessly rude. What would you speak of to pass the time with your invalid?' He settled back on the pillows and smiled in what he hoped she would find an encouraging fashion.

She did not answer for a time, but he saw her slip a glance at him. At last, she seemed to take courage and lifted her head. 'You have come from the hall of the High King?' Gawain nodded. 'Tell me of Camelot.' She whispered its name, and Gawain was not certain whether she thought it a word of blessing or a curse.

Whatever it was to her, Gawain was glad to oblige her request. He told her tales of the proudest names, of Arthur, Lancelot and Bedivere. She asked him shrewd questions that told him she'd heard some of the wilder stories and sensibly doubted their veracity. He was pleased to be able to tell her the far finer truths. He spoke of feasts and pageants, and of the queen, of course. All the while, he saw Rhian's image before him, how she stood so fair and proud beside Guinevere, how she kept her face so solemn as she made some jest, how she held her own even with Kai playing against her.

But this lady knew something. There was something about her lord that kept her from speaking even though she knew he could not hear. If he could make her his friend, if he could bring her to trust him, she would speak. If she could tell him what she feared, he would help, and in return she would tell him where the Green Temple was.

Where, despite all his hopes and his pride, he would face his death.

Gawain's tale faltered.

Ailla rose from her seat, leaning towards him. 'Is your fever returning, Lord Gawain?'

'No, lady.' He held up his hand, although it would have been pleasant enough to feel her hand on his brow again. 'It was . . . an unwelcome thought.'

She sank back into her chair. 'Because you seek the Green Temple?'

'Yes my lady.' *What made you ask that, my hostess?*

Flustered, the lady looked down again at her hands. Her fingers twisted tightly together. 'It is only . . . such a place as that must be . . . no one would seek such a place save for some great and terrible need.' She stood abruptly. 'I must see to the ordering of dinner. I will have one of my women bring you your meat.' She turned her back to him, and Gawain suddenly felt that she did not want to have to look at him anymore.

'Then let me bid you goodnight, my hostess, since I am not to see you again.'

Her shoulders sagged for a moment and then straightened. 'God be with you this night, Lord Gawain.'

She was gone, and Gawain was alone with a rush light and the remains of the broth and the bread and his own uneasy thoughts. He tried again to stand, but he made it no more than two steps from the bed before his knees began to buckle under him. He could do nothing but lie in his bed and stare at the boards and buttresses over his head, and wonder – what did his hostess know, and where did Rhian bide, and what did she suffer?

Be brave, be brave my love. God grant me my strength again. Let me find her whole.

There was no way to tell how much time passed before he heard the thudding of bootsoles on stone. The door slammed open and Belinus strode up to the bed, a bloody bone in his hand.

Without concern or ceremony, he tossed the object onto the bedcovers. It was a boar's curling tusk.

'The whole of the beast is in the yard. I did not think my lady would like me to drag it up to the sick room!' He bellowed with laughter at his own joke. 'A poor thing, skinny from winter and not yet fat for summer, but fought like a tiger. I've a man who will be showing his scars to his grand-children.' He folded his arms in great satisfaction. 'That is what I have gained today, my lord. And you?'

'Several hours fine conversation with my most courteous hostess,' said Gawain promptly. 'I will do my best to return them to you, my host, but I may have to beg you to have mercy on my weakness.'

Belinus laughed heartily at that. 'We must get you well soon, my lord, I should dearly love to hear how you spoke to my wife! But although I've hunted a boar today, I've an appetite like a bear and my meat waits in the hall. Goodnight, my Lord Gawain. We will talk soon, you may be sure of it!'

When he was gone, and the door was closed, Gawain picked up the tusk that had been left to decorate his sick bed. It was warm, as if it had been freshly torn from the newly dead beast. It had an edge that could cut a man's hand were he not careful. The place where the tusk had lain was spattered with drying blood, reminding Gawain of the blood he had imagined on the edge of his bowl of broth, and the blood he'd smelled in his dream. It seemed to him that the smears and spatters shifted beneath his sight, and he fancied that if he looked long enough, he might read them like old runes.

Gawain rubbed his eyes. *What is happening to me? That fever is not so far gone as my lady promised.*

Setting the tusk carefully on the table so he would not be seen to show disrespect to his host's token – though in truth he would have tossed the grim thing aside if he could – he lay back on his pillows to wait for supper and then for sleep, and to pray for tomorrow and strength and health, and after that . . . and after that . . .

After that, for life.

That night, Rhian dreamed. The door to her cell was diffuse, like mist. The threshold around it sagged unevenly and was made of only rough and broken stones. Rhian started forward, only to realize her wrists and ankles were weighted down with chains of iron, so heavy she could barely move. She struggled, against the chains and against the profound weariness that filled her. She had to climb the stairs, she had to. So she walked out into the corridor, which was black and dank and solid. She toiled up the worn stairs, her chains scraping on the stones, a harsh grating noise.

Outside, the courtyard was nothing but a ruin. Yet, she could still discern hints of Euberacon's palace. The memory of clean and gleaming marble coated the filthy, tumbled stones like a silver mist. The tiles were the barest hint of colour gleaming thinly across a churned sea of clay and mud. The fountain was a muck-filled bowl in which a little dirty water bubbled up fitfully. The jagged ends of roof beams lay beneath the moon like a giant's broken bones. Only one tower stood whole, a thick, inelegant edifice, built for keeping watch against some enemy.

Rhian stood there, gaping, at a loss as to what to do next.

Then, she saw a woman trudging towards the broken fountain. In her hand she carried a sieve made of wood and hair. Her face was sunken with woe and despair. She dipped the sieve into the dirty water and watched, tears running down her face as the water ran out onto the muddy ground. Rhian saw then that she had no eyes. She had only pearl-grey spheres where her eyes should have been, spheres to cry and to suffer, but not to see.

Head hanging low, the woman turned and walked one weary step at a time back the way she had come.

Rhian stared after her, a lump rising in her throat, her own woes forgotten for that moment.

Then, she saw the others.

In the manner of dreams, she saw them one at a time. As soon as she turned from one, that one was gone, and she was alone with another person, entirely different, but just as blind, just as suffering.

She saw a youth wielding a broom as tall as he was, frantically sweeping at the clay and mud of the courtyard. The broom bristles swished against the ground, sounding so much like the sea Rhian thought she might see the foam from the breaking waves.

A man, chained like she was, dragged his shackles up the winding stairs to the south-east tower. Each step was an unspeakable strain. His face, his whole being was slack, devoid of hope or any plan beyond the next step. Two demons – red-skinned, black-horned and leather-winged, fluttered around behind him, laughing at his struggle. The man's strength failed him and he crumpled forward, dashing his chin against the unforgiving marble, his body a helpless weight in its chains. He rolled down the hard and unforgiving steps until he lay still, bruised surely, perhaps broken, at the bottom.

The demons leaned over his still body, sniffing like dogs over a kill.

'Is it dead?' asked one.

'It wishes it was,' replied the other, pawing delicately at the man's head. 'But it will be here again tomorrow.'

Then the other one looked up, and saw Rhian.

'What's this? What's this?' shrieked one, leaping into the air. 'Is it flesh or is it foul?'

They dived towards her, as the ravens had done. Panic
and fury lent Rhian strength despite the chains, despite the
weariness, and she swung her arms, swatting at the fiends,
but they just cackled in delighted laughter, flying out of her
reach.

'Again! Again!' cried one in foul delight. 'The others do
not give such sport as this! Again!'

Its companion swooped low, and Rhian ducked. 'How is
it she has eyes and they have none?'

'Ah! For it is her body he wants confined, her mind he
has other uses for.'

'Him! Him!' screamed the first of the fiends. 'Has he fallen
yet? Has he?'

They flew away, up into the night sky, like leaves caught
in the wind, and up at the top of the tower, balanced on the
slumping stones of the battlements, she saw Euberacon.
Around him in the air there hung a flock of demons, shining with their own eerie light. They were bloated and
grotesque. They were pinched and withered with long grasp-
ing fingers. Some were as beautiful as angels, others had red
and black faces distorted by fury. They slumped in the air as
if as weary as Rhian, or they gambolled, displaying their
bodies to him, enticing him to reach out, to stretch his arm
too far, so that he might lose his careful equilibrium.

They were waiting for him to fall.

'Yes,' she whispered. *Fall, fall! Let them take you, let them
break you on the stones.* 'Yes!'

She wondered for a moment whether Euberacon saw the
demons before him, or if he was as blind as the others she
had seen. But then he looked down past his shoulder onto
his tiny, dark domain and she saw his face clearly. She
expected him to smile, to gloat at her bound in chains of
nightmare, but he did not. She saw only fear written across
his face. Around him the demons flocked, greedy and ready.

Then, it was over and Rhian woke. Dawn's light streamed in through the tiny window and showed her the solid stone walls and the closed door. All was as it had been when she fell asleep. Including, she tightened her fingers and relief rushed through her, the knife she held hidden in her sleeve.

What was that dream, or could it have been another vision?
What does it mean?

The cell offered no answers. The stones around her looked and felt as solid as they had been before. There was no way to make any ablutions or to refresh herself. She smoothed her hair down with her free hand, then she worried one of the ribbons out of her loosening braid. Clumsily, she bound the knife to her forearm, her heart in her mouth the whole time. What if the invisible servants were here to watch what she did? What if they had alerted Euberacon? Or would they just dart their clawed hands down and seize her only hope?

Were they demons like the ones she had seen in her dream?

She stood and folded her arms, letting her sleeve fall over the knife and its hasty binding. She could feel its edge against her skin. It would cut her if she moved too quickly. Worse, the ribbon would not hold for long. She would have to find her chance or make one quickly.

Remembering how it had gone the previous day, Rhian tried the door. It swung open easily. Evidently, the sorcerer desired her presence.

Good, she thought grimly, steeling herself. *For I would be near to him.*

Rhian mounted the stairs to the courtyard. The sun poured down, careless of Rhian's captivity. A table covered in cloth of silver had been set beside the fountain. Euberacon sat there, loaves of bread and bowls of jellied meats before him. A woman bustled to and fro, setting down another bowl, this one of deep red preserves, adjusting linen and setting out another cup and knife. But that was not what caused Rhian to stare. She knew this woman. This was the one she had seen the night before in her dream, trying to draw water with a sieve.

How is it she has eyes and they have none?

Ah! For it is her body he wants confined, her mind he has other uses for.

The woman curtsied to the sorcerer, her face serene and alert. Rhian could not see her eyes. Euberacon nodded, and the serving woman took her leave.

'You are prompt this morning,' said the sorcerer. 'Good. Come here.'

Yes. Rhian did as she was told, coming to stand before him, arms folded tightly across her chest.

The sorcerer spread a slice of fresh brown bread with jellied meat and took a bite. Rhian was ashamed to find her mouth watering.

'Tell me what you saw last night,' he ordered.

The details of her nightmare sprang instantly into her mind's eye, but Rhian just tightened her hold on her own forearms. She felt the shape of the knife beneath the cloth of her sleeve. The ribbon was already loosening.

Find the chance soon or make it.

'Did you hear me?' the sorcerer's voice took on a dangerous edge.

'I saw nothing last night,' she said. 'I slept in a cell behind a locked door. What could I have seen?'

'You are a liar,' said the sorcerer coolly. 'I will allow that once only. What did you see last night?'

What could concern you about my dream? The sorcerer's eyes were boring into her mind and fear shrank Rhian's heart, but still she said, 'I saw nothing last night.'

The sorcerer rose slowly to his feet. Rhian looked up and

deliberately shrank in on herself, shoving her hands into her sleeves. He stalked around his chair. His shadow fell across her. His eyes drew her close, and she felt her mind slip away from her, all volition draining towards him.

Clamping down hard on the last of her will, Rhian drew the knife. Its edge sliced a fiery line across her skin. She swung it out, but she swung too wide, and only grazed his hand.

'Slut!' he shouted. Rhian did not give him time to say any more. She darted in, knife raised and ready, aiming for his belly. She stabbed upward. Cloth tore and the blade sank quickly through flesh, until her arm jarred against bone.

Euberacon clouted her hard across the ear, and Rhian toppled backward, seeing stars.

Before Rhian's sight cleared, Euberacon was beside her, his hands gripping her arms, twisting, and his fingers gouging into her tendons. 'What? You think I keep my life where such as you can find it?' He dragged her to her feet, and she saw the knife on the tiles. There was not even any blood on it.

But I felt it, I felt *the blow!* her mind wailed.

Euberacon twisted her arms harder, forcing them up and behind her. She kicked backward, but her feet found no purchase.

'You will learn, you whore. You will learn who your master is.'

Euberacon twisted her arms until the pain burned from shoulder to finger-tip. He kicked at her knees and calves, driving her forward towards the fountain. She struggled but it did no good. The sight of the clear, sparkling water in its beautiful tiled basin filled her with terror. Euberacon gripped the back of her neck, his fingers digging deep into the flesh. The world swirled red and black before her eyes.

'So you still think you will be saved? Perhaps you think

that your knight will have you back and be enchanted again by that pretty face of yours. It has opened so many doors for you, that face. I think it is time you learned I own that face as I own all of you.'

He thrust her downward. Rhian cried out, but her scream was muffled by the water. It filled her mouth and stopped her ears, a gout of it dragging painfully down her throat into startled lungs that gagged and dragged in more water. She thrashed aimlessly, the panicked instinct for survival wiping out all else. But Euberacon's arm was like an iron bar, pinning her remorselessly down. Drowning, she was drowning. She saw black again and flashes and lines of gold, and her lungs were more filled with water than air, and over the churning of the water she heard distantly a voice chanting, and thought she heard another answer, and then the blackness drew its cloak closer.

Mother Mary, help me!

But this time, the Virgin did not answer. This time, something else happened. She felt it in her bones and in each joint. They twisted, warped and crushed themselves together. The muscles of her face dragged themselves out painfully, snapping and tearing. Her aching eyes screwed in tightly to her skull, shrinking almost to nothingness, while her teeth fought to tear themselves from her gums. The pain overrode the terror of drowning and Rhian struggled to scream and not to scream and felt herself tear in two for death to enter in.

All at once Euberacon's arm dragged her up out of the water and dropped her onto the tiles.

For an eternity, all she could do was retch and try to breathe. Her lungs burned. She vomited up clear gouts of water onto the tiles, soaking her hands, sleeves and skirts. At last she was empty, and her breath rasped in and out, and she blinked her eyes clear of tears and ice-cold water, and she could feel again.

She could feel her eyes, small and round and set too close to a nose suddenly too broad and protruding. Her jaw was heavy as a stone, but her head where she was accustomed to the weight of her hair was feather-light. She pushed herself up on her hands, and stared down at them, her tiny, piggish eyes trying to strain out of her misshapen skull. Her hands were unrecognizable. The skin on them was scaled and scabbed. The fingers were splayed and twisted and the yellow nails curled like the talons of some bird of ill-omen. Her wrists stuck out inches past her sleeve, the filthy, yellowing skin clinging slackly to the bones. The only thing left that was recognizable was the ring on her right hand with the great, square emerald winking mockingly in the brilliant sun.

Rhian screamed. She couldn't stop herself. Terrified at the sight of her own hands, she slapped at them, trying to pull off skin and nails as if they were a pair of gloves. Over her head, she heard Euberacon laugh.

'It is well you cannot see that face now!' he crowed, and he seized her collar, dragging her again to the fountain, and leaning her over it. And Rhian looked at the wavering water, and she could not help but see.

Round black eyes that belonged in the face of an animal blinked and stared. Skin stretched tight over jutting brow but hung slack and hollow against cheeks, and a jaw that jutted out beneath a spatulate snout where her nose had been. Her teeth, jagged and speckled with black, protruded over her sagging lip. Already, a stream of spittle ran from the mouth she could not close down to her long, wasp-thin neck.

But her hair, her hair, that her mother had combed and perfumed and braided, her hair that Gawain had called fairer than any crown of gold, her hair was little more than a scattering of black bristles over a scabbed and mottled scalp.

'Now, listen closely to me,' Euberacon said, his voice barely louder than a whisper cutting through the roaring that seemed to have filled her ears. 'I am inclined to turn you out into the world as you are to see whether it is men or the wild beasts that hunt you down first. But if you show me your obedience, if you serve me without question, then I will return your beautiful face, and yes, that mane of hair you are so proud of. It is all for you to choose now.'

He released her and stood back. Weakened as she was, Rhian nearly fell. She barely caught herself on the edge of the fountain. She looked up at him. His snake's eyes glittered with their triumph. She looked back at her wavering and distorted reflection in the water. She did not need to see what he had done. The smallest movement screamed with the pain and the wrong of it. Fear, fury, wretched sorrow swarmed and sang through her mind. A thousand thoughts wailed like ghosts, first among them the urge to murder the man who stood before her and then take her own life, dashing herself down from the tower against the tiles so no one could see the monster she had become.

'Well, woman, what is your choice?'

And she remembered what the witch had said, and she remembered how Gawain had looked at her in love, and she saw again the horror of her own hands and face and looked up into the black and shining eyes of the man who wielded his power without mercy, and she knew she had no choice. Not anymore.

Slowly, painfully, as if she were an old woman wracked with rheumatism, Rhian knelt. She bowed her head until her forehead touched the sun-warmed tiles at his feet.

'Please, Master,' she said. The voice in her new throat was harsh and her new teeth slurred and slushed the words so they were barely comprehensible. 'Please, do not send me away.'

'Very good.' He touched the back of her head, and she flinched like a whipped dog. 'Your name is Ragnelle now, and will be until I say otherwise. So. Follow me, and learn your new duties, Ragnelle.'

He walked away across the court and did not look back. Ragnelle, who had been Rhian of the Morelands, climbed painfully to her feet and followed behind.

NINETEEN

Gawain woke to the same stone walls, the same bed and sparse furnishings. He had no idea what time of day it was. The rush lights burned, so there must have been daylight enough for the servitors to be awake and to come and kindle them.

He swung his feet over the side of the bed and planted them on the rushes. No dizziness came over him this time, and he stood, and remained standing. A few steps across to the chest where his clothes and gear waited told him he was still weak, that his rib still had not healed, but he was better than before. Healed enough to feel the stone walls as a cell about him.

I need to walk and see the sky, see this land I am in.

He had only enough time to lace up his breeches before the door burst open, to let in Belinus with Ailla a step behind.

'Ah!' he cried with satisfaction. 'The young eagle is testing his wings! How does this morning find you, my Lord Gawain?'

Barefoot and barely dressed, Gawain found it difficult to pull together his dignity, but he managed a small bow. 'Much better, my host, thanks be to God and your lady.'

'A dab hand at many things, my Ailla.' Belinus threw an arm about his wife's shoulders and hugged her roughly. Ailla seemed nothing so much as resigned to the gesture. 'Has she told you aught of this Green Temple you seek so eagerly?'

Did his face seem more shrewd as he asked that question. He did not let go of his wife. 'No, my host.' Gawain did not look to the lady to see how she took this query. He did not want to give her away if she was trying to hide something from this man. 'She has not.'

'Ah well.' Belinus released his wife and clapped his hands together. 'Perhaps I will bring back news of it today. Rest well, Gawain!'

He strode away, leaving Gawain and Ailla standing awkwardly before each other. She'd dropped her gaze so she would not have to look at the half-dressed stranger in front of her.

'If you are feeling well enough, my lord, I would be most pleased if you would join us at board.' Evidently deciding Belinus was far enough away she added, 'I imagine seeing nothing but these walls is beginning to pall on you.'

'I will join you with a good will, my hostess,' replied Gawain and he was rewarded with a quick smile before she retreated to let him finish dressing.

Perhaps today you will tell me what is wrong with you. Perhaps you will let me help you before I must leave. The idea pleased him. Merlin had warned him to remember his honour. Here was a chance to do honour in aiding a lady. If only she would speak and tell him what she held so tightly within her heart.

Belinus's hall was an ancient place. No tapestries or banners hung from the rough stone walls, nor even any trophies of war. There were no hearths. The fires burned in the centre of the floor, filling the long chamber with smoke and ash. The place held more dogs than servitors. There was no dais. The tables were roughly planed boards with only short cloths to cover them. Lady Ailla stood before one of the fires ladling porridge into a wooden bowl. It struck him how out of place she was here, a delicate flower in a thicket of thorns. Who were her people that they had given such a lady into such a place?

He walked up to her and bowed before her as his hostess. What few men were in the hall, all dark-eyed with untrimmed beards, glowered, as if they thought her unworthy of such a gesture. Ailla herself seemed flustered and curtsied with the bowl still in her hands. None of the squat, square women came forward to take it from her, so Gawain did so, with another bow. The contents proved to be a thick porridge of lentils and oats. Plain fare, but strengthening. He sat to eat and Ailla served him herself, bringing watered wine and fresh baked bread, butter and honey. For the first time since he had arrived, Gawain found he had a good appetite and he ate with a will. All around the hall, Belinus's people watched him and their lady, and said nothing at all.

Well let them stare. There is nothing improper for them to see. 'My hostess,' said Gawain. 'I would be grateful to see my horses, and something of the land I am in.' He needed to get his bearings, needed to decide what road to take next, and if he could do this and get Ailla out of this dank and smoky place into the wholesome air for a time, that was all to the good.

She looked to the door almost wistfully. Was that a frown from one of the black-bearded men? What manner of place *was* this?

'Of course, my Lord Gawain,' she said with the air of someone who has reached a decision. 'If you are finished . . . ?'

He was, and, he found, glad to be so.

The day outside was fresh but damp. It had rained

overnight, and the land was still given over to mud and mist. Still, the air was clean, and he could feel the sun despite the clouds. The fog would soon burn away and he would be able to see just where he was.

In the meantime, Lady Ailla led him to the stables to see Pol and Gringolet. Having now seen the state of the hall, Gawain was worried about the conditions in which his horses had been housed. He needn't have been. If anything, the stables were better made than the hall. They were certainly cleaner, and there were several lanky blood mares housed there with his horses. Gringolet greeted him cheerfully from a wide, roomy box filled with fresh straw, which Pol was munching with enthusiasm. Gawain checked the ankle beneath the poultice. It seemed tender, but not badly so. Pol only snorted with mild discomfort as Gawain probed the place. He rewrapped it and straightened up.

'I have great cause to thank my Lord Belinus,' he said as he patted Pol's back.

'My husband has a great admiration for fine horses,' she answered, her voice carefully neutral. 'He would not have permitted two such as these to come to any harm.'

'He is a deep and complex man, your husband,' said Gawain, searching for an opening through which he might see his answers.

Ailla hung her head. 'Not so. He is simple to understand, if one understands that he is of the oldest ways.'

He decided to take a small risk. 'Are you far from home here, lady?'

'Farther than you know, sir.' She straightened. 'But come, I cannot be melancholy today while you are trying to regain your strength. Nor can I keep you out in the damp. The chill will only do you harm.'

Gawain insisted he felt quite well in the fresh air, but the lady would not be gainsaid and insisted he return to his little room. She sat beside him, but this time, Gawain noted, she left the door open. Every now and then, he saw a graceless, shadowed figure pass by in the corridor. The certainty grew in him that her lord was having her watched.

Suppressing a growl of frustration, Gawain leaned back against his pillows. He was far weaker from his brief stroll than he would have liked to admit. 'So, my lady, what shall we speak of today.' *Let you pick the topic with those suspicious eyes at your back.*

'My Lord Gawain will think me foolish.' A blush touched her cheeks. 'But I would like to hear more of Camelot.'

'Not at all, my hostess.' *But when will you speak of yourself? When will you help me, and help me to help you?*

So Gawain entertained her with more of the merriest tales that he knew, gratified to hear her laugh and to see the light returning to her eyes. It was a shame that such a beauty need be so sad. He wondered what Rhian would think of her, and what she would advise him to do to bring her situation some ease.

Something must have showed in his face with those thoughts, because the lady lowered her voice and asked, 'Have you a lady love?'

Now it was his turn to lower his gaze. 'I do.'

'And is she fair?'

'Most fair.'

'What makes you sad, my lord? Is she . . . have you lost her?' He could barely hear her, she whispered her question so softly.

Gawain lifted his head. She was afraid now, holding herself like a deer, thinking she might need to run, but not certain yet. 'Yes, lady, I have lost her. I seek her now.'

Ailla's face paled a little. 'You said it was the Green Temple you sought. Is she there?'

'I do not know where she is.' Gawain's heart twisted. He

did not want to speak of this. But to remain silent was no way to draw out the lady in front of him, especially now that they stood so close to the goal. 'What I seek at the Green Temple . . .' he shook his head. 'Repentance, perhaps.'

She seemed genuinely surprised to hear this. 'What can such a man as you have to repent?'

Despite his resolve to speak openly, Gawain found his throat closed around those words. 'Do not ask me that, Lady Ailla,' he could only say. 'The answer would take far too long to give.' *That is not true, but to see my shame reflected in your eyes . . . I am that much of a coward.*

'I think your lady must be very lucky.'

If you knew the truth you would not say so. 'Oh?'

Her veil had fallen partway over her face, screening it from him. 'Her lord seeks after her, he does not abandon her to her fate.'

Greatly daring, Gawain reached out and touched Ailla's hand. For a moment, he smelled the perfume she anointed herself with. A rare and delicate scent for a rare and delicate lady. 'And who has abandoned my lady?'

But that was pressing too far. She pulled back immediately, clutching the back of her hand where he had laid his fingertips. 'If I cannot ask you of your repentance, I beg you do not ask me of my abandonment.'

Gawain bowed before her as deeply as he was able. 'I ask your pardon.'

'No, my lord, I beg you forgive me. It has been so long since I have had anyone to talk to . . . I have forgotten how to guard my tongue.' She still held the place where he touched her. Did she wish to discourage the repetition of such a liberty, or did she not wish to let it go?

As gently as he could, Gawain said, 'I should be very sorry if our talk caused you any worry or grief, my lady.' *And that is nothing but the truth. God grant she believe. God grant she trust.*

'You do not know how much happiness you have given me.'

'I would do more, if my lady would tell me how.'

She smiled in sad contemplation. 'There is nothing that can be done for me. My fate is long sealed.'

'It is said that hope remains as long as there is life.'

'Not here. Not . . .' She stood abruptly. 'No. I must not say anymore.'

'Why not? We are alone here.' *I will see when any comes past that doorway. Please, lady, speak. Tell me how I can help Rhian, and you.*

'Because my lord will question you on your return, and you must give him what you yourself were given today.' Her fingers laced together in her nervousness and she looked over her shoulder towards the shadowed corridor, listening for breathing, looking for spies.

'That is but a jest my lady,' but even as he said it, Gawain was not so certain. His bedcovers were still stained with the boar's blood from the day before.

'No. No jest my lord. It is in earnest, I assure you. He follows the oldest laws and will not shy away from them.'

Gawain felt the skin on his arms begin to prickle. 'Do you say I am in danger here?'

'Not yet.' She rose. 'Let me go, my lord, before I say any more.' She leaned over swiftly and kissed his cheek. 'At least let me know I will not bring your downfall as well.'

And she was gone before he could ask any more. Gawain pressed his hand against his mouth so that his curses and frustration would not burst forth and be heard by whoever loitered out there still. So close. She was so close . . .

The answer was so close. That is what I meant. The answer was so close. Rhian's answer.

Gawain repeated that to himself until he could at last believe it. Suddenly he could not bear the idea of lying here in idleness and isolation. He got to his feet, forcing back the weariness that came over him. He had felt far worse. He could master this. He would find his answers and he would find Rhian.

His stride was steady if slow when he gained the hall. The servitors in their shadows turned to regard him, but none made any duty or reverence, and none came forward to greet him. They only watched as he left by the hall's single door.

The afternoon's sun was still shining brightly as Gawain crossed the tiny, dusty yard. All around him, he could see nothing but rolling meadowland that retreated rapidly into forest that climbed unbroken up the sides of the great hills looming on every side. He could see no cleared fields, no dwellings beyond the outbuildings of the hall. A woman toiled beneath a yoke of buckets filled with milk, her uncombed hair falling across her face. A man herded a pair of pigs out of the trees and back towards their pen.

It was then Gawain realized what he did not see.

There were no children. There was no boy helping with the pigs, no girl to carry another bucket of milk. No little ones running about the hall or the stables. No women with babies tied to their bosoms while they worked, no grandmothers hushing the infants balanced on their hips.

It was possible a hall, especially a small one such as this, might subsist on what could be gleaned from the forest. But how could there be no children? It was unnatural.

Gawain turned on his heel. He was in the centre of some great riddle, its threads and hints stretching out on all sides of him. Did one of them lead to Rhian? Which one would it be? And how could he hope to unravel it when the one he was bound to follow led to death?

One thing was clear. He needed to leave this place, and quickly. He needed to find Ailla and persuade her to come with him.

But even as he thought that, he heard the sound of distant hoofbeats. Belinus, riding a bright bay horse, cantered across the untamed fields at the head of an unruly cluster of men on shaggy ponies. He saw Gawain standing out in the yard, for he raised his hand and urged his horse forward at even greater speed.

The hall's door came open and its meagre population scurried out to greet their master's return. Ailla, of course, came with them. Gawain moved towards her, trying to catch her eye.

I know there is something very wrong here, he wanted to say. *You can trust me. I will help you.*

But she would not look at him. She rigidly focused all her attention on her returning lord.

As he drew closer, Gawain saw the results of the day's hunt. A stag's carcass had been tied to the rump of Belinus's horse. Its rack had been torn free already, and its shorn head flopped ludicrously as the horse cantered forward.

'Ha!' exclaimed Belinus as he reined his horse up. 'It is the young eagle! How are those wings now?'

Gawain bowed. 'Ready to fly, my host, and I thank you.'

'Excellent!' He swung himself onto the ground. 'Although I think my wife will be sorry to see it.' Businesslike, he undid the knot holding the carcass to the horse's back. The stag slid to the ground, lying contorted there, its glassy eyes staring up at Gawain, its red-stained throat pointed to the sky as if offering itself up to the knife.

'There you are, Lord Gawain.' Belinus planted his hands on his hips. 'I had thought to have it for your board tomorrow, if you are still with us. Be that as it may, this is what I gained today. What of you?'

Gawain could not help but glance at Ailla. She had not gone forward to greet her lord, but stood with her head bowed and her hands folded. She did not look up, or give any other sign.

Very deliberately, Gawain walked forward and kissed Belinus on the cheek. 'That is what I gained this day, my host.'

Belinus threw back his head and laughed. 'And such a treasure too! You will think my wife a miser if this is all you receive in my hall!'

'I think your wife a fine and noble lady and a courteous hostess.'

'I would be most disappointed to find you thought otherwise, my lord.' He lingered over the last word, drawing it out, bringing to it the slightest hint of discourtesy. But then that moment was gone. 'Come! Let us go in to board.' And he strode into his dark hall. His men lifted the stag's carcass and carried it in behind him, followed by the other dark and silent servants and his pale, modest wife.

Gawain had no choice but to follow.

It was nearly dark when Euberacon summoned Rhian again. The pain still burned in all of her crabbed and contorted joints, made worse by the weariness that turned her blood to water.

This fortress of dreams and nightmares did have a kitchen and a scullery, and Euberacon had left her there, presided over by the woman, Nessa, who had laid the breakfast, and by a cheerful stump of a man named Drew, who took one look at Rhian and declared that she should be left in the pen with the pigs.

'Well, if we don't take her, who will?' chided the woman as Rhian hunched before her. 'Hands is hands. Let's get to work then, girl.'

They could not possibly see the full horror of her. Euberacon's spells apparently sheltered their minds from the strangeness around them. They blinked very little this pair, and as she watched them, they sometimes moved around as if there was something in their way that they saw but she did not.

If it was true they did not see the fullness of her monstrosity, this fact won her no respite from the work heaped upon her. She drew water and scrubbed the floor, cleaned up after the dogs and plucked the birds the man brought back, after she had cleaned up from their slaughter.

She looked hard at them to see if they had been killed with an arrow. If there was a bow . . . her hands could still shoot, her eyes could still see.

No. Don't think it. Bury it, bury it deep. Don't let him hear. Don't think how you know when he's afraid. Not yet. Not yet.

But the birds' necks had been snapped. Drew kept snares. She plucked furiously at the birds, quills cutting her fingers and their blood mixing with her own.

Now she hunched in front of Euberacon. She stank and she was covered in the filth of her work over the hideous form forced on her. She tried to still her mind, tried not to think, tried most of all not to hate. She tried not to see that in his hand he held a copper collar and that it was attached to a copper chain.

'Come here,' he ordered as if she were a recalcitrant hound, and as if she were that hound, she cringed even as she obeyed.

She knew what he meant to do. There could be only one thing. She tried to hold silent, but as he snapped the collar around her neck she heard a whimper come from her throat, and her malformed hand went instantly to the collar.

'Oh, no.' The sorcerer smiled. 'No hand but mine removes that from you now.' There was a staple driven into the ground beside the fountain that she had not seen before. The other end of the chain had been attached there.

'Now,' he said. 'We wait.'

It was almost past bearing. She tried to stand, to keep that much of her dignity, but the exhaustion and pain were too much, and she was forced to sit at his feet before she fell at them. Slowly, the darkness around them deepened. There was nothing to do but wait. Even the work in the scullery had been better. At least there was a task, something to occupy her body if not her mind. Now, there was nothing to do but feel the weight and the wrongness of her own body, to try not to hate, to try not to weep. She was hungry. She was thirsty. The edge of the copper collar slowly chafed and cut into her skin.

Bury it deep. Bury it all.

Slowly the sky turned to black. Slowly, the quarter moon rose over the fortress walls. As it did, Rhian saw shadows moving in the courtyard. She blinked the tiny eyes she had been given, and looked again.

She saw her nightmare.

She saw the marble fortress and the gilt-roofed towers fade like morning's mist. She saw the kitchen woman trudging across the rutted yard of mud and clay with her sieve in her hands, blank, silver orbs where her eyes should be. She saw the little boy, who she now knew kept the stables, sweeping frantically at the dirt with his pitiful twiggy broom and heard again the rush of the sea, saw Drew who snared the birds and kept the gardens, struggling up the stairs in his chains. Impossibly, over it all, she saw Euberacon perched on the sagging turret, and saw the demons flocking to him, waiting for him to fall.

And yet he still sat beside her, calm and regal in his chair.

But not so calm as he had been in the day, for now his hands scrabbled nervously at the chair arm.

Above, his image was afraid. Below, his body was afraid. He had said he did not keep his life within him anymore. Was that his soul up there? Was that what the demons were waiting to take?

'What do you see?'

You do not see this? You can't *see this?* 'Nothing, Master,' she tried.

The blow he dealt her was casual, but it knocked her flat to the ground with its strength, making her ears ring and making her ragged teeth grate the inside of her cheek. 'You lie.' He did not even give her time to pick herself up. 'What do you see?'

Drew fell, tumbling down the stairs, breaking his body and his will. Nessa wept as her water ran onto the ground.

The demons circled around Euberacon, gloating, goading, tempting, and he swayed and he was afraid. Two more demons sat on the rim of the fountain and laughed, jeering at the spectres, and at their kin, enjoying all the games.

'Nightmares,' whispered Rhian. Her own chain rattled as her spindly arms pushed her back into a sitting position.

'Tell me.'

Rhian shook. *He cannot see. Not at night. Not everything you can see.* 'I see you,' she said. She tasted her own blood as she spoke. Her voice shook, her hands shook, her whole crooked body was wracked with tremors. 'I see you perched on a ruinous tower with demons all around you. They are waiting for you to fall. I see two more demons sitting on the fountain, watching all that occurs.'

'Is that all?'

'Yes, Master.' *He'll hear. He'll hear the lie. He'll hear my heart pounding. He'll do something worse. He'll find something worse than this.* The cook was heading back to her kitchen now, weeping copious tears. The man lay still and broken in his chains. The little boy swept on, tears rolling down his sunken cheeks.

Euberacon nodded judiciously. His fingers still scratched nervously at the chair arms. He still knew his fears. *Good. Good.* 'Kerra was right. You have sharp eyes.' He stood. 'You may keep watch here tonight. Perhaps tomorrow you may return to your room. We will see how pleasant you are when the sun rises.'

He left her there, collapsed in the mud at the foot of his chair, and it seemed to her that he vanished. His spectre, or perhaps it was his soul, remained where it was, high on its precarious perch, surrounded by its demons. Too far, too long. Was it weary? Would it fall?

'Fall, yes fall, and take us all down with it!' cried one of the two who sat on the fountain. 'Then my pretty lady would weep for sure!' It leapt into the air, dancing before Rhian's eyes. She knew better now than to swing at it. It would only fly away.

'Oh, poor spiritless thing!' squeaked its companion. 'It's all crunched up and has no fight left.'

'Shall we bite it, shall we pinch it?' asked the first, darting in so close that Rhian shrank back involuntarily. 'Watch it dance? It dances for the master now.' The creature's fangs gleamed in the moonlight as it grinned with hideous merriment at her.

Its companion on the well's cracked bowl scratched itself. 'While it wears the chain, it dances like a bear. But does the master see the bear for the skin? Does he see the virtue for the sin?'

'Let's see! Let's see! He maybe has a dainty for us. Maybe doves, maybe better while he works!'

That seemed to please the other and they both took off into the air and were soon lost to Rhian's nightmare sight and she was alone.

Now was her chance, if she had any, to lay a plan, to find a weakness.

But what chance could she have? The ruined courtyard with its overlay of dreams stretched before her. Euberacon stood on the parapet balancing himself before the swarm of demons that watched him greedily, furiously, impatiently, waiting for his slip, for his last mistake. Turn, and there was the stableboy sweeping furiously to the sound of the sea. Turn, and there was Drew, broken on the ground. Turn, and there was the cook trudging back again, with her empty eyes and her weight of weariness and her sieve.

Euberacon stood over all, lord and master of these horrors even caught in his own fears. All he had to do was look down and he would see her and what she did. All he would have to do was turn his head from the demons.

Which was all the protection she had. If he glanced away, if that shape of him aloft there looked away, what would they do? She had no way to know if it truly was vigilance that kept him aloft on that perilous height.

But he cannot see, she reminded herself. His omniscience was illusion. There lay her chance. She must find her way to use it. If not, day would come again soon. It would come and it would go and she would be lost in whatever slavery he commanded of her, and every night would be this horror until . . . until what?

Until Gawain came for her? But what if Gawain did not come? What if he did not come soon enough?

Why should I even try? asked a treacherous voice in the back of her mind. *Euberacon commands demons and I command a few peasants' tales. I am lost and gone. God has already condemned me.*

No. No. I mustn't. Despair is also a sin. Think. This is the stuff *of those peasant tales. What would happen in one of them?*

Absurd. Ridiculous.

No, it was the reality that moved around her. It was in Drew's chains as he toiled up the stairs. In the sieve in the cook's hand as she waded through the mud yet again.

An idea came to Rhian then and nearly hysterical hope made her move, shuffling forward to the very limit of her copper chain as Nessa slogged towards the well. The woman did not look up, did not hesitate in her endless task.

Stretching her arm to its fullest length, Rhian lifted the sieve from Nessa's loose fingers. The woman opened and closed her suddenly empty hand. With a whimper of despair, she plunged her arms into the broken basin, seeking the sieve she must have dropped. Rhian fell to her knees. With cold and trembling hands, she dug into the mud and clay at the base of the filthy, shattered fountain. She packed the clay and soaked grass into the sieve, blocking the mesh, stopping the holes. Praying with all the strength her weary and battered soul had left, she dipped the sieve into the water, and filled it to the brim. Then, she settled it into Nessa's hands.

The woman's blank eyes stared down, her face gone slack with dumb surprise. She dabbled her fingers in the cloudy water, disbelieving.

Hurry, hurry, begged Rhian silently. *Whatever you must do, do it quickly. This trick will not work for long.*

Nessa gave a shriek of delight and scurried back towards where the kitchen would have been. Rhian heard the splash of water, presumably into some vessel, and then Nessa came running out, staggered in the mud, and froze. She blinked.

She had eyes.

The scales had fallen from them, perhaps into the water she had carried, and now she could see. Nessa took several steps forward, her mouth agape. Rhian straightened up, so she was among the things that were seen.

Nessa screamed, a high, insane sound. Fear of discovery lent Rhian strength and speed. She slapped her hand over the terrified servant's mouth and dragged her close. Nessa's eyes bulged in their sockets and for a moment Rhian thought she might faint. She could feel her panting breath against her palm.

'By that God who loves us both, Nessa, hold your tongue.

I know how I look, but if you scream you'll bring worse down on us.'

Slowly, Nessa nodded, although none of the terror left her eyes. Cautiously, Rhian removed her hand.

'What . . . what . . .' stammered Nessa.

'A prisoner, even as you.' She did not give her time for questions. 'What do you know of your state?'

She swallowed. She was a solid, plain woman, obviously of a practical turn of mind. Devils and true monsters did not swear by holy things.

'My master sold me to . . . I don't know. He had black eyes. That is the last I know.'

As quickly as she could, Rhian explained to whom she had been sold into service. The woman clutched at her apron as if it were her telling beads to keep back the devils that must surely be about to jump forth. But she did not scream, nor did she deny what she heard.

'What of my man?' Nessa croaked. 'How long have I been here?'

'Drew will be with you in the morning, but he won't know anything's wrong. He's been enchanted, just as you and I have been.' *Yes, pay attention. This is not the truth of me any more than that struggling blind creature is the truth of you.* 'If you listen, and if you'll help, I think I can set us all free.'

Nessa wadded her apron up in both hands, but still, she made her decision. 'What must I do?'

Nessa's question ringed around Rhian's mind and she frantically tried to think. There must be a way. Could Nessa steal the key to Euberacon's tower? Impossible. But where else could his weaknesses be found? How else could they be discovered? Rhian glanced furtively at the tower, as if she feared to see Euberacon scowling down at her. But he was as before, balancing on his strange and precarious perch, surrounded by all the demons.

Rhian's breath froze in her lungs. Not all the demons. Where were the other pair? The two that were invisible during the day, that came and went from his study and seemed to know all that occurred within these walls?

And what if they could be made to tell what they knew?

She had it. The oldest stories and her own desperation showed her what to do. There were ways to trap demons, ways to make them speak, and they were told round the fire on a winter's night. Now was the time to find out if those tales told the truth.

Rhian gripped Nessa's hand tightly.

'At day's end, you must take your largest covered kettle and put in it some of the hops, barley and malt for the brewing, a fresh egg, a length of rope and all the things needful to make a fire. Repeat that.' The woman actually looked affronted. She was used to receiving complex instructions, Rhian reminded herself, but nonetheless, she made her say it. When Nessa had successfully repeated that much, Rhian kept going. 'Make sure everything is left by the fountain before you go to bed. If any sees you, you'll have to make some excuse. It must be there tonight, by the fountain, nowhere else. If you fail . . . we are all here lost.'

'But . . . but what if I am questioned?' Nessa stammered, fear beginning to return. 'What if I am discovered?'

'You must not be. You must go about your day. Serve as you would serve any other master. Do not question anything you see, that is the most important thing. Can you do this? Your freedom and your man's depend on it. There's a boy here too. They have no one but us to save them.'

That seemed to steady her. 'I . . . I can try . . . mmm . . . mmm . . .' She was trying to say 'mistress', but the word would not come.

'Then try, and pray for your soul that your trying is good enough. Go now, before anyone comes.'

Nessa nodded and scurried away, relief plain on her face. Again, Rhian wondered what she saw around her. It didn't matter. As long as she did what Rhian asked. As long as her guesses proved correct.

Too tired to stand anymore, Rhian, greatly daring, curled up in the chair Euberacon had left behind. Perhaps she could find her way to sleep from here, and dream of Gawain, of her freedom. She looked up to the turret so she might again see Euberacon afraid and use that as fuel for the small sparks of hope inside her.

But Euberacon was not there. The demons bobbed and swooped like so many confused and angry bees. The turret was deserted of its spectre, and not one of the monsters could tell what had happened.

Where had he gone? What had he done? Rhian gaped.

He had saved himself, pulled his soul down from the precipice and regained that part of himself lost to nightmare, and she had helped.

How much more would he be able to do come the daylight?

She gripped the chair arms and struggled not to cry out as the fear swelled and bubbled and coiled within her. He could do so much, even when he was in danger, what would he do now? What would he force her to do?

Hold on, hold on. God give me strength. Help me. He doesn't know what I have done. He can't know. If he knew he would be down here now. He still can't see. He knows only what I told him, nothing else. He can't see for himself.

Yet.

But Euberacon did not appear, not to her, not to the demons, for all they searched, frantic in their outrage. Nessa stayed away. Drew lay broken in the mud, and the little stableboy still swept. There was nothing to do, nowhere to go. Her copper chain held her fast. All she could do was pray, for strength and for calm, and that the morning would come again.

Rhian knelt and the mud and clay were cold beneath her aching knees. She bowed her head and clasped her twisted hands.

Help me, she prayed, for it was the only prayer she had left in the whole of her tattered soul. *Help me.*

TWENTY

Gawain woke in his bed. Darkness surrounded him. His dreams had been confused. There had been a chase, and blood in the greenwood. He rubbed his eyes. He did not even remember going to sleep. He had meant to stay awake and walk the hall after dark to see what he could find. He had sat at board, there had been strong wine, and . . . he was here.

What had woken him?

Then, he heard it. A soft scratching at his door. He stood, grabbing up his tunic to cover his nakedness, and then he opened the door.

Ailla stood in the dark corridor, a rush light burning low in her hand.

'My lady . . .?'

But even as he spoke, she pushed her way past him. 'Close the door. They mustn't see the light.'

Gawain did as he was told. She used her light to kindle the candle at his bedside, then she placed the rush in a wall sconce. Gawain watched her swift and graceful movements, trying to clear the last of the heavy sleep from his head.

Ailla faced him. 'You know,' was all she said.

Precious little, though. But what he said was, 'I know this is no natural place, lady.'

She nodded. 'There is much I cannot tell you, but I can answer some of your questions if you ask them now.'

Gawain frowned at the closed door. 'But it is night. If your husband . . .'

'It must be now,' Ailla cut him off. 'He cannot question you about what you've received. It falls outside the bargain. Quickly, ask what you will.' She perched on the chair, her gaze darting anxiously between his befuddled countenance and the door.

With an effort, Gawain pulled his wits together. 'Where is the Green Temple?'

Ailla nodded, as if approving of his choice of beginnings. 'In the centre of the great northwood.'

'What is it?'

'A green mound without tree or brush growing on it and a clear stream running down its face.'

A strange temple for a strange apparition. Gawain found his mind clearing. What had taken him so deeply into sleep? Was he ill again? Or was there something else happening to him? 'Who is Belinus?'

Ailla dropped her gaze to her hands clasped tightly together on her lap. 'That I may not say.'

Gawain leaned forward, and put his hand beneath her chin, lifting her face towards him so that she had to look into his eyes. He wanted her to see his honest desire to help her, he wanted her to see she could trust him. 'Who are you?'

But she only pulled herself away from him. 'A prisoner, even as you are.'

'How can I free you?'

'You cannot.'

I do not accept this. 'There must be some way . . .'

'There is none,' she announced, her voice flat and hopeless. 'Listen to me, my Lord Gawain. I know what game you have committed yourself to play. Do you want to live to find your lady love?'

'With all my heart.' *But do not say I must leave you here to do so. There must be a way to bring you out of this place, to thank you for all you have done.*

She regarded him for a moment. Did she doubt him? No, she was saddened. She had no one she believed could save her, and yet her generous spirit drove her to try to save another in a similar plight. What a miracle to find such a one in such a place. 'I can help you, but it must be done in secret. Tomorrow, your horse will be fit for travel. Come to breakfast with my husband. Do not be certain when he asks if you will leave. Say you are going to exercise your horse and ride out southward. Do not take your arms, or they will know something is wrong. You will find a track, and near it there is an oak that was split by lightning. I will meet you beside that oak.'

'I cannot ask you to risk yourself for me.'

'You do not ask. I do it gladly. If I cannot be free, then let me know that you are.' She stood, answering some inner warning. 'I must go.'

She took her light and left him then, closing the door softly behind her. Gawain stared for a moment and then ran both hands through his hair, trying to think.

What he wanted to do was grab up sword and spear and fight his way out of here, dragging Lady Ailla with him, as the Pictish men were said to do with brides they favoured. He did not want to wait anymore. She needed him, she was risking everything for him, and he could do nothing. Imprisoned, she said. How? By whom? There must be some way to find out, some way to set her free.

And what of Rhian? asked a quiet voice in the back of his mind.

Rhian. God in heaven, he had forgotten her for a moment. The realization appalled Gawain. How could he have ceased to think of her, even for a heartbeat? How could he find another woman fair or worthy when his betrothed had vanished, carried away by vile magics to what fate, God alone knew. How could his heart be so wayward.

Or so uncertain.

No. There was no doubt in him. No true doubt. He loved Rhian, heart and soul. He would save her. He would marry her. Gawain leapt to his feet and began to pace, cursing his weakness and his confusion. It was this place. The wrongness of it was infecting his blood. He had to get away from here. The way had been opened for him, he had only to take it. When he found Rhian again, his eyes would clear and there would be no doubt left.

There was some glamour on this place. It was deep and it was subtle. He could not trust anything.

Not even Ailla?

He dismissed the thought. Even if she was not all that she seemed, she was risking all to help him. Should he open the door? Should he take his weapons and both of them out of here by force if he must?

No. She had some way to help him survive what must come at the Green Temple. To seek escape now would be to lose that chance. He must stay. He must endure the remainder of this night, and then he and Ailla both would be free. He would see to that. Then he would find Rhian. He would find Rhian if he had to split the world in two to do it. She was his love, she and no other.

Knowing sleep to be impossible, Gawain took up his sword and began a series of practice exercises, parries, cuts, thrusts, counters. The chamber was small, but there was just room enough to swing the blade, to dance with his shadow in dangerous play, cutting at the air as if he could slice through the tangle of mystery that held him, as if he could cut the yearning to see Lady Ailla smile once more for him from his mind.

In the morning, Gawain washed his face and hands. Regretfully leaving his arms behind, he went into the hall and for the first time since coming to this grim place, he joined his host in breaking his fast. Belinus consumed massive quantities of the simple porridge his wife served, washed down with more ale than Gawain would have thought it possible for one man to consume. Ailla did not look at him once during the meal.

'Well, my Lord Eagle!' Belinus slammed his noggin down on the table, making all the bowls and spoons rattle. 'Do you fly away from us today?'

'I mean to take my horse out for exercise,' Gawain replied, hoping he did not sound too much as though he were being careful with his words. 'If all be well then yes, I mean to continue on my journey.'

'Well, some of us will be sorry to see you go.' Belinus winked broadly at Ailla. 'But if you are still not able to tear yourself away from our merry hall, you are welcome to stay and see what this day brings you.'

'I thank you for your most generous hospitality, my host.'

'Rather you should thank my wife!' Ailla was passing Belinus's chair with an empty bowl and he grabbed her around her waist, planting a great kiss on her cheek before releasing her. Gawain had to force himself to remain seated. She was his wife, all rights were his, but . . . a serving girl would not be handled this way in Camelot, never mind a lady. Arthur would have never permitted it. 'It is a treat to have her so blushing and lively! I would have you stay all the summer to quicken her blood with your tales of Camelot. But tell me,' his voice dropped into tones of conspiracy, 'were you able to winkle the secret of the Green Temple while I left you two alone these past days?'

I will get you out of this place, he swore silently as Ailla returned to the fire to fill the bowl once again. Gawain chose his words carefully. 'My hostess has told me nothing of the Green Temple on any day.'

'Bad luck, bad luck!' Despite his words, Belinus looked quite pleased. He pushed aside the bowl of porridge Ailla placed in front of him. 'To horse then, my Lord Eagle. Let us fly!'

Gawain accompanied Belinus out into the yard. His men were already mounted on their uncombed ponies and his great roan stallion was saddled and waiting for him. He swung himself up easily into the saddle, raised his hand to Gawain, who returned the salute, wheeled the horse about and cantered away into the woods.

Gawain waited where he was until the forest had closed completely about his host and the sound of hoofbeats was lost beneath the sound of birdsong. Then, he ambled towards the stable as if reaching his horse was less important than enjoying a morning where the sun shone brightly for a change and the mist was already burning away.

There was no immediate sign of the stablemaster, and Gawain did not seek him out. He examined Pol's ankle and found that the swelling was gone, and there was no pain when he probed the spot, nor did Pol seem to be favouring it at all. He found Pol's harness hanging on wooden pegs outside the box. Gringolet gave an anxious snort as his master began to saddle the other horse.

'Do not worry, my friend,' he said. 'I will be back for you, without fail.'

You and my lady. Neither of you are staying here.

The sky was clear and taking his bearings was a simple matter. He had crossed only a handful of acres before the trees began to close about him, and he found the track Ailla had told him would be there. It was rutted and faded, but still easy enough to follow, and soon he came to a towering oak, the side of which had been burnt black and flayed open almost to its heart. It would not live much longer.

As he pulled back on Pol's reins, Ailla stepped out from behind the tree. She had come on foot and she must have run for she was flushed and breathing hard. Her eyes were brighter than he had seen them before.

She could come this far, why could she not go farther?

'How is it you are able to walk free?' Gawain could not keep himself from asking the question.

Ailla twisted her hands together. Gawain wanted to reach down and separate her hands. He feared one day she might hurt those delicate fingers with that rough gesture. 'There are ways, my lord, but they will not last long.'

'Do you work magics?' Wariness rose in him, for all he at once told himself that this lady had done nothing but aid him since he had come to this strange place.

'My husband is not the only one who follows the old ways, my lord. Please, we must hurry.' She held up her hands. 'We have some way yet to go.'

Gawain reached down and pulled her up before him. She found her seat easily. It was obviously not only her lord who liked to ride.

'You must tell me where, my lady,' he said, reaching around her to take up Pol's reins.

'Follow the track,' she said. 'But I must ask you to be silent. What we need to find will take some looking.'

'As my lady says.' Gawain put his knees to Pol's side. The horse, thoroughly tired of being cooped up for days on end, stepped up quickly and lightly.

Gawain soon found himself wishing he was at leisure to enjoy this ride. Ailla's body was warm against his chest. Despite her silence, she seemed at ease, as if savouring the measure of freedom she gained in the greenwood. *What holds you in that hall?* he found himself wondering yet again. *Why will you not speak to me of it?*

Could Belinus be a sorcerer? There was magic here. Was her fate what Rhian's would have been had he not found her?

What Rhian's fate is. He reminded himself sternly. *You have not saved her yet.*

The heat of the day was growing, even beneath the forest canopy. Two days of inactivity and an interrupted night followed by the steady rhythm of a walking horse lulled Gawain into a kind of waking sleep. For a moment he thought it was Rhian he held, and he longed to take her into his arms, to remind her of his love the best way he knew how . . .

'There, my lord.'

Gawain's head jerked back, and the world snapped into place around him, and Rhian was gone, and Ailla was in his arms, pointing off to the left. Gawain reined Pol to a stop, and tried to see what Ailla meant to show him.

At first he saw only the trees and the rough ground between them. Then, gradually, he realized what he had at first taken for a small hillock was in fact a hovel of bark and mud, and a human figure squatted on the ground before its dark doorway.

Ailla slipped down from Pol's back. 'The one we are going to see has great power in this place, Gawain, although it will not appear so. Treat her as you would the High Queen in her hall.'

Gawain nodded, tethered Pol to a tree and followed Ailla into the trees. As they approached the hovel, he saw that the human figure was an ancient woman. Her hair was lank and yellow-white. Her dress was so filthy and tattered it was impossible to tell what colour it had once been. It was only the constant breeze that kept the smell of the place tolerable. Her eyes though, her eyes were still a young woman's, sharp and watchful, and almost entirely black.

Ailla knelt before the hunched and haggish figure. Gawain, mindful of what she had told him, did the same.

'Mother,' said Ailla humbly. 'I am come to beg a favour of you.'

The crone shifted her weight left, then right. She peered closely at Gawain, and Gawain could feel the power of that gaze.

'I know what you're here for,' she said. Her voice was harsh as a crow's, as if she were unused to speaking. 'It can be bestowed only once, daughter. I've told you that before.'

'I know, mother.'

The dim gaze seemed to grate across Gawain's skin, raising goosebumps. Then, she turned her head and spat. 'Is he worthy of such a gift?'

Gawain opened his mouth, but Ailla spoke first. 'For my sake, mother. I beg you.'

'Well. Well. So it shall be then.'

The crone shuffled into her hovel. Ailla wrung her hands in her nervousness. Gawain had to resist the urge to put his arm about her, to comfort her, to try to find some way to make her believe that he would not abandon her.

When the crone returned, she carried a roll of leather in her arms tied with a grease-stained thong. The bundle was black and cracked with age and stank from damp and mould. Slowly, she set it on the ground and slowly she knelt in front of it. Her sharp fingers worked the knot and slowly unrolled the leather wrapping.

Inside lay a sash the colour of emeralds. It was a hand-span wide and looked to be half an ell long, the cloth of it as finely woven as Egyptian linen. The old woman picked it up lovingly in her crooked hands.

'The knight who wears this shall not fall before any blow, no matter who deals it out,' she said, caressing the fine fabric. Then she said sharply to Ailla, 'You know the price of what you do, daughter?'

Gawain could not remain silent. 'If there is a price for this, mother, let me pay it.'

The crone only shook her head and spat again. 'I do this for my daughter's sake. What she does after that is up to her.' She handed Ailla the sash, and Ailla stood only to curt-sey deeply. Gawain stood beside her and bowed with all solemnity.

'Take her from here, Sir Knight,' said the crone. 'And do not forget what she has done.'

'Never in life, mother.'

She nodded, seemingly satisfied. 'Get you gone then.'

Thus dismissed, Gawain and Ailla walked side by side back to where Pol waited nosing about the undergrowth. She did not seem inclined to talk, even when she hung the sash about her shoulders and allowed herself to be helped up onto the horse's back.

The day was cooler now, and the forest far dimmer. Clouds were gathering. It would rain again soon. Ailla held her peace, but Gawain felt her back and shoulders stiffen and draw tighter the closer they came to her home.

When at last they reached the forest's edge, she touched Gawain's hand. 'Let me down, my lord,' she said in a voice made husky by tears long withheld.

Gawain reined Pol to a halt. 'Lady . . .'

But she shook her head, her jaw clenched tightly closed and dismounted.

Gawain followed suit. She was staring at the distant hall, and for the first time, he saw hatred plain on her face.

He could stand it no longer. He touched her arm. 'Lady, you are free of the place now. Let me take you to Camelot.'

'No. It cannot be.' She faced him and took the sash from her shoulders. Swiftly, she wrapped it around his waist and tied it tight. As she completed the knot, Gawain felt a new wellbeing take him, as if he were rested and refreshed and all the world around were sun and summer. 'There.' Ailla stood back. 'Now, no matter where you go, no blow can harm you. You will be safe.' She turned swiftly away as if she could no longer bear the sight of him. 'Go back to the hall. You must retrieve your arms, and ride at once to the Green Temple.'

But Gawain did not move. 'I will not leave you in that place.'

Again she shook her head, and again he heard the tears unshed in her voice. 'You cannot save me.'

This time though, Gawain was not content to leave the matter at her word. 'Why not? Why is it so impossible? You know the answer, my lady, I am sure of it. Speak to me.'

'If I could . . .'

He put his hands on her shoulders. 'You can. I will believe whatever you say, however fantastic.' She leaned close, her mouth open, longing to speak, longing to tell him all her secrets, to let him save her as she had saved him.

He was kissing her. He did not know who had moved towards whom, but she was in his arms and his mouth pressed against hers and she was warm and she was soft and she pressed herself against him with a kind of frantic need, as if he were all in the world that was good and safe. She would give herself to him, here, at once, if he would accept the gift, and he wanted her, oh, how he wanted her.

As he had wanted Pacis. As he had wanted Rhian.

No.

Gawain raised his head. Ailla looked up at him, confused.

Not as he had wanted Rhian. With Rhian it had been heart's tenderness, not wild desperation. With Rhian it was a beginning, a promise, a gift yes, but not like this, not given in fear or despair. He had made that promise with her. To do this now would be to break it open, to break his word, and Rhian's heart.

'My lord?' asked Ailla timidly, laying her hand over his heart.

His heart. It drummed hard against his ribs for wanting her, she was so warm, so near, so desirous of his touch and the strength and comfort that were his to give.

Gawain opened his arms, and stepped back.

'I'm sorry, my lady. I cannot give you what you ask.'

She stared at him, dumbfounded. A tear trickled from her eye and she turned quickly away. 'My fault.' She buried her face in her hands. 'I forgot myself. I just wanted so much. . .'

'No, lady, it is not your fault.' But he did not move. To draw close to her again would be to smell the intoxicating scent of her, to feel her warmth again. He must not or he would be lost. 'It is mine. I have promised my love to another. To take yours now would be to do so falsely.'

Hesitantly, she turned and took a step towards him. God Almighty, she was beautiful. 'And if I ask nothing but this once?' she asked. 'This once so that I might at least dream I have known love?'

Let me dream the dream that is you . . .

'No, my lady, and I am sorry.'

Ailla retreated, her eyes wide with shock. But shock melted quickly into anger, and then, to Gawain's horror, contempt.

'Love?' She sneered. 'You do not love, Gawain. You need. You want a woman to save, that's all. As soon as your little

Rhian was safe and sound, you would tire of her.'

'R . . .' Gawain stammered. 'I did not tell you her name.'

She tossed her head back contemptuously. 'What does a name mean to you? One will do as well as another. It will never be enough because you can't ever save the one you've already lost.'

This was impossible. This could not be happening. Ailla had loved . . . he had loved . . . it was Belinus who was . . .

'No,' he breathed, with that one word trying to deny so much of the truth that fell like stones into his heart.

The woman before him, the witch whatever her name might be, only smiled. 'I meant to make this pleasant for us both, Gawain. It still can be.' She slipped up to him so that he must breathe in her heady perfume and remember how it had felt to have his arms around her. Her mouth was wide and red, and her eyes wide and knowing. 'Come now, kiss me. Your doom is already sealed, but if you please me in this, perhaps I can make it easier for you.'

It would be so easy to do as she wanted, what he wanted. So easy to fall into that dream.

'No!'

The witch shrugged. 'Very well then. That is your choice.' She retreated three steps and looking steadily at him she opened her mouth and screamed.

The terrified sound startled him and Gawain fell backward a step. Still screaming as if murder had been done Ailla ran towards the hall, clutching at her bosom.

The realization of what she meant to do hit Gawain in the pit of his stomach. Before he could think, he ran after her, tearing across the meadows all the way to the muddy yard of Belinus's hall. But for all his desperate speed, he could not catch her, and she collapsed before the hall door, sobbing as if her heart would break. The silent servitors gathered around her as if she were some curious breed of animal.

Gawain brushed past them, and they did not move. 'Stop this!' he cried, seizing her by the shoulders.

She only screamed again. Tears streamed down her face and to look at her was to see only the hysteria that came with utter terror. 'Let me go! Let me go!'

Then, Gawain heard the drumming of hoofbeats. He did let go, and he stood and backed away. He cursed himself for a fool; it was all far, far too late.

Belinus and his men rode swiftly across the meadows, lashing the horses to gain speed. Ailla saw them coming and screamed once more, leaping to her feet and dashing to meet them. Belinus threw himself from his horse and ran to his wife. She threw herself into his arms.

Gawain felt all the blood drain from his heart.

'My husband! My husband!' she sobbed.

'What is it my wife?' Belinus drew her close, but he was looking at Gawain. He ought to run, before they surrounded him. He had no proof, no witness, no friend beside him. His name meant nothing here.

'I have been . . . he tried . . .' Ailla buried her face against her husband's shoulder. 'I swore I would die first . . . he laughed and said force would make it all the sweeter . . .'

With a gentleness Gawain would not have believed him capable of, Belinus set Ailla aside. He stalked forward, moving like a mountain. Over his shoulder, Gawain saw Ailla's expression of pure triumph even as the tears dried on her cheeks.

Then Belinus stood directly before him, blocking out all other sights. He was breathing hard, as if he had just carried some great weight a long distance and his huge hands opened and closed, looking for something to seize upon in his rage.

'I have sheltered you, my Lord Gawain.' Belinus spat his name. 'I have treated you fairly and with honour, and this is how you repay me, guest to host?'

I'm going to die, thought Gawain, surprised at how calm he felt now that the moment had come. *Very well then.*

Slowly, his back straight and proud, Gawain knelt before Belinus. 'My Lord Host, I swear to you, by my life, my arm and God Most High that I have taken nothing from this woman but what she did freely give me, and here I give you all she gave me this day.' Gawain pulled the green sash from around his waist and held it up to Belinus.

Belinus bent down and stared into Gawain's eyes. Gawain realized he could not have looked away if he had wished to. Then, he realized his host's eyes were not brown as he had thought before, but green, as forest pools, as the shadows in the wildwood . . .

As the Green Knight's.

'Well,' Belinus said softly as he straightened up. 'It would seem, woman, that you have failed.'

Behind him, Ailla stiffened. Slowly, as comprehension came over her, her triumph peeled back and fell away, leaving only fear.

'No,' she whispered. 'No! He did as I said. He lies . . .'

Belinus's green eyes glittered. 'Be quiet.'

Ailla turned to run. She lifted her foot, she set it down, and tried to raise the other, and failed. She struggled for a moment, and then she screamed, and this time the terror was real.

Roots were spreading from beneath her skirt. They burrowed eagerly as hungry worms into the earth. Her fingers lengthened and grew crooked and brown. Leaves sprouted where joints and nails had been. A skin of brown bark crept up her dress to her waist, to her torso, to her throat. She threw back her head to scream once more, but the brown bark sealed over her mouth and then her eyes. Then, there was nothing left of the woman. There was only a thorn-apple tree in full flower standing where she had been.

Gawain turned to stare at Belinus, but he saw his host for only the blink of an eye. It was not that Belinus changed, it was as if Gawain had not looked closely enough before to see the Green Knight standing before him, his fist on his hip and his great axe in his hand.

The hall and its folk was gone, the fields were gone. The wildwood crowded on every side. Behind him, instead of a gate, was a mossy mound.

The tree still stood, the tree that had been a woman.

'Well done, Gawain, Lot's son,' said the Green Knight in a voice as soft as the whisper of wind through leaves.

Gawain's tongue froze to the roof of his mouth. What reply could he make? It was too much to comprehend. He could not take his eyes from the tree. Three petals fell like tears onto the forest loam.

'Lord, the woman . . .'

'Made her bargain as you made yours.' The Green Knight still spoke softly, but now there was danger beneath his words. 'Do not ask after her again.'

Shaking, Gawain turned away to face the giant. He should have felt some measure of relief, he supposed. She had clearly meant to trap him, to take his life because he would not give her what she wanted . . . but he only felt sorrow.

'There is still a matter to be settled between you and I, my Lord Gawain.'

Gawain swallowed. He had not forgotten. It was not possible to forget, even as his mind reeled from all that had occurred.

God forgive me, he prayed. *Rhian, forgive me*, he begged with all the love in his heart.

He lowered himself onto his knees, and bowed his head, letting the gesture indicate his readiness. The blade, at least, was very sharp, and he had no doubt the headsman had a steady hand.

He heard the whistle as the axe swung up. *Our Father who art in heaven . . . oh Rhian . . .*

The air over his head rushed as the blade came down. *Hallowed be thy name. Give us this . . .*

Something hot stung the skin on the back of his neck, like a fly's bite, and there was silence, and stillness.

Gawain's ears rang. His heart pounded against his ribcage as if seeking release. His hands began to shake, and the tremors ran up his arms and down again into his torso.

'Such is my blow, Lord Gawain,' boomed the Green Knight. 'Can you stand?'

For one delirious moment, Gawain was not certain that he could, but he stiffened his sinews and willed his limbs to movement, and they obeyed. Gawain rose smoothly and stood on his own legs before the Green Knight.

The Green Knight laughed the booming laugh that Gawain had heard from Lord Belinus, and failed to recognize. 'Very good, man! Very good indeed!'

A little warm wetness trickled down the back of his neck. Gawain put a hand to it automatically and when he brought it back down, a red streak of blood smeared his fingertips.

'That cut is for the kiss.' The Green Knight grinned. 'It will heal in time, but perhaps the scar will give you something to think on, eh my lord?'

Gawain did not understand what was happening. He wished fervently that Merlin were here. This much was clear, this apparition was a power, one of the old ones whispered about around the fire at night, perhaps, and reviled by the priests as devils and demons of the forest. This was no devil. Gawain knew that much.

And how much might such a power know? But how little were such creatures disposed to speak?

He also knew that where there was no other answer courtesy was all, and he went down onto one knee.

'My lord,' he began, then stopped. 'I know no proper way to address you.'

'Belinus will do.'

'My Lord Belinus, I seek a woman who was taken from Camelot . . .'

'Ah! Rhian of the Morelands.' Belinus planted the butt of his axe against the ground and leaned over it. 'You want to know where the eastern sorcerer has hidden her, do you?'

'Yes, my lord.'

'And for that knowing, what would you give?'

'Anything.' Gawain knew a moment's regret at that word, but he made no attempt to retract it.

'Anything? You say that before *me*, Gawain? Do you mean it?'

Gawain felt suddenly profoundly weary. He remembered the night in Pen Marhas when he had said to Rhian that she was too tired to say anything but what she truly meant. That was how tired he felt now. Let the giant do to him what he would. He had no more heart for this fight. 'My Lord Belinus, I don't know, and I am not certain that I care. I am tired. I am tired of magics and riddles and bold gestures and wondering whether or not I am worthy of my place and my love.' He raised his head and met the old god's gaze. 'I know that Rhian has been taken against her will, and that I want to find her and see that she is set free. After that . . . after that it shall be as it please God. I will make no more bargains and play no more games. Let her come to me fully of her own will or not at all. It is the only way we will either one of us be free to live the lives we were meant to have.'

The Green Knight looked long at him. Gawain felt all fear, all hope, all thought drain from him like water from a sieve. There was nothing left to him but those last words. To his relief and amazement, he knew in his soul that for this once what he had done was right, and it was enough.

The Green Knight nodded his great head, and Gawain was himself again, heart, mind and soul.

'Very well, my Lord Gawain. Leave here without looking back. Walk away from my mound, turning neither left nor right. Take with you what you find, and if you can find your lady on the way, you will have her.'

And he was gone. Only the mound and the spring, the forest and the thorn-apple tree remained. Gawain, long past wonder and surprise, began to walk.

TWENTY-ONE

'You may return to your cell, Ragnelle.'

Rhian lifted her head. She had slipped onto the courtyard floor at some point during the long night. Cold and damp cramped her already distorted joints, and she could not make herself stand. Euberacon loomed over her, tall and imperious, blocking out the sun.

Biting her lip against the pain, even though she tasted her own blood, Rhian unbent her legs as far as she could.

Return to your cell, her fogged mind repeated the order. No. That would leave Nessa alone, and the woman might not be able to last out the day. And if she could not, it was over. Everything depended on Nessa's strength. She could not be shut in.

'But Master,' her tongue was as thick and heavy as her thoughts. 'Should I not . . .'

'You should do exactly as I say.' To her shame, the anger in his voice made her wince. 'Question me again and I may forget I meant to feed you when I return.'

Hunger raged in Rhian's stomach. She had drunk a little from the fountain last night, but that had stilled it for a few hours only.

Then something else he had said repeated itself in her confused thoughts.

Return?

He was leaving. Leaving!

'Do not look so pleased,' he snorted. 'Shall I tell you where I go?' He bent close. 'The Saxons are riding up from the south to join their brethren in the west. The timing is most propitious too, for the best of Arthur's knights are haring off across the countryside looking for a lost lamb.' He straightened, grinning broadly. 'My little witch is busy at present, so I needs must make sure their road is clear.' He grinned and then spoke to the air above her head. 'Take her.'

The taloned hands seized her at once and dragged her across the tiles, then across the stones and down the stairs. Rhian barely felt the bite of them.

Euberacon was leaving. The Saxons were rising. Gawain was gone searching for her. The Saxons were rising.

Euberacon was leaving.

The hands threw her roughly into the cell, and barred the door behind her. Rhian curled up on herself, nursing her hurt, nursing her hope.

Euberacon was leaving and she was unchained. All she had to do was wait for darkness. That was all.

But that waiting was the hardest thing she had ever done. Through the window, she heard Euberacon cry out some incomprehensible words and then there was the clop of hooves on the tile, and a wind blew through the little portal, and then there was nothing at all. She paced awhile. She had stood on tip-toe until her ankles cried out in pain trying to see if Nessa was able to place the kettle by the fountain, but her little window did not let her see so far. Hunger and thirst made her dull. Waiting made her frantic. He had lied, she told herself. He was watching her. He was testing her. He must be. There could be no other explanation. He knew, he knew, and if she tried to move he would come for her, he would do something worse, God she was so hungry . . . She dropped into fitful sleep, for she did not have the strength to stay awake.

And she would doze for awhile only to wake and have her thoughts begin their whirl once more.

Then came a time when she started awake, and her cell was dark. Night had come. The time when the marble fortress dreamed of its true shape. Rhian pushed herself to her feet and stared eagerly at the door of her cell, waiting for the illusion to part, waiting to see nothing there but dust and splinters.

But the door remained, as did the walls, and outside in the moonlight the marble and the tile court was still whole and beautiful.

What had happened? How was this? Last night she had seen the nightmare played out even though she was awake.

Last night, she had worn Euberacon's collar and chain. Had they been enchanted in some way to let her see with both her waking and sleeping eyes? She'd told him she saw the ruin. Did she really believe he would have put her in here if he had known the room could not hold her?

No. Oh, no. No. She ran to the door. She pushed at it and it did not move. She pounded at it with her fists. It remained closed. Splinters dug into her scaly skin.

It would be there as long as she was awake. It would be gone only when she dreamed, when she was powerless to act.

He knew that. She'd told him herself, while she thought she was being so clever with her lies.

Rhian slumped down to the floor, burying her face against her knees like a child. The grotesque tusks that grew from her mouth tore at her skirts. She wept. She could not stop herself. She was so tired. She was so hungry. She hurt so badly. She could not last, not anymore. She had shot her one bolt. For Nessa would be discovered soon, and the kettle could not be left out there more than one night.

She was lost.

She had no power, she never had. She had eyes to see, and that was all, and now her eyes were not even her own. Rhian of the Morelands had been sewn up tight inside the skin of the slave-monster Ragnelle, and she would die in there, pining for want of air.

Pining for want. What is it every woman wants? He thinks he knows what women want. Trapped inside. Trapped inside the mists and fog. Sewn inside . . .

Slowly, Rhian lifted her head. Carefully, she wiped away her tears.

She had the answer. She knew. She had seen it.

The ruin was inside the marble fortress, sewn inside it, as she was Rhian sewn inside the skin of Ragnelle. There was no sewing in the world that did not leave a seam, and seams could be felt, even when they could not be seen. If you were careful. If you knew what you were searching for.

Rhian closed her eyes and laid her hands against the door. She felt the knotted wood beneath her fingers, pitted and aged, but solid. She held her breath and in her mind's eye, she pictured the empty threshold she had seen in her nightmare. She strove to remember the way the stones had begun to sag and separate, the way the boards had lain like jackstraws on the earthen floor, how she had dragged her nightmare chains across them.

The door stayed solid beneath her palms. Despair sent shivers down her arms. She squeezed her eyes more tightly closed. She must not give in. There must be a way.

I saw it. I saw it. The threshold was empty. The door lay in pieces on the ground . . .

On the ground.

Rhian knelt. The door was in splinters. It had rotted to pieces. It lay there, useless to anything but the worms and the beetles.

Her hand touched the soft and crumbling fibre of wood succumbing to age and damp. Her heart leapt into her throat and her eyes nearly tore themselves open. Like a blind woman, she felt her way forward. Damp splinters brushed her skin. Dank and spongy wood parted under her palms and shifted beneath her knees. Biting her lip hard, she reached to her side.

She felt the empty threshold and the cool, broken stones.

Rhian crawled forward on hands and knees. The rotting wood gave way to dank earth, and her forehead brushed more rough-cut stone.

Holding her breath, Rhian opened her eyes. She was in the corridor. She saw the stones beneath her hands, but she felt cold dirt. She had it. She *had* it.

She moved carefully. The footing was treacherous, for although her eyes saw smooth and well-fitted flags on the steps, her feet felt the broken and crumbling stones. She sloshed through mud as she made her way across the wonderful courtyard. It was dizzying, seeing one thing and feeling something completely different. Her mind rebelled against it.

No. Rhian closed her eyes to let herself concentrate on touch, on truth. *Do not give in to the lie.*

The kettle waited beside the fountain, just where she'd asked for it to be when she thought she would be spending another night in chains. Rhian ran to it, slipping in the muck she could not see. She all but collapsed against it, gripping its iron sides with both hands.

And for an instant, she saw the ruin, the muddy yard, the broken fountain. Then it was gone, and there was only the illusion, serene in the moonlight.

She lifted the kettle's lid, and inside saw her treasure trove: a length of rope, a bundle of hops, a handful of barley, a screw of cloth that surely held the malt, kindling and flint, and nestled among it all, a single brown egg.

This is ridiculous, said the part of her mind that had already sunk beneath her fear. *This is insanity.*

Yes. But there is only one place where I might find my answers, and it is only insanity that will get me there.

She laid out a small nest of kindling. Her hands shook, but she stilled them. What she did now must appear natural, casual, an everyday thing. That was how it went in the story that told of a young woman who needed to lure a demon from her family's mill. By going through the motions of brewing in eggshells, so the tale went, she had roused the thing's curiosity, it had come too close and she had been able to trap it.

Whitcomb had once said there was truth in the oldest tales. Now Rhian would find out if her old friend had been right this one last time.

Her hands shook again. Rhian bit her lip with her jagged teeth and tried to concentrate. What would it be most natural to do now? Softly, carelessly, Rhian began to sing.

'Oh, have you seen John Barleycorn, and whither has he gone?
Oh, have you seen his golden beard and heard his whispering
*   song?'*

She cracked the egg on the side of the kettle, and spilled its meat out onto the ground.

'Oh, they have broken all his stems, oh they have ground his
*   bones to dust,*
Oh, they have baked him in the fire, and tell you this sad news
*   I must . . .'*

She tried to see again. It was easier nearer to the iron of
the kettle. She could almost see the broken stones, and just
make out the shadows of Drew and the stableboy struggling
at their impossible tasks.

She could just barely see the shadows of two demons flying
like foul bats above her head.

'What is this one doing? What is it doing?'

'Has the master set its task? What must it do then?'

She filled each half of the eggshell with water from the
fountain, and then with the greatest of care, she set them
upright in the kindling nest, so that each made a little brown
cup. It would have been nearly impossible, but her fingers
felt the mud and clay and were able to use the soft ground
to help balance the fragile shells on their ends. She sprinkled
a few grains of barley into each, and scooped in a fingerful
of malt, and then, last, she crumbled the dried hops over the
absurd brew.

'What's it doing? What's it doing?'

'I cannot see. I cannot tell. Its eyes are clear. It is not
blind.'

She picked up the flint and struck spark to tinder beneath
the brimming eggshells. They trembled. She prayed. If they
spilled out now, she would have to begin again and she did
not know if she had the strength.

Something brushed her shoulder.

*'Oh, they have taken off his head, they've taken out his heart
so hale . . .'*

She struck another spark. The tinder was slow to catch.
*Keep your mind on what you're doing. You know nothing
but what's in front of you. Nothing but what's in front of
you.*

'She sees, she sees, but what does she *do*?'

'*Oh, they have boiled him in a vat, and called him nut-brown ale . . .*'

'She brews!' laughed the demon, just beside her ear. 'What fish or fowl or great fool brews John Barley's blood in an *eggshell*!'

Rhian snatched at the air beside her, and her hand closed around a skinny, wiry body. Its skin burned her, its scales cut her, and the pain shot up her arms. She threw it hard into the iron kettle and clapped the lid down over it. Gasping, tears of pain and triumph rolling down her cheeks, she leaned against the vessel as it rocked and thumped from the struggles of the thing within.

'Sneak! Sneak!' it cried. 'Thief!'

'Oh dear!' She caught up the rope and wrapped it around the kettle, tying the lid down tight as the demon beat against it. 'The bird I caught for the stew must not have been sleeping. I must build the fire up.'

'Sneak!' cried the voice inside the kettle.

Rhian hummed loudly as she struck the flints beside the kettle, the better for the creature inside to hear them knocking together. 'Oh yes,' she said, her heart hammering so hard and fast in her chest she felt dizzy, terror singing so strongly through her it felt like elation. 'Pile the fuel good and high. This is a fine bird for stewing.'

'No!'

Rhian struck the flints again.

'No, mistress, please! Let me out!'

'Hear the little bird!' She made herself laugh and struck the flints one more time. 'How funny it is! I have not eaten in days. What could a little bird give me that would be better than dinner?'

'*Whatever you want!*'

Rhian's whole body shook. Nausea filled her empty stomach. Her ears rang with fear and hope. 'Whatever I want?'

'Yes, yes, mistress, please!' The kettle rocked furiously.

'Do you swear it? Whatever I want?'

'I swear! By my right hand and my left eye, I swear!'

Rhian loosened her knot. She lifted the edge of the kettle lid just far enough to see the scrawny winged creature crouching within. 'I want the answer to a question.'

'Yes, mistress.' It bobbed its head frantically. 'Of course, mistress.'

Cautiously, Rhian lifted the lid away. The demon crawled shivering out of the kettle and perched on the edge of the fountain. Its brother fluttered down beside it, and plucked at its skin as if to give comfort.

Rhian looked sternly down at the creatures. 'Euberacon said he doesn't keep his life where such as I can find it. Tell me where he does keep it.'

The demon cringed. 'No, mistress. Do not make me say!'

There is no time for this! 'Where does Euberacon keep his life!'

Then, the demon smiled, and a warning sounded in the back of Rhian's mind. 'He keeps it in the place that may be seen with both eyes, waking and sleeping, left and right. He keeps it in foul and hides it with fair.'

'What do you mean?'

'Ha!' The demon leapt from the fountain's edge, clapping its wings. 'Mistress said a question! Mistress said *a* question! Mistress may not ask another! I am free! Free!' It grabbed its brother's arms and they rolled and tumbled in midair, screaming out their glee at her foolishness.

'It should not have insulted you so, my brother!'

'Indeed it should not! Now we must tell the master!'

'Yes! Yes, the master! It thinks distance matters to such as he! Oh, he will shout when he hears what it did to us!'

Cackling in anticipation, they vanished into the night sky, leaving Rhian gaping up at them.

She clenched her fists until her nails cut into her skin. She had known Euberacon could come and go in the blink of an eye. How could she have not stopped to think any watchmen he set would be able to do the same?

Stop it. Think, Rhian. It gave you an answer. There must be meaning in it. There must.

What was there in both eyes? What did she see waking and sleeping? Rhian stared about her, turning in place. The wind blew hard and cold, the fountain splashed. She saw white marble, but she knew grey stone. She saw beautiful tiles and she felt the mud. She saw the fountain clear and beautiful, and she felt its broken edge.

The fountain!

Could it be? So close?

Close enough to be well guarded. Hidden by illusion from those who could not see. Hidden by filth and ruin from those who could.

Rhian shut her eyes and plunged both hands into the fountain. Her hands felt the muck built up after years of neglect. She groped frantically, blindly, up to her elbows in the silt of decaying leaves and mud and ice-cold water. Her fingertips brushed something smooth and she seized it, lifting it high.

To her eyes, it was as if it had just appeared in her hands. It was a small, cylindrical casket. It was heavy enough to make her think it was gold she held. It was about the width of a broom handle and the length of her hand. It was made in two halves that fitted snugly together to keep safe whatever lay within.

Rhian pulled and the two halves came open to reveal a roll of creamy parchment.

As she did, she heard a scream of outrage so strong and so terrible it might have come from Hell itself. Her heart froze in her chest, even as she tossed aside the case and unfurled the parchment. She had barely time to take in the runes and sigils that crowded the whole of its surface before the gates flew open and Euberacon, still astride his miraculous horse, galloped through, his robes flying around him as if he might take wing. Rhian was barely able to scramble out of the way. He pulled the horse up short and wheeled it around. His face was fury incarnate and her pain and her weariness made her shrink back, but at the same time she held the parchment up in both hands.

And Euberacon froze where he was. Moving no more than one muscle at a time, he dismounted the horse.

'Give that to me,' he croaked.

Rhian straightened. She smiled as far as her crooked mouth permitted. 'Why?'

'Because I command it!' he shouted. He should have flushed with anger, but instead his skin had gone white as snow.

'I found it in the mud,' said Rhian. 'It cannot be that important. I thought to tear it in two. It will do admirably to feed the kitchen fires.'

'Whore!' screamed Euberacon. He made to run forward, but Rhian only held the parchment higher, and he reeled back, as if she had dealt him a physical blow.

'So,' said the sorcerer, his voice suddenly filled with honey. 'So. I underestimated you. I thought you were a barbarian, fit only for slavery. I see now I was wrong.'

He took a step forward. Rhian clutched the parchment tighter. He froze.

'It was my ignorance that did this,' he said softly. 'I did not expect to find such a pearl here among the swine. You know only some of what you can do with your heart and will. I can teach you the rest. You can be queen of this isle, or empress in Constantinople, if you so desire. All you need do is pledge yourself to me, and I will show you the whole world.'

'What good will the world do me when all the world sees a monster?' asked Rhian.

'I have told you, what has been done can easily be undone. I can even teach you to change your own appearance as you need or desire. You can be anything you wish.'

'Do you think you are tempting me?' cried Rhian. 'I have seen how you treat those who serve you. I know who you ally yourself with!'

'You know only what you have seen, and I tell you there is a whole world that yet remains hidden to you. It is just in sight, if you choose to open those eyes that are inside you.'

Rhian swayed. Would it be worth it? With magic, no one could harm her again, no one could frighten her, sell her, starve her, imprison her again. She would have her own power and would be dependent on no one, not kin nor stranger.

'No.' She shook her head, trying to clear such thoughts from her mind.

Euberacon straightened. He was a storm cloud towering over her. He was death itself. 'Listen to me, woman. Do this thing and you will remain as you are now. This will be my final word and it shall not be undone until the Doomsday come. You will be forever a monster. Rhian of the Morelands will be gone, and there will only be Ragnelle the Loathly Lady.'

A vision assailed her. She saw the hideous, tusked monster she had become walking towards the great church of Camelot. All the court spread out on either side in silence. Men stood grim and stoic. Women turned their faces away.

A child screamed. Gawain stood on the church steps beside the pale and tremorous bishop, and in his eyes there was no more love, only pity.

Rhian shook her head. Tears stung her eyes. The parchment wrinkled in her fingers. *No. Not that. Anything but to be pitied, to be feared and loathed. No.*

'Give me the parchment, and you will have your beauty and your knight, and all shall be for you as any woman could want.'

Want. Need. Choice. The riddle from the beginning of all this nightmare came winging back to her.

'As any woman wants?' She lifted her head. 'Answer me this. What is it *every* woman wants?'

The sorcerer looked at her blankly. 'The same as every man. Sovereignty.'

'Wrong, my lord.' And with a single motion, Rhian tore the parchment in two.

Euberacon threw back his head and howled in pain. A wind from nowhere suddenly blew hard, catching up his robes to tangle his limbs. He threw up his hands, to ward off what, even Rhian could not see. Thunder sounded, overhead and from the ground. All the world pitched and shuddered, and Rhian fell backward. The scraps of parchment flew from her hands, caught up by the wind. Euberacon screamed again and clawed for them. A second thunderclap sounded and beneath the sorcerer's feet the beautiful tiles he had made with his magic split open. The rage and pain turned to terror, and Euberacon fell into the earth. Rhian threw her hands over her head, but could not block out the sound of the sorcerer's fading scream.

Silence returned but slowly. Rhian lifted her head. The fortress was gone, and there was only the ruin. Where Euberacon had stood there was a jagged, black crevice with no bottom she could see. The parchment scraps had landed on the near side of it and lay in the mud. Unwilling to trust her legs to hold her, she crawled forward and picked them up. They seemed to tingle slightly in her hands.

If I took these back to Merlin, she thought. *If I could learn to read these things, then perhaps I could learn his secrets. I could win back my true shape . . .*

And she thought of the demons, she thought of the bargains that were surely written there in blood.

Rhian tossed both halves into the crevice. 'Freedom,' she whispered as they fluttered down into the darkness. 'The answer is freedom.'

The ground rumbled and she heard a loud sigh, and the crevice snapped shut so tightly, it was as if it had never been.

She stared at the place for a long time.

'Mistress?' said a tremorous voice behind her.

Nessa. 'Yes?'

'Mistress, is it over? Are we . . . are we . . .'

Rhian lifted her head. She stood in the middle of the ruinous fortress. Nessa, Drew and the stableboy all huddled beside the fountain. Drew had his arms protectively about the other two. All around them stretched the tangle of the wildwood. A bird complained at being woken. Another answered. A third called in defiance of the first two and soon the air was filled with chatter, complaint and merry song.

'Yes,' said Rhian. 'Yes. It is over. It is morning and we are all of us free.'

'What do we do now?'

What do we do now? Rhian stared at the broken walls.

Searching the countryside for his lost lamb. But what countryside? Where?

She pulled together her torn thoughts. 'If there is any food, bring that. If there is a cloak, bring that too. I fear we must walk out of this place.'

*   *   *

The forest of the Green Knight offered Gawain neither sun nor shadow to guide himself by. All was twilight and the air was heavy with approaching rain. Still, he did not look behind him. He sighted on the trees ahead to keep himself moving in a straight line. He looked neither left nor right, partly because he had been so instructed.

Partly because in his heart, he was not sure what he would see if he did.

A pair of shadows moved and shifted directly ahead. Gawain walked towards them, and as he drew near he saw they were horses; Pol and Gringolet, saddled and harnessed, and looking a little affronted, as if they wanted to say 'what took you so long?'

He found he was not at all surprised. He tied his charger to his riding horse and mounted. The forest was old enough that the way between the trees was clear of underbrush and tangling limbs. It was almost as easy as riding on the highway.

A little while later, they came to the pile of his gear, and Gawain reclaimed sword and shield, mail-coat and spear.

And Gawain rode on.

While Nessa and the stableboy, Donat, scrounged for food in a kitchen that proved to be little more than an oven and an open yard, Drew helped Rhian search the ruins that had been Euberacon's fortress. There was one whole room, down in the cellars where Rhian's cell had been. In the illusion, this had been his tower workroom. The tools of his trade remained, as did the animals in their cages. All these they threw open, letting the creatures fly or scurry to their separate lives. They found a chest of robes and cloaks. Although her skin crawled at the thought of touching something that once belonged to him, it would be far worse to be seen on the road as she was.

He had not lied. The whole of her monstrous form remained, and though she railed inside it, her mind and heart pounding against it as her fists had once pounded at her cell door, it did not change.

Drew helped her into the cloak. She forgave him for looking relieved as she drew up the hood to hide her face.

All at once, she heard the thudding of horse's hooves. Her heart seized up in terror, as if she had forgotten any other way to respond to some unexpected thing.

'Wait here,' said Drew, hurrying from the room.

But she could not wait, not here, not alone. Instead she crept to the shadows of the doorway where she might see, but not be seen.

A rider on a black gelding came through the gate. He had a white charger tied to the riding horse, and a silver shield hung from the saddlebow. But Rhian needed no such token to know at once who she saw.

Gawain. Rhian pressed both her fists into her mouth to stop herself from screaming out his name. What little strength she had fell away and she staggered, catching herself against the wall.

Nessa had preceded Drew into the yard. Gawain looked down at her, seeming a little dazed, as if he had been too long in the sun. 'Who is lord here?'

'There is no lord here, not anymore. There is a . . .' Nessa's voice faltered. 'There is a lady.'

'I would speak with this lady.'

'Sir,' Drew stepped up, bowing his head humbly. 'We're nothing here and nobody. If it's help or house you're looking for . . .'

She could remain in hiding. She could creep away. She could find her cure first. There must be a way. There were cunning men in the far west. Merlin had come from there.

He did not have to see her as this monster.

'I would see the lady of this place,' said Gawain.

For all she had seen, for all she had done, nothing felt more difficult. Rhian walked out into the sunlight, face and figure obscured by the black cloak, and faced Gawain.

Then, she drew back the hood.

The black horse whickered and danced in consternation at the sight and stench of such a creature. Gawain stilled it with his expert skills. His face remained calm as he dismounted.

'Are you the lady of this place?' he inquired with quiet courtesy.

'Yes.' *It's me, Gawain!* cried her heart. *It's Rhian!* But her tongue would not move.

He looked at her little, piggish eyes. He looked long and he looked hard and he did not flinch, nor did any pity or fear cross his face.

And then he spoke.

> *'The nymph is all to laurel gone;*
> *The smoothness of her skin remains alone.*
> *Yet Phoebus loves her still.'*

He threw his arms around her, catching her up and holding her to him so tightly she thought they might meld together and never again be parted.

After a little while he did loosen his embrace. Sadly, she stepped away and stripped off the cloak. *Look again, Gawain. See this crooked body, see this monster's face. See what price I've paid for fighting my doom.*

'This is what I am Gawain. This is what he said I must remain.'

'I don't care.'

He kissed her then, with all the love he had given her so freely when she was beautiful, and though the tusks and the jagged teeth cut at him, still he did not hesitate. Rhian threw her arms around his shoulders, answering kiss for kiss, heart to heart.

And the pain was gone, and she felt each joint, each bone, straighten into their proper places, and the scales drew themselves back and her skin grew whole again, and her hair blossomed forth, cascading down her back, and her face, the face she had wept and mourned and screamed over, grew round and fresh again, and her mouth resumed its rightful shape.

She pulled back and regarded Gawain, weary, unshaven, and alight with happiness with her own eyes. He did not appear at all surprised

'Come, my lady,' was all he said, taking her arm in his and pulling her close. 'Let me take you home.'

EPILOGUE

It was midday when the aging woman came to the centre of the forest, but the heavy shadows of the trees made all as dim as twilight. She bowed to the mound and looked longingly at the fresh stream that chattered down its side to pool at its feet. There was great power to be had in those waters, if one could find a way to harvest them. Perhaps one day . . .

But today she had other business. Amid this ancient forest of oaks and maples, ash and alder, there stood a single thorn-apple tree. It looked lost and small, trying to spread its blossoming branches to catch what meagre sunlight the other trees permitted to fall so far. It did not look like it would live for long and another witness might have wondered how such a tree came to be in such a place. A lone raven sat in its branches, croaking angrily at the intruder.

But Morgaine just laid her hand against the thorn-apple's bark.

'I truly am sorry, Kerra. If there had been another way, I would have done it. But you see, you liked your power too much. You tasted what it was to rule over men, and would no more have been content to wait at my side until stars and men were ready. So when I needed a sacrifice, I'm afraid you had to be the one.' She snapped off three blossoming twigs. 'These yet will serve, as you ever have.' She held them up as if the tree could see. 'You did well,' she added as she stepped back. 'Without your interference with the girl, the Easterner might have had his way and brought Camelot to its knees. It is not time, though, my dear. Not yet.' She turned her face towards the west. 'Soon though, Arthur, my love. Soon.'

And she was gone, and there was only the whispering of the trees to the wind and a soft, distant sound that might have been a woman's tears.